Reader Pr

"Wow. Schatz has done it once again—the best of the series…"

"A fast paced fantabulous thriller story of mystery…"

"You don't even have to like baseball to love this series…"

"A 'who dunnit' with twists and turns to keep you interested…"

"Schatz has delivered another 'perfect game' for all of us fans…"

"This story will keep you guessing… Another masterpiece!"

"I am a fan for life! Well done, and keep 'em coming!"

~*~*~*~*~*~*~*~

See more reader reviews and ratings of Allen's books online at
Amazon.com, Barnes & Noble.com, Smashwords, and elsewhere…
Visit **www.allenschatz.com**

RALLY KILLER

Go TEAM MORGAN!

Also by Allen Schatz

Game 7: Dead Ball

7th Inning Death

RALLY KILLER

Allen Schatz

ISBN 13: 978-1-466-31224-1
ISBN-10: 1-466-31224-6

Cover art by Adam McFall. File conversion help by writer Sean Sweeney. Thanks, guys.

For Sandy, Michael, and Samantha
The best support system ever.

"You may be deceived if you trust too much, but you will live in torment if you do not trust enough."

Dr. Frank Crane, Author of *Everyday Wisdom*

PROLOGUE

Early October
New Yankee Stadium
The Bronx, New York

I'm not sure how long it was before I moved forward and knelt next to the fallen body. Alive, but struggling to breathe, when he tried to speak, he coughed up more blood than sound. I took a direct hit from the red spray, but ignored it and leaned in closer, not wanting to miss whatever came next. I had the feeling it would be his last words.

"I *trusted* you—"

Whatever else there might have been got cut off by another wet cough, and as the sound died, the sharpness in his eyes went with it and his entire body sagged. Any thoughts of trying to revive him faded, too. There was nothing I could do, and seconds later, he was gone. The answers to my questions were going to have to come from someone else—if they came at all.

"Shit, shit, shit," I said, before reaching down and gently closing his eyes.

I stood, but couldn't stop staring at the growing pool of blood near my feet. Within seconds, I could see a distorted reflection of myself in the dark plasma.

"What a goddamn mess," I said to my sanguine twin.

"Profound as usual, Connors," a familiar voice said, from somewhere behind me.

A two-staged click followed. The sound reminded me of the one that came from pulling the chain on the ceiling fan in my parents' kitchen. Yeah, if only, I thought, as I slowly raised my hands.

"I try," I said, before turning.

I knew what I was going to see, but my heart skipped a beat anyway as my eyes were drawn to the darkness at the end of the gun's barrel. The tiny black hole began sucking me in. If nothing else, at least I had an answer for what the dying—sorry, *dead*—man had been looking at instead of me, and for what his last words had really meant. Those answers were helpful, but not the ones I needed.

After a few seconds, I broke free from the trance and looked up, into the gunman's eyes. The answers there weren't much better.

"And Thomas isn't here to save your ass," the man said, as if somehow reading my thoughts. "This time, you're on your own."

And there it was.

"Shit, shit, shit," I said again.

My mind started racing, but all roads led back to an unarguable conclusion, that this was all wrong. "Kill the umpire" had always been just a stupid thing people said out of frustration, a sometimes annoying part of the game. But that was the point: Baseball was *a game*. It was supposed to be fun. It wasn't this—whatever *this* was—and it sure as shit wasn't supposed to include any actual murders.

So why the hell was it happening *again*?

Chapter 1

About four weeks earlier
LOVE Park
Philadelphia, Pennsylvania

Thomas Hillsborough sat alone on a slab of cement that passed for a bench, a handful of leaves floating through a low-lying layer of cooler damp air the only blemish on the stillness around him. The leaves, prematurely aged and chased from the trees by unseasonably cold weather, were a reminder that all things must die. Thomas didn't need the admonition.

In his world, both past and present, death was a given—and far too often intentional. He'd spent seven years with the CIA, in places and situations conducive to kill or be killed, experiences that had left him with scars seen and unseen. In the years since, more deaths and scars had been added, but such came with his job, it was the path he'd chosen.

The same could not be said for Thomas' close friend, major league baseball umpire Marshall Connors. Marshall's job was supposed to be less harrowing. He was arbiter of a boy's game played by men, a pastime meant to be a diversion from the struggles of day-to-day life. It was supposed to be fun, but in recent years had become something else, something darker.

That Thomas had twice pulled Marshall back from that darkness was never in doubt. In his mind, he had an unending debt to his friend, dating to their college days. Marshall had saved him from a fire in their dorm building. The selfless act, by a man closer to being a stranger than a friend, had left as profound a mark as any of Thomas' subsequent wounds. Marshall now believed the note was paid in full, but Thomas had no plans to stop the payments.

He should have died in that fire.

That he did not meant the answer would never be: We're even.

Adding to that conclusion was Marshall's recent propensity for stepping in shit. The umpire felt the deadly situations were coincidental, a string of disconnected events, a run of bad luck. Thomas knew better. Coincidences didn't happen. There was always an underlying reason, a starting point to the chain. Worse, in his experience, such bad trends rarely changed tack, even for the best of sailors, and he knew that with each added link, the chain became stronger, the course harder to correct.

Worse still, Thomas was fighting a growing realization that he himself had cast the first link.

The time was nine years earlier, in the barren landscape southeast of Wajir, Kenya, near the Somali border. None of Thomas' prior CIA assignments had been as difficult. Not so much the task, but the impact of what he saw there. He'd been helpless to intervene, ordered to observe and do nothing more, a fact that had not sat well for a man of action, one unaccustomed to standing idle while others suffered.

"Never again," he said aloud to the growing memory.

A breeze ran under the bench and tossed some dirt in the air. Thomas' eyes closed and Africa returned. He was stomach to dirt in the shallow hills above the remnants of a small village. The setting sun's fading light doing little to mask the devastation below. The sounds and images were as fresh as the day they'd occurred...

"We should have stopped this," Thomas said, turning toward another man crouched nearby. "*You* should have stopped it."

The words carried a noticeable edge, a rare outward display of anger, but the other man was unmoved. That man, Dikembe Dukabi, former leader of the marauders ravaging the defenseless villagers, was not the sort to be easily swayed by a harsh tone alone.

"Such was not our deal, my friend," Dukabi said, his deep voice carrying a clipped-English accent. "These men now act of their own accord. It is what you and your government have created. You were a fool to think my situation would alter this outcome. Desperation and weapons do not mix. Not here. This is Africa."

Thomas shook his head.

"No," he said. "*This* is murder."

Dukabi laughed.

"*Murder?*" he said. "Don't be a fool, Mr. Hillsborough. This is about survival. This you should know."

Thomas *did* know. People had been struggling all across this land, unable to defend themselves from the savagery, natural and otherwise. It was ugly, but there was much ugliness in this strife-torn country. A years-long drought had brought despair and death. It was brutal, but acceptable, Nature's will in action, survival of the fittest. It made sense.

Nothing of what Thomas saw in the village made any sense at all.

The gang—and others like it—was a different kind of brutality, a man-made phenomenon more deadly than anything found in nature. The CIA's funding of these so-called "local coalitions for change" had been meant to influence Kenya's upcoming democratic elections. It would, but not in the manner hoped.

After the elections, the gangs didn't disappear. Many became rebels, pillaging remote villages out of the eye of the newly formed government. Others were recruited by that same government, an extension used to keep people in line as much as fight the rebels. The colossal error in judgment, hatched by the suits in a political sub-committee sitting in a cozy office in Washington, D.C.—men and women clueless to understand the realities of the world, their naivety matched only by their cowardliness—failed miserably.

The failure would echo for years to come.

Cooperation earned Dukabi a safe passage from Kenya. Once in America, he was passed off to the FBI, but the Bureau was preoccupied with the post-9/11 war on terror and had neither the time nor interest for what it saw as glorified babysitting duty. Dukabi skillfully exploited the situation, establishing a highly-profitable gambling operation out of his home in the years that followed.

The invitation-only poker games were frequented by many celebrities, including more than a few professional athletes who had money to spend, but a preference to do so out of the spotlight. Such paparazzi avoidance came at a heavy price, however. When you lost to Dukabi—and most did; the games were rigged—you paid, and those with outstanding chips quickly discovered the man's collection methods were not exactly consumer-friendly.

One such episode drew Thomas—and Marshall—back into Dukabi's world. Ultimately, Dukabi's role was discovered to be secondary, but he made sure it stayed that way by hatching another deal, just as he had done in Africa. It had led to the capture of a serial killer, but Dukabi was again given a pass by the FBI in exchange for a promise to end the games and leave the country.

Thomas had come close to killing Dukabi for endangering his friend, but accepted the deal with an expectation it would be his last encounter with the African, the end of the chain. The request two days ago for a meeting now told him otherwise. The chain remained intact. Worse, it meant he'd been wrong. Thomas did not like being wrong.

Being wrong got people killed…

"A fool indeed," Thomas said under his breath as he opened his eyes and pushed the memories aside.

Another chilly breeze came and stirred up some leaves near his feet. He followed the movements until his eyes settled on Philadelphia's City Hall. The windows of the historic building were mostly dark, but its brightly lit tower was shrouded in a thickening fog. Below the willowy grayness, the plaza was empty, the usual collection of pedestrians and vagrants inspired to find more suitable environs as much by the hour—eleven P.M. on a Sunday—as the chill.

Thomas didn't mind either factor.

The setting was intentional, an attempt to add discomfort to the situation. That discomfort was personified in the form of a lone figure emerging from the shadows at the far side of the Hall. The laboring stride might have been mistaken as that of someone fighting the cold, but Thomas knew the weather merely added to the limp caused by the bullet he'd delivered to Dukabi's leg years ago.

Slowed by the impediment, it took Dukabi the better part of a minute to traverse the courtyard. When he reached a small traffic island at the intersection of JFK Boulevard and 15th Street, he paused to allow a lone car to pass before stepping across the road. At the sidewalk on the opposite corner, he paused again to scan the area.

When he took notice of Thomas on the bench, Dukabi's body seemed to expand. That was followed by a small movement from a large hand, not quite a wave, but an acknowledgement of recognition. When Thomas did not respond, Dukabi nodded, and the hand returned to its coat pocket as he stepped from the curb and quickly covered the final thirty or so feet to a pair of shallow steps near the bench.

"Mr. Hillsborough, my friend," he said. "I trust all is well in your world?"

The accent, the bass, the inflection—all of it was the same, yet somehow… *different.* Thomas' right eyebrow went up in response, his version of a shrug and something of a trademark. When he spoke, his words came in a flat tone, another trademark.

"It was," he said.

Dukabi nodded again before a sound similar to something you might hear from a dog, a tentative bark at an unfamiliar situation, escaped his mouth. As the noise faded, he scaled the steps and moved to a bench on Thomas' left, where he began a struggle to situate his girth on the unforgiving hardness.

"You look uncomfortable," Thomas said. "I take it this setting is not to your liking."

Dukabi's head turned. Something that might have been anger filled his expression.

"*Nothing* here is to my liking," he said in a matching tone.

Thomas' eyebrow went up again.

"And yet, here you are," he said.

The eyebrow movements, the tone, his attire, all were precise without being pretentious. His looks, handsome without the need for artificial enhancement, added to the picture. In short, he was well-put-together and clearly in control of the situation. Dukabi, on the other hand, was uncomfortable in every way imaginable, something his next words confirmed.

"Yes, leaving Africa was not an easy decision, nor was *this*," he said, adding a sweeping motion with his right hand.

He stopped when he was distracted by another car out on 15th Street. His eyes followed then lingered there. Thomas guessed the man did not like what he saw—or rather *didn't* see. For just as the skateboarders who frequented the park loved a crowd when they performed their tricks, Dukabi undoubtedly would have preferred the same now.

Again, that was the point.

"It seems anything is tolerable when one has proper motivation," Thomas said.

Dukabi's head slowly turned back.

"Touché," he said. "But let us dispense with game play. There is much to discuss."

A fresh breeze kicked up another small cloud of dirt. Dukabi began waving at the tiny specks. Despite the size difference— Dukabi was a touch over six feet tall and north of 350 pounds, a few degrees more so than the last time Thomas had seen him—the pollution was easily victorious. Several particles landed on the man's overcoat. The darkness on his face intensified as he stared down at the invasion. A second later, his two huge paws began aggressively removing the dust.

"Such filth saddens me," he said as he worked. "It is shameful."

"I wasn't aware you'd become an environmentalist," Thomas said.

Again, Dukabi's eyes came back to Thomas'. This time, the fire was less intense.

"Yes," Dukabi said. "There is much you do not know."

The tone had lost some of its edge as well. Thomas, extremely skilled at reading people, detected both changes and added them to the list of signals Dukabi had already given.

"I take it you're here to educate me," he said.

Dukabi's head shook.

"Educate? No," he said. "I come with a simple request."

Dukabi's last "simple request" of Thomas had come near the end of the Marshall incident, a proposal to join forces. There was a mutual respect between the men despite their opposing positions, but the appeal never had a chance. Helping Dukabi in any way was never going to happen—*then or now*. Thomas let the statement hang as if to make the point.

"I see," he said; then after another pause. "I'm afraid we're wasting each other's time. I've let you live twice. *Nothing* could top that."

The intensity was beyond anything in Dukabi's arsenal. He backed off a few inches out of reflex before recovering.

"Yes, my friend, that may be, but as I said, there is much you do not know."

In an expansive but sparsely furnished apartment near Penn's Landing, less than two miles from LOVE Park, another man was searching for answers. Unlike Dukabi, this man had no one like Thomas to turn to. Even if such a savior was available, it probably didn't matter. Edward James—"Eddie" to most people—Booker was going to die, if not this day, then one very soon. Of this, there was no dispute. The only questions now were how and where. Why was no longer in doubt.

Eddie was going to kill himself.

He had played major league baseball for sixteen years. Coaching and managing took up the next six. The twenty-two years, nearly half his forty-six year life, was part joy part sorrow, moments of extreme highs interrupted by abyss-like lows, a thrill ride matched only by the best roller-coaster Six Flags had to offer.

But somewhere along the line, Eddie's coaster car had left the track. It would have been better had the resulting crash been like a bug against a windshield, instantaneous and painless, a result of events it could not control, but Eddie's wreck was different. It came in stages, a series of mistakes anything but coincidental and more than preventable—and every one of them hurting like hell.

The pain had started innocently enough. A tweaked right knee suffered late in his playing days turned out to be a full-on ruptured ACL. Surgery and months of rehab followed. With the window of his career closing faster than he cared to admit, Eddie was desperate to get back in the game and overdid the therapy. New injuries sprouted, pushing him to opt for an approach more dangerous than the knife.

The exact day steroids entered Major League Baseball was debatable. The impact was not. Many records once thought untouchable were shattered by muscled-up cheaters, and a lot of the game's innocence was lost. Eddie lost his innocence as well. He knew juicing was wrong, but chose to ignore that in exchange for a few more years in the game. For him, not juicing would have been the idiotic response. He wasn't a superstar. No records would bear his name. He just wanted to heal so he could keep getting paid.

Eddie wasn't proud of that. The destructive properties of steroids had been well-documented. Sure, he got stronger and healed more quickly, but he was in constant pain of a different sort. When the steroids weren't enough, he moved on to painkillers. When that failed to numb, he added alcohol, and by the time he retired from the field, he was completely fried.

The derailment came after that, during his years as a coach, courtesy of a kink in the track otherwise known as Dikembe Dukabi. Like many retired athletes, Eddie had an endless need to replace the rush of the game with something else. For him—as it was for Michael O'Hara, a central figure in Marshall's run-in with Dukabi— that something was gambling.

Sadly, as it was on the ballfield, aided by or perhaps because of his addictions, Eddie was no more than passably average at the poker table. There, unlike on the diamond, he was a roster of one with no protection from better hitters in the line-up. That left him vulnerable, and in a high-stakes game like Dukabi's, vulnerable and passably average equated to big loser.

And losing big to Dukabi was a very bad idea.

In fact, it could kill you.

Chapter 2

LOVE Park

Dukabi's version of Eddie's story left out the ex-player's addictions. The omission didn't matter.

"As I said, you're wasting your time," Thomas said when the big man finished the tale. "I don't do collection work."

"Yes, I don't imagine you would," Dukabi said. "Such is not the request, however."

"Since when does he not care about money?"

The last words came from a third voice, one heard only by Thomas and belonging to an ex-FBI agent named Sandy Hood. Sandy now worked for Thomas—OK, "worked for" was a stretch. Thomas treated her as an equal in his firm, the previous one-man shop he'd started after his CIA days. The services offered were a mix of consulting, security, private investigation, and a few other things not easily described. How, when, and for who such services were rendered was at Thomas' sole discretion. Sandy was OK with that. Thomas almost always made good decisions.

She hoped he was about to make another.

"Please don't tell me you're thinking about helping this monster," she said.

She was communicating with him via micro-sized devices she and he were wearing, some of the many toys at their disposal. Sandy's presence—in a well-hidden place elsewhere in the park— was due to the fact one didn't come alone to a meeting with a man like Dukabi, no matter how talented one might be. That would be a good idea exactly never.

Sandy's disdain for Dukabi, something worn more openly than Thomas', stemmed from the events involving Marshall. Damien Hastings—Sandy's FBI partner and lover at the time—was murdered by a serial killer, the revenge-seeking madman named Andrew Singer. Hastings was the second person close to Sandy murdered by Singer and she blamed Dukabi by extension for both deaths. Fortunately—or maybe not—the big man's next words kept her from dwelling on it.

"I need assistance in finding Mr. Booker before he does something drastic," Dukabi said.

Sandy held her tongue and waited for Thomas to respond.

"Explain 'drastic,'" he said. "Why would I care?"

"Locating Mr. Booker has more to do with the well-being of others than of my own."

A slight frown came and went on Thomas' face. Dukabi had just pushed one of Thomas' buttons, a big one, that of protecting innocents.

"Explain," Thomas said in a tone no longer flat.

"Whoa. Hold up."

The reaction from Sandy wasn't in reference to the sharpness in her partner's voice, but from something else she heard, a faint sound originating from a source other than the two men on the benches.

"I think we have company," she said, following up on the interruption.

She adjusted her sightline and began to scan the area around the park. The noise came again, from her left. She looked across 15th Street, toward the entrance of the Philadelphia City and County Building. At first there was nothing, but then she saw it, in the alcove, two forms, hiding in the darkness.

"Yep, we have two bogies at eight o'clock from your position, across Fifteenth," she said.

Thomas showed no outward reaction to the revelation. He wasn't surprised. Dukabi was smart and not likely to have come alone to the meeting, either. Still, it changed things.

"Tell me about these others," Thomas said.

The statement was as much for Sandy as Dukabi. She responded first.

"Hard to tell—they don't look friendly. I think we need to end this. I'm getting a bad feeling."

At the benches, Dukabi again adjusted his body. It appeared the cement was still winning that particular battle, but his words said he was more interested in the other duel he'd been waging.

"Ah, yes, I see you are interested," he said to Thomas.

He had misread the situation, an error Thomas moved to correct.

"I said no such thing," he said.

Dukabi didn't miss the message, and his large frame seemed to stiffen.

"Is there a problem, Mr. Hillsborough?" he said, discomfort also sounding in his voice.

Sandy caught the reaction.

"He catches on fast," she said into Thomas' ear.

He remained focused on Dukabi.

"I won't know until you make your request," he said.

Dukabi slowly nodded before taking a deep breath. The exhale sounded like a blast furnace.

"Yes, very well, I believe I understand," he said; then after a pause. "Mr. Booker was scheduled to make final payment two days ago. He did not. I can no longer locate him. Soon after, I contacted you."

Thomas let the words marinate for a few seconds. The taste was off. He flashed on the unknown guests. His eyes narrowed slightly before relaxing again.

"Are you having labor issues?" he said.

The question caused yet another movement in Dukabi's body, not quite a twitch—something that big didn't twitch—but a reaction nonetheless.

"I—I don't understand," he said.

"Simple question, really," Thomas said. "Why did you call *me*?"

He thought the implication obvious. Outsourcing was not Dukabi's style.

The big man took another deep breath and pushed it out loudly.

"As noted, I would rather not see the situation escalate to include unintended victims."

There it was again, "unintended victims." Thomas' frown returned and stayed in place this time. Dukabi was definitely trying to pull the strings, but why? Sandy was right to have a bad feeling. Something was clearly amiss. It was time to find out exactly what.

"I don't believe you're telling me everything," Thomas said.

He stood. The sudden movement seemed to startle Dukabi.

"And this means?" he said after recovering.

"This means nothing," Thomas said. "I simply need time to verify what you've said. If I can determine the truthfulness, I'll consider your request."

Without another word, he turned and walked away, toward the center of the park, leaving Dukabi alone. Sandy remained in position to monitor the reaction—at the benches and elsewhere. The first came from Dukabi. He stood and moved off in the same direction from which he had come, his pace a little stronger than his approach had been.

A few seconds later, the two figures across the street stepped from the shadows, and Sandy got her first good look at them. Both men were as dark as Dukabi, but smaller in size. Not so much in height, but in width. Sandy got the feeling that wasn't necessarily a good thing, but was more surprised when the men turned away from City Hall.

Instead of following Dukabi or Thomas, they walked back along the sidewalk on 15th until they disappeared from her view after turning the corner. The retreat made no sense to Sandy. Then again, most of the past half-hour hadn't. She came out of hiding and hustled out of the park. When she reached her car, she checked in with Thomas via the transmitter.

"I'm not sure what just happened," she said. "I don't think those guys were with Dukabi."

"I agree," Thomas said.

"Wait, what?" Sandy said. "Which part? You mean you know who they are?"

There was a slight delay before Thomas replied.

"Yes."

Thomas couldn't see it, but the cryptic one-word reply had generated a scowl on Sandy's face. Her next words did the job of conveying the emotion.

"Why do you do that?" she said.

"Do what?" Thomas said.

"Piss me off sometimes more than the bad guys do."

Penn's Landing

Eddie being pissed off had as much to do with himself than any of the perceived bad guys, not that the latter didn't exist. In fact, the face of one of Eddie's enemies was on a flat-screen TV hanging above the fake fireplace in his living room, that of a reporter named David Donovan, baseball beat writer for the New York *Daily News*.

Donovan was part of a panel appearing on the MLB Network to discuss various topics, including rumors of a renewed interest in steroids among the players. He was considered something of an expert on the subject, having penned several books about the game's sins and sinners. His latest effort—titled *It's Only Cheating When You Get Caught*—featured a few of Eddie's exploits.

The revived notoriety was something Eddie could have done without.

A short glass, once filled with whiskey, now mostly-melted ice cubes, rested atop his lap, held in place by an unsteady hand as he watched the program. Besides his labored breathing, the only other sounds came from the TV, where Donovan was in the process of sharing one of the passages from the book. It was a memory Eddie wished he could erase.

"Booker's July 2002 arraignment in U.S. District Court in New York on tax evasion charges was especially entertaining if for no other reason than it started out badly and went downhill from there. I'm not sure Eddie would agree with the entertaining part. The hearing was the stake to the heart of his baseball life.

His fall had been spectacular and he saw the faces in the room, especially the reporters—me included—as a tank full of piranhas waiting to feed on his carcass. Others in the press had first shown their teeth in a series of brutal attacks leading up to the trial, stories light on facts but heavy on damage. None of it was necessary. Eddie had done enough damage on his own.

His feelings about the trial—and the judge—were just as bad. He once told me he hated when people used his full name. It was something his mother did and he admittedly hated her. He would later tell me the judge reminded him of the wretched woman—his words—which was probably why he ignored her plea question at first.

He was alone, having fired his legal team, and was clearly overmatched and overwhelmed by the situation. I felt bad for him, but that lasted only until he finally entered his plea.

It went something like this: 'I plead... I plead... fuck you, *bitch.'*

It was then I stopped feeling bad for him..."

The F-bomb was bleeped out on TV, but Eddie heard it anyway. He'd been there, but had no desire to go back, and there was no bleeping *his* reaction.

"Fuck you, Donovan," he said to the TV. "What the fuck do you know?"

He reached forward and pushed a button on the cable remote, sending the screen to black. It was a perfect reflection of how he felt as he looked around the suddenly darkened room. The furniture— what little there was—was like him, a ragged shell of what it used to be. Despite the millions made during his career, he had little to show for it now. That realization redirected Eddie's anger.

"Fuck me," he said aloud as he sank further into the cushion of the well-worn sofa.

He closed his eyes, but the added blackness made things worse. More bad memories came, racing past his mind's eye, adding to the discomfort in his body. As much as he wanted to forget them all, to erase everything, he knew he couldn't. At best, he would have to settle for the temporary respites brought about by the alcohol and whatever other drugs he could find.

As the latest doses thereof began to kick in, Eddie dozed off.

Seconds later—seemingly—he found himself somewhere else, somewhere familiar, but equally as uncomfortable as the beat-up cushion. He was in Mark Rosenbaum's office, the commissioner of baseball's office, sitting in a chair in front of Mark's desk. Mark was on the other side, standing at a window, looking out at New York. He was wearing a dark suit—maybe navy blue?—and looked his usual dapper self. Eddie never remembered seeing the man as anything less.

"You've put me in a bad spot, Eddie," Mark said without turning. "I promised I would reconsider. There was never a promise of reinstatement."

Eddie glanced around and caught his own reflection in a mirror on the far wall. He was unshaven and disheveled. He couldn't remember ever seeing himself as anything more. When he turned back to Mark, he wanted to speak, but couldn't find his tongue. Panic began to seep in and he started to sweat.

"The answer is no," Mark said as he turned from the window. "You may have been acquitted of tax evasion, but I can't ignore the other findings. You have jeopardized the integrity of the game. I can't have that."

Eddie tried to stand, to protest, but couldn't find his legs.

"I'm sorry, Eddie," Mark said. "You are no longer welcome in my game."

"NO!"

Eddie's eyes snapped opened. The shout had been real, but had again fallen on deaf ears.

"Damn it," he said to the memory in a tired voice.

He winced and tried to find a better angle to combat the spasms racing through his body. He ended up in a slouched position on the cushion, his feet resting on a coffee table in front. The combination worked and his body relaxed a little. *A little* would have to do. He couldn't expect anything more. Not at this point.

As he sat there, his sweating increased. He tried to wipe it—and the memory of Mark—from his face, but stopped when he felt the room begin to spin. He reached out and grabbed hold of the sofa on either side of where he sat, waiting for the sensations to end. He needed it to end, all of it, not just the spinning, but the drugs and drinking and poker losses and bad memories, all the shit adding to the pain.

Ten minutes passed before the spinning subsided. As it did, Eddie loosened his grip and slowly opened his eyes. He was soaked through with sweat, but had no desire to seek dry clothes. In truth, he had no desire for anything.

"It's not like anyone is gonna miss me."

Chapter 3

West Philadelphia

The short drive from Center City to the West African restaurant located on Locust Street had taken less than ten minutes. The slight deviation was worth it for the pleasant reminder of home, something a few others must have been craving, because the dining room was crowded when the two men arrived and they had to settle for a small table near the front window.

Five minutes passed before a waitress appeared. The young woman took their order and returned within seconds with two glasses of auburn-colored liquid. The smaller of the two men sampled the beverage. The homemade ginger juice was like a time-machine, transporting him back to the dusty village of his earliest memories.

"Excellent," he said in his native tongue. "Thank you, my dear."

"You're welcome, kind sir," the waitress said in the same language.

She smiled and stepped away.

"Drink, my friend," the man said to his partner.

Each was wearing similar attire, black from head to toe, matching the darkness of their skin. The second man sampled the juice and nodded. Apparently, it was acceptable. The first man smiled and pulled out a cell phone. After dialing, it was several seconds before he spoke.

"He met with someone," he said in near-perfect English. "I do not know the man's identity, but he appeared to control the conversation."

The man's multi-lingual abilities were no surprise. Zende Ibori, nicknamed "Jamie" because of a resemblance to American actor Jamie Foxx, was Nigerian by birth. His exact age was uncertain—a true birth certificate never existed—but mid-thirties was a reasonable guess.

Jamie had migrated to Kenya as a boy after his parents had died of malaria. He was adopted there and moved to America by his foster parents. In the States, he was given access to the best things in life, including a Harvard education. He'd made good use of it. His accent was similar to Dukabi's, but there was something different, an edge cultivated from the harshness before the American excesses. Fondness for the juice aside, it was a past of which people would be better off not learning, including the person on the other end of the cell phone conversation.

"It would have been unwise to follow," Jamie said into the phone. "We were being watched."

His features began to take on an ominous appearance as he listened to the response. He deflected some of the growing anger with another drink. A memory of his mother's version of the beverage came to mind—his real mother, not the American—but faded quickly.

"Your concerns are irrelevant," he said after swallowing. "The situation is in hand."

He closed the phone with a loud snap. The man across the table looked up. His name was Shahidi—pronounced Shady—Okonjo. Sudanese by birth, Shady had also been raised in Kenya as an orphan, after the rest of his family had been murdered during an ethnic cleansing campaign.

It was in the sullen confines of that temporary home where he and Jamie first met. The men quickly bonded, the seal forged by their mutual loss. Shady was several years younger than Jamie, but was never adopted and until recently, had never been to America. His education was of a more primitive nature. One need not have books to learn.

"Drink your juice," Jamie said. "We must go."

Shady's eyes took on a look of disappointment.

"Are there problems?" he said.

The rest of his features also carried innocence, matching the tone, but Jamie knew the truth behind the façade. A small grin appeared.

"With you, my friend, there are *never* any problems."

Wayne, Pennsylvania

It took Thomas and Sandy close to forty minutes to get back to their office, located in the largest unit of an apartment-condo complex on Lancaster Avenue in Wayne, part of Philadelphia's famous Main Line. The set of six buildings was one of many assets held by the Hillsborough family estate. Thomas and his younger sister, Jennifer, a psychologist living and working nearby, were the last direct descendants.

Neither was married—Jennifer was divorced—and neither had kids. There was a time when Jennifer was the more likely of the two to change that, but after a recent brush with death, another link in the chain of events involving Marshall, she had no interest in the job. Thomas wasn't without the occasional companion, but none of the relationships ever got close to escalating toward marriage.

The best chance had come back in college, but that ended the day Thomas announced his intent to join the CIA. It was a universally unpopular decision for those close to him, including his parents. They'd wanted him to assume control of the family businesses, but his interest for that was something that *did* die in the fire.

It was true the family's wealth had opened doors, but it had done so in a cold, heartless manner. Money could buy many things, but happiness wasn't included. That realization grew in Thomas after he and Marshall became close friends. They were opposites in almost every way, but that turned out to be a good thing. It opened Thomas' eyes to the concept of "the simple things matter most."

In a world of opulence, nothing was simple. Experiences were purchased, not felt. It was part of what drove Thomas to the CIA. He saw that as another opportunity to learn how to feel. The ability to express such was another issue—and still very much a work-in-progress—but Marshall's yin to Thomas' yang was a good starting step. They filled in each other's blanks.

Sandy had learned a lot of this early in her relationship with Thomas. Relatively skilled at reading people, but not nearly as strong as Thomas, she had noticed the guarded nature in many of his actions. It wasn't reluctance, but something else. She had yet to completely figure it out, but was pretty sure there was plenty of time to solve the mystery.

Her two years with Thomas—after her six at the FBI—had been great, and she wanted it to continue. On top of the work, there was a mutual attraction and hint of something other than professional between them. To date, it hadn't gone beyond that, but it was better that way. In their work, a significant other gave the bad guys some leverage. It had happened to Marshall, and Thomas and Sandy knew a lot more bad guys than the umpire.

After the events at the park, Sandy had a feeling the two strangers she'd seen were among them.

"OK, start talking," she said. "What do you know?"

She was in one of two armchairs facing Thomas' desk. He was on the other side, in a well-worn high-back leather chair that had been in his family for more than one hundred years. Keeping it was part of Thomas' continuing education into how to hold on to the things in life that really mattered. The wall at Sandy's back was another example.

The shelves were lined with a collection of antique trinkets and books. Many were cracked and tattered, but their value could not be measured in money. They were there out of loyalty, either to the source or the story behind the acquisition. Figuring out how much happiness Thomas got from the possessions was still on Sandy's to-do list, but for now, she was content to leave it alone.

Other issues had her attention.

"C'mon, spill it," she said when Thomas failed to reply. "What are we dealing with?"

"I can only venture a guess," Thomas said.

Sandy shook her head.

"No way," she said. "You said you knew. Tell me."

Thomas sat forward and used his index finger to guide a folder across his desk. Sandy reached up and grabbed it. Within seconds her brow knitted up as she read the contents.

"How... I mean, where... *Shit*," she said before blowing out a long sigh.

She returned the folder to the desk and folded her arms across the front of her body. She was mad, but she wasn't, partly because Thomas was seemingly always ahead of things. It was a valuable skill, but not knowing how he got there ate at Sandy.

That great unknown was another part of the wedge between them. She was convinced Thomas was still connected to the CIA— or to some agency—in more than a "service provider" manner, but like any personal feelings he might have for her, knew he would never confirm it. And like the contents of the folder, it was very frustrating.

"OK," she said as she eyed him warily. "Did you have this *before* we went to the park?"

Thomas nodded.

"Yes," he said.

"So... I guess it was for *your* eyes only, huh?" Sandy said, not trying to hide her disappointment.

Thomas raised his eyebrow.

"Not any longer," he said with his flat tone firmly in place.

Sandy caught on that the shrug and tone were an apology without the actual words. "Sorry" would have been better, but she had learned to take what she could get from him and her expression bounced around until it settled on something more upbeat. Not quite a smile, but close.

"Fine," she said. "Give me the damn thing again."

She reached up and grabbed the folder and flipped it open. As she re-read the information, she took a drink from a bottle of water she'd been carrying. After wiping her mouth, her head began to bob from side to side, something she did when thinking.

"OK," she said without looking up. "So our two friends are known associates of Dukabi's. Says here the running presumption is they're his new help. So why did he ask for ours?"

She looked up.

"Good question," Thomas said.

Sandy's face scrunched up a little.

"What do you think?" she said in a slow cadence that emphasized a return of the frustrations.

Thomas ignored the tone.

"I don't, not yet," he said. "I'd like your theory first."

Sandy sighed slightly before relaxing again. After a second, she looked down at the folder and flipped a page. After reading, she looked up.

"Hmm, OK," she said. "Maybe Dukabi is in the middle of something, but has lost control. For that reason, he can't send the muscle. Or maybe the muscle can't handle it. This info would suggest otherwise, at least from a talent perspective. So, does that mean Dukabi lost control of these guys and *that's* why Booker is missing?"

Her eyes went wide to further emphasize the question.

"Valid concerns," Thomas said.

Sandy's head bobbed again for a few seconds, but she suppressed the urge to sigh again.

"Yeah, but are they *ours*?" she said.

"I haven't yet decided. We need to know more."

Sandy nodded.

"Yeah, no kidding," she said before standing. "I'll go break out the shovel."

The "shovel" was a program Sandy had created during her days as an FBI analyst. Never registered as theirs and not left behind when she resigned—not exactly kosher—if Google Search was a gorilla in the information jungle, Sandy's algorithm was King Kong, and the beast was even more powerful because of access to databases she'd previously only read about. The access furthered her "Thomas still works with someone" feelings, but was gladly accepted.

The program was loaded on two separate computers in her office, each machine's CPU providing obscene amounts of capacity. After leaving Thomas' office—and a quick detour past the kitchen for another bottle of water—Sandy made her way to her desk. Despite the late hour, she dove right in. Of course, she wasn't sure she would find anything Thomas didn't already know—something that happened a lot—but the workaholic in her was always more than happy to make the effort.

As the computer hard drives began to spin, Sandy retired to a spare room adjacent to the office. Her one-bedroom apartment, overlooking Philadelphia's Rittenhouse Square Park, was a forty-five minute drive on a good day. Sandy loved the place, but schlepping back and forth was often a traffic-induced nightmarish headache. She would rather get headaches from her work.

At least then she could do something about it.

Sandy awoke the next morning around seven. After a quick shower, she headed back to her office, but wasn't surprised to find both machines still processing. There were a lot of sources to dig through, and, she hoped, an equal number of treasures to be found. Undaunted, she made her way to the kitchen.

Thomas was already there. Despite the same amount of sleep as her—or less, she wasn't sure—he looked completely refreshed. It was another trait Sandy found appealing. No matter the situation or circumstances, he never seemed to get flustered. He was, in a word, unflappable.

"Sleep well?" he said when he saw her.

Sandy shrugged as she grabbed a muffin from a basket on the counter near where he stood.

"I'm not sure I actually slept," she said, parking on a stool. "My brain wouldn't shut off."

"Understandable," Thomas said.

"So, I guess we need to go call Alex, huh?"

"We do," Thomas said. "In one minute."

Sandy picked at the muffin as he diced a small melon. The dexterity and speed of his fingers and hands was impressive—and mesmerizing. Sandy got lost in the movements for a few seconds and an unprofessional thought danced across her mind. She was pretty sure she shook it off before he noticed.

"Done," Thomas said, recapturing her attention. "Let's go chat with the director. I'm sure he'll be interested."

"No doubt," Sandy said.

Alex Harris was director of the FBI field office in Philadelphia, and had been Sandy's former boss. Of the many possibilities, he was about the only thing Sandy truly missed about the Bureau. He'd been great to work for, although, at times, it was almost as if she'd never stopped.

Alex and Thomas had first met years ago, when Thomas was still at the CIA and Alex was with MARSOC, the Marines' Special Ops unit. They'd remained close—personally and otherwise—after moving into their current occupations. Thomas often consulted on cases for Alex and the Bureau. There was also the occasional *unofficial* lead passed Thomas' way, work better off not being handled by the FBI.

The former had been the situation on the Andrew Singer case. Thomas and Damien Hastings had worked together years earlier. Alex thought reconnecting them might help. It mostly did—until Damien was killed. That was the first of several cracks caused by Marshall's troubles. Sandy understood why. Thomas didn't trust his friend's safety to anyone, not even Alex. That left him prone to act outside normal channels. Alex didn't have the same luxury. He had to play by the book, and the conflicting priorities added the stress that led to the fissures.

Sandy wasn't sure how deep they'd become. She hoped not very.

She also found herself hoping this latest link wouldn't add to it.

A minute later, they were in Thomas' office. He used the speakerphone on his desk for the call. The first several minutes were devoted to an edited version of the Dukabi meeting. Alex's initial response was silence. Sandy understood, she'd been on that side of the table once, too. Alex was looking for a way to say something without saying anything. It was often an awkward dance. This one was more so given the participants.

"That's... *interesting*," Alex said when his voice returned. "The player you refer to reminds me a lot of Babe Ruth."

Alex, like Sandy, was a big baseball fan. Neither came close to Marshall, but both far outdistanced Thomas. A raised eyebrow told Sandy he needed help with the code Alex had just used. She held up three fingers, the Babe's uniform number when he played for the New York Yankees. Translation: three out of ten, meaning Dukabi was a name on a list in a file folder stuffed in the draw of a desk at which no one was sitting.

"Ah, yes," Thomas said. "I'm familiar with Mr. Ruth. What's your opinion of the others?"

Sandy heard what might have been a sigh through the line.

"I don't have one," Alex said.

Sandy was more worried than surprised. The words meant Alex couldn't say anything, not even a coded comment. That meant Thomas had gotten the earlier info from some other source. It also meant there were active files—and eyes—on the two men, but not necessarily Alex's.

"Damn it," Sandy said under her breath as she began to wonder if she'd missed more at the park.

Thomas eyed her for a second before responding to Alex.

"It would seem they have similar standing elsewhere," he said.

Sandy wanted to ask where that might be, but decided to quit while she was behind.

"Just be careful," Alex said.

"Always," Thomas said.

"Hmmm, like last time and the time before that, huh?" Alex said; then after a pause. "Listen, guys, I love you both, but try not to push it, OK? Don't get anyone else killed, especially yourselves."

There was a click and the speaker went quiet. Thomas reached up and tapped a button to close the connection before sitting back and eyeing Sandy.

"That went well," he said.

Sandy shook her head and frowned.

"I'm glad *you* think so," she said. "Christ, I missed enough stuff to get us in serious trouble—or worse."

Thomas nodded. Apparently, he agreed.

"A problem I'm sure you'll soon correct."

Chapter 4

Wayne

"Soon" ended up being late the following morning, not because of any additional failings, but because Sandy's program did its job. The digging produced a lot of information and she needed time to sort through it. She'd learned long ago the devil truly was in the details.

"OK," she said. "I'm not sure where to start."

She was with Thomas again in his office. He motioned with his chin toward the sizeable stack of paper on her lap. There were three separate subsets, each bound by a large clip.

"Your work, your choice," he said.

She nodded and looked down, her head bobbing for a second before she lifted the top stack.

"Well, it seems Mr. Dukabi lied," she said. "He *did* leave the country, as requested, but he didn't stay gone. He was back two months later. So were the poker games."

Something flashed across Thomas' face and Sandy stopped. She wasn't entirely sure what the expression was. Sometimes it was really hard to tell. In this instance, she made a guess.

"Yeah, it pissed me off, too," she said. "He's back doing the same crap that got a lot of people killed."

Thomas nodded. Sandy concluded she'd guessed correctly. She continued.

"That's where the relationship with Booker comes in," she said. "It's hard to tell exactly how big of a hole we're talking about here. From the financial info that came up, Booker's been in a mess for a long time. He got banned from baseball a few years ago and it looks like it wiped him out pretty good. It fits that he'd have outstanding markers. That makes me wonder if this thing is another 'Michael O'Hara repayment plan' situation."

O'Hara's scheme to repay Dukabi ultimately led to Marshall being dragged into the chaos two years ago—and to Damien being killed. Neither Sandy nor Thomas wanted to think something similar could be happening again.

"That would be most unfortunate," Thomas said.

Sandy caught the slight edge in his voice, but let it pass. Again, she agreed.

"Yeah, anyway, I found something else," she said, quickly changing the subject. "Dukabi has been back and forth to Africa more than a few times. The first was right after we closed the Singer case. But in the park, he said leaving wasn't easy. I think I might know why."

She took the next five minutes to give a quick story about the new lines of business some of the CIA-created gangs—and shaky governments—had gotten into.

Illegal drugs exploded across the Dark Continent in the years after Dukabi first left for America. The political instability was a perfect breeding ground for trafficking. Cannabis was the first and most widely-produced product to appear. Heroin joined later, imported from India, Pakistan, and Thailand, destined for markets in Europe. The Latin American drug cartels got involved after that, and the result was a market that saw close to thirty percent of the cocaine used in Europe and the Gulf transited through the region.

"Says here the activity is worth close to two billion a year," Sandy said, holding up the second stack of notes. "Tapping into that would be worth pursuing, especially for someone like Dukabi. That could be the link to the guys in the park. Maybe they turned him onto it and he restarted the games to launder the cash. It would explain why they're being watched. It could also mean *they're* running things, not Dukabi."

Thomas' hands came up and interlocked in front of his chin, his index fingers extended up toward his mouth. Sandy's father used to do something similar when she was a little girl. "Here's the church, here's the steeple, open the doors and see all the people," was the jingle the man would sing to her in a cutesy voice. The last words came as he opened the "door"—his thumbs—and began wiggling the fingers inside.

Sandy knew Thomas wouldn't take it that far, but the memory did draw a slight smile on her face as she waited. In Thomas' version, the steeple began working at his lower lip. It was one of his "I'm thinking" tells. Sandy used the time to steal another drink of water, and it was close to a minute before Thomas finally spoke again.

"I agree," he said.

Sandy's smile disappeared and she resisted a new urge to sigh. Thomas had managed to consolidate what had to be extensive thoughts into two words. It was infuriating.

"OK, well, anyway," Sandy said after a pause of her own. "The rest of this stuff on Booker is pretty straightforward. He got reinstated recently—sorry, *partially* reinstated—to be a players' agent, but I can't find any active relationships. Again, that fits the 'out of money' theory."

"Interesting," Thomas said.

"Yeah, I thought so, too," Sandy said. "I also found some stuff about rumors of steroids. Booker's name came up in a new book about it. Maybe that's why he doesn't have any clients."

Thomas nodded. Sandy finished off the last of her water.

"I'd say we have two things to follow up on," she said. "First, we need to have another chat with Dukabi about his activities. This drug thing could be bad."

"Agreed," Thomas said. "And part two?"

"I think we should call our favorite insider and see what he knows about these steroid rumors. I hear he's gonna be in New York in another day or so."

~*~*~*~*~*~*~

New York City

Mark Rosenbaum was trying his best not to get annoyed. The reporters on the other end of the phone weren't making that easy.

"Listen, gang," Mark said. "I don't think there's anything else to add. The quotes attributed to me in the book are accurate, but Mr. Donovan's conclusion is his own. I have no comment about whatever he said the other night on TV. That's his opinion. I have no issue with his right to have one. We all have that right... *even you guys*."

A knock on his open office door made Mark look up. He held up a finger to the man standing there before returning his eyes and attention back to the phone.

"Fellas, I gotta go," he said in a firm tone. "As far as Eddie Booker is concerned, the decision has been made and we're moving on. The man has paid his debts. Case closed."

The visitor at Mark's door—Gabi Loeb, MLB's Director of Security by title, but Mark's right-hand man in practice—moved a few steps into the office. Together for the better part of ten years, the two men had a seemingly strong relationship, one that saw Mark consulting the younger man on every significant decision. His trust of Gabi and his abilities ran deep.

Gabi mouthed "Reporters?" as he neared Mark's desk. Mark nodded.

"Guys, *enough*," Mark said into the phone. "We're done. Good-bye."

He slammed the handset back into the base unit. A small piece broke off.

"Ouch," Gabi said. "You OK?"

Mark looked up. His face was pained.

"Not really," he said. "Eddie keeps getting fired, but all the press seems to care about is why I reinstated him in the first place. I'm beginning to wonder myself. What has this guy gotten himself into here, Gabi? What are you hearing?"

Gabi settled into one of the chairs fronting Mark's desk.

"I don't know," he said.

"Look at this shit," Mark said.

He held up the New York *Daily News* and pointed to the headline on the back page: GOT JUICE? The connections were obvious—and a painful reminder to the past.

"Saw it," Gabi said. "Donovan already called. He seems to think we're hiding something. I told him there's nothing to hide. We're not aware of any new steroid issues."

Mark exhaled loudly and shook his head.

"Doesn't mean they aren't out there," he said, before turning away.

Gabi caught the sting in the tone. Steroids—more so than Eddie Booker—were a sensitive subject, one that tended to grate on everyone's nerves, Gabi's included. Mark's venting was understandable. He'd thought the problem solved, that the juice had run dry. If that *wasn't* the case, well, more people than Eddie would be in trouble.

"I understand," Gabi said. "Hey, listen, you got time for lunch? This shit isn't going anywhere."

Mark turned back. His features slowly brightened as he caught on to what Gabi was doing.

"Good idea," he said. "Are you paying?"

"Absolutely," Gabi said. "I'm thinking you could use the break."

"I like the way you think," Mark said with an exaggerated nod.

Eight minutes later they stepped to the sidewalk on 47th Street in front of the MLB offices.

"Lead on," Mark said.

Gabi nodded and they headed southeast to Lexington—avoiding Grand Central Station—and then five blocks south to 42nd Street. From there, it was a half-block southeast past the Chrysler Building. Mark's smile returned when they stopped in front of the doors of the Capital Grille.

"I *definitely* like the way you think," he said.

"Hey, it's why you pay me the big bucks," Gabi said.

Mark faked a frown.

"I thought I did that so you could keep me out of trouble."

"Trouble," Gabi said. "*What* trouble?"

A chuckle replaced Mark's faux frown. He shook his head.

"Ha, I wish."

~*~*~*~*~*~*~

Penn's Landing

There was nothing fake about how Eddie felt. He'd awakened with a groan. That he awoke at all might have shocked a lot of people. Between the whiskey and sedatives ingested over the past two days, a weaker person might be in a coma or at least be suffering from the world's worst hangover when they got out of bed, but Eddie's hangover days were long gone. What came now was in an entirely separate category.

Eddie would have gladly traded.

It was already after nine-thirty, but he had no desire to move. Moving would bring back the spasms and the sweat and the other aches and pains. Not moving meant the only thing he had to deal with was the mental anguish—not that that was any better, thanks to David Donovan.

"Fucking asshole," Eddie said under his breath as he stared up at the ceiling.

Almost ten minutes passed before he finally rolled over. The small victory of actually making it to the bathroom and then the shower was forgotten by the time he finished thirty minutes later. The high-pressure water pounding his muscles hadn't helped. Neither had the handful of something he'd grabbed out of the medicine cabinet. He wasn't surprised. At this point, he was resigned to finding relief only after he was dead—and even then, maybe not.

Too bad he was too afraid to test that theory.

In the next few minutes, he rummaged through his clothes for something clean, settling on a long-sleeve blue polo shirt and jeans. Before pulling on the pants, he found himself staring at the long scar extending down from the kneecap of his right leg. The once-sutured flesh was bright red, probably from the hot water or maybe the alcohol—or maybe just because.

Eddie ran his fingers along the reminder of the damage he'd done.

"I was fine before *you* came along," he said in a tired voice.

The mark didn't argue.

In the next hour, he finished dressing and made his way on foot to his office. The rental space was located in an aging building at the corner of 9th and Race streets in Philadelphia's Chinatown section. He'd walked because he couldn't remember where he'd left his car—not that he was in any condition to drive anyway—and he hadn't felt like waiting for a cab.

Like taking the sedatives, he wasn't sure why he'd bothered making the journey. Maybe both were simply habits he could no longer break, like a lot of things related to his present condition. Everything in the office—including Eddie—was beyond its best days. He was alone there, having fired the last of his agency staff months earlier. No clients meant there wasn't any need for employees. The days when it was otherwise weren't coming back anytime soon.

He wandered into what passed as the main office of the suite and parked on a beat-up love seat pushed against the side wall. There was a phone on a nearby side table. A small red zero told Eddie what he'd already figured to be the case. No messages. The handful of mail grabbed on the way in had been nothing but junk and was already in the trash. As he sat there, in the middle of the nothingness, the thoughts from two nights earlier returned.

"Ain't no one gonna miss me," he said aloud. "I should just do it and get it over with."

He let his head fall back. It wasn't very comfortable, but he didn't have the energy to move and it wasn't long before his eyes shut and he faded off. No dreams came this time, but the nap was rudely interrupted by voices coming through the thin wall next to him.

It took Eddie a few seconds to realize it was his neighbors, the Asians working at the Chinese take-out next door. A passing thought of food came along with the lunchtime smells seeping through the cheap wood. Eddie loved oriental cuisine, but quickly dismissed the urge. He was certain today would be a bad day for it. The odor alone wasn't mixing well with the two days of alcohol in his system. He was doing all he could not to puke from it.

"Yo, Wong," he said in something close to a yell as he bounced his fist on the wall. "Shut the fuck up already, will ya?"

A squeaky reply that may or may not have included the Chinese version of "Fuck you, Eddie" came back in his direction, but he didn't have time to dwell on it. The phone on the small table had starting ringing. Eddie stared at it for a few seconds before touching the *SPKR* button on the base. Static quickly filled the air.

"Yup, Eddie here," he said. "I'm not really here, so—just leave a message."

The static remained.

"Hullo?" Eddie said to it. "I was kidding. Who's there?"

"Time to pay, Mr. Booker," a mechanical-sounding voice said.

Eddie mistook the distortion as something caused by the cheap phone.

"Huh?" he said as he jiggled the base.

"All debts must be repaid," the voice said.

It took much longer than it should have, but Eddie finally caught up. As he did, his hands began to shake—or maybe they'd already been shaking. He wasn't sure.

"Uh… yeah, I, uh—I don't have your money," he said.

In his mind he added: "Even if I did, there's no way I'd give it to you now," but he didn't have the balls to let that thought get past his lips. When there was no reply, however, he began to think maybe he'd accidentally done so.

His entire body started to shake and a new round of sweat erupted from every pore—or maybe he just began to notice it. Either way, fear had replaced lethargy as a new thought filled his head. Killing himself might no longer be required, especially if the person on the phone was in fact who Eddie now thought it was.

"Hullo?" he said again. "Did you, uh, hear me? I don't—"

"We heard," the voice said, cutting him off. "That is most unfortunate."

There was a click and a staticky dial tone returned. Eddie stared at the phone, but couldn't remember how to make the noise go away.

Chapter 5

Queens, New York

"It's nice to see you again, Mr. Connors."

An appropriate response would have been something like "Same here," but that's not quite what came out.

"That makes one of us," I said instead.

In my defense, I was brain-dead—which is what happened when airport delays turned a supposed two-hour flight into a red-eye marathon. The fact the clerk knew my name wasn't helping, either. On one hand, it was a nice touch, the hotel had attentive staff. Good. On the other hand, it meant this particular bundle of excessive perkiness remembered me from one of my many prior visits over the years. Not good.

Travel was a big part of my job. I should have been used to the crap that often came with it, but there were times when it beat me down. Too many days got lost in an endless cycle of packing and unpacking, sleeping in strange beds, eating bad food, and everything else that came with life on the road. If it wasn't for my job as a major league umpire—the greatest job in the world, in my opinion— I think I would have lost my mind long ago.

I could do without people yelling at me, *a lot*, and expecting me to be perfect, *all the time*, but still, it wasn't the clerk's fault. She didn't deserve some dickhead doing the same thing to her. She was just doing her job. And besides, that wasn't what really had me down.

"Hey, uh, listen, my bad," I said after realizing the mistake. "I'm a little tired."

"I understand," the clerk said, most of her perkiness still there. "Don't worry about it. We're *always* glad to see you anyway."

Her tone said she was flirting with me, but I didn't want to go there.

"Yeah, I have that effect on people," I said with a half-smile and a shrug.

In my head I thought I'd nicely avoided her advance, but the clerk's smile got bigger.

"Oh, I'm *sure* you do," she said with a look that left no doubt I'd failed.

Normally, I would have continued the dance, but I let it die without a word. True, she was cute and it might have been fun, but recent events had more than convinced me to stay out of any relationships.

"Here you are," the clerk said after about a minute, handing me a card key. "You're in room eight-two-five. Your partner is already here."

That much I knew. I was the only one in my four-man crew stupid enough to try for a later flight. I had a good reason, catching up with an old friend. Too bad the simple change became anything but. The umpires union had done wonders with improving our standing in the game, but we still flew commercial, with all its inherent joys. Translation: Endless and mystifying delays.

"Is there anything else I can do for you?" the clerk said.

She was still smiling and I let my tired eyes wander down to her name tag. She'd known my name, I wanted to learn hers. It seemed like the polite thing to do, but I lingered a little too long and I think she thought I was checking out her breasts. I was actually trying to figure out why a location was so important it had to be included on the tag. No, really, that's what I was doing.

"*Mr. Connors?*" Monica Myers of South Bend, Indiana, said in a tone less flirty than before. "Is there anything else?"

"Oh, shit, sorry," I said as I realized my latest error. "No, I'm good, thanks."

I forced a smile, picked up the key, and shuffled away from the counter. I think Monica was happy about that. The misplaced stare—not that I was looking at her curves; well, not on purpose—was another example of my dangerous habit of being in the wrong place at the wrong time lately, especially when it came to women.

Just ask my ex, the stunningly beautiful and way-too-good for me Suze Keebler. Suze had figured out there was a lot more to it than bad luck. In my adventures, people got hurt, and in some cases—*too many* in fact—ended up dead. That's not what Suze had signed up for when she decided to date an umpire.

No one would sign up for that.

Suze lived and worked in New York, her job executive assistant to MLB Commissioner Mark Rosenbaum. I lived in Radnor, outside of Philadelphia, but was mostly on the road, in a new city every three or four days, working ball games. Ours should have been a safe albeit long-distance relationship. It should have been a lot of things, except what it turned out to be.

The beginning of the end had come when Suze almost got killed after being kidnapped by a seriously messed up man named Andrew Singer. When I got kidnapped by another whacko a year or so later, she was done with me. I was lucky the breakup was the only price I paid. If not for my best friend, Thomas Hillsborough, Suze and I might also have been among the dead.

Thomas was very good at the hero stuff. Me? Not so much—although there was one time I managed to pull it off, back in college. It got Thomas into my life, but I've tried to tell him he doesn't owe me anything for it. He doesn't listen.

Actually, now that I think about it, I was kind of glad for that last part.

Anyway, after slinking away from Monica Myers, I headed to my room. There was a note from my roommate—he'd gone to lunch—so I was alone. Outside of thinking up an appropriate recovery response for the next time I saw Monica, sleep was the only other thing on my mind, but the sound of my phone changed that.

Put me in, coach, I'm ready to play...

The John Fogerty song ring-tone was assigned to Thomas, but I hadn't expected to hear from him, at least not yet. We had a simple system. Barring unusual circumstances, like kidnappings, murders, good stuff like that, we'd touch base whenever my schedule permitted, usually when I had games in Philly or when I was in New York or D.C.

The visits were a nice break from the day-to-day grind of the season. Thomas didn't much care about the game, but was always willing to let me blather on about it. In addition to being a great fixer, he was an even better listener. I think that's why I got worried at hearing the phone. I hadn't told him I was going to be in New York. That meant he had something to say, and for the better part of the past two years, when that had happened, more bad than good had followed.

Of course, could be I was just tired and over-thinking it. It wouldn't be the first time.

"Um, should I be worried?" I said after answering.

"Hello to you, too," Thomas said.

In the years I'd known him, I'd gotten fairly good at reading the at-times-annoying flatness in his voice. When I could see his face, I could usually decipher the underlying meanings, not that he made a lot of facial expressions, but it helped. In this case, without the visuals, I wasn't sure what might be going on. My exhaustion pushed me to use a direct approach to find out.

"So, what's up, spy boy," I said. "You never call unless someone is in trouble."

"We need your assistance."

And there it was, I thought, before taking a deep breath. A second later, I slowly let it escape.

"*We* need it?" I said. "Does that mean Sandy is with you?"

"Hey, Marshall, I'm here," she said. "You sound tired."

She was almost as good as Thomas at reading things. In her case, though, she didn't mask the reactions. It was probably why the two of them worked so well together. Suze and I had once tried to push them into something more, but it didn't happen—at least I don't think anything happened. I'd since given up trying. Either way, they were a good team.

"I am," I said to Sandy's comment. "And there's a nap here with my name on it."

She laughed. She had a nice laugh. Thomas could do worse if there was something more going on, but it wasn't like he would ever tell me. After a second or two, I chased those thoughts away and tried to refocus.

"Alright you guys, what's up, what's this assistance?" I said, getting back on point. "I hope whatever you need is a quickie."

There was a too-long delay before Sandy's voice came back.

"I don't know about that," she said. "Do you have time to talk about Eddie Booker?"

I suddenly no longer felt tired. I knew a lot about Eddie "Don't call me Edward James" Booker—and pretty much none of it was good.

"Uh… yeah, no," I said. "There isn't enough time in the day for that."

Penn's Landing

Eddie didn't hang around the office waiting for another phone call—or whatever else the strange voice might have had in mind. He'd been expecting something to happen because of the money he owed Dukabi, but thought he could make it go away by avoiding it. He knew now there were no more chances of doing that. The phone call meant this shit wasn't going anywhere, and so did something else, an unexpected gift.

The process of locking up the office, walking a block to Market Street, and hailing a cab there had taken five minutes, max. The ride back to his apartment had taken maybe twelve minutes. Total time after finally hanging up his end of the phone call: Twenty minutes. That there was a package waiting for him at the lobby desk of his building when he stepped through the street-side doors meant that the other end of the odd call had been somewhere close, *too close*, as in someone was watching him.

That thought was scarier than anything his aches and pains had produced, but the package itself was worse. The doorman couldn't say who'd left it. It had just "shown up" the man said. He never saw who dropped it through the slot. Inside was an unmarked envelope, no return address, no stamp, no nothing. Inside the envelope was a single sheet of paper.

"What the fuck is this?" Eddie said aloud after the first read-through.

He was in his bedroom, sitting on the edge of his unmade bed. He read the message again, but the answer didn't come. He set the sheet next to his hip and put his head in his hands. Instinctively, he started to work his temples with his thumbs. He had a headache. He almost *always* had a headache. But now, on top of it, he was confused.

"No fuckin' way can it be that easy," he said as he processed the note. "No way—"

He was cut off by a fresh round of spasms. He fell back on the bed to ride out the attack, but each misfire felt like the snap of a whip, only from the inside—a more conventional lashing would have been less torturous.

Five, then ten minutes passed as he did his best not to move. The sweating, now a constant, was a blessing, the feel of the damp shirt against his skin a welcome relief from the pain. Above him, the dusty paddles of the ceiling fan were doing slow turns. Unnoticed at first, the movements began to draw him in, until suddenly, the fan was no longer spinning, *he was*.

The sensation was worse than that from two nights earlier and he was unable to hold back the vomit. The contents of his stomach exited with a vengeance. Most of the gunk hit the floor, but a handful splattered across the bed. As the heaves subsided, he fell back again and closed his eyes, having failed to notice that much of the puke was blood.

He stayed in the same position for another ten minutes, concentrating on nothing other than his breathing. When the spinning finally ended, he slowly opened his eyes, but made sure to look away from the fan, lest it return. The pain would be back soon enough, too, but for a brief moment his body relaxed.

Clear of interference, his mind circled back to the sheet of paper and the option he'd been given. The simple instructions seemed to make sense, except that they didn't. He tried to weigh it against what he'd been contemplating, but it didn't add up. There was no comparison, unless maybe there wasn't supposed to be, like maybe *that* was the point.

In the quiet, his head began to shake as a new thought surfaced.

"What the fuck have I done?"

~*~*~*~*~*~*~

Wayne

Sandy filled her afternoon adding Marshall's tidbits about Eddie to what she'd already learned. It left her thinking there might be something to the steroid angle, but she couldn't see how it connected to Dukabi. It did further her desire to get another meeting with the man, and she set out to bounce the idea off Thomas.

She found him in the kitchen. Correction, she was lured there by a strong smell of food and he happened to be the force behind it. In addition to his spy skills, Thomas was a first-rate cook. If Sandy had to rank it, his food acumen would be near the top of the already crowded assets side of his ledger.

"That smells *really* good," she said after reaching the kitchen. "Is some of it for me? Please say yes. I was destined for a Wawa hoagie on the way home, but that looks a lot better."

Thomas raised both eyebrows.

"I was hoping you'd join me," he said.

A big smile filled Sandy's face.

"Nice," she said in an exaggerated Philly accent.

She parked on her usual stool at the kitchen counter and watched as he put the finishing touches on two Panini sandwiches. The aroma of spinach, mozzarella, roasted red peppers, and various spices was already overwhelming. When Thomas set the sandwiches on a griller and closed the lid, the scents intensified. She closed her eyes and let them sink in.

"*Wow*," she said. "Let's get married."

Her eyes shot open. The reflexive statement was a slip. Freud would have appreciated it. Sandy wasn't so sure about Thomas, but she found a smile on his face. It was slight, but it was there, and her cheeks started to get warm.

"Sorry," she said as she tried to shake off the rising blush.

"Have you made any progress?" Thomas said.

It took a second to process the words. Sandy was relieved he was way ahead of her in this instance. Changing the subject was a great idea. She chased away the rest of her embarrassment and followed his lead.

"Yeah, I should have something by morning—if there's something to have."

"Is there a problem?" Thomas said.

"No, no," Sandy said. "I've been thinking about the guys from the park. I can't see Dukabi letting them be in charge. Sure, they're nasty, but it doesn't fit him, you know what I mean? If they really are running things, it's gotta be bad."

She waited as Thomas set out two plates and silverware.

"Go on," he said.

Sandy adjusted herself on the stool, leaning forward further onto her elbows—mostly to get closer to the smells coming from the toasting sandwiches.

"Dukabi doesn't give up control, *ever*," she said. "Hell, even after you guys lured him from that gang in Kenya he was still pulling the strings. But what do you think would happen if the rest of the gang didn't buy the cover story? Would they be pissed if they found out he was still alive? And could they be looking for a payback?"

There was a small beep. Thomas pulled the sandwiches from the griller, sliced each in half, and arranged them on the plates. A fresh dill pickle was added along with a handful of kettle chips, barbeque-flavored. He slid one of the plates in front of Sandy.

"Time out," he said.

Sandy got the message and took a bite of her sandwich. Her eyes closed and she slumped slightly. One of her friends called the move a "food-gasm." It felt almost as good as the other kind of gasm—not that Sandy had had one of those in a while.

"*Oh. My. God,*" she said after swallowing. "I'm never eating at Wawa again."

Thomas bowed his head slightly.

"Thank you," he said through a slight grin.

For a few minutes the food took center stage. Sandy finished off hers first.

"OK, where was I?" she said after her last bite.

"You were suggesting an internal conflict," Thomas said.

"Right," Sandy said; then after a pause. "If Dukabi was running from these guys, might he be inclined to reinstate some of his past activities?"

"Explain," Thomas said.

Sandy grabbed one of Thomas' chips and popped it into her mouth.

"I can see him messing with the drugs for the money in it," she said. "This steroid thing, though, that doesn't seem like something he'd get involved with. But what if Booker was the one to raise the issue?"

Thomas picked up a chip, but didn't eat it.

"The O'Hara scenario," he said. "It is plausible."

He crunched into the chip. Sandy began to nod.

"We gotta go find out," she said. "We need to fill in some of these holes."

"Agreed," Thomas said.

A quiet descended. Both seemed to be lost in thought. Sandy was first to air hers.

"Hey, can I ask you something else?" she said.

Thomas nodded.

"Do you ever go out?" Sandy said. "I mean for stuff that isn't related to work? I've known you, what, three years? I don't think we've ever—I don't think I've ever heard you talk about it. And I've certainly never seen you with anyone."

Thomas eyed her. He wanted to say "And you never will" but chose another path.

"Acceptable?" he said.

"Huh?" Sandy said, clearly confused.

Thomas motioned to her plate. Sandy realized he was changing the subject again. A sound of disappointment escaped her mouth.

"Yeah… it was great," she said, the dejection thick.

She stood and carried her dish to the sink. More than a few heavy sighs escaped as she helped clean up the remnants of the meal. She was mad at him for being so goddamned stoic. She was mad at herself for being mad at him. She was the one who'd allowed her feelings to peek out from under the covers. She needed to tuck them back in. Nothing was going to happen. It *couldn't* happen. It was too dangerous in too many ways. She'd been there, done that, with Damien. She couldn't go back.

"Thanks for dinner," she said after stowing the last of the dishes.

"My pleasure," Thomas said.

Sandy let out one last sigh and nodded. It was time to get back to work.

"So, Dukabi, tomorrow?" she said as they left the kitchen. "I don't like how familiar this is all starting to sound. He's involved with another baseball player with outstanding debts. He's having trouble with his hired guns. He's coming to us for help."

"It does have certain déjà vu-esque qualities, yes," Thomas said.

Sandy nodded.

"Yeah, that's what I'm afraid of."

Chapter 6

Suburban Philadelphia

This is Eddie. Leave a message after the beep…

The familiar instruction dissolved Paul Bischoff's focus into a splintered mess, and the thick rush-hour traffic around his car faded to a status of barely registered. Bischoff was a prime example of why "no cell phones while driving" laws were necessary. He had trouble with basic multi-tasking, like walking and talking at the same time. Adding technology to the mix made it worse, and when the beep sounded, "barely registered" became non-existent and Bischoff's gaze dropped from the road.

After a couple of seconds, he shouted into the quiet.

"Dude, where are you?" he said. "You're startin' to piss people off, me included. What the fuck are you doing, Eddie? You better not—"

He stopped mid-sentence when the glare of brake lights in his eyes ignited one of the few other functioning brain cells in his head. The spark's message was "You're in a car," but it took another few seconds before another spark told him "You're *driving* the car."

"*Shit,*" he said in a half-shout as his reflexes kicked in.

He swerved the Bentley to the right. Any thought that another vehicle might be already occupying that space never had a chance. The air outside the $200,000 blue-crystal Continental GT Speed filled with the sound of blaring horns and screeching tires. A heavy foot to the accelerator pedal confirmed the manufacturer's claim this was their most powerful production car ever, and the sleek vehicle shot past the unfortunate victim of Bischoff's lack of attention to details. Contact was avoided.

A handful of quiet seconds later, the car's fifteen-speaker audio system re-engaged the CD player. The sound of the Foo Fighters returned to Bischoff's ears. "The Pretender" was playing. It was fitting. Paul Bischoff was the ultimate pretender, a forty-four year old walking billboard for his company, Bulge, Inc., maker of supposedly healthy and natural supplements. Bischoff's physique suggested said something was anything but "natural." The claims by angry customers in a few pending lawsuits left "healthy" up for debate as well.

Bischoff didn't care.

As displayed by his driving, he tended to leave the details to others. He was more a big picture type, an idea man—one idea at a time, of course, but still, an idea man nonetheless. Unfortunately, the idea currently bouncing around his overtaxed brain had run into trouble. He was working hard, without much success, to understand the implications.

"What the fuck are you doin', Eddie?" he said again.

The sounds of Dave Grohl and his band mates were replaced by a female voice.

Did you say, contact Eddie?

Bischoff had no idea who the woman was or how she got into the radio. It was borderline scary, causing him to quickly push a button on the steering wheel. Pristine silence followed, but the lack of sound was equally as eerie and he stabbed at another button. The female voice returned.

Command, please.

It took Bischoff a few seconds to respond.

"Uh, call Jason," he said in another shout toward the dash.

The car's owner's manual explained there was no need for anything more than a normal speaking voice when dealing with the automated system. Shouting was Bischoff's solution to the technical dilemma of having never removed the manual from its plastic wrapper. Sophisticated electronics couldn't overcome stupidity.

Did you say, check ignition?

"Wait. What? No," Bischoff said.

Wipers on...

"Goddamn it," Bischoff said as he stabbed at the controls.

Another few seconds passed before he got it right and the computer dialed a number. As the tones played out, Bischoff checked his reflection in the car's rearview mirror. The acne-scarred bulbous face looking back was streaked with sweat. A wondering question about that began to form. but it was chased away when a new voice replaced the ringing.

"What's wrong, Paul?"

The voice belonged to Jason Adley, Bulge's thirty-nine year old lead chemist and Bischoff's partner. The partnership was about the only thing these men had in common. Where Bischoff used brawn to get by, Jason used brains, and similar to the hands-free system in the car, often overwhelmed the burly man's grey matter to the point of uselessness. The simple question had done so again.

"Huh, whataya mean?" Bischoff said.

Bischoff couldn't see it, but Jason's head began to shake. The doctor was used to the bewilderment, but it was beyond annoying. So was something else. Bischoff was a shyster, a snake-oil salesman who could get people to do things they'd otherwise never think of— or even want to think of. Whether it was ladies lifting skirts or athletes dropping drawers, Bischoff had a knack for pushing the right buttons. It was one of the few things Jason's IQ couldn't solve.

"Paul, *focus*," he said in a sharp tone. "You called me."

"Oh, yeah... right," Bischoff said. "I can't get holda Eddie. I think something's wrong."

An exaggerated sigh came through the speakers.

"I don't know about Eddie," Jason said. "But you're right. We do have a problem, a big one."

Dynamic Combinational Chemistry (DCC) was a powerful new technology. Jason—with the help of Bischoff's money—was at the forefront of its development. If DCC worked as promised, chemists would be capable of creating almost limitless undetectable designer steroids. It would give new meaning to the term "performance-enhancing drug."

Steroids had a complicated four-ring carbon structure. Any attempt to change the anabolic, estrogen, and androgenic properties of a substance—testosterone for example—had to be done one part at a time. That meant development was a slow process. DCC changed that. Chemists would no longer be limited by the complex structure. Synthesizing and testing hundreds—if not thousands—of unique and potent steroid compounds would take mere minutes. The possibilities were endless.

Jason hoped to do something good with the tool, possibly extend its benefits to the fight against cancer and other life-threatening diseases. Bischoff didn't care about that. He merely wanted to get rich. At the moment, neither man's goal was likely to happen.

Jason's first creation using DCC was labeled "The Cure" by Bischoff. It was a mutation combining the fat reduction properties of Masteron, a powerful anabolic—think Ephedra times one hundred—and the mass gain effects of Equipoise, a veterinary steroid developed for horses. Having never attempted such a combination, Jason had no idea what "The Cure" might do to a user. That's why it needed extensive testing and why it was so dangerous.

Again, Bischoff didn't care about the danger. The only thing he could see was that "The Cure" was undetectable by any testing system used in sports. It was, literally, a cure, a way to beat the system, to cheat. For him, it was a three-for-one deal. It was going to be easy to produce, easy to distribute, and easy to charge a shitload for. He'd already identified a client base, arranged for a conduit to said clients, and contacted a distribution partner.

All he needed now was the inventory.

"What the fuck is *that*?" Bischoff said.

He was standing in the lab on the second sub-level of Bulge's office building, motioning to a table. Jason was on the other side. Between the men, on top, a splayed-open carcass of what used to be a hamster stared up at them.

"*That* is what happens when you screw with Mother Nature," Jason said.

The muscles in Bischoff's jaw began flexing repeatedly, turning the rumpled skin on his face bright red as blood rushed into the potholes. It was as unpleasant a sight as the dead rodent, and as more confusion set in, additional muscles began to flex. The stress on the weave of the loud shirt Bischoff wore, already clinging to his body like sausage casing, increased.

Jason wondered how it held up. He never took such chances, clothing or otherwise. He, too, was something of a health-nut, but unlike Bischoff, steered clear of anything the company produced. He knew better. The same was true of his attire, his normal and current outfit being jeans, t-shirt, and white lab coat. It screamed "Nerd" but it was comfortable. He was content to let Bischoff be the flashy one, the strung-out, stressed-out freak.

"Fuck that, Doc," Bischoff said, proving that very point. "You need to make this shit work. I got a lotta people waiting for it."

Jason sighed and shook his head.

"They're going to have to wait a long time," he said.

Bischoff's expression worsened and he began to look around the lab. He already hated spending time in the windowless pit on the best of days. All the equipment was confusing enough. The dead thing on the table made it worse.

He shook it off and refocused on Jason.

"What?" he said. "Because a few fucking rats died?"

"That's right, Paul," Jason said. "Better them than an actual person."

A ripple ran through Bischoff's body. It was as if every muscle had suddenly spasmed. The weave on the shirt stretched thinner. Despite that, and the heat and smell emanating from the man, Jason did not flinch.

"There's no way I'm releasing this stuff," he said.

Bischoff's bully façade cracked and his eyes began to bounce around to everything in the room except Jason's.

"Yeah, well, if you don't fix this the rats won't be the only dead things," he said.

Jason backed off for a second and then leaned forward again.

"A threat?" he said, his eyes narrowing. "You're kidding, right?"

Bischoff shrugged.

"Paul?" Jason said. "What's going on? *What did you do?*"

"I—I didn't do anything," Bischoff said. "It's just—it's a little fuckin' late for this."

Jason shook his head.

"No way," he said. "I told you from the beginning it would take time. No one has ever done anything like this. You can't just... you have to... *Goddamn it, Paul, I need more time.*"

Bischoff eyed the dead hamster again before backing away.

"Shit, Jason. We're outta time."

An hour later, Jason was alone, standing in front of a small cage along the back wall of the lab. From inside the cage, another pair of lifeless black eyes stared back, the tenth such set in the past month. He wasn't quite sure what Bischoff had done or what Eddie's absence might mean, but the eyes in the cage kept him from dwelling on it.

"I'm sorry little fella," he said.

With a heavy sigh, he opened the gate and gently removed the latest victim. He silently cursed Bischoff as he carried the animal to the table in the center of the lab. After placing it next to number nine, he dropped onto a stool and stared at both for a long moment. A single tear escaped his eye.

"Goddamn it, Paul," he said again in a soft voice.

He would go through the motions of another autopsy, but knew the results would be the same. The cause of death was no longer a mystery. What these creatures had endured was nothing short of torture. On so many levels it was wrong, and despite the prospects for something good, Jason knew it had to stop.

He just hoped it wasn't already too late.

Chapter 7

Philadelphia

"Forgive me when I say it feels like we've been here before," Sandy said.

"I agree," Thomas said.

They were in Thomas' car, parked just off Chestnut Street, around the corner from Dukabi's building. For strategic reasons, they'd arranged to meet with Dukabi on the big man's turf, an apartment suite remarkably similar to the one the African had occupied several years ago. A layout of the suite filled the screen of an iPad resting in Sandy's lap, her head bobbing as she studied the schematic.

"So, how you wanna play it?" she said, looking up. "Show and tell, twenty questions?"

"A bit of both seems to be in order," Thomas said.

Sandy nodded.

"That works for me."

Eleven minutes later, they were in the room Sandy had identified as Dukabi's office. The lack of interference in getting there was glaringly noticeable. Dukabi had met them alone, furthering the doubts about the strangers from the park. Now, as they sat, he joined them on the guest side of a humongous mahogany desk, in a collection of matching armchairs there.

Dukabi was dressed in his version of casual: Black slacks, black shirt, black sport coat, black shoes, no tie. Thomas was in an outfit similar to the one from the park, stylish without effort. Sandy was wearing something in-between. It wasn't sloppy, but somehow seemed so to her. Then again, clothing wasn't her specialty.

"You mentioned additional questions," Dukabi said, starting the conversation. "Please, ask."

The bass in his voice sounded friendly and he added an inviting gesture with his arms.

"Mr. Dukabi, are you dealing drugs?"

The straight punch from Sandy shattered all pleasantries. Dukabi reacted with his version of a fidget—to the extent something so large could fidget—but the lack of space in the overmatched armchair gave the movements an almost comical awkwardness. No one laughed.

"What type of question is this?" Dukabi said after he stopped moving.

"The type you need to answer if you want our help."

The words were Thomas'. Dukabi's gaze shifted and darkened.

"I have explained my travel," he said.

Sandy shot a quick glance toward Thomas. A barely noticeable eyebrow shrug yielded the floor to her. She eyed Dukabi again.

"I didn't ask about your travel," she said. "I asked about drugs. We know you're associated with people who are in the business. We need to know how much of that business has spilled into your lap. It would help fill in some of the holes in your earlier stories."

Dukabi looked back and forth between his two guests. A single bead of sweat appeared above what used to be his hairline and made a slow, wet descent toward his jaw. It hung there for a long second before falling and disappearing into the dark fabric of his shirt.

"Yes, I suppose such an assumption may exist," he said. "However, I can assure you, I do not deal in drugs. They are a most foul creation for which I have no taste."

The words were met with a skeptical look from Sandy.

"I didn't mean to suggest you were a user," she said. "We're more interested in how you feel about the money side of things."

Dukabi's eyes narrowed.

"Please do not insult me with such accusations," he said.

The room went quiet. Another unspoken gesture between Sandy and Thomas passed the baton back to him. He pulled a single sheet of paper from the inside pocket of his jacket and handed it to Dukabi. The paper practically disappeared in the man's large hands.

"What can you tell us about these men?" Thomas said. "We were hoping we might meet them in person."

Sandy caught an odd reaction in Dukabi's facial features as he eyed the material. A second later, his right hand closed into a fist. The sheet of paper let out a crinkle of a cry in protest.

"They are no longer associated with me," Dukabi said in a tone as dark as his expression.

"Is that why you came to us?" Sandy said.

Dukabi turned to her. She did not scare easily, but the look she saw on his face came close to doing it. Ominous would be an understatement, and she was sure Thomas' presence was the only thing keeping him from lunging at her.

"In part," he said.

Sandy held firm.

"*Which* part?" she said.

Dukabi's dark skin could not mask the micro expressions racing across his face. Sandy caught most of them. Thomas caught them all.

"Let us just say, Ms. Hood," Dukabi said. "All involved would be better off if these men were… *elsewhere*."

The pause before and emphasis on the last word left a confused look on Sandy's face.

"That's not really—"

A raised hand from Thomas stopped her.

"I believe what Mr. Dukabi is trying to say is that he doesn't need help locating Mr. Booker," he said. "He needs help locating his friends from Africa. They are the ones likely on the verge of something drastic."

Sandy's eyes got wide as she looked first at Thomas, then at Dukabi, then back to Thomas again. She was even more confused than moments before. She was upset, too. It wasn't from Thomas being several steps ahead of her. It was because he'd had ample opportunities in the last two days to share the theory he'd just put forth. She decided to step back and simply let things play out, whatever the hell things were.

"You assume these men frighten me," Dukabi said into the growing tension. "I assure you, such is not the case."

Sandy found herself doubting that, but said nothing. This was Thomas' show. Let him return the volley. He obliged.

"That may be," he said. "But something has you on edge. Care to explain?"

Dukabi deflected.

"Yes, it would appear you have decided not to assist," he said. "That is most unfortunate... *for everyone.*"

Thomas' eyes narrowed.

"A threat, Mr. Dukabi?" he said.

Dukabi brushed at something on his slacks only he could see. After glancing at Sandy, he refocused on Thomas.

"*A fact*, Mr. Hillsborough," he said.

"Whoa," Sandy said under her breath as some of her confusion lifted.

Dukabi turned to her. An understanding—albeit wicked—smile appeared on his face.

"Yes, Ms. Hill, I concur," he said "Very much so."

A large black SUV pulled to the curb outside the building. Jamie was behind the wheel. Shady slid into the passenger seat without a word. It was two blocks before either spoke.

"What have you learned?" Jamie said in his native tongue.

Shady turned.

"It seems the plans have changed," he said in the same language. "Dukabi again met with the strangers. I was unable to complete my task."

Despite the message, Jamie smiled at the younger man's mastery of the dialect, never an easy thing. As with his other skills, it was impressive.

"I see you have been practicing," Jamie said in English.

Shady's face showed a passing hint of confusion before he offered up a slight shrug.

"Nevertheless," he said, also in English. "I have failed."

Jamie's smile returned.

"Fear not, my friend," he said. "You will have an opportunity to make amends."

"What has happened?" Shady said. "Do we have new orders?"

"No," Jamie said. "The orders are no longer relevant."

Shady listened intently as Jamie provided the details. When he finished, Shady nodded, but remained quiet. A left and two rights put the SUV onto JFK Boulevard, face-to-face with 30th Street Station, Philadelphia's Amtrak depot. Shady glanced at his partner. The older man saw a question in the look.

"I promised a trip to New York City one day," he said. "Today is that day."

Shady nodded.

"A new game," he said, almost as an aside.

"Yes, my friend, a new game indeed."

Sandy slammed the car door harder than she meant to, but didn't apologize for it. The expensive vehicle should be able to handle the abuse. Sandy hadn't been abused, but she sure felt like it, and it was ten minutes before she spoke. That Thomas allowed her to sulk that long only made things worse.

"OK, you need to explain what the hell just happened," Sandy said. "How do you... *why* do you... *damn it*, you could have told me that's where your head was."

She was staring at him through a pronounced glower. His eyes remained on the road.

"I find the element of surprise adds effectiveness," he said.

Sandy's scowl gave way to something closer to the confused look she'd displayed during the meeting with Dukabi. She looked away from Thomas then back to him again.

"How?" she said. "We're supposed to be on the same side."

"We are," Thomas said.

"Don't you think that would be easier if I knew what you were going to do *before* you did it?" Sandy said. "Maybe then I could actually contribute something."

Thomas' features didn't change. Sandy fought back an urge to smack a look, any look, *onto* his face, something other than the damned flatness.

"You did contribute, extensively," he said.

"How... *grrrrr*," Sandy said, the growl noise followed by a long, loud exhale. "Like I said, feel free to explain. I'm all ears."

"I wanted you to follow your instincts in an unbiased manner," Thomas said. "You did that. Mr. Dukabi's response solidified my conclusion. Such may have been 'where my head was,' as you suggest, but it was by no means firm until I saw his reaction."

He hadn't shouted, yelled, or emphasized any one word above the next, but the lack thereof served the same purpose. Sandy got it—what Thomas had been doing at the meeting—and most of the tension and frustration left her face.

"Oh... OK," she said; then after another pause. "Still, you coulda told me."

The last part came as she looked away from Thomas. After another minute or so, she turned back toward him.

"So, where does that leave us?" she said. "On the case, I mean. Are we actually going to help him? Or is it fourth and long and time to punt?"

The sports analogy elicited a half of a grin at the corner of Thomas' mouth. Marshall was fond of using similar words—too often if Thomas were pushed to opine on it—and Sandy's use reminded him of how similar his two friends were. The fractional grin survived longer than that thought before Thomas refocused on answering Sandy's question.

"I suspect if I were to simply say yes you might be inclined to harm me," he said.

He shot her a quick glance. Her eyes had narrowed slightly.

"You'd be lucky if that was the only thing I did," she said.

Thomas nodded.

"Indeed," he said. "I shall refrain."

"Gee, thanks."

Eddie made three phone calls before leaving his apartment for the last time. The first two went unanswered. He didn't leave a message—he'd be able to do so in person soon enough. The third was answered, but Eddie did all the talking.

"I don't really know what's going on, but you should be ready, just in case. I'm not sure what's gonna happen, but it ain't gonna be good—for any of us. You were right. I never shoulda let Paul convince me to do this. I'm sorry... *for everything*."

No turning back now, he thought, as he closed the phone and dropped it into a trash can on the sidewalk. He was standing in front of a parking garage near the Philadelphia Convention Center. He'd finally remembered where he'd left his car in an odd moment of clarity, clarity that also helped him find some of his missing courage. He was going to need all of it.

He'd decided to complete the tasks on the strange note from the unmarked package, but on his terms. He knew the changes would generate retribution from the source of the mechanical voice—or from elsewhere—but he no longer felt afraid. The game was over.

It was time to end the pain.

Chapter 8

Philadelphia

Step one of the instructions told Eddie to wear a very specific outfit. He complied, with the exception of a green shirt instead of blue. It was a subtle difference, and most likely wouldn't be noticed should someone be following. The shirt was all but fully covered by an overcoat. You'd have to be looking very closely to catch it. Eddie banked on that not being the case, at least not yet.

Step two said to take a cab to 30th Street Station. Eddie's adjustment here was less subtle. He drove his own car and parked it in the Amtrak garage at the Cira Centre, across Arch Street from the station. The tweak, aided by the plodding pace brought about by the pain raking his body, was captured by a significant number of mechanical eyes. Eddie thought he noticed twelve. The actual count was sixteen.

That count went up when Eddie stopped several times, first at a Dunkin' Donuts in the corridor near the stairways to the commuter line tracks, and then across the same walkway at a Hudson News stand. He paid for the transactions with a credit card, adding excessive tips on each slip. The clerks on the receiving end thereof would definitely remember the man, as would the handful of commuters who witnessed the exchanges.

Step three directed Eddie to the self-serve kiosks to purchase a ticket for New York. His alteration again bordered on daring when he bypassed the machines and got in line at the regular ticket window instead. His time to complete this task was captured by another six security cameras and not less than seventy-five sets of human eyes.

Ticket in hand, Eddie moved on to step four. That took him to a baggage counter adjacent to the ticketing area. Thanks to post-9/11 changes, the station's public storage lockers had disappeared, a reasonable act given the circumstances of that horrible day. All temporary storage was now handled in person and required a valid ticket and matching Photo ID. The days of anonymous activity were no more.

As Eddie waited in line, a man there recognized him and started up a conversation. Eddie politely endured the man's diatribe on why football was somehow better than baseball. Apparently steroids were OK when everyone was trying to kill each other. The chat was both short and long enough to be forgotten or remembered, depending on one's perspective.

When it was Eddie's turn at the counter, the female clerk on the other side gave him a dead stare over the edge of her reading glasses when he took longer than necessary to retrieve his driver's license. Eddie apologized—loudly—to the four others waiting in line. This latest temporary inconvenience caused by the disheveled limping man who may or may not have been famous would be memorably forgotten until it wasn't.

It took the clerk three minutes to fetch Eddie's package. For the first time since he'd left his apartment, he lost a little of his nerve in the wait. That increased when the clerk dropped the black and gray backpack on the counter. It was a fair match of Eddie's version, but that's not what scared him. The fear came from sight of a small travel lock sealing the main compartment.

"Sign," the clerk said.

"Huh? Oh, yeah, sure," Eddie said.

He autographed a form on a clipboard before sliding along the counter to his left. He began to rub at the stubble on his face as he stared down at the bag. He never locked his and the instructions hadn't mentioned anything about it. Something's not right, he thought, as he lifted the bag to test the weight. It was heavier than he'd expected, about what he'd feel if his laptop were inside.

"Shit," he said under his breath.

"Excuse me?" the clerk said, turning the first word into three syllables. "Is there a problem?"

She stretched the last word into four parts. Eddie didn't notice.

"Yeah—I mean *no*," he said. "It's, uh, nothin'. I'm good."

"Well, OK, then," the clerk said. "Go on now, scoot. You can't stand there."

She added a motion with her hand, like she was shooing a fly.

"Sure," Eddie said out of reflex.

Despite the confusion and rising fear, he remembered to make sure to take one last look into the cameras over the woman's shoulder before stepping away from the counter. He was moving slowly, but it wasn't because of the pain. He had left his MacBook on the table in his dining room, but the feel of the bag pushed him into wondering if it was still there—and if he was no longer the only one making changes to the plans.

Distracted by the thoughts, it was another five minutes before he made his way to the gate for Track C. He found some empty space on the long benches there and sat. The bag went next to him and he again found himself staring at it.

"What are you doing?" he said to the bag.

The question was as much for him as for the mysterious voice from the phone call. A man seated nearby heard it and gave Eddie a questioning look. Eddie responded with a forced smile before waving him off. The other man shrugged at the rebuke and went back to his newspaper. Eddie used the distraction to look around the expanse of the station.

In another life he was a fan of classical architecture, but the magnificence around him failed to register. There was no focus in his eyes. He saw, but didn't see any details, not at first. He was locked in the mental struggle of deciding if he should sit and fret— and probably lose the rest of his nerve in the process—or do something about it.

Something in the window of a convenience store on the far side of the concourse pushed him to choose the latter.

Queens, New York

The cold air I felt as I stepped out of the cab was a welcome slap in the face. I was still tired and trying to forget about Eddie Booker, but the chill, along with the sight of Citi Field, home of the New York Mets, gave me a boost. It was time for work, my work, umpiring a baseball game. That's what I did best. Thomas and Sandy could deal with Eddie—and whatever else might be going on. That's what they did best.

I paid the cabbie and took an extra minute to soak in the scene. Fans were filing into the gates, a scene I normally missed—I usually arrived a lot earlier—and there was an audible buzz in the air. The race for the postseason was in full swing. The Mets and visiting Los Angeles Dodgers were locked in a duel for the National League Wild Card spot. The winner of this three-game series would get a step closer to that prize. That I would be a part of it was pretty cool.

Not everyone shared that opinion. More than a few people seemed to think the wild card concept took away from the game. I felt the opposite was true. This system gave life to what would have been otherwise meaningless games, ones with players going through the motions in order to get to their end-of-season vacation plans. To me, that kinda thing fucked with the game, not this.

This was exciting.

I had no idea it was about to be even more so.

Philadelphia

Eddie took a window seat on the train, away from everyone else. He'd endured another bout of spasms in the wait to board, but it was the dejection of not finding what he needed in the store that had drained off much of his resolve. They didn't carry the brand of travel locks used on his bag. The man working there suggested trying again in New York, but by the time the train departed, Eddie had given up on the idea of opening the backpack.

As the train started to move, his mind drifted to the final step of the instructions. On paper, it was the simplest one. Take the bag to Citi Field and leave it with one of the players on the Mets, a former client by the name of Mike Coakley. The "former" part was a recent occurrence. Few knew of the divorce, but lack of disclosure was not an omission. The break-up was part of a different plan that Eddie had screwed up—or so he thought.

He turned to the bag resting on the seat next to him. The lock was swaying slightly from the motion of the train. Eddie stared at it. What if this wasn't unrelated? What if it was all part of the same game? What if he had inadvertently stepped back into the shit he thought he'd escaped? With each question, fear replaced resolve until there was little left of the latter. When his hand reached into his pocket and came up empty—a reminder he'd tossed his phone—the conversion was complete.

Everything in his body said "run" but he couldn't just leave the bag, not without knowing what was inside. He reached down and looped an arm through one of the shoulder straps and pulled it closer to his body. His free hand did a quick pass along the outside, but the squeezes and pats—not his first such attempts—were sufficiently impeded by the padding. The contents would remain a mystery.

"Goddamn it," he said in a mumble as a chill ran up his back.

He shook it off as he propped his weary legs on the empty seat in front of him. When he was as comfortable as he could hope to be, meaning not very, he let his head fall against the window. The coolness of the glass and gentle vibrations of the train's movements were oddly relaxing, and without meaning to, his exhaustion got the better of him and he dozed off.

A bump in the tracks an hour later bounced his head off the window, waking him. As he opened his eyes, he found he was no longer alone. The dark face of the stranger sitting next to his feet seemed familiar, but with the fog in his eyes, Eddie couldn't place it. He reached up and pinched the bridge of his nose before rubbing his eyes, using the time to search his memory.

"This is not as we instructed," the stranger said.

Eddie's eyes went wide.

"Oh, shit—"

~*~*~*~*~*~*~*~

"Hey, man, you OK?" a voice said from somewhere in the periphery of Eddie's mind.

Images of a garden—his mother's?—faded as other synapses fired. The realization he wasn't dead or dreaming came quickly. His eyes popped open and he turned toward the window. The train was no longer moving.

"Where are we?" he said, his voice groggy.

He turned back. The stranger was gone—had he ever been there?—replaced by the stern-looking face of an Amtrak conductor standing in the aisle. A rush of panic came and went when Eddie found the bag still entwined around his arm. He pulled it to his lap and sat up as his breath returned.

"Penn Station, last stop," the conductor said. "It's time to go."

Eddie nodded and ran a hand through his hair as he tried to regroup. The fingers then moved to his neck and began rubbing out the kinks there. He stopped when he found a small bump. The spot was tender. He was familiar with the sensation.

"What the fuck?" he said as he touched at it.

The conductor mistook the words.

"*What the fuck* is that you gotta go, man, as in beat it, ride's over," he said in a nasty tone.

Eddie looked at the conductor, then his hand, then out the window again. After another few seconds, the hand curled into a fist. He turned back to the conductor as he stood.

"Goddamn right it is."

Queens

The cab ride took forty-five minutes, more than twice as long as an MTA Long Island Rail Road train from Penn Station to the Mets-Willets Point station would have. The extended trip pushed Eddie perilously close to missing the start of the game. It also pushed him perilously close to a full-on panic mode, and when he got to the Press Entrance at Citi Field, his face and body was wet with sweat.

"Cheese-Louise, Mr. Booker, you look like you been out for a run," the guard at the gate said as Eddie arrived there.

The man's heavy Brooklyn accent turned each "you" into a "youze."

"Running late is all," Eddie said.

The guard nodded.

"Well, youze can relax," he said. "Youze ain't missed nuttin'."

Despite the reassurances, Eddie didn't relax. He couldn't. Not now. He had to fix things before it was too late. He started forward, but stopped suddenly.

"Ah, shit," he said; then after regrouping. "Hey, I uh, forgot to go grab my ticket. Ya think you can help me out?"

The guard scratched at his head for a few seconds and made some odd faces.

"Wow, I don't know," he said in wary tone. "I could get in trouble."

The normal practice saw players leave tickets for agents and others at Will Call. Eddie truly did forget to stop there, but it wouldn't have mattered anyway. There were no tickets because he no longer had any clients. He wasn't sure if the guard knew about that last part and he held his breath as he waited to find out. It seemed a lot longer than the three seconds it took.

"*Gotcha,*" the guard said as a big smile filled his face. "I had youze goin' there, didn't I?"

"Haha," Eddie said. "Yeah, ya did."

He wiped a new round of sweat from his brow before passing through the gate into the stadium. A few places back in line, another man running late had noticed something familiar in Eddie's odd movements and voiced his concern when he reached the guard.

"Hey, Booker looks messed up again," David Donovan said. "You guys might wanna keep an eye on him and make sure he doesn't do anything stupid."

The guard's big smile returned and he shook his head.

"That ain't my job, Mr. Donovan. The guys inside can worry about that shit."

Philadelphia

"It happens tonight."

Dukabi's massive thumb smothered the *End* button. Several additional heavy clicks deleted the contents of the phone's Inbox—including the message just played—as well as all the call logs. He then set the device on the desk in front of him and let his fingers linger on the antique wood. The feel of the mahogany was comforting. The huge desk was one of few things to have survived the turbulent times of recent years.

Dukabi's thoughts drifted to some of the losses. Chief among them was an image of a man named Hudson, technically Dukabi's butler, but much more in practice. He'd been Dukabi's friend, in many ways his version of Thomas to Marshall. Hired muscle came and went, but Hudson had always been the grounding constant in Dukabi's life once he left Africa.

Andrew Singer had changed all that.

Despite evidence to the contrary, Dukabi abhorred violence. It was as distasteful as the dirt that had polluted his coat at the park. His contempt for it was why he'd brokered the deal that ended Singer's life. Singer was lower than dirt, a sick man who believed in violence for violence's sake. He had murdered innocent women for no reason. He had mistreated the baseball official's romantic companion out of spite. He had killed Hudson.

It was all unacceptable.

Dukabi lifted the phone again and dialed a now too-familiar number. As he waited for the call to go through, he found something in his memory, words Thomas had said years ago, the simple but pointed message delivered in the hills above the burning village.

You could have stopped this.

The thought evaporated under the sound of a robotic female voice in his ear, instructing him to leave a message. Dukabi disconnected without doing so, and returned the phone to the desk before standing. Seconds later, he was at the room's window.

The sky outside was dark, but the lights of the cityscape shone brightly beneath. The ships of Penn's Landing were in front of him. Across the river, on the far side of the Benjamin Franklin Bridge, Camden, New Jersey, twinkled in the night. Further still, to the north and out of sight, was New York City. It was there Dukabi's eyes settled, staring for a long moment before turning away.

"And so it begins."

Chapter 9

Citi Field

Eddie had his head down as he walked the corridor toward the team clubhouses. That he didn't have the appropriate ID hanging from his neck went unnoticed. The few who recognized him did nothing more than offer up small nods of recognition. Eddie was glad. He didn't have the strength—or time—for small talk.

"You're sure I can count on you?" he said a minute later to a younger man standing in front of him.

They were at the door to the Dodgers clubhouse. Eddie had missed the chance for the face-to-face meetings designed to replace the incomplete phone calls—the players were already out on the field. Something creative was needed to compensate; Eddie had found the idea during the long cab ride.

"No problem, Mr. B. I'll go do it right now."

Eddie handed the attendant a small white envelope.

"Put it where he'll find it," he said.

"You got it" the attendant said.

"Thanks, kid," Eddie said as they shook hands. "You're a life-saver."

There was a lot of truth in that statement, but the young man missed it, distracted as he was by the crisp currency in his hand, left there during the shake. He remembered his manners and didn't unfold and count it. He simply disappeared through the door without another word.

Eddie turned and made his way to his next stop, the door for the home team's sanctuary. His job there was going to be more difficult. Even if he had active clients, he wasn't allowed access to the clubhouses when the players weren't around. As with the entrance gate, a work-around was in order. It came when the old man working the door recognized Eddie right away.

"Aw, there he is," the man said. "My favorite Met."

Eddie regretted that he couldn't remember the old man's name.

"Hey, thanks, bud," he said. "I, uh, I know the guys are out, but any chance I can get in? I gotta leave something for Mike C."

He reached up and shook the backpack. The oldster never hesitated.

"Anything for you, Eddie," he said. "I'm fuckin' eighty years old. Whatta they gonna do, fire me?"

When I realized as a teenager that I couldn't hit for shit, umpiring became the next best thing. I started when I was eighteen, working my up through high school- and college-level games, before trying out for the majors after graduating from Temple U. Some might say I got fast-tracked to the big leagues—a story for another day—but the truth was, I was good and I earned it.

I also loved this game like no other, something I was thinking about as I wandered out into shallow left field after the seventh-inning stretch ended. It had been a great game so far, as expected. The Mets were up, four-three, and had just killed a Dodgers rally. The buzz from before the game had gone up a few notches.

I was taking a minute to soak in some of the murmur and ant-like movements of the crowd. The adrenaline of working had erased my fatigue and I'm pretty sure I was smiling. That such would be the case was never in doubt, not for me anyway. It'll be the day when that *doesn't* happen—a day hopefully far in the future—that I'll know it's time to find a new vocation. Even then, I don't think I could do anything not related to this game. This was what I was meant to do, where I was meant to be.

Of course, I might have changed that last part had I known what was about to happen.

Manhattan

The New York FBI field office occupied several floors of 26 Federal Plaza, on Lafayette Street. It was two skinny blocks from New York's City Hall and a sniper's rifle shot from the former site of the World Trade Center towers. Despite the time—pushing ten P.M.—there was still a relatively large contingent on hand. For at least one person working late, being there was better than the alternatives.

Gus Pappas—a fifty-two year old, more-than-slightly overweight, twenty-year veteran and current Assistant Director of Counter Terror—had nowhere else to be. He wasn't married. He didn't have a girlfriend. He had no children. There were acquaintances, but no real friends. Simply put, people didn't like the man. "Let's go out" was a request Gus rarely heard.

For the most part, the FBI was it. Gus' job there, as he put it, was to "catch the motherfuckers responsible for the 9/11 attacks." It was his sole mission in life. It's what got him out of bed every day. Six of his friends had died among the several thousand killed that day, and he'd been trying to avenge those deaths ever since. Business lately had been slow.

All that changed with a single phone call.

"This is Pappas."

Gus was at his desk. The call had come to one of his cell phones, a number not too many possessed. That should have been the first clue something was wrong. If not, the twenty seconds that followed listening to the caller made sure of it.

"What did you just say?" Gus said at second twenty-one. "*Who is this?*"

His neck began to turn red as he listened again. Another eighteen seconds passed. His eyes got wide and he broke out into a heavy sweat.

"But... *wait.*"

A second later, he pulled the phone away from his face and stared at it until his eyes began to water. He blinked at the moisture and his head began to shake. The parts of his shirt not already wet quickly caught up. His laundry service was going to have its work cut out.

If nothing else, at least he was about to have someplace to go.

Citi Field

The explosion was louder than anything I'd ever heard in my life. In the process of being knocked to the ground, something that might have been "Holy shit" or "Holy fuck" or "Ah" with a lot of H's came out of my mouth. A split-second later, pieces of something began to land near where I'd ended up in the outfield grass. I covered my head with my arms and hoped none found me.

I'm not sure how long it was before I found the courage to uncover and look up. What I saw made me flinch again. Below a rising mushroom of billowing smoke, I saw that a portion of the Pepsi Porch, the seating section above right field, was missing. It was called "Porch" because it hung out over the playing field like— well, like a porch, and "Pepsi" because they had paid a ton of money to stick their name on it.

I'm not sure that money was going to be worth the infamy of being associated with whatever-the-fuck had just happened. The same was true about most of Citi Field, the eight-hundred-fifty million dollar replacement for the Mets prior home, the dump that was Shea Stadium. I had never minded Shea. Sure, it was a sty, but that's what made it great. It was old school. This overpriced abomination named for a failing financial institution reeked of greed and phoniness.

And now it reeked of something else: Death.

I'd thought the shit was gone from my life, that after the last episode everything was returning to normal. I guess I should have known better. I had no idea what "normal" was. But still, this was even more unfathomable than the last two circuses I'd endured.

Those events had seemed focused, specific attacks on specific people, me included.

This was—well, I had no idea what *this* was other than really, really bad.

Manhattan

Alarms sounded outside Gus' office exactly four minutes and twelve seconds after the Citi Field explosion—and exactly one minute more than after the strange phone call. Recognition of the connection was instant, but Gus did his best not to dwell on it. At first, many of the late workers around him thought the alarm a drill, but when a recorded voice over the intercom confirmed it seconds later as otherwise, the place erupted into a frenzy of activity.

Gus found enough composure to seamlessly blend in with the controlled chaos. He began working two cell phones, masterfully directing his teams to action. A Code Red alert was issued, sending a large force of agents and support teams to the ballpark, and other smaller units to strategic locations around the city. Every other FBI office in the country was also notified, as was the rest of the Homeland Defense system. The entire operation appeared flawless, but like far too many things in life, Gus knew looks could be deceiving.

It would be a few more hours before he figured out just how much so.

Citi Field

A part of me wanted to run, but for reasons I would never understand, I didn't. Around me, the stadium was in full panic mode. Pieces of seats and concrete and other flaming debris littered the playing field below the Porch. Everywhere else, people were screaming and running toward the exits. It wasn't any different on the field.

"*Jesus Christ,*" a harried voice said from somewhere behind me.

I turned to find Travis Mackenzie of the Dodgers, moving toward me. His head was shaking and his eyes were as big as silver dollars. I'm sure I looked the same to him.

"Travis, you OK?" I said.

"Fuck—*no*," he said; then after a pause to look around. "Shit, man, how could I be?"

He had a point. I think I might have nodded as I noticed another group of guys running at us from the bullpens. It was hard to concentrate on any one thing, any one face. It was hard to do anything at all.

"*RUN!*" someone in the group said in a shout.

Travis did so, but again, my legs wouldn't work. I did manage to turn just in time to see my umpire partners making their way down into one of the dugouts. A shot of relief came and went, but I didn't join them. I just stood there, watching the backs of the players as they moved away. I don't know if it was shock or what, but I didn't move. It was surreal, like a movie, only I was *in* the movie.

"C'mon, Marshall, *do something*," I said into the din around me.

My hand found its way into my pocket, to a small black object there. Not my clicker, but something else, a device I kept with me at all times, one supposedly for emergencies only. Thomas had given me the toy years ago. It was a quick way to contact him and had come in handy on more than one occasion in the past.

Given what was happening all around me, I figured now would qualify as another appropriate moment of use. I think I knew it was probably too late, but like I said, Thomas was good at dealing with this shit.

If anyone would know what to do, it was him.

Manhattan

Gus ended up in a crowded conference room. Within ten minutes of the Code Red, a new call had come in to the cell phone now pressed to his right ear. That the Vice President of the United States had personally called—and not some aide—would have been stressful enough. That Gus had to lie about why he didn't already have an answer for the cause of the explosion made things worse.

The VP was of the mindset that the country had suffered another terrorist attack of the 9/11 variety. That wasn't entirely off base. In FBI parlance, if a crime endangered someone or in some way intimidated or influenced someone—be it their policy or opinion—commission of said crime was deemed to be an act of terrorism.

The Citi Field explosion certainly qualified, but it fell under the heading of domestic terrorism instead of the other kind, an attack inflicted by a mysterious and lethal group of fanatics, preferably of Arab decent. With what he already knew, Gus was looking at a hard sell to make that latter theory fit.

"Yes, sir, we've already dispatched teams… As soon as I know, you'll know… No, sir, there was nothing to suggest this was imminent… Yes, sir, I understand… Yes, sir, we'll get you the answers…"

The two-minute call seemed a lot longer to Gus. When he finished, he closed the phone and looked around the room.

"Where's Dreisdale?" he said in a shout over the noise.

Kurt Dreisdale headed New York's JTTF—Joint Terrorism Task Force or Jay Tiff—the FBI's largest such unit. He also worked for Gus.

"He's with team one, sir, at the field," a voice said from somewhere to Gus' left.

Gus turned, but couldn't find a source.

"Fine," he said; then after a pause. "Someone have my car brought around."

He then stood. All eyes turned in his direction and the noise dropped off dramatically.

"And in the meantime, would someone please figure out what the fuck is going on?"

Wayne

"You have lived an interesting life," Sandy said.

She and Thomas were in his office. They were taking a break—at least Sandy was. Her mood had markedly improved. She'd pushed past the earlier blow-up and was happy to be busy on the mystery again, even if she was close to information overload. The Dukabi meetings, the searches, Thomas' revelation, all of it was daunting at best, troublesome at worst. The momentary respite of the glass of wine and casual conversation was helping her get past it.

"I've been fortunate," Thomas said in reply to her comment.

He'd been more than that. His family was rich. There was no other way to put it. Still, he had managed to remain humble. It was another endearing trait in Sandy's eyes. The money was a means for him to pursue his passions, but he wasn't bound by it. She was fairly certain he'd have been exactly the same way without it.

At the moment, she was eyeing the antiques on the shelves. She turned back to Thomas, smiled, and lifted her glass toward one of the trinkets, a small figurine.

"What's the story behind that one?" she said.

In addition to the family heirlooms, the Egyptian relic—a small cup near the middle of the shelves—and a few other pieces had been obtained during Thomas' trips to places exotic during his CIA days. This particular red terracotta piece was maybe five inches high, a few more around. There was a chip in the rim.

"Don't tell anyone I still have that," he said.

Sandy tilted her head and a small frown appeared.

"Why, did you steal it?" she said in a kidding tone.

Thomas' eyebrow went up.

"Not exactly," he said. "But the Egyptian Minister of Defense is under the impression I've returned it."

Sandy smiled.

"*Ooh…* Thomas Hillsborough, criminal-at-large," she said through the grin.

"Indeed," he said.

A quiet moment followed as both let their eyes linger on the shelves. Sandy was thinking how totally cool it all was, not just the pieces, but the stories behind them, too. Like the man, they were fascinating. Thomas, on the other hand, was thinking about the prices paid, not in dollars, but in time lost and opportunities missed.

His parents and grandparents were gone, the money, artifacts, antiques and properties the only remnants of what they'd accomplished. Thomas and his sister were remnants as well, but unless something changed, they would be the end of the line. The material possessions would disappear to wherever and the

Hillsborough family would be no more. It was sad in a way that Thomas couldn't express.

He moved his eyes to Sandy. He'd long since memorized every line of her face, every contour of her body. That wasn't unusual. He did the same thing for everyone and everything he encountered. He paid attention to details. It was how he was wired. But in her case, it was different. As his eyes lingered, a fraction of a smile came to his lips.

The smile disappeared when she suddenly turned.

"It is perhaps a more fortunate destiny to have a taste for collecting shells than to be born a millionaire," she said, quoting Robert Louis Stevenson. "You, Mr. Thomas Hillsborough, have experienced both."

Thomas' eyebrow went up again.

"Don't judge each day by the harvest you reap but by the seeds you plant," he said.

It was another Stevenson quote. Sandy's eyes suddenly filled with intensity.

"And where do you plant your seeds?" she said, her tone equally as strong.

The answer on his tongue would have surprised her, but before he could voice it, he was interrupted by a sharp beep coming from somewhere on his desk.

"Is that—*is that Marshall's pager?*" Sandy said. "But... but he's at—"

The sound of Thomas' cell cut her off. Within seconds of answering, his face darkened.

"Thomas?" Sandy said with a lot of concern in her voice.

Without a word, he grabbed a remote from his desk and pointed it at the shelves. A flat-screen TV embedded there came to life. Sandy turned to find a clearly distracted talking head having trouble talking. The graphics encasing the female anchor explained why: Terrorist Attack at Citi Field? The question mark did nothing to alleviate Sandy's concern.

"Oh, shit," she said, almost to herself. "Marshall's there."

Thomas nodded through the emotions filling his expression. Sandy had never seen the looks, but made no attempt at decoding.

"It appears to be his gift," Thomas said.

Sandy knew he hadn't said it to be funny.

Chapter 10

Philadelphia

The Philadelphia FBI building was at the corner of 6th and Arch, across from Independence Park and the U.S. Constitution Center. That historic area was the first section of the city locked down in response to the Code Red. Other key locations had followed quickly, and within hours, the city was secure.

It was now after three A.M., but the office was still buzzing. If anyone was tired, it didn't show. Alex was seated at the head of a large table in a conference room on the fourth floor. The chairs around him were filled by agents and analysts hard at work coordinating state, city, and local law enforcement. Everything was running smoothly, a fact that bothered the director.

"Has anyone heard anything from Jay Tiff?" he said into the hum. "Has anyone heard anything from *anyone*?"

The connotations were obvious. A younger-looking Hispanic man looked up. Special Agent Carlos Santiago was a demon on all things technical, and had been promoted shortly after Sandy's departure. Originally a sound technician, computer prowess and sharp ears were his trademarks, and he'd quickly replaced Sandy as

Alex's favorite. The director could never publicize that fact, but the rest of the staff knew. Alex didn't care if any were bothered by it. He wanted all his people to bust ass like Carlos did. If a little favoritism helped make that point, so be it, especially at times like this.

"Nothing yet, sir," Carlos said in response to Alex's questions. "So far, all's quiet."

"Good or bad quiet?" Alex said.

Carlos' face contorted through a series of movements as he checked some notes on the table in front of him. When he looked up again, Alex saw that confusion had won the battle.

"Neither, sir," Carlos said. "There's nothing, no claims of responsibility and no chatter box activity. Everything is quiet. I'm not sure what's going on, but if this was a terrorist attack, we missed it."

Alex frowned. The lead-up to the 9/11 attacks had been missed, too. Obvious clues were ignored by people at pay grades several notches higher along the food chain. Alex hated to think the same might have happened again.

"It wouldn't be the first time, but I hear you," he said. "This doesn't smell right."

New York

Mark Rosenbaum had been at home when the explosion occurred. In the hours since, he'd been glued to the TV, watching the rescue attempts unfold. Much of that time was spent talking with various people on the phone. About the only calls that didn't annoy him were Gabi's.

"I'm going to Citi," Gabi said to start the latest one. "I can't get anyone to answer my questions on the phone. I'm not sure that'll change in person, but figured you'd want me to try."

Mark nodded, forgetting Gabi wasn't there to see it.

"Yeah, yeah, that's good," he said; then after a pause. "What the hell is happening?"

"I don't know, but I'll find out," Gabi said into his ear.

The strength in the tone gave Mark a shot of confidence, but he was going to need a lot more to ever feel good again.

"Jesus, Gabi," he said. "This is a fucking mess."

Gabi agreed. It was a mess, a lot more so than it should have been, and as much as Alex was bothered by the subsequent lack of activity, Gabi was bothered by how much had already taken place. That feeling wasn't one he planned on sharing with his boss—or anyone else. Not yet anyway. For now, he would do his best to stay firm. He had a job to do.

"I initiated our disaster plan," he said to Mark. "Games in process were stopped and those on the west coast were postponed. All the stadiums were cleared without incident. Everything is OK."

It took him a second to realize the mistake in his words.

"Shit, sorry," he said. "I mean everything else is OK."

Mark didn't seem to catch the slip or the recovery.

"I don't know, Gabi," he said. "How is any of this OK?"

He meant the game itself. Baseball—the return of baseball—had been a big part of the healing process after 9/11. When the game came back, it had lifted the country's collective spirit, becoming the lead car in the somber parade down the path of recovery. But now… if this was another attack, an attack on the game, who or what would come to the rescue this time?

Mark shuddered at the thought.

"Do what you can," he said into the phone.

"I will," Gabi said. "Trust me, I'll find out what went wrong."

The last words were another slip Mark missed. Gabi did, too. Discovery and realization of the error—and a few other things— would take a little longer.

Citi Field

Once at the ballpark, Gus made his way to the concourse at the top of the Pepsi Porch. The damaged area and destruction was directly in front of him. Most prominent in Gus' view was a collection of yellow tarps covering much of the area on either side of a missing jagged semi-circle. He knew what was beneath each piece of plastic. They weren't going to be the first dead bodies he'd ever seen. Still, he wasn't in any hurry to get a closer look.

"OK, people, talk to me," he said to a group standing to his right. "What am I looking at?"

He turned just as Kurt Dreisdale stepped away from the others.

"We're looking at a serious mess," Kurt said.

The director's face morphed into something that reminded Kurt of a rotting apricot.

"Really, Kurt, ya think?" Gus said; then after a pause. "Fuckin' tell me already."

The sarcasm and disrespect did not go unnoticed. Kurt's jaw muscles flexed several times before he looked down to a small note pad he was holding.

"This is preliminary," he said in a matter-of-fact tone. "We have twenty-two confirmed dead, forty-three injured. Both counts will go up once we get coordinated with the nearby hospitals."

"And when might that be?" Gus said.

Kurt sighed. The heavy noise replaced what he wanted to say. He knew it was no time for petty squabbles. Remaining professional was the least he could do for the people under the tarps.

"As soon as we get it," he said.

Gus nodded and looked past him.

"Fuckin' towel-heads," he said under his breath; then to Kurt. "Fine… what about the bomber? You got anything on that yet?"

Kurt sighed again before motioning toward the playing field and the sizeable collection of law enforcement and medical personnel milling about in various places, a group that included teams from the FBI, NYPD, FDNY, and New York State Troopers.

"We think what's left is down on the field below us. It'll take forensics a while to come up with an identity."

Gus nodded and made a noise that sounded like a grunt—or maybe a pig in heat.

"What about witness statements?" he said. "Got any yet?"

A third sigh escaped Kurt.

"That's gonna take a while, too," he said. "People didn't exactly hang around to see if there was gonna be another blast. We'll need to research things, ticket purchases and the like. My guys are already working on the warrants, but it won't be easy chasing down all these people."

Gus couldn't really argue that point, but the apricot face returned anyway, a little more rotten looking this time. Kurt recoiled a few inches.

"Who the fuck ever said this job was easy?" Gus said in a tone as ugly as the expression.

Kurt's response was to flip the notepad closed and walk away. Gus followed with his eyes until his focus shifted to the field. The blast zone was significant, but something about it was bothersome. He couldn't put a finger on it and started to look away, but stopped suddenly when he noticed something in the space at the end of the third base dugout. One of the TV cameras was angled upward, as if still focused on the Porch and the workers there.

It took Gus a few seconds to do the math.

"Hey, what about TV?" he said in a shout toward Kurt.

Kurt turned, but said nothing. Gus pointed to the camera box.

"There's gotta be a shitload of pictures."

Philadelphia

Alex was in his office, two hours later, checking over more reports that contained nothing new. It left him tired and cranky, but he did his best not to let any of that show. As it had been for Kurt, Alex also felt an obligation to the people under the tarps and knew it was his job to make sure no one else joined them.

A soft rap on his open door caused him to look up.

"Excuse me, sir," Carlos Santiago said.

"Come," Alex said.

Carlos moved to one of the two chairs in front of Alex's desk. Prior to being promoted, the agent's specialty had been audio. When Kurt had called and asked for help analyzing the video from the bombing, Alex hadn't hesitated in assigning Carlos to the task. The young man could seemingly hear things normally reserved for the canine world, and from the look on his face now, Alex had a feeling it had happened again.

"Sit," he said, motioning with his chin to the folder in Carlos' hand. "Whataya got?"

Carlos handed the folder across the desk.

"It's from SNY, sir, Sportsnet New York," he said.

Two minutes later they were on the third floor, in an area affectionately known as "Dorkville." The moniker was a badge of honor for the techs working there. Field agents had guns, but the "Dorks" had brains, and without the latter, the former was useless. The agents were too macho to ever admit that, but Alex knew how important the "Dorks" were to the success—and failure—of the FBI's work.

"OK, walk me through it," he said.

They were in the main video room with its set of four twenty-five inch flat-screen monitors. At the moment, the top two were dark, but the bottom pair had still shots of Citi Field.

"Technically, all of this video belongs to Major League Baseball," Carlos said. "You know, 'without express written consent' and all that stuff. Gabi Loeb was more than happy to release it without a warrant. You're gonna wanna thank him."

"I will," Alex said. "Now, what are we looking at?"

Carlos pointed to the monitor on the left.

"Third base dugout camera," he said; then moving his hand to the right. "And home plate press box camera. This is just after the seventh inning stretch. The audio is going to be from a crowd mike near the foul pole in right field."

"All right," Alex said. "Let's see it."

Carlos touched a button on the control panel and the small room filled with noise. It was raw feed without any announcer voice-over interference. The screen on the left showed a man walking away from a microphone. Alex recognized the face, but couldn't remember the singer's name. A split-second later, a loud scream filled the room. Both screens went out of focus as the cameras' angles changed. The background filled with a growing murmur as the images zoomed in and refocused on a man near the bottom railing of the Pepsi Porch.

The man's mouth was moving as if he was talking. Alex leaned in.

"Can we get a lip-reader to see what he's saying?" he said.

"No need, sir," Carlos said. "Hang on."

He worked the controls again. The video stopped, then slowly rewound, creating awkward-looking reversed movements. Alex focused on the man. He was wearing an overcoat and had a Mets cap on his head, making it hard to see the face. More prominent, though, was a backpack hanging from the man's left shoulder. Alex moved in closer.

"He looks Caucasian," he said more to himself than Carlos, his tone a mix of surprise and confusion. "No wonder no one has claimed responsibility yet."

"I kinda thought the same thing, sir," Carlos said. "I hope you won't mind. I sent the stills to New York. Maybe we'll get lucky and get a hit on facial recognition. In the meantime, at least we have the transcript."

Before Alex could respond, Carlos touched *Play*. The bomber's words were somewhat muted, but clearly discernible above the din around him.

"I never wanted any of this. It was only supposed to be me."

Carlos stopped the video just as the man stepped from the railing. Alex stared for several seconds before sitting back, a deep frown on his face.

"What the hell does *that* mean?"

Chapter 11

Queens

I'd lost track of time, but I think it was after four A.M. by the time police gave me the go-ahead to leave the ballpark. I was happy to get away, despite the fact it was dark and I would have to walk back to the hotel. No cars were allowed near the field. That meant no cabs were available. I didn't mind, though, because the crisp air felt good. Not like before the game, but good in a relative sense.

In truth, *everything* was relative. I was alive, but a lot of others weren't. It was both scary and comforting, leaving me relieved but feeling guilty at the same time, and by the time I reached the hotel I was numb again. There were a handful of people in the lobby bar, watching the news. I didn't bother to join them. The images from the field were already forever burned into my head. I didn't need a TV replay or idle chat about it. I wasn't going to be forgetting anytime soon.

Once upstairs, I found my roommate and umpiring partner, Bartolo Casaba, still awake. After a firm handshake that turned into a quick bear hug—a Bartolo trademark of sorts—we didn't say much else before I made my way to the shower. The warm water felt good, but the stink, like the images, wouldn't leave. Maybe the smell was only in my mind, but I couldn't seem to get rid of it.

I finally gave up after about thirty minutes, when my fingers started to wrinkle. After getting out of the tub, I stood in front of the bathroom mirror for a long time. I felt sick, but not in a "throw up" kind of way. This was more of a gut-wrenching empty feeling, like when you lose someone or something close to you. I'd had it a few times before, most recently in the days after Suze broke up with me. I'm not suggesting the break-up compared with what happened at the field—there was no comparison—but it was still a loss. Maybe it was more of my innocence going bye-bye, I didn't know for sure.

What I did know was that it sucked.

I can't say I'm religious, but as I stood there, I started to think that maybe someone was trying to send me some kind of message, that maybe I needed to get away from the game. I didn't want to believe that, not really, but I had to wonder. Once was random. Twice was problematic. But now, for the third time in as many years, people had died around me. And each occurrence had been in an increasingly brutal way. It had to mean *something*.

Too bad I had absolutely no idea what.

By the time I came out of the bathroom, Bartolo had drifted off to sleep. There was no chance of that for me, so I got dressed in the dark before moving to the windows. I didn't know if the answer—the *something*—was out there, but I stood there, staring, for a long time. The first hint of morning was visible at the edge of the sky. It should have been seen as beautiful, but knowing how much bad stuff was lurking in the shadows left me shaking my head in disgust.

"What a goddamn mess," I said under my breath.

I started to think about Suze. She was out there, too, probably scared like a lot of people. I thought about calling her, but it didn't take long to kill the idea. I could never lie to her. That meant if I called I'd have to tell her I was at the game. I'd put her through enough already. She didn't need the added burden of knowing I'd been in danger—*again*. That would just bring back the painful memories. No, I decided, it was better this way.

I was the King of Shitsville. The best thing was to reign alone.

"Fuck me," I said before turning from the window.

A second later, my cell rang with Thomas' ringtone. Bartolo stirred a little, but didn't seem to wake up. I stepped back into the bathroom and closed the door anyway, just in case, parking on the closed toilet seat. If I had been paying attention, there was probably some irony or something in that choice. I wasn't much paying attention.

"Hey," I said after answering the call.

"My God, Marshall… Are you OK?"

It was Sandy. I took it to mean they were using the speaker on Thomas' phone. I didn't mind. I was just happy to hear a familiar voice.

"I have a headache, but I'll survive," I said.

"Where are you?" Sandy said. "We tried to reach you."

It made sense they couldn't. In the moments after engaging the pager, I'd made my way into the mess in right field to try and help. My participation wasn't exactly appreciated and it wasn't long before I'd been forcefully ushered off the field.

That was followed by a drilling by an FBI agent for close to an hour. I had to wait another ninety minutes after that to get back in the locker room to collect my stuff. Citi Field was a crime scene and every nook and cranny had to be checked and rechecked, every witness interviewed and re-interviewed.

I'd been a suspect until I wasn't.

"Yeah, sorry, it was a little crazy," I said into the phone. "I saw you guys tried to call. Where are you?"

"Office," Sandy said.

I looked around the still-damp bathroom. It was a lot smaller than it had seemed just moments ago.

"Wanna trade?" I said.

"It seems we should be asking that question."

Those words came from Thomas. I think I might have smiled after hearing his voice.

"You do have a serious knack for bad timing," Sandy said.

Yeah, no kidding, I thought, as I flashed on the bodies I'd seen on the field. Besides several fans and one of the Dodgers, their rightfielder—killed, I think, by falling debris—there had been another. At least I think there'd been another. There wasn't much left of the body, but I was operating under the impression it was the terrorist, the suicide bomber, but I'd been too afraid at the field to ask. I still was, despite being pretty sure Thomas and Sandy probably already knew the answer.

"Timing never was one of my strong points," I said instead.

"This, I know," Thomas said.

He did know—too well—but that was because he cared and was always looking out for people, for me. I could do a lot worse for a friend. I was an only child. It left me close to my parents, but I was envious of some of the kids I'd grown up with, the ones with brothers and sisters. Sure, I saw a lot of dumb-ass fights for dumb-ass reasons, but the fights were good because at the core they arose out of the love only relatives can share.

I knew now my relationship with Thomas was as close to that as I would ever get. As I sat there, thinking, that fact started to sink in even more. I realized that I'd never really told him how I felt, what he meant to me. It would have sucked big time if I had been one of those killed at the stadium—or in either of my earlier adventures. Then it would have been too late.

I sat up straighter.

"Uh, hey, Thomas, there's something I need to tell you," I said.

There was a slight pause.

"Marshall, it's OK," he said. "I know."

His flat tone wasn't so flat. Somehow, he'd figured out what I was trying to do, to say. I shouldn't have been surprised. He was usually five steps ahead of everyone, and in this case, it gave me a shot of energy—or maybe courage—and I circled back to the elephant in the room.

"So… you guys got any idea what's going on?" I said. "I heard some people talking about terrorism or something."

"Plausible," Thomas said.

The flatness was back. The tender moment was over.

"We're looking into other theories that might better fit the circumstances."

It took me a second to catch the first word. I sat up straighter.

"*You're* looking?" I said. "Why am I not surprised?"

Citi Field

"Everything is secure on our end," Gabi said. "All games are cancelled until further notice."

He and Gus were surveying the destruction from the Press Level. Despite Gabi's status with MLB, that was as close as the FBI—read: Gus—would allow. Given the number of tarps littering the landscape, Gabi didn't argue the decision.

"Any ideas about who might be responsible?" he said.

He thought the query valid. Gus making the pig noise again before shaking his head.

"*No,*" he said in a dark tone; then after a pause. "Tell me again why you don't have better security at these places? Haven't you guys learned anything from that shit last year?"

Gabi's reaction to Gus was similar to Kurt's earlier, except he didn't walk away from the attack. His eyes narrowed and he turned toward Gus. What he was thinking was "that shit last year" could have been avoided, or at least been less deadly, had the FBI done a better job. What he said instead was a little less combative.

"Our security is more than sufficient."

Gus grunted again.

"Oh, yeah, fuckin' looks it," he said. "How's about you just stay out—"

He got cut off by a loud buzz from one of the cell phones on his belt. He snatched it from its holder and turned from Gabi before answering. Gabi eyed the back of the director's head and waited. Seconds later, Gus slapped the phone shut without having said a word. After a few more seconds, he snatched another from his waist and flipped it open.

"Get my car ready. I'm goin' back to the office."

He turned to Gabi. The rotting apricot had returned, but Gabi thought it looked more prune-like.

"Is everything OK?" he said.

"No, Mr. Loeb, everything is not OK. Someone blew up part of my city and people are dead. You need to stay the fuck outta the way until we figure it out."

He stormed past. Gabi turned back to the field.

"You aren't going to figure this out," he said under his breath.

A minute or so later, he pulled out his cell phone. Mark answered after the first ring.

"The FBI says they have everything under control," Gabi said.

Mark didn't miss the obvious undertones.

"How bad is it?" he said.

Gabi took a second to do another survey of the field. "Very."

Manhattan

"I am not to be disturbed," Gus said in a shout as he reached his office.

He didn't wait for his assistant's acknowledgement, slamming the door shut to make the point. On the way to his desk he threw his FBI field jacket toward a sofa along the far wall. It missed and slid across the floor. Gus ignored it as he dropped like a rock into his desk chair.

The first call, before the bombing, had been bad enough. The second, interrupting his chat with Gabi, was worse. Of the two, however, that was the one he needed to listen to again. That wouldn't be a problem because all calls to and from his phones were recorded. The problem would come if anyone else heard it first, because it had a lot of bad implications.

First was the national security issue, the potential lead into the bombing; the caller had provided a name. Second was the threat of a more personal nature, one that would raise a lot of questions that would jeopardize more than Gus' career, questions he wasn't prepared to answer.

He was going to need more time to find a workable solution, but got interrupted by a sharp buzz before he could start. He reached forward and punched a button on his desk phone.

"Are you that fucking useless," he said in a shout. "I said *no interruptions.*"

The silence in response added to Gus' surly mood.

"Fuck, speak already," he said. "*What do you want?*"

The reluctant voice of his assistant came through the line.

"Sir, Director Harris is on the line. He says it's urgent."

"No shit," Gus said out of reflex.

"Sir?" the assistant said.

"Put it through already."

Gus sat back and flashed on a memory, the day Alex Harris replaced him as director in Philadelphia. Gus had never been in the military. He was a lifelong civil servant, first as a beat cop and detective with Philly PD, since with the FBI. Never pretty, he did his job the best he could. He made mistakes, but still got results, his creed similar to that in sports: It doesn't matter how you win, only how many. His superiors didn't agree.

They felt the FBI needed something more polished. Their solution was Alex, a highly decorated and well-traveled Major in the Marine Corps. They felt someone like that could do a better job, especially in relation to public perception. They'd since been proven correct, but Gus still held a grudge. In his head, Alex stole the job, plain and simple.

He sat forward and punched the phone again.

"I'm a little busy, Alex," he said. "What the fuck do you want?"

"Did you get the package?" Alex said.

"What—"

Gus was interrupted by a knock on his door. A young man stepped in.

"Sorry, sir," he said as he placed a blue folder on the desk in front of Gus.

He turned and quickly disappeared without another word. Gus eyed the folder. A yellow stickee note read *From Philadelphia*. Reluctantly, he opened the folder. Inside were several photographs, obviously taken from a TV feed, and a sheet of paper. Gus remembered his comment to Kurt about television. The rotting apricot-plum-prune face returned.

"Where'd you get this?" he said after a few seconds. "I told Dreisdale—"

"I know," Alex said, cutting him off. "Kurt called and asked for my help. I helped."

"Yeah, right," Gus said; then after a pause. "So, what then, what is this? You want the case? My job wasn't enough?"

On his end of the line, Alex sighed.

"I don't want the case," he said. "And let it go already, we don't have time for that dance again. How about we just stick to figuring out the bombing?"

There was a longer pause as Gus eyed the phone and the file.

"Fine" he said. "So what am I lookin' at here?"

"The snaps are from the ballpark video," Alex said. "Kurt's crew is working them through the recognition protocols. The script is what the bomber said before he blew up."

Gus looked at the pictures. He doubted they'd produce a suspect. The man's face was close to completely blocked by the hat. He then scanned the script. The words made no sense, but after a few seconds, they did give him an idea about how to handle the battle he'd been waging before Alex called. He set the folder aside and leaned in toward the phone.

"OK, you want to help," he said. "Does the name Dikembe Dukabi mean anything to you?"

Philadelphia

More than professional acquaintances, Alex and Thomas were friends. That friendship was pushed at times, especially when work got in the way. Now was one of those times. Had it been anyone else, Alex would have been livid. As it was, he was somewhere between simmer and boil, probably a touch closer to the latter.

"How could you not say anything?" he said. "This leaving me in the dark shit is getting old. I went with your plan on the Singer case because I was paying you for it. I went with you on King because— well, *because you're you*. I'm not driving the bus on this one, Thomas. Too many people have died. Looking the other way is not an option."

Thomas wasn't fazed by the fire in Alex's voice. It would take a lot more than that.

"I wouldn't expect you to do so," he said. "That does not change the facts, however. I did not know. My involvement with Mr. Dukabi may not be connected."

"*Bullshit*," Alex said. "You don't believe that any more than I do. There are no coincidences. That's what you always say. So tell me what's going on?"

Thomas remained unfazed.

"Alex, I assure you, I do not know."

Alex let out a heavy sigh. Most of him knew Thomas would never jeopardize innocent civilians. Still, it didn't change the facts at hand. Thomas had been in contact with Dukabi. Dukabi was now linked to the explosion. If he was behind it—as the second call to Pappas suggested—that made Thomas a potential co-conspirator. At the very least, it meant he had information vital to the investigation.

"Damn it, Thomas," Alex said.

"Alex, I understa—"

"*Shut up*… No, you don't understand, but that's my problem."

"Alex—"

"No, *stop*," Alex said, again cutting Thomas off. "I need whatever you have and I need it yesterday. And don't even try to suggest you aren't already looking. Just don't get in any deeper."

He hung up without waiting for a reply. A deep frown set in as he shook his head. He sat back, staring up at the ceiling tiles of his office. They'd recently been replaced and the once prominent stains were gone. It made the room brighter, but didn't help his mood. Too much about the events in New York didn't make sense.

Unlike the tiles, Alex had a feeling that wasn't about to change any time soon.

Wayne

"I don't think I've ever heard him so pissed," Sandy said.

"Indeed," Thomas said.

His tone wasn't the normal flat. Sandy got that he shared Alex's sentiments, but wished he would open up and talk about it, at least a little. After a few seconds, she pushed that thought aside because it wasn't going to happen, not today.

"Could this have been what Dukabi was talking about?" she said. "I mean, there's nothing to suggest Booker had anything to do with it, but…"

The words faded off into an exaggerated shrug.

"True," Thomas said. "It was drastic, but does seem excessive based on what we know of the situation."

"What do we really know?" Sandy said.

"Go on," Thomas said.

Sandy nodded and looked down at the spiral notebook in her lap. She was tired, having skipped sleep since the explosion—for obvious reasons. Alex had been right about that, the chase was well under way and her program had spit out a lot of new info. Sifting through it and making sense of it would take time. She'd already spent the past four hours or so getting started.

After a sigh, she looked up from the notes.

"There's a lot here," she said. "It'll take more time."

"We have time," Thomas said.

"OK," Sandy said. "Booker owes Dukabi money. Dukabi's having trouble collecting because he has an issue with his staff. He comes to you for help with that problem. One theory is he needs the money because he's on the run from something. He may or may not be mixed up with drugs. Booker, on the other hand, has no apparent link to drugs. But then a bomb goes off at a baseball game and someone says Dukabi did it. Booker used to be a ballplayer. So it's all either connected or it's not."

She stopped with another shrug. Thomas watched with an even expression, but as usual it belied his emotions. Dukabi being implicated gnawed at him. On a scale of one to ten, it was around four, like a puppy nipping at his ankle. Not painful, but annoying enough to notice. It was a feeling he got when information was lacking. Sandy shared the feeling. They were definitely missing something, as her synopsis had just proved. The holes were many and large.

That wasn't the only thing biting at Thomas. He was angry and it was growing because of Marshall's proximity to the blast. It had refreshed the feeling that his friend appeared destined to find trouble at every turn unless Thomas could somehow break the chain—and as much as Alex didn't want him involved, that reason alone would ensure he was.

Sandy's voice put a temporary halt to the angry thoughts.

"I don't know, like I said, there's a lot of stuff here," she said. "Not just on Dukabi, but on Booker, his friends, associates, et cetera. I need to keep crunching, but I think we need to keep an eye on Booker—at least for a while, see what he's up to. Maybe something will pop."

Thomas nodded.

"Agreed," he said. "Of course, there is the impediment of Director Harris' request to refrain from further activity."

"Yeah, so," Sandy said. "When has that ever stopped you?"

Chapter 12

New York City

That David Donovan couldn't sleep was understandable. Every time he closed his eyes, the stark images from Citi Field were there, replaying in an endless loop.

Mistimed and off-sounding crowd noise from the rightfield stands cause him to look up from his work. A man is running down the steps. The murmurs turn to gasps as the man steps to the railing. The gasps turn to screams as he jumps. The screams are erased along with everything else in a blinding light...

David's seat in the press box had provided a perfect view of the devastation. But like Marshall's reaction, for reasons unknown and despite the chaos, David had not run away in the aftermath of the explosion. As those around him scrambled for safety, he instinctively shifted gears from "sports reporter" to "first man on the scene" and the game summary he'd been working on morphed into a narrative of what he was seeing and feeling.

> At that moment, everything stopped. That the Mets had let the Division slip away, and soon, if they didn't wake up, the

Wild Card, no longer mattered. Theirs and everyone else's
wake-up call had come in a different form, one this city and
its millions of residents had seen before, and hoped to
never see again. But we knew the day would come. It was
inevitable. Death is inevitable. I have now witnessed it first-
hand. I won't ever be the same…

Some would later call the first-hand recital Pulitzer-worthy.
Other reporters would compile similar recaps, but there was
something about David's that lifted it above the rest, a strength in the
words that made it more than the typical over-dramatized
accountings often accompanying disasters such as this. He'd been
right there as it happened, and his words put the reader in the middle
of the action as well, more so than his usual game-synopsis skills.

The collective strength of this city can never be
questioned. We'd proved it once, on another September
day. We proved it again on this night. The reaction of a
handful of heroes was instant and nothing short of
miraculous. At times, it seemed as if as many were
running to the damaged area of the Porch as were running
from it. It will be some time before the box score of the
dead and injured is fully compiled, but I can say without
doubt, the numbers would have been far higher if not for
those swift-acting New Yorkers…

The link to his story was picked up by virtually every newspaper
in the country shortly after it was posted to the *Daily News* website.
Combined with a series of stunning photos captured by an equally as
courageous AP photographer, the later written version drew just as
much, if not more attention, something that added to David's
insomnia. In the hours that had followed, he was interviewed by
every New York network TV affiliate and became something of an
instant albeit reluctant celebrity.

He hadn't wanted to be part of the story, no reporter would.
He'd simply done his job and would have gladly traded the
accolades for a few minutes of sleep. It wasn't about him. It was
about those who'd come for a ballgame, but went home in a body
bag. Pennant chases no longer mattered. People had died, at a
baseball game. That kind of thing wasn't supposed to happen. Not
like this. Not ever.

Baseball was supposed to be fun.

> I don't know who did this or why. I don't know what point
> they wanted to make. I just know that the game, my game,
> is never going to be the same again. The events at last
> year's All-Star Game were tragic. The two deaths there
> may not have been avoidable, but they were contained to
> those involved. The deaths tonight, at Citi Field, were
> neither contained nor avoidable. The victims never had a
> chance. I wonder if any of us do...

"Yo, DD, you still with me?" a voice said, jolting David from the latest rewind playing in his head.

David's eyes opened and his fingers came up to rub at them. After a second or two, the hand moved away and he looked at his boss, the paper's managing editor, a man David didn't much care for. The two were in the editor's office, David in a guest chair, the editor leaning against a desk, a copy of the *Daily News* and several other papers behind him.

"Yeah, I'm here," David said before a massive yawn overcame him.

"Nice, DD," the editor said in the middle of a chuckle.

David hated when the editor called him "DD" but was too tired to protest. He was trying to conserve what little energy he had left for another struggle he was facing. He'd seen something else, just before the bomber and a few other souls were deleted from existence. At first he'd told himself he was wrong, that his eyes had been fooled by fear. But then he saw the video, being aired in another seemingly endless loop on every newscast.

A hat had disguised the bomber's features, but that wasn't what David had seen. As much as he would have liked to forget the explosion and its aftermath, part of him wanted more to forget he'd seen that something else, the backpack hanging from the man's shoulder, because now, the reporter in him would never let it go.

Eddie Booker had been carrying the exact same bag at the press gate before the game.

"This is some goddamned good writing," the editor said, rapping his knuckles on the desk on top of one of the newspapers.

The sounds once again jostled David from his thoughts.

"Huh? Oh, yeah, thanks," he said in a distracted voice. "It, uh, kinda wrote itself. I just gave it some paper."

The editor stopped knocking and shook his head vigorously.

"*What?*" he said. "Shit, you did way more than *that.*"

David closed his eyes again, squeezing tight to bring on the darkness, hoping maybe he could delete the editor from existence. The man's over-amped attitude made worse the fact so many had died, a fact seemingly lost on the man—and a lot of the media. The part of David that wanted to forget about the backpack also wanted to mourn that loss of life. Such would have been appropriate, but again, the reporter in him knew it had to wait.

The airing of the video had created a monster and the beast was hungry for more. It was quite possible David possessed that "more" but he had no intentions of tossing it into the cage, not yet, not until he knew for sure, because as sobering as the deaths had been, the magnitude of Eddie's potential involvement was mind-numbing.

After a deep breath, David reopened his eyes. He needed to get to it, to confirm it, one way or another. He had to know if Eddie was involved. First, he had to get out of the M.E.'s office.

"I, uh—I just did my job," he said. "I'm not sure it's much more than an obituary."

"*What?*" the editor said again.

He picked up the *Daily News.*

"This is no obit, man, *this is huge.*"

"Whatever, I just… whatever," David said, his tone shifting to annoyed.

The editor missed the change.

"Listen, we have a ton of follow-up to do," he said. "I want you in on it."

No shit, David thought as he stared up at the man, shut up already and I will. Despite an overwhelming urge, he managed to keep that thought under wraps.

"Hey, I'm on it," he said instead, retaining most of his professionalism. "I'm already putting together a piece on the cancellations."

Along with MLB, every spectator sport in the U.S.—professional and otherwise—had ground to a halt. It was probably an over-reaction, but until the FBI or Homeland Security or some other authority gave an all clear, no one wanted to be first in line to resume play. That would appear insensitive, and political correctness in the face of tragedy was a touchy subject.

"Come on, DD, I'm not talking about *that*," the editor said. "People want to know what the hell is going on, if we're gonna have more explosions. You were there, partner, so who better to figure that out and tell us?"

David's eyes narrowed. Again he wanted to scream out *NO SHIT*, but managed to keep it inside.

"Eh, I'm a sports writer," he said, deflecting. "Give the conspiracy shit to the hacks downstairs. I already got plenty to keep me busy."

The editor's smile grew, exposing most of his cigarette-stained teeth.

"Shit, David, this *is* sports."

King of Prussia, Pennsylvania

Sports News Network—SNN for short—was headquartered in a converted warehouse in the suburbs west of Philadelphia, near the sprawling King of Prussia Mall complex. Real estate was cheaper there and saving pennies mattered at a place like SNN. They were a distant second to ESPN in ratings and every other category, and where the Worldwide Leader had Disney's deep pockets to help in rough times, SNN had no one. They had to fight for everything—and what little they got wasn't much. To industry insiders, working there was something of an insult, sloppy seconds if you will.

Alyson Lane didn't care.

For her, SNN was a chance to live out a dream. She knew television was a cut-throat business—especially sports television and especially for women—but like the network itself, she was willing to do anything to see that dream through. At the moment, "anything" was being stretched to its limits. As David's ME had suggested, there was a story out there, something bigger than the games, and Alyson was determined to find it first.

"I'm guessing you won't say no to me again?" she said.

A harried but satisfied looking man was in front of her. As he fumbled to rebuckle his pants, Alyson calmly brushed at her knees.

"I, uh, no—I mean, *yes*," the man said. "You're right. I won't."

Alyson smiled and closed in. The man staggered back against his desk as she reached behind him, for a tissue from a box there. After pulling one out, she backed off and dabbed at the edges of her mouth with it while the man tried to remember how to breathe. Alyson's effort was more successful—the man gasped when she grabbed the remnants of his erection through his pants.

"I'm *always* right," she said with a squeeze.

She had intercepted the man, her executive producer, on the way to his office. The poor fool never had a chance, not that he was the only one who had enjoyed the not-so-spontaneous blow job.

"By the way... *nice cock*," she said in a whisper into his ear before releasing her grip.

She gave him a wink before turning and unlocking the door.

"You'll, um—keep me informed?" the EP said to her back.

"I'll let you know as soon as I have something," Alyson said over her shoulder.

She turned the knob and left the office with a smile. More than a few co-workers shot angry glances in her direction as she walked past. It didn't take a rocket scientist to know what she'd done. Truth was, most of the others were just pissed they hadn't thought of something similar first.

"You are such *a whore*," a voice said to Alyson when she reached her cubicle.

There was a chuckle as a smiling female face appeared at the top of the partition.

"I know," Alyson said. "But I got it."

"Damn. I wish I could be like that," her cube neighbor said.

Alyson's smile slowly faded as she considered the words.

"No, you don't."

Queens

There wasn't much to Mike Coakley's apartment, his latest temporary home, but that was on purpose. Mike didn't buy property. His journeyman career included a track record of being traded and married far too often. He found the fewer assets in his possession, the better. There was less to lose that way—and Mike had lost a lot already.

The thirty-eight year old middle reliever for the Mets was a hanger-on, someone who bounced from team to team, a body needed to fill out a roster. It was the kind of thing that happened a lot in baseball, mostly because of expansion in both the major and minor leagues. Mike, and others like him, should have been gone from the game long ago, but every spring, there they were, doing whatever it took to last another season, to cash another paycheck.

Mike was a lot like Eddie and Alyson in that respect. *Whatever it took* wasn't about cheating, it was about survival. It was also about choices and the consequences thereof. As the saying goes, you dance with the one that brung ya, even if the dance wasn't always pleasant.

Mike feared he'd just stepped into a really bad one.

"Ah, man, what did you do?" he said aloud.

He was alone in his bedroom, sitting on the edge of his bed, a small slip of paper in his hand. It had been in the pocket of the pants he'd worn the night before, found as he was repacking those trousers along with most of his other clothes for the extended road trip that was sure to be brought on by the disaster at Citi Field. There was no way the Mets were going to be playing there again this season. If they played another game at all was still to be decided.

When—and if—that occurred, their games would get switched to the opponents' parks or maybe Yankee Stadium, but it was going to be a while before the team played a *home* game. Mike was OK with that; he could never go to Citi again and be just fine. He'd been in the bullpen, and along with some of the other players there was first to try to help the Dodgers rightfielder after the explosion. It was an ugly memory, one suddenly made worse by the note.

"No, no, no… Eddie," he said after reading it again.

He put his head in his hands as his thoughts began to race. A growing fear added to an already strong sadness, and both emotions left him unable to control the flow. Distracted by the confusion, it took five rings before he reacted to the sound of his ringing cell phone. When he saw the name on the caller ID—*Travis Mac*—he just let it ring and closed his eyes again.

Unlike Mike, Travis Mackenzie possessed an abundance of natural talent, but that was never enough. *Nothing* was ever enough for Travis. *Whatever it takes* in his world wasn't about survival, it was about more—more money, more cars, more houses, more women, more attention, more everything. And as is often the case for people like that, the shortest distance to more was to cheat.

Travis Mackenzie cheated a lot.

In fact, to many, Travis was the King of Cheaters. The thirty-four year old reigning National League MVP was cocky and arrogant and universally despised. Sure, he had skills, but like a few other players before him, people blamed a growing hat size on more than just an out of control ego. Worse yet was the fact he got away with it. Unfortunately—or fortunately in Travis' eyes—to date, no one had been able to directly link him to any evidence of illegal substance use. Along with the shitty attitude, that fact put Travis at odds with reporters, fans, and other players, players who knew the truth—players like Mike Coakley.

It wasn't the only truth Mike now knew.

A beep sounded from the phone, kicking him out of his self-pity. It meant Travis had left a message, but it took a few more minutes for Mike to find the strength to operate the phone's buttons and listen.

"Mike fuckin' Coakley, you better call me... now."

Mike began to shake from an onslaught of new emotions—Travis had a way of doing that to people—and it was another five minutes before he could steady his nerves and return the call. Travis picked up after the third ring.

"Michael, Michael," he said in a nasty tone. "Are you fuckin' screenin' my calls now?"

"You, uh, I was—"

"Shit, Mike, talk already," Travis said, cutting him off.

Mike swallowed. It was difficult.

"No—I mean, you called me," he said. "I, uh—is this about the note?"

There was a noise in Mike's ear. He couldn't make out the source.

"Note," Travis said. "What note, Mike? What the fuck are you talkin' about?"

Mike shivered, maybe from the tone, maybe from something else. With no hair to stop it, the sweat was pouring from his head. He did his best to wipe it away with his free hand.

"C'mon, Travis," he said. "I know Eddie left you a note, too."

He wiped at the sweat again as he waited for a reply.

"I have no idea what you're talking about," Travis said.

Mike lowered his head and a handful of drops fell to the bed.

"Don't be like that," he said in a low voice.

"Be like *what*, Mike? Eddie ain't my fuckin' problem."

More drops hit the bed.

"How is this *not* our problem?" Mike said.

"Don't get stupid," Travis said.

Mike wiped at the sweat again and stood. As he began pacing the bedroom, his anger grew.

"Fu-fuck you, Travis," he said. "Don't forget, I know, too."

There was a sharp laugh in his ear.

"You don't know *shit*," Travis said. "And who would believe you anyway? Wake up Mike, you're a fuckin' nobody. Ain't no one gonna care about what you might have to say."

Mike reached into the bathroom and grabbed a hand towel. As he wiped his head, Travis' voice came back to his ear.

"Are we clear, Mike? *Nothing* changes."

Mike tossed the towel into the sink.

"But what about—"

The line went dead before he could finish. He snapped the phone shut, spun away from the bathroom, and fired the device across the bedroom in the same motion. The plastic fastball exploded into a hundred pieces when it hit the far wall. Mike thought about doing the same thing to Travis' head the next time they faced each other on the field.

The fucker definitely deserved it.

Chapter 13

Manhattan

About three minutes into the conversation with Alex, Gus had realized Dukabi was a dead end. Scratch that. What he'd realized was that the name was nothing more than a diversion, something on which the FBI would waste time. By adding the second part, the personal part, the caller had ensured that would happen. The person was smart. He—or she; it was hard to tell because of the mechanical overlay—knew Gus couldn't ignore the calls, but would somehow have to. He would have to act without acting.

Gus wasn't a very good actor.

Eventually, someone was going to find out. It wasn't obvious but it was there, and if they dug deep enough... Gus didn't want to think about that. What he needed was to buy some time, so he had framed his instructions in such a way that his staff would have to concentrate on the African. It was risky, but given the circumstances, it was the best he could come up with on short notice.

As head of the bombing investigation, all eyes were on him at the moment, and he didn't have the luxury to be overly creative. The caller had constructed a neat little box and Gus was stuffed firmly inside. There wasn't a lot of room to breathe. He figured that was the point. Whoever this caller was, they knew an awful lot about how the Bureau worked. It was a scary thought.

So was something else.

Despite the forewarning, the rush Gus had felt after hearing the alarms had been invigorating, the sounds a justification that his job meant something again. He'd been telling everyone for years that the bad guys were still out there, still trying to hurt us, and this attack proved it. Except, of course, for the fact none of the existing evidence backed up those feelings.

Gus knew why: It was another side of the box. The caller had been *very* smart.

A new blue folder rested on Gus' desk, delivered by Kurt Dreisdale, who was now sitting across from Gus, waiting. In the twenty-four hours since the explosion, Jay Tiff—in coordination with Homeland Security—had worked through every high-priority target on the current Watch List. None had claimed responsibility. In fact, several went so far as to deny involvement. As Dreisdale put it, "Nothing was missed. This was not a terrorist attack."

Gus was going to have to work hard to change that assessment.

"I think you're wrong," he said.

He eyed the folder again before shifting his gaze to Kurt. The Jay Tiff leader's expression was solid. Gus' feigned uncertainty. Of the two, the former was more convincing.

"Fine, whatever," Kurt said. "Technically, you're right. It was a terrorist incident, but it sure as shit didn't have anything to do with the Taliban or Al-Qaeda or any of the thousands of other nutbag groups out there. If that's where you want to go, good luck, you're on your own."

Gus began to strum his fingers on top of the folder, slowly at first, then faster, until ending it with a bang from the edge of his fist.

"Then it's a good thing you're not in charge," he said. "You don't have the balls for this job."

Kurt held his tongue. Like at the ballpark, he simply gathered up his belongings, stood, and left without a word—and without closing the door. Gus stared at the opening for a long minute.

"Fucking coward," he said under his breath before bringing his eyes back to his desk.

There was another folder resting next to the blue one. It held the latest casualty report. Gus was familiar with that content as well. Eighteen people remained in critical condition. Eight were not expected to survive. Depending on those outcomes, the final death toll could reach as high as thirty. Gus sat back and thought about the numbers.

After a series of huffs and puffs, his mind went back to the original phone call. He bounced it around and added in the bomber's words. The longer he thought, the more he realized there was a flaw in the math. Thirty was a lot, but not nearly enough. Kurt was right, a real terrorist would never settle for such a paltry amount. They would have put ten people in the stadium with bombs and taken *three thousand* souls to a better place.

"You said a statement needed to be made," he said to the memory of the call. "Shit, twenty-nine innocent people and one asshole. What kind of statement does *that* make?"

After several seconds, he abruptly sat forward.

"Hold the fuck up," he said.

He began to rifle through the other papers and folders on his desk. After another minute or so, he located the projected timeline. Using the surveillance video, most of the bomber's movements had already been tracked. There were still a few holes—the biggest being that no one had seen him enter the stadium—but Gus found what he needed.

He sat back again.

"Son-of-a-bitch," he said aloud. "Stupid fuck wasn't trying to kill anybody but himself. What the fuck is going on here?"

Philadelphia

Alex was right, Thomas did not believe in coincidences. Things happened as a direct result of other things, cause and effect, links in a chain. An anonymous call is only so for the receiver, not the deliverer. It was done for a reason. That reason would answer a lot of questions. Thomas had a few ideas, but couldn't be sure, not yet.

What he did know was that someone knew enough about the system to know how such a call would be received. Because of that, he went into Dukabi's apartment alone this time. Sandy stayed back to keep tabs on the easily spotted FBI surveillance teams around the building. None of the agents appeared to have noticed Thomas' arrival. Either that or they didn't care.

Thomas knew that might change. He kept the conversation short.

"Someone wants all eyes on you," he said to Dukabi.

They were seated opposite each other in the living room portion of the suite. Despite the relaxed clothes adorning the big man's body, he was clearly anything but. Thomas was calm on all fronts, dressed in a version of his usual attire—never too business-like, never too casual. In truth, he could make any outfit look good. Sandy always noticed. Dukabi did not. His thoughts were on things other than fabrics and fashion.

"I have no reason to lie," he said. "The event in New York was not my doing."

Thomas nodded slightly.

"Maybe not, but you knew something."

The flat tone was also close to normal, but there was something just on the other side. Unlike the conversation at LOVE Park, Dukabi picked up on it this time, and another layer of concern crept onto his expression.

"Is that another accusation?" he said.

"Not at all," Thomas said. "You feared a drastic action. The event in New York was drastic. I'm merely trying to determine why the caller suggested a connection to you."

"I am not comfortable with that suggestion," Dukabi said.

"I would think not, especially if the event was not as expected."

Dukabi's dark eyes narrowed.

"How do I know you are not once again working with the FBI?"

Thomas shrugged an eyebrow.

"You don't," he said.

Dukabi smiled ever so slightly.

"Yes, I suppose this is an issue of trust," he said.

He adjusted his bulk in the chair.

"Very well, Mr. Hillsborough," he said, continuing. "The answer to your question is no. The event in New York was not entirely as expected."

"Not entirely?" Thomas said. "Explain."

Dukabi adjusted again. The chair he was in creaked out a complaint.

"It seems my expectations were flawed," he said.

Thomas remained unmoved.

"Flawed as to which aspect?"

Dukabi stood.

"Multiple reasons, Mr. Hillsborough," he said as he began to pace the room. "Most concerning is the severity. I did not expect such damage. It does not match my understanding of the events taking place."

Thomas eyed the big man's slow pace around the office.

"The events taking place," he said. "Events you knew about, but don't know about."

Dukabi stopped and tilted his head, a subtle version of a nod.

"You need to explain that concept a little better," Thomas said.

The comment was met with a more pronounced nod.

"All in due time, my friend," Dukabi said. "Let us first discuss the authorities."

"OK," Thomas said. "The FBI has several teams outside. I suspect they will arrest you or at least bring you in for questioning. I take it such would be fruitless."

Dukabi began pacing again.

"Yes, they are, shall we say... *misguided.*"

"Am I misguided?" Thomas said.

Again, Dukabi stopped. His expression was between angry and impressed. His tone matched.

"You and I have differed on many occasions."

Dukabi was trying to say a lot without saying anything, to help himself as much as others. The FBI was doing the same thing. Either they didn't believe the tip or there was more to it. Thomas flashed on something Alex had said.

I'm not driving the bus this time.

That was definitely true because whoever was calling the shots was firing mostly airballs. Thomas began to wonder if that was on purpose, and it brought him back around to Dukabi.

"True enough," he said to the big man's last words. "But I need more to work with."

Dukabi held Thomas' eyes for several long seconds.

"Yes, I agree," he said before returning to his chair.

Thomas shrugged the eyebrow again.

"You agree it's true or you agree I need more?"

Dukabi sat and a more pronounced smile worked onto his face.

"Both, Thomas, I agree with both."

Ten minutes later, Thomas was back in his car with Sandy. She had nothing to report. The FBI teams had made no movements. Thomas wasn't surprised. It fit with everything else not happening and not making sense.

"How'd it go upstairs?" Sandy said.

"Pretty much as expected," Thomas said.

Sandy frowned.

"So, what now?" she said.

Thomas started the car's engine.

"I think we need to have a chat with Mr. Rosenbaum," he said. "I want to run something by him and Mr. Loeb."

Sandy's frown deepened.

"You think this is about baseball?" she said.

If she was confused or worried before then, what Thomas said next made it worse. It was something she'd never heard, at least not from him.

"I'm not sure what to think."

Chapter 14

New York City

Gabi and Mark were in Mark's office, seated in the guest area off to one side of the room. The Commissioner was on a leather sofa, Gabi in one of two facing armchairs. On a coffee table between them were copies of the morning papers. Next to the papers was a speaker phone, its tiny green lights blinking. Mark was staring at the lights, his face locked in a heavy frown. Gabi's expression was slightly less tense.

"Shouldn't the FBI be telling me this?" Mark said toward the speaker.

"The FBI is distracted," Thomas' amplified voice said.

Mark's eyes shifted to the newspapers. The headlines confirmed Thomas' statement.

"I can see that, but I take it you're talking about something else?"

"The investigation is being led by New York," Thomas said. "Their information does not necessarily match mine. I believe it may be some time before they become as well-versed."

Mark closed his eyes and pinched the bridge of his nose.

"Jesus, Thomas, I really don't like the sound of that."

"I take it you're not officially involved," Gabi said.

"A fair assessment," Thomas said.

Mark looked at Gabi, then back to the phone.

"What is your involvement?" he said. "This is all starting to sound scary."

"At the moment, consider me a concerned citizen," Thomas said.

"Concerned for your friend, right?" Mark said.

It came out more like an aside. Thomas didn't respond. Mark released the nose-pinch and moved the hand to the top of his head. After finger-combing the brown and gray locks there, he began to furiously scratch at his scalp. Gabi knew it signaled frustration. He jumped in to try and relieve it.

"OK, Thomas," he said toward the phone. "As a concerned citizen, if we restart the games without the FBI's blessing, won't that piss someone off?"

Mark stopped scratching and sat forward.

"That's a good point," he said. "They're saying this thing is a terrorist attack. I'll look like an ass. No, I'll be crucified if something were to happen at another game."

There was a pause. Mark stood, but sat almost as fast. Gabi almost smiled at the odd movements, but recovered quickly.

"You and me both," he said.

"I understand," Thomas said. "There is an element of risk involved, however, I believe that risk exists whether or not you choose to play."

Mark's frown returned and he looked at Gabi, then the phone, before his head dropped.

"Shit," he said before pausing. "So, this *does* have something to do with baseball?"

"If for no other reason than the location of the explosion, yes," Thomas said.

Mark emitted a loud sigh and flopped back onto the sofa. His eyes opened and closed a few times, like he was trying to blink everything away.

"So that must mean there are *other* reasons, too," he said.

Gabi jumped in again.

"Thomas, do you have any idea how long before the FBI catches up, before New York catches up?" he said. "I'd hate to trigger something too soon."

"A valid concern," Thomas said. "My advice would be to make a call to our mutual friend in Philadelphia. Allow him to provide you with something more official."

"Jesus, guys, this is fucked—"

Mark cut himself off from finishing. His head then began to shake.

"Does Alex know what you know?" Gabi said toward the phone.

"Doubtful," Thomas said. "He knows enough, however."

"In other words," Gabi said. "This conversation never happened. We'd be making the suggestion on our own."

"Indeed."

David shook his head and a slight chuckle escaped his mouth as he read the headline on the front cover of the *Daily News*: SWING AND MISS. A Photoshop-created graphic under the words had a shadowy ballplayer swinging a bat overlaying an overhead shot of Citi Field, post explosion. At the bottom, in smaller letters, the sub-heading read: Baseball to blame for attack?

Sure, the *DN* was a tabloid and stuff like this was to be expected, but David had to give the copy editors some extra credit for creativity. The story—stories—on the pages were enough to stand on their own, but he knew the play on words on the cover would attract a few more eyeballs, and any eyeballs that sent messages to the brain to signal the hands to reach for a coin or two was always a good thing.

Journalistic integrity wasn't entirely a thing of the past, but more and more the newspaper world was all about the money. Ad revenues were down. Subscriptions were down. Costs were up. There was unrelenting pressure from the blogosphere and online sites. Times were tough. Still, no one wanted to see good writing overlooked, forgotten like a piece of candy collecting dust under the seat of a car driven by the bottom line.

David wasn't as seasoned as the greybeards in the newsroom, but he held the same belief. The ethics of the Fourth Estate—truthfulness, accuracy, objectivity, impartiality, fairness, and public accountability—meant more than a P&L in the black. He believed he had an obligation to get things right. In relation to his latest effort, he wasn't sure he'd been successful.

He flipped to the story that had been teased on the cover, his story, and a frown filled his features. It wasn't what he'd wanted to pen, but it was his only option. Like a few of the paper's other writers of lesser talent, he gave in to his deadline with a collection of rumors, innuendo, and historical tidbits thrown together to get the managing editor off his back. It mostly worked, but left him feeling dirty. There was a better story, the Eddie story, but it needed more work before it could be printed. There were too many holes.

David turned the paper over and paged in from the back. Despite the lack of games, he had gone ahead and filed his regular weekly Baseball Notes feature, a collection of news and fodder from around the league. About halfway through was mention of Eddie in a blurb about agent activity. Mike Coakley had confirmed the firing about two weeks earlier, but David had been holding off mentioning it for some other day.

Inspired by frustration—at his boss, at his crappy story, at his lack of confirmation that Eddie was involved in the bombing—he'd dropped the firing in as a tease, hoping maybe it would be a breadcrumbs trail that someone would follow and show up and fill in the blanks. He figured it would take some time before that happened, if it worked at all.

Turned out he was wrong on both counts.

"I don't like this."

The words came from a man seated with Jamie on a bench near Central Park's Conservatory Pond. 5th Avenue was at their backs. Traffic there was light and the area around the pond was quiet. It was after rush hour but before the dead of night. Most of the joggers had come and gone and the homeless and late night partiers had yet to arrive. The park was relatively safe after dark, much more so than years past, but Jamie had no fear of that. Most of his life had been spent in the dark. He was very much at home there. The same could not be said of the man with him.

That was the point.

"This isn't the best idea," the man said. "You could have just called."

"Yes, but I enjoy it here," Jamie said. "It gives us a chance to become more... *personal*."

The emphasis on the last word was as much a message as the setting. Several days of inactivity had left Jamie and Shady restless, the younger African more so. Idle time was not something either was used to. Both were happy it was coming to an end. Whether the other man agreed was debatable.

"I'm not sure I like all these changes," he said. "None of this is what we agreed to. Things are out of control. I wanted you to make a statement, nothing more."

"Statements were made," Jamie said.

His face was like a black hole in the dim light coming from the lamps along the path. The other man shivered.

"Not like *this*," the man said after recovering. "I'm paying you guys to make sure things *don't* go wrong. From where I'm sitting we're well past that."

He placed a newspaper on the bench between them. It was opened to the page with David's baseball notes. The man tapped a finger on the words about Eddie.

"People are gonna figure it out," he said. "You need to fix this."

Jamie looked down. After a few seconds, he nodded and stood. The black hole seemed deeper than before.

"Then it shall be fixed."

An hour later, David's shoulders sagged when his desk phone rang. He dropped back into his chair and stared at the noise. It had been a long day—check that, days—and the story-writing frustration had added to the severe lack of sleep. His last drops of energy drained away at the thought of having to deal with anyone, and it took until after the seventh ring before he reluctantly lifted the receiver.

"Daily News sports," he said without even the slightest hint of caring.

"David Donovan," a strange voice said.

It was a statement rather than a question and elicited a shot of adrenaline. David sat forward slightly in his chair.

"Whoever this is, I'm really not in the mood," he said.

"Your mental state is of no concern."

Crank calls were usually reserved for political reporters and gossip columnists, not so much Sports guys. David had fielded a few over the years, but the distorted mechanical voice told him this was different. He sat completely upright.

"OK, enough with the funny voice," he said. "Who is this? I'm not in the mood for games."

"I assure you, Mr. Donovan, this is no game."

As the adrenaline did its work, David's entire body began to shake. He made a mental note to ask some of the players how they dealt with the rush as he tried to catch his breath.

"*Who is this?*" he said with as much force as he could muster.

"My identity is also of no concern."

David's breathing degenerated into short puffs.

"You don't seem to be too concerned about anything," he said. "So what do you want?"

"Be careful where you tread, Mr. Donovan."

The shaking increased as David tried to get a full shot of air. During the effort, his eyes tried to find something on which to focus. They landed on today's paper, front cover up on his desk. A thought blossomed, the breadcrumbs.

"Are you talking about my story?" he said. "Is this some kinda threat?"

The line was quiet.

"*Hello?*" David said in a shout. "Are you still there? What the hell are you talking about? What is this?"

"Tread wisely, Mr. Donovan."

Gus moved most of the crap from his desk to a chair off to the side. The only items not relocated were a newspaper—the New York *Daily News*—and a folder containing the preliminary forensics report. Gus scratched at his chin as he picked up the paper. He hated reporters in general and would have ignored the tabloid completely if not for the uncanny coincidence one of his analysts had found inside.

He exchanged the paper for the folder and lifted out the report. The bomber's identity was the same name this reporter, this David Donovan, had mentioned in a throwaway sidebar. The match had raised some red flags in the analysts' room. It had also raised some serious issues for Gus, not the least of which was the fact it could be the final nail in his terrorism theory if the name got out.

According to the forensics, the bomb had been in the man's backpack. That much was never in doubt, at least not for Gus, but confirmation of it didn't make him feel any better. The munition of choice was C-4, the most common variety of plastic explosive. It was stronger than TNT and had a relatively simple structure: explosive, plastic binder, plasticizer, and usually a chemical marker for identification. This particular batch was traced to a manufacturer in China. Gus was sure that meant nothing. Pretty much everything was made in China these days.

C-4's popularity came from its stability and flexibility. It could be easily molded into any shape, making it a favorite of suicide bombers. Triggering was achieved by introducing heat and a shockwave, such as that produced by a detonator or firing cap. The resultant explosion had two phases. The first caused most of the damage. After detonation, a variety of gases—mainly nitrogen and carbon oxides—were released. The gases expanded at close to 26,000 feet per second. At that rate, there was no outrunning the second phase of the blast. Destruction was instantaneous.

The deaths and damage at Citi Field were testament to that.

There was nothing overly sophisticated about the bomb. The detonator was triggered by a cell phone. Several stills from the video showed a phone in the man's right hand. Most of that communications device miraculously survived. Investigators found it and the bomber's severed appendage imbedded in what was left of a Subway Sandwich sign on the façade of the Porch.

The phone was of the pay-as-you-go variety, available at any convenience store, but the hand gave up a full set of fingerprints. The images matched those in a file already in the FBI's extensive database. They did not belong to a terrorist. They belonged—at least in Gus' mind—to someone far worse.

"A fuckin' baseball player," he said aloud.

He picked up a coffee mug resting next to his computer monitor and took a drink. The beverage was cold, causing a return of the rotting apricot face, and he emptied the liquid into the dirt of a large plant next to his desk. Seeing as he wasn't much for watering, the parched Dracaena appreciated the moisture, caffeine infused or not.

Gus passed on seeking a refill and returned his focus to the report. Being a baseball fan, he knew all about Eddie Booker's tainted history, but couldn't connect any of it to what had happened. Why would the man do something so horrific, no matter how sordid a past? Gus couldn't get his mind around it. He gets a call. A bomb goes off. He gets another call. He's given the name of an African mobster. None of it made any sense. Neither did something else.

His eyes went back to the newspaper.

"OK, Mr. Donovan, how the fuck did *you* know?"

After the phone call, David didn't move for close to five minutes. It took that long for enough of the adrenaline to wear off so he could think straight. Then, just as he was close to fully functional again, the face of one of the paper's interns appeared above his cubicle wall.

"Excuse me, Mr. Donovan," the young woman said in a hushed tone. "I, uh—I think you need to come out front."

David looked up. There was hesitation on the girl's face. David misread it and sighed.

"Please, Linda, I told you. Don't call me *Mister*," he said.

The intern looked offended. David quickly recovered.

"Sorry," he said. "Why do I need to come out front?"

The intern seemed to shrink a little as she leaned in.

"There's, um—there's two men here from the FBI," she said in barely more than a whisper. "They said they need to talk to you. They don't look very happy."

David's glands produced another rush of epinephrine. The nervous excitement of the call was back, joined by a healthy—unhealthy?—dose of confusion and concern as he stood and looked around.

"Mr. Donovan?" the intern said.

David refocused on her.

"OK, go tell them to wait," he said. "And make sure security doesn't let them in yet."

She hustled off. David followed with his eyes, and when she was out of sight, he looked around the office again. Everything seemed normal—except that it didn't. He knew now the breadcrumbs had worked, but not in a good way. The single word that escaped him as he stood there summed it up nicely.

"Shit."

Chapter 15

Manhattan

In an ideal world, the sequence of events that followed would have been something like this: David goes to the night desk editor and tells him what's going on; said editor makes an urgent call to the paper's First Amendment lawyer; David and editor wait patiently, out of sight of the FBI visitors, until said lawyer gets to the office; lawyer and David then sit together with the FBI representatives; David is *never* alone and reveals *nothing*.

That's not what happened.

In addition to the First Amendment, New York State's Shield Law—one of the strongest in the country—protects the right of news reporters to refuse to testify about information obtained through news gathering. There is no federal equivalent, at least not yet—a version had passed the House but awaits a vote by the full Senate—but most competent lawyers can get past that.

What they can't get past is the Patriot Act and section 215 thereof. It overrides state shield laws and federal common law protection for journalists' source materials. Gus was a big fan of that particular nuance of the law. David? Not so much, especially after he ended up leaving alone with the two agents. He wasn't arrested, but wasn't exactly treated with kid gloves. To say it was unpleasant would have been to drastically understate the experience.

He was driven to the FBI field office and ushered into a small interview room where, for almost two hours, Gus worked him over—hard. David was smart enough to know when someone was fishing, and the fat, slightly odorous agent was seriously working the line. Whatever the FBI was chasing, he had no intention of being the catch and did his best not to take the bait, clinging to his severely beaten rights, hoping the paper's attorney would get there before things got too far out of hand.

It almost worked.

"Mr. Pappas, I don't know what else to tell you," David said. "The notes don't have anything to do with anything really. Seriously, I was just filling space. I honestly have no idea where Eddie Booker is or what he might be up to."

Gus' face seemed stuck in rotting-fruit mode. David saw it as more of a peach than an apricot. He didn't much like either fruit.

"For the last time, it's *Director*," Gus said in a matching nasty tone. "*Director* Pappas."

David closed his eyes and shook his head. A lot of his earlier fatigue had seeped back in. He didn't give a shit about Gus' title. He just wanted the interview to be over so he could get back to doing what the FBI now also appeared to be doing, looking for Eddie.

"Fine, whatever," he said. "I still don't know where Eddie is."

Gus' jaw began to move as if he were chewing a steak. David mostly ignored it and the following half-hour of more Eddie-related questions, "mostly" because somewhere in that time something clicked in his head. The FBI's fascination with Eddie didn't make sense, unless—

"*Director* Pappas, hold up," David said, interrupting Gus—and sarcastically emphasizing the first word. "Are you trying to say that Eddie Booker was the bomber?"

Gus' breathing faltered; it may have been a gasp, but sounded more like a leaking tire. David's eyes widened at hearing the sound. He'd found the Holy Grail, the missing piece for his story.

"Son-of-a-bitch," he said; then after a pause to process. "Oh, shit… it *was* him I saw."

He pushed back from the table as the weight of the realization pressed down. His thoughts went to the weird phone call, but Gus interrupted before he could connect all the dots.

"What did you just say?" Gus said. "What do you mean you saw him?"

David looked away for a second, his mind still trying to work out the logistics. What he came up with wasn't quite the answer he was looking for, but he ran with it anyway.

"I told you," he said. "I saw Eddie at the Press Gate, before the game. He was having a conversation with the guard there. To me it looked like he was having some trouble. I told the guard I thought he might be drunk and maybe someone should keep an eye on him."

"No, no, no, that's not what you meant," Gus said in a combative tone. "You saw something else. What was it?"

David's expression changed, his concern giving way to annoyance.

"Huh? No. What?" he said in a matching tone. "I didn't see or mean anything else. Booker is—was a loser. The man's been an alcoholic and drug fiend for as long as I've known him. It looked like he was off the wagon again. Frankly, I'm surprised he can still get out of bed. He's a fuck-up, Director."

Gus made a note on a pad on the table, his head shaking the entire time.

"Yeah, but is he fucked up enough to do something like this?" he said.

David hesitated. There it was: confirmation. This guy is an idiot, he thought, as he sat back.

"I don't know," he said through a smirk. "What exactly did Eddie do, Director?"

Gus stopped writing and made another odd noise before looking up and manipulating the fruit expression for a few seconds. David was watching, but not seeing, distracted by all the calculations going on in his head. One of the answers was to not share his strange call. As much as he didn't want to admit, he was intrigued by it, despite the fear it had generated. And now, based on Gus' slips, he knew it was all connected—and it was big.

"OK, Mr. Reporter, here's what happens next," Gus said, jarring David back to the present. "I am not confirming or denying anything you've said. You are to tell no one of the contents of this meeting. It is protected under Federal law. I don't care how much your boss and lawyer bitch about it. None of your rights were violated. Patriot beats Shield. Make up whatever you want—you're good at that—but it better not be the truth. This is an active investigation. Any disclosures could jeopardize things."

Telling a reporter to stay away from a story was like telling a four-year-old to stay away from the cookie jar. There was no way it *wasn't* going to happen.

"Mr. Donovan, are we clear?" Gus said in a fierce tone.

David nodded, doing his best to suppress a grin. The toddler inside him was up on the chair, reaching for the jar, and Mommy was in the other room. Whatever had caused Eddie Booker to lose it in such a spectacular fashion was beyond tempting—and David now had the inside track to be the one to tell the world all about it.

"Sure thing, Director, all clear," he said with as straight a face as he could manage. "I understand *everything*."

"Keep an eye on him," Gus said. "And keep it quiet."

He hung up the phone and took an inventory. He had been busy since David was dismissed. It was bad enough he'd screwed up and the reporter now knew Booker was the bomber. Gus couldn't afford to let anyone else come to the same conclusion. He pulled some strings, flexed his rank, and called in a favor or two, and was able to put the kibosh on any further airings of the explosion video. Keeping it off the Internet would be more difficult, but he was assured by tech support and legal it would be taken care of. Gus silently thanked the Patriot Act again as his last call went to Alex.

The fact he woke the man was a welcome bonus.

"Gus? What's wrong?" Alex said into his ear. "What time is it?"

Gus smiled at the grogginess in Alex's voice.

"You said you'd help."

There was a pause. On his end of the line, Alex sat up in bed.

"Geez, I did, but it's what, three-thirty?" he said. "Can't this wait a few hours?"

"Not really," Gus said. "A person of interest needs to be interviewed. I'm sending the script to your office."

Alex was now fully awake.

"What person of interest?" he said. "You have something new?"

"It's all in the script," Gus said. "Call me when you're done."

He disconnected and sat back in his chair. The red numbers on the small black digital clock above his door caught his eyes. He was a little surprised by the read-out: *03:31:14*. He watched the seconds roll over a few clicks before a satisfied smile filled his face.

"OK, this is OK," he said. "Time is still on my side. This'll work."

Despite sleeping on the sofa in his office, Gus was only slightly more rumpled than usual several hours later as he made his way back to the interview room on the tenth floor. The fresh shirt and tie, pulled from a supply kept in his closet, couldn't mask the fact he was still wearing the same suit as the day before. A quasi-shower—some splashes of cold water out of the men's room sink—and generous slathering of deodorant covered up most of the odor—most, but not all.

Gus didn't care.

Identification of Booker as the bomber led to a long list of questions. First up: Why was he at Citi Field? The answer to that was in the file under Gus' arm: Two of Eddie's clients—check that, former clients—were playing in the game. That made the ballplayers, Mike Coakley and Travis Mackenzie, persons of interest. Of the two, Gus figured Mackenzie less likely to cooperate. The man was a diva asshole. He was also in route to Philadelphia, which was why Gus pushed that task to Alex.

Gus was content to stay in New York and go after Coakley. He had spent the past hour reviewing background information on the man. He'd highlighted more than a few items in the notes, facts he was sure when shared would elicit something useful. He didn't have the same feeling about Mackenzie, but again, that was Alex's problem. If the hotshot ex-Marine fucked up, so be it. Gus would use it against him later.

All in all, he felt reasonably good as he walked the hallway leading to the interview room. Coakley was already there, having offered no resistance when Gus' agents fetched him from his apartment. After some initial concern caused by the agents' misreading the collection of packed bags—they took them to mean he was fleeing—the player seemed to be in a cooperative mood.

It didn't last. But that was Gus' fault.

Something about seeing Coakley in person triggered a reaction. Gus had enjoyed baseball when he was a kid, but weight issues kept him on the sidelines. Still, he considered himself a fan and was very familiar with players like Coakley, would-be high school coaches who somehow got paid seven figures. Gus only made seven figures if you counted the pennies. And even with that, he was expected to keep the spoiled athletes safe.

He hated that fact, but not as much as something else.

"Mr. Coakley, why did you take steroids?"

The question wasn't on Gus' script. It was asked out of anger. Mike responded as might be expected, meaning badly.

"*Excuse me?*" he said with disgust. "I've been cleared of that. Is *that* what this is about?"

Gus noticed the excessive sweat on Mike's head. He forgot about the man's ridiculous salary.

"Are you OK, Mr. Coakley? You seem nervous."

Mike eyed the agent carefully.

"No—I mean yeah, kinda," he said. "It's been a tough week."

"It has," Gus said. "No worries. I'm just tryin' to establish some background, it might be important."

"Yeah… um, OK, sure," Mike said. "I guess I understand."

He didn't, not really. His steroid use was more embarrassment than anything else. Unlike Bonds, Sosa, McGwire, Travis, and others, Mike never cared about getting bigger, better, and stronger. He just wanted to make sure his options were picked up. He got caught, served his suspension, and moved on. Knowing what he knew now, he wished it had never happened.

The same was true about something else.

Gus' expression accelerated the sick feeling in Mike that began after reading Eddie's note. If the FBI somehow knew—panic began knocking at the door in Mike's head. He frantically wiped at the sweat running down his cheeks and looked around the room. He caught glimpse of his reflection in a mirror on one wall. He figured someone was on the other side of the glass, watching. He wondered if they thought he looked as bad as the face he saw.

"You didn't answer," Gus said.

After a few seconds, Mike turned from the mirror and moved his eyes back to Gus'.

"Huh?" he said.

"The steroids," Gus said. "Why'd you take them?"

Mike wiped away more sweat.

"Uh, I uh—I guess the short answer is it seemed like a good idea at the time," he said. "I, uh—I needed the money mostly. I know my three ex-wives all agreed."

He laughed at his own statement, a nervous hack of a sound. Gus' eyes narrowed.

"Is that how you met Mr. Booker?" he said.

Mike reached up and scratched at his head. His fingers came back wet.

"I, uh—*Eddie?*" he said. "Nah, nah, that's not, no—Eddie was my agent."

The sick feeling, the face in the mirror, the walls of the small room, all of it was beginning to close in. It reminded Mike how he felt during the drilling he'd taken years ago at the hands of Gabi Loeb, just before he'd been suspended. He'd managed to survive that interrogation and avoid a lifetime ban by using lies and half-truths. He wasn't sure it would work again.

"Why did you fire Mr. Booker?" Gus said.

There was another round of scratching and wiping. Mike's eyes couldn't find anything on which to settle.

"No, I don't... uh, I *didn't*," he said. "No, no, it's nothing like that. I meant that's how I met him, when he became my agent. I'm not the one who fired him, no."

Mike was right about there being an audience on the other side of the two-way mirror. One observer, a body-language expert, could barely keep up with all the signals he was emitting. The man's report was going to be long.

"So, he's *still* your agent?" Gus said. "Paper says you fired him."

More wiping and scratching as Mike shifted in his chair.

"Eh, yeah, right," he said.

Gus leaned forward.

"Why? What happened?"

In Mike's head he heard a door slam shut. He knew he didn't have the key to reopen it.

"Uh… you should ask him," he said in a low voice.

"OK," Gus said as he sat back. "When was the last time you saw Mr. Booker? Do you know how I can reach him?"

There was no reply.

"Mr. Coakley?" Gus said.

"I don't know," Mike said.

His voice was barely audible. Gus leaned in again. Mike caught some of the man's smell. He almost gagged from it, but managed to get away with a small cough.

"You don't know *which*, Mr. Coakley," Gus said after the sound faded. "When you last saw him, or how to reach him?"

Mike coughed again. He was having difficulty breathing.

"I don't know," he said again.

"I think you *do* know," Gus said. "I think you know *a lot*."

Mike hacked out another sound, made painful by the knots in his stomach. He swallowed hard and tried to clear his throat. Gus' eyes narrowed as Mike's hands worked through another round of sweat removal.

"Mr. Coakley?"

Mike stopped wiping.

"Yeah, Eddie… uh," he said with great effort. "Let's see… well, it had to be—yeah, it was before the last home series. What's that, about a week ago?"

Gus' expression darkened a few notches.

"Are you asking me, Mr. Coakley?"

"No, no, sorry," Mike said. "It was, definitely. He was, uh—he was supposed to stop by after the game, the one with the attack. We, uh, we haven't been able to connect since."

Gus leaned in further. Mike almost retched again from the odor.

"Why, Mr. Coakley? Is there something I should know?"

"He, uh, he's my agent—I mean my friend," Mike said. "Friends do stuff like that."

"Stuff like *what*, Mr. Coakley? Schedule a meeting and not show up? Leave you wondering where they are, whether they're OK or not? That doesn't seem very friend-like to me."

Mike heard a few more doors slamming.

"Can I, uh—you guys got any water?" he said. "I could really use a drink."

He ran his shirt sleeve across his forehead. The flow instantly returned.

"No, Mr. Coakley," Gus said. "Not until you tell me what happened to Mr. Booker."

Mike shook his head.

"I don't know, man," he said. "Like I said, we, uh, we never hooked up."

"*Why*, Mr. Coakley?"

Mike slammed his hands on the table. The slap echoed around the room.

"I don't know."

Gus didn't back off.

"You're lying," he said.

Mike tried to outstare him, but failed.

"I guess he's busy," he said, reluctantly. "Maybe he's in trouble again. All this shit going on… we're all in a little bit of trouble, you know?"

The tone was a mix of anger and panic. Gus pushed on.

"Are *you* in trouble, Mr. Coakley?"

Mike closed his eyes and pictured the note again. Along with the warning came a request for a simple favor, a last wish from a dying friend: *No police. You guys have to fix this on your own.* Mike began to shake his head as he opened his eyes. Despite the intensity in Gus' and the pressure from the questions, he would stay strong and see it through. He would not betray the friendship.

"No sir, Director Pappas. Everything is good."

Chapter 16

New York

In the week following the explosion, theories expressed in the media had been numerous and varied, assigning blame where there was none, suggesting nefarious plots that didn't exist, creating a renewed sense of "us" versus "them" if for no other reason than to boost ratings. None were remotely close to accurate, but a glaring lack of "official" pronouncements only served to add to the clutter of misinformation.

There was no denying something bad had happened, people had died, but that was no longer the point. As they so often did, the talking heads and media pundits had somehow made it about them instead, as if the insult wasn't against the victims and their families, but against the right to know—or in this case, the right to say you were first to know.

Mike Coakley hadn't said anything about being questioned, not directly, but that didn't matter. Slowly, via leaks, hearsay, and "unconfirmed sources" within the FBI and elsewhere, others figured it out. There truly are no secrets in the media. It's all about timing, as in how fast can you get it printed under your masthead or plastered across the screen? With the advent of the Internet and its uncountable outlets, the answer was almost always "not fast enough."

The first post came in a blog. A friend of a friend of a secretary working for the Mets caught wind of something said in a team meeting. It wasn't that Mike had been interviewed—twice—by authorities. Hell, everyone with anything to do with the team and ballpark had been talked to, some more than others. That part made sense. The oddity was that Mike had been dropped off at the field with his bags packed, as if he was going somewhere.

That was followed by pictures posted on Facebook, of other team members arriving. Then more online chatter, from people both in and outside the organization. The Mets weren't the only ones reconvening. The Los Angeles Dodgers were also on the move. They'd been holed up in New York, en masse, a victim to the travel restrictions enacted within hours of the bombing. But now, another blogger wrote, they were headed to Philadelphia, by train. Not because it was an alternate escape from New York, but for a far less clandestine reason.

The bombing was not as it seemed. Baseball was coming back.

Philadelphia

The travel arrangements had been harried, but the Dodgers arrived in Philly seven days after the explosion, ready to resume their playing schedule. The announcement, a simple statement two days prior, released by the commissioner's office, had come as a surprise to everyone. "The best thing we can do now is do what we do, play ball." There was no press conference. Mark wasn't taking interviews. That was it; game on.

The Dodgers would return to New York at some point to make up the lost series. Few were happy about that; most on the team would just as soon never return to the city. Fewer still were happy about playing at all, at least again so soon. The loss of the teammate and ugly circumstances surrounding the death were hard to bear. Playing a game wasn't going to be easy.

Travis Mackenzie was the lone exception. He could not have cared less about the deaths, teammate or otherwise. He was more concerned about being hauled out of the visitors' clubhouse at Citizens Bank Park by the FBI, an hour after arriving. "Hauled" might be too strong a word, but that's how Travis saw it. He considered anything not done on his schedule an insult. The train trip had already pissed him off. This subsequent detour made it worse.

Alex Harris wasn't entirely convinced the questioning was necessary, but stuck with his offer of cooperation with Gus' work. The two had blessed—off the record—Mark's decision to resume play. Alex, if not Gus, understood the bigger issue was finding a motive for the bombing. If the ballplayer had information that helped, he was all for it.

Carlos Santiago was assigned the unenviable task of digging for said knowledge. Alex, watching from the other side of the interview room's mirror, was confident the young agent would keep at it until he found a crack in the thick ice of Travis' façade—if there was one to find. Travis' attitude was anything but cooperative, his expression saying "I'm too cool for this."

Carlos remained undeterred by the ballplayer's attitude and stuck with Gus' script. The first set of questions centered on the relationship between Travis and Eddie. Travis confirmed the two were no longer associated professionally, but offered little else, spending most of the time fiddling with his cell phone. The disinterest did not go unnoticed.

"Mr. Mackenzie, when was the last time you saw Mr. Booker?" Carlos said.

When Travis failed to answer, Carlos repeated the question with more force. Travis took a long, slow breath, and as he exhaled, his left hand came up to his face and he used the middle finger to scratch at a spot just above the eyebrow.

"Couldn't tell ya," he said.

The finger lingered for a second before he dropped his eyes and hand back to the phone. Carlos nodded before making a note on the edge of the script. His next question wasn't on the paper.

"When was the last time you spoke by phone?" he said.

Travis looked up again. "Too cool" had changed to something less arrogant. It was as telling as the middle finger. Carlos imagined Travis a lousy poker player. Subtle the man was not.

"Couldn't tell ya," Travis said again.

Carlos pointed to the phone with a pen.

"Why don't you check your phone log? I'll help if you don't know how."

Travis' eyes narrowed. The insult had scored.

"I know how," he said in a pointed tone.

There was another scratch—all four fingers this time—as he eyed the agent. After a few seconds, he looked down and began to thumb the phone's controls. When he looked up again, the anger was more obvious. Carlos saw it. On the other side of the room's mirror, Alex did as well.

"Nice one, kid," he said under his breath as he watched. "Keep at him."

"Mr. Mackenzie?" Carlos said. "Do you have the date?"

Travis turned to the mirror. A curled lip confirmed what Alex had already seen. Slowly, Travis returned his gaze to Carlos.

"Yeah, sure," he said. "It was the day the shithead killed himself."

Radnor, Pennsylvania

The sudden reset of the playing schedule wasn't all bad. It put me in Philly for a few nights, and a chance for some time in my own bed. Hanging around New York hadn't been easy. I kept expecting something else to happen, especially after the chat with Thomas. Feeling that way sucked, but there wasn't a lot I could do about it. My life had gone past crazy, what with the World Series mess and the All-Star Game fiasco—and now this.

I found myself bouncing between angry and scared. I don't know if it was survivor's guilt or something else, but I don't think I was the only one feeling it during the long week. There'd been an odd vibe to the city. Not entirely unexpected or hard to understand given the similarities between 9/11 and this latest bombing, but still, things there were far too tense for my tastes.

I was surprised there wasn't more of an exodus, at least from what I could tell. The train I'd boarded out of town wasn't crowded. I guess it was natural people were reluctant to travel, despite nothing else blowing up. I think that last part was why Mark went ahead and restarted the season. Admittedly, I was worried, because I hadn't heard about a lower threat level, but it wasn't like I was in the loop either.

In truth, *out* of the loop was a good place to be. I wasn't avoiding the situation—or Thomas—on purpose, but I'd made no effort after the initial calls to change that. I left the TV off, didn't bother with email, and pretty much kept to myself. I simply didn't want to know what was going on. I'd been too close to too many dead people, in situations I was not cut out to handle. I needed a break. Yeah, I know, that's selfish, but I needed to find some stability again.

It almost worked, too.

And then the phone rang on my second night home.

"Hey, you," Suze said into my ear.

A mix of emotions flooded my brain. Suze had been in the middle of my comfort and discomfort over the past two years. We'd found each other before the shit started, but lost each other because of it. OK, I lost her. Seeing as how I'd stepped it in again, she was right to have moved on. I won't lie, though. The sound of her voice made me smile, but left me forgetting how to talk.

I think she sensed it. She was good at that. Then again, I was easy to read.

"I heard you were at the office the other day," she said into the void I'd created. "Sorry I missed you. Gabi said you looked tired."

Another couple of seconds went by before I found my tongue again.

"Me, too—I mean, I was," I said.

A giggle came through the line. I think she was laughing at my mangled syntax.

"Sorry I missed you at the office, too," I said, correcting it. "And yes, I was tired. It's been hard to sleep."

"I guess so," she said. "Gabi told me what happened."

A "shit" slipped out on my end. I'd been hoping she wouldn't find out I was working the game. That was probably stupid on my part seeing as she worked at MLB.

"Marshall?" she said into the quiet. "Are you OK? I was worried."

"Yeah, yeah, no need to worry," I said. "I'm OK. I'm home now. And I'm talking to you. How could that be bad, right?"

She didn't fall for the happy tone.

"You really do suck at lying," she said.

It was obvious from her tone that she cared. Then again, caring about people was never a problem for Suze. It was one of many reasons I'd fallen in love with her. It was also why we were no longer together. Caring about me almost got her killed.

"Yeah, I know," I said. "So, uh, how are you doing? The office looked pretty nuts."

"To say the least," she said. "Mark's not doing too well."

"I imagine not," I said. "I'm not sure Thomas helped much, either. He kind of dropped a bomb—"

I cut myself off, but it was too late.

"It never stops with you guys, does it?" Suze said in a sharp tone.

I'd flipped the switch.

"Suze, wait—"

"No, just no," she said. "Listen, I'm glad you're OK, but I gotta go. I can't do this. Take care of yourself, Marshall."

She was gone before I could reply. The next "shit" that followed wasn't a slip. Suddenly, being home wasn't any better than being in New York.

"Way to go dumbass," I said aloud as I closed the phone.

As my head began to shake, I headed for the kitchen. Something alcoholic was in order. Luckily, I found a few beers in the fridge. The first one disappeared as I stood there, pouting. The second was emptied on the short walk to the living room. I managed to stretch the third and final can over the next ten minutes, until I was interrupted when my phone rang again. My first thought—hope?— was that it was Suze, calling back, but I was greeted instead by *Unknown* on the caller ID. It was disappointing, but only until I answered.

Then it got worse.

"Marshall, glad I caught you. It's David Donovan. You got a minute?"

Two hours later, and several drinks stronger than beer, I broke the silence with Thomas. I should have known better than to talk to Donovan. The only time guys like him—meaning reporters—called was for something bad, like to ask how I could have possibly blown a call for example. That would have been a lot better than what he told me.

"I don't know why. I don't want to know why," I said after a retelling of the conversation. "I simply told the man I would talk to you. Whatever you decide to do is your problem. I'm out of it."

"Marshall, I understand," Thomas said.

The use of my first name was meant to be reassuring. Normally, Thomas' existence alone was all I needed for that, but in this case, neither was doing any good. After Donovan's call—more shit I never wanted to know—I doubted I'd ever feel good again, Thomas being around or not.

"Listen, I'm headed west after tonight's game," I said. "I'll be gone for two weeks. I won't mind not hearing from you. And I won't lose any sleep over it, either."

"Again, I understand."

"Yeah, well, that and seventy-five cents will get me a bag of M&M's at Wawa."

Whatever was going on, whatever Donovan knew or *thought* he knew, or thought he needed Thomas' help with, I had no desire to join him. I'd stepped off that ledge too may times. I was an umpire and the only thing I wanted was to get back to umpiring.

"Travel safe," Thomas said.

"Eh, fuck you."

I was mostly kidding—mostly. I think Thomas knew that, but I didn't care. It was time for me to get back to work, *my work*, not his.

"Good night, Marshall."

I closed the phone and turned to my reflection in the mirror on the back of my bedroom door. Despite how bad I looked and felt, a realization begin to creep in. I sighed and let my head drop.

"Yeah, right, you're out of it," I said. "Shit, no way you could be that lucky."

When I looked up again, my reflection didn't argue.

King of Prussia

"End of discussion," Alyson's EP said. "You have one week."

Alyson didn't argue, either. Getting another week was good, but it might not help. She was a lousy investigator and worse researcher. Of course, neither skill was part of her job description. Her usual task was to look good and read scripts written by others, her input limited to make-up and clothing selection—and even there used sparingly. At best she was a talking head with the occasional wide shot of cleavage.

She needed to change that perception and had hoped to find something to show the Citi Field bombing was more than terrorism, that it had something to do with baseball itself. It had been a far-fetched idea to begin with. Now, with the games resuming and her work turning up nothing, it was more so. The previously cooperative producer had lost patience. With football back in swing as well—college and pro—Alyson would need more of a hook than another blow job to avoid being reassigned.

"What did he say?" her cubicle friend said after Alyson returned from the EP's office.

"He said I'm a twit," Alyson said.

The friend moved around the partition.

"No he didn't," she said.

It came out more like a question than a statement. Alyson managed a smile.

"Nah, he didn't," she said. "I said that."

The friend frowned.

"Hang on, I found something that might help."

She went back around the wall and returned not five seconds later.

"Check this out," she said.

She handed Alyson a book. A couple of the pages were marked.

"What is this?" Alyson said.

The friend smiled. Alyson caught a touch of evil—not the bad kind—in the look. She narrowed her eyes as she waited for a reply. The friend touched the cover of the book.

"Like the title says, it's only stealing if you get caught. Don't get caught."

~*~*~*~*~*~*~

Three hours later, Alyson swallowed her doubts, took a deep breath, and dialed the number.

"Yes, hi," she said into the phone. "I'm trying to reach David Donovan, please. My name is Alyson Lane. I'm with SNN—yes, I can hold."

A sorry-sounding cover of what might have been a Rolling Stones song hit her ear. She pressed the *Speaker* button and set the receiver on the desk. Holding it had been difficult. Her hands were shaking, caused by what she was about to do.

It had taken most of the afternoon—and more help from her friend—but her desk was now covered with copies of every story David had penned about the bombing. The original story was there. So were various follow-ups. A few more pages of the book had been marked. Alyson had to admit she was impressed—and a bit envious as well. David was good at what he did.

His latest contribution was in the form of a recap. Alyson re-read the story. It was her friend who picked up on the veiled accusations, hidden by David's skilled writing. Why hasn't the FBI been able to find who was responsible? Why would MLB commissioner Mark Rosenbaum resume play without formal clearance? Did the FBI and MLB know more than they were telling the public?

They were hard questions and exactly the kind of thing Alyson had set out to uncover from the beginning, but failed so miserably to produce.

That was about to change.

Manhattan

Gus had no need to change anything. He had the bomber's identity, a solid but slightly fabricated theory on motive, and control over the media. He also had everyone's attention on things other than his personal affairs. That left him in a good mood as he prepared for the latest status update conference call. He was connected in from his office, with Kurt Dreisdale and the head of forensics. On the line from D.C. were his boss—summoned to the

Capital hours earlier—and that man's boss. Alex was tied in from Philadelphia.

The first ten minutes were monopolized by the forensics agent and his report on the technical aspects of the bombing. Gus followed with a convoluted yarn that had Eddie, via Dukabi, being recruited by an as yet unnamed organization. He spun in bits and pieces from the ballplayer's life and personality characteristics that made it seem he was a prime candidate for such activity.

Next up were recaps of witness statements and POI (persons of interest) interviews. Gus stretched and pulled Mike Coakley's words to support his theory. It was reasonably creative, especially coming from him. He tied it up by conveniently omitting mention of the less than subtle warnings delivered to David Donovan or part two of the original Dukabi tip call.

He was confident he could convince his bosses—and some others not on the call—that everything was moving in the right direction, he was making progress, and with just a little more time would soon have all the answers.

The first inkling of a problem came when Alex presented Travis Mackenzie's disclosures.

"How he knows is unclear, but Mackenzie's assertions support what we heard on the video and what Director Pappas has already reported. Booker acted alone. He committed suicide."

The conclusion was followed by a long, quiet pause. Gus' boss' boss broke it.

"Wow... wow," he said. "This is beautiful. You guys are telling me there was never any indication this thing was terrorist related? Is that right?"

As in the military, shit flowed downhill at the FBI, but it took a few ticks longer than it should have for Gus to realize this particular pile of crap was all his. As the words sank in, Kurt was pretty sure he heard a fart come from Gus' side of the desk.

"*Pappas?*" the boss' boss said in a shout.

"I, uh... we—well, no, not entirely, sir," Gus said.

Kurt's hand came up to his nose as the smell reached him—definitely a fart.

"Not *entirely?*" the boss' boss said. "What does *that* mean? It either is or isn't, and seeing how Alex just Swiss-cheesed everything you've been saying, I'm leaning toward the latter."

There was another round of dead air as Gus stared at the phone, unable to process what he was hearing. Kurt and the forensics man were secretly enjoying the situation—not the smell, but Gus' general discomfort—and neither came to the rescue.

"Yo, Pappas, are you still with us?" the boss' boss said in another shout.

"Uh, yeah, yeah, I'm here," Gus said. "I, uh... I... yes sir, it is terrorism. At least until we know with absolute certainty otherwise."

A loud sigh came through the speaker, emitted from the boss' boss.

"Oh, well, OK, *that's* a big relief," he said, his tone surprisingly level. "I know the President will be happy to hear he can save billions of dollars on homeland defense by just relying on the extremely questionable intellect and judgment of Gus Pappas."

There was another pause before the man's voice returned.

"Are you fucking insane?"

"Sir, if I may—"

"No, Pappas. No you may not. We all want to make up for that mess nine years ago, but this is not how we're going to do it. I won't even mention all the shit I've taken about how we fucked up with that kook down at Fort Hood. If there was ever a time I needed sharp from you, this was it. I'm not seeing a goddamn thing close to sharp."

The man provided his own segue with another loud sigh.

"Can someone else please give me something of substance," he said. "Alex?"

There was a rustling sound over the speaker. Gus barely noticed. It would be another few seconds before he caught up again.

"Yes, sir," Alex said. "Dukabi and Booker have a past relationship. There may be a connection to Dukabi's former life in Africa, a drug connection. One theory has the bombing as a retaliation of some sort. We're looking into that aspect."

Gus seemed to snap out of his funk and his eyes bulged. Why was Alex looking into *any* aspect? This wasn't his case.

"OK," the boss said; then after a pause. "Pappas, you're out. Alex, I want you to take the lead. Find me some answers—like *yesterday*. For now, I need to go tell the President he can drop the alert level. And I swear to God you all better keep me in the fucking loop. Am I clear?"

The line filled with "Yes, sir" responses in various tones and volumes. Kurt and the forensics man added theirs and left Gus' office without another word. Gus remained silent, crushed under the weight of what just happened. The rotting apricot was bright red and ready to burst. It took a full three minutes before he recovered enough to reach for the phone and bang out the digits for a new call.

Alex picked up on the second ring.

"Harris, *you fuck*," Gus said. "You set me up."

"No, Gus, you did that all by yourself."

Chapter 17

Central Park, New York

"Are these reactions not as you expected?" Jamie said into his cell phone.

He kicked at some stones along the path at his feet. Shady was at his side. His expression filled with a question. Jamie lowered the phone and pressed a button to engage the speaker.

"Some are. Some aren't," a voice said. "I think we need to stay flexible."

"We are nothing if not flexible," Jamie said.

He smiled as he watched Shady shake out his hands, shrug his shoulders, and twist his head from side to side. "Flexible" was an accurate description of the movements.

"You better be," the voice on the other side of the speaker said. "The FBI is no longer our only concern."

Jamie hesitated before responding.

"Yes, I have spoken to the reporter," he said.

"I'm not talking about the reporter."

Shady made a few more interesting movements. Jamie nodded.

"Ah, yes, I believe I understand," he said. "We shall see to it."

He closed the phone and slipped it into his jacket. Shady stopped moving.

"Come, my friend," Jamie said. "There is more work to be done."

~*~*~*~*~*~*~*~

New York

David folded and unfolded the pink slip of paper five times before setting it on top of the other four already on his desk. Save for the handwriting, each was exactly the same.

Message from: <u>Alyson Lane, SNN</u>
Message: <u>Please return call ASAP</u>

He sat back and turned toward his computer. The screen was filled with an image of Alyson on the sidelines at a college football game. It was a nice picture. Her light brown hair and pretty face played for the camera perfectly. The angle of the shot was such that it included more than just her head and shoulders. David guessed that wasn't an accident, but a budding daydream was interrupted by a firm tap on the shoulder.

"Nice," a female voice said. "You're a pig."

A yellow folder slapped down on his chest with a little too much force.

"Hey," he said as he grabbed it and turned. "Totally work related, I swear. Look."

He pointed to the address of the website to make the point the picture was from SNN and not a site that somehow got past the paper's network filters.

"Whatever," the co-worker said. "Have a nice trip."

Several replies came to mind, but David refrained. He turned back to his desk and focused on the folder. In it was his travel itinerary for the next two weeks. He would accompany the Mets on their extended road trip, including stops in Cincinnati, D.C., Atlanta, Florida, and Philadelphia.

"Shit," he said as he flipped through the papers.

It wasn't so much the travel that bothered him—he never minded being on the road—but rather the fact his capacity to continue digging was about to be greatly diminished. He was hoping to get Thomas, through Marshall, to investigate Eddie's past, at least the parts that weren't public knowledge, but Thomas had yet to respond. Without the man's help, David knew the chance of delivering a blockbuster story was going to be extremely difficult.

He tossed the travel package to his desk. It kicked up a breeze and one of the pink message slips floated onto his lap. He stared down at it for a few seconds before shifting his eyes back to the computer. An idea not related to sex began to form, and seconds later, he was dialing the phone.

Alyson answered before the first ring ended.

"David, oh wow, thanks for calling back," she said.

David caught the hint of desperation in her voice.

"Uh, yeah, apparently," he said, eyeing the message slips. "I guess you're welcome."

Alyson chuckled.

"Five calls a little too much, huh?" she said.

"A little, but I have that effect on women."

Alyson chuckled again.

"I'll bet you do," she said.

David perked up at the flirt and looked again at her image. He began to wonder if some of the stories he'd heard were true. She was a hottie, but before he slipped back into the daydream, he remembered why he was calling.

"Hey, um, are you busy over there?" he said.

"Not as much as some would like me to be. That's why I've been calling you."

David sat up.

"Really?" he said.

"Hey, it's no secret we're in trouble," Alyson said. "I got to thinking a story like yours could give us a boost. I was hoping maybe you'd consider a collaboration of sorts?"

"Really," David said again, but not in a questioning way.

The whole Citi Field thing had lost its glamour, now that any Arab boogey men had been ruled out by the recent FBI announcement. David knew why, of course, which was the only reason he still gave a shit about it. His mind began racing between everything he'd done and everything he still wanted to do in relation to that fact.

"David?" Alyson said into his ear. "You OK?"

David shook away the thoughts.

"Yeah, yeah," he said. "It just so happens I was thinking the exact same thing, about a collaboration I mean."

"*Oooh,*" Alyson said, drawing the word out. "Great minds think alike, huh?"

The purr-like tone of the first part had already pushed David's eyes back to the computer screen and he missed the second part as a smile worked onto his lips. Alyson's mind wasn't the only great thing she had going. After a long second, he recovered.

"OK, let's do it."

Philadelphia

Alex slowly looked around the room. Most of the staffers and agents there were pleased he was now in charge of the investigation, but it didn't change the fact the case was a mess, maybe even more so given the latest revelations. Eddie Booker wasn't exactly the kind of bad guy they'd been expecting.

"OK, walk me through it," Alex said. "What do we know and what are we looking at?"

Carlos Santiago was first to respond. He had a stack of notes in front of him on the table.

"The general consensus is that whatever Booker was involved with went terribly awry and he snapped. Based on the interviews, it appears both of his ex-clients knew or sensed something was wrong with the man. Coakley exhibited extreme distress during his chat. Mackenzie was just the opposite. Some of that is for show, but he got genuinely angry right before saying Booker committed suicide. Or maybe disappointed is a better word, I'm not sure."

"Agreed," Alex said, remembering back to what he'd seen during the session with Travis. "Let's set up another interview with each."

Carlos made a notation as another agent raised a hand.

"Go," Alex said.

"Sir, we have surveillance in place for the ballplayers," the agent said. "Someone will be on them at all times. It won't be hard to spot anything unusual. Do you want us to add phone taps?"

Alex mulled over the question.

"No, not yet, it would probably be too much of a stretch to get a warrant for that," he said. "Let's just stay with the visuals for now. And I want the interviews done ASAP. Now, what else do we have?"

"We're also looking into the players' finances," Carlos said. "Both make seven figures, but that doesn't mean there isn't something wrong."

"OK," Alex said with another nod; then after a pause. "OK, where's our friend Dukabi fit in to all of this?"

A third agent raised a hand.

"On the surface, sir, it's hard to tell," he said. "Outside of the poker debts, there doesn't seem to be any connection between Dukabi and Booker, or Dukabi and the other two. We're working with our friends over at the CIA to see what they may know about the drug angle Mr. Hillsborough mentioned."

Alex nodded, but it belied his feelings. His was still a bit annoyed by Thomas' involvement, but more concerned the CIA wouldn't be overly cooperative.

"Well, play nice with our friends at Langley," he said. "We need all the help we can get."

The words pushed him to think more about Thomas and Sandy. They'd been overly quiet. He knew that didn't necessarily mean they were following his directive to stay on the sidelines. In fact, he was sure they *weren't* doing so, but shook it off and refocused on the agents with him at the table.

"OK, is that all?" he said.

Carlos made a movement with one of his hands.

"There is something else," he said. "I think Director Pappas was right about one thing. I don't think Booker meant to hurt anyone else. In fact, I think he was trying to be stopped."

Alex's brow knitted into a frown.

"Why do you say that?" he said.

"Well, for starters, he left a long trail."

The frown got more severe.

"OK, explain," Alex said.

The room took on an eerie quiet as Carlos flipped a few pages in his notes.

"Going in reverse order from the time of the explosion," he said. "Booker appeared on the concourse ten minutes earlier. He was captured by all four security cameras there before moving to the stairs. In the fifty minutes before that, he was captured by others throughout the stadium, including two near each of the team clubhouse doors. We think that's when he attempted to contact Mackenzie and Coakley, or at least that was how Mackenzie figured out what happened. The glaring thing about the long walk was the obvious attempt to make sure he was spotted."

Alex's right hand came up and he played with his bottom lip for a few seconds. Carlos waited.

"Oh, shit, sorry," Alex said. "Continue."

"Yes, sir," Carlos said. "Going back further, based on Donovan's statement, we found Booker entering the press gate right before game time. The guard there gave us a statement that Booker was 'a little off' is how the man put it. Donovan corroborated that fact. The guard told us Booker said he was running late because of the trains. We confirmed that with Amtrak. Booker used a credit card to pay for his ticket. His train was late leaving Philadelphia. There, he was captured on every camera at Thirtieth Street Station, including the ones at baggage claim. It was obvious—"

Both of Alex's hands came up to cut Carlos off.

"Wait a minute, *baggage claim*," he said "Why was he at baggage claim?"

Carlos flipped a page before continuing.

"We believe that's where he picked up the computer bag, the bomb."

Alex sat back, his eyes narrowing. A few seconds passed before he spoke.

"So he didn't bring it from home?"

It came out almost as an aside, but Carlos answered.

"We thought that at first, but—"

Alex sat forward and cut him off again.

"Whoa, what do you mean *at first*?"

Carlos looked down to refer to something in his notes.

"Uh, says here, per the logs, the bag was left at the station approximately two hours before the train was scheduled to depart. Booker checked it, then came back later and picked it up."

Again, Alex sat back, this time adding in a deep breath as he looked around the room. It was hard to tell if he found what he was looking for, but no one else made a sound to interrupt the effort. After a handful of seconds, he sat forward again.

"Do we know if Booker had the bag when he left his home?" he said.

Carlos scanned his notes again. When he looked up, his features reflected disappointment. His tone confirmed it.

"No, sir, we don't," he said.

"Find out."

Chapter 18

Wayne

Sandy stepped into Thomas' office and sat in one of the armchairs. He was on his cell phone. A raised index finger told her to wait.

"I understand," he said into the phone.

He closed the phone and set it on the desk. Sandy detected agitation in his movements.

"Problems?" she said.

"No. What do you have?"

She frowned at the harsh redirect, but quickly erased it. She knew he would explain the call at some point—or not. It didn't matter at the moment. She started in on her findings.

"Before becoming a players' agent, Booker had a PR firm and did some work for a company called Bulge, Inc. I don't know if any of Marshall's baseball stories mentioned Bulge, but they were connected to some of the steroid problems a few years ago."

"It sounds vaguely familiar," Thomas said.

"The charges weren't all that surprising," Sandy said. "Bulge's CEO, a sleazebag named Paul Bischoff, played ball in college and was suspected of juicing. He was caught several times and eventually got kicked out of school. One of his teammates happened to be Booker. The two stayed close over the years and when the company got in trouble, Bischoff hired Booker's firm to help with damage control."

"Where does our client come in?" Thomas said.

Sandy shuddered slightly. Thinking of Dukabi as a client ate at her senses, but she shook it off and continued.

"Booker was one of Dukabi's regulars."

Thomas began to nod. After a few seconds, he stood and began to pace the office, one of his "thinking-mode" tells. Sandy stayed quiet and let him process. It took about thirty seconds.

"Mr. Booker loses money to Dukabi," Thomas said. "Want of financial means to repay leads him to introduce Dukabi to his client, Mr. Bischoff. Dukabi sees potential in Bischoff's activities. Bischoff sees potential in Dukabi's clientele, most notably the professional athletes. Booker suggests a mutually beneficial arrangement. No more Dukabi problem."

"Nice theory," Sandy said. "Except how do we explain the part where Dukabi comes to you? What went wrong?"

"That is the outstanding question," Thomas said.

Sandy nodded.

"I'll start on Bulge, see what they're into. Maybe that's where the missing pieces are."

She was about to stand when she caught something in Thomas' expression.

"What?" she said.

"Director Harris would like us to keep him informed," Thomas said. "Otherwise, we're on our own—*for now*."

Sandy did the math in her head. The answer made sense.

"Fair enough," she said.

She stood to leave, but after two steps stopped and turned back.

"Hey, um, can I say something?" she said.

Thomas' eyebrow shrugged.

"This is personal for you isn't it, with Dukabi I mean?" Sandy said.

The eyebrow relaxed, before something unpleasant flashed across Thomas' features. It was gone in a split-second, but Sandy caught the intensity. When he spoke, his tone had the same.

"Yes."

Citizens Bank Park, Philadelphia

As it was most nights, reporters flocked to Travis' locker after the game. The man was usually good for something controversial and tonight figured to be more of the same. Despite three hits from the star, the Dodgers lost to the Phillies, 7-4, and dropped into a tie with the Mets for the last playoff spot. There might not be an "I" in team but there was "ME" and more than a few bets were saying Travis would throw someone under the bus.

On this night, however, the bus hit him first, courtesy of a question from Alyson.

"Travis, did you know your agent was suicidal?"

The other reporters, reacting as if someone had passed gas, all backed off in unison, a collective *"What was that?"* expression on their faces. Once the initial surprise wore off, they closed ranks, inspired by the chum in the water.

"What the fuck are you talkin' about?" Travis said.

The tone was sharp and the feeding circle got tighter.

"Eddie Booker," Alyson said. "Did you know about his problems and the fact he was suicidal? Is that why you fired him?"

Travis looked away and began messing with some items in his locker. The movements were like a new scent and the predators edged closer, jostling each other for best position.

"Everybody knew Eddie had problems," Travis said, his back to the group.

"*Had* problems?" Alyson said.

Travis turned again. He was oblivious to the others as he eyed her. There was a hint of worry on his face, but it slowly turned into a layer of nastiness in the form of a scowl.

"I'm sure he *still* does," Travis said. "Why don't you go ask him?"

If the other writers hadn't come into the room with thoughts about Eddie's issues, they had them now, and the recorders and microphones pushed closer.

"I'd love to, but he doesn't seem to be around," Alyson said. "Do you know where I can find him?"

Closer came the circle.

"I have no idea," Travis said. "But it sounds like you might, like maybe you know somethin' about it. You sure you wanna go down that road?"

Alyson held her ground.

"What road is that, Travis?" she said.

Travis scoffed and slowly shook his head.

"Nice try, bitch," he said. "We're done."

"People deserve to know," Alyson said. "I'm just trying to get them there."

Travis laughed.

"I know *exactly* what you're tryin' to do."

Philadelphia

Jason Adley carried the bowl of Ramen noodles back to his desk. The wisps of steam rising up from the cardboard container bore the scent of excessive sodium. The rare violation to an otherwise strict diet was brought on by an unshakeable need to find a respite. The soup was the closest thing in the lab to comfort food.

Jason dropped onto a stool and mindlessly stirred the broth. He usually liked to read when he ate, but there was nothing new within reach, having long since burned through the stack of *Scientific American* issues he kept on hand. The only other option, a pile of newspapers, garnered little interest. That pulp was on hand to line the hamster cages, nothing more.

With nothing to occupy his mind, he slurped in a spoonful of noodles. As he chewed, his eyes wandered to those cages. All were empty. The last two habitants were now pinned to trays on the examining table in the middle of the lab in front of Jason's desk, ready for their final contributions to the spectacular failure that was "The Cure." Despite adjustments to the formula, made to appease Bischoff, the experiment was over.

Making the man and his partners understand that was becoming as dangerous as the steroid itself. The first attempt had killed more than the rodents. Jason closed his eyes and tried to shake off the guilt. He still had work to do, but wasn't sure how much time was left. With a loud exhale, he pushed the soup aside and moved to the exam table.

He eyed the latest victims for several seconds before lifting a small digital recorder to his face. After a deep breath, he focused on the corpse on the right and began to dictate.

"September twenty-four, ten-twenty P.M. Test subject eighteen, a male, deceased after twenty-one days. Cause of death most likely organ failure, however, exact determination is difficult. There is severe muscle and tissue degradation throughout the body. There may also have been loss of cognitive function."

He stopped and looked back to the cages. He closed his eyes again and let the recording of the hamster's final days play out in his mind. His head began to shake at the memory of the animal as it endlessly circled the cage without pause for food or water. It made no sense. The thing had literally run itself to death.

When Jason opened his eyes again there were tears there.

"What have I done?" he said into the empty room.

Several floors above Jason's head, a similar question was being asked.

Paul Bischoff was at his desk, staring at his computer screen and the four images fed there from the building's security system. The lower right-hand view was from behind his secretary's desk. She was clearly stressed, but that wasn't what caught Bischoff's eyes. Two dark-skinned faces coming toward the camera got credit for that.

"What are you guys doin' here?" Bischoff said to the picture.

How the two men had gotten past the guards in the lobby never entered his mind. He was more worried about something else, something in their stride. When they reached the desk, he held his breath. The shorter of the two men did a slight bow.

"Madam," he said.

His voice came through the intercom connection the secretary had left open.

"Um, may I help you?" she said.

"You may. We need to see Mr. Bischoff, please.

"I, um—I'll have to see if he's available."

Bischoff watched as she fumbled beneath the counter, the sounds magnified through the speakers. Her effort was cut short by Jamie's voice.

"No need to search, young lady. We know he is here. He is available for *us*."

Chapter 19

Philadelphia

"Mr. Bischoff reiterated his promise of delivery," Jamie said.

He was behind the wheel of a black Navigator, seemingly speaking to no one. The big SUV was parked in the lot of an empty playground, a mile or so from the Bulge building. Outside the car, Shady was working through an exercise routine of sorts, a mix of karate-like moves accompanied by a machete. The sharp blade twinkled like a Christmas tree as it twisted and turned in the moonlight. Jamie smiled at the beauty of the movements.

"I'm guessing you made that an easy choice?"

The voice came from the car's speakers. Jamie returned his focus to the dashboard.

"The penalties were explained," he said. "Mr. Bischoff understands."

"Make sure that doesn't change."

Jamie looked out again at his partner. His smile broadened.

"It will not."

~*~*~*~*~*~*~

Bischoff's head was about to explode. The visit from Jamie had done a lot of damage, but the scientific mumbo-jumbo Jason was spewing was far worse. Most of the words were like a foreign language, but a few managed to stick...

"The Cure doesn't work."

"There's no way to change that."

"It doesn't matter what they want."

Bischoff did his best to focus, but it wasn't easy. He was about to be out some serious cash. He was also out of options, something Jamie had explained in detail.

"Jesus Christ, Jason, shut the fuck up already," he said, cutting off whatever the doctor was saying. "I ain't fuckin' tellin' these guys it doesn't work. Not now. *Not ever.* You better come up with something fast because if they have to come back, we're both dead."

Citizens Bank Park

"Are you sure?" Alyson said into her phone; then after a pause. "OK. Call as soon as you have it. And thanks."

Within seconds her phone buzzed again. It was David.

"Hey, how's D.C.?" Alyson said.

"Not as good as Philly," David said. "I heard about your run-in with Mackenzie. You're the talk of the press room."

"It wouldn't be the first time," Alyson said. "But in this case, I'll take it as a compliment."

David resisted an inappropriate follow-up. Maybe later, he thought.

"Hey, you planted the seed in him," he said instead. "Now we wait to see if anything grows."

Alyson smiled. She was proud of herself for pushing Travis. It had been exciting.

"It was kind of fun," she said. "He's definitely hiding something."

There was a pause. If it was awkward, neither of them mentioned it.

"What about you?" Alyson said. "Did you talk to Coakley?"

"Not yet. I'm hoping to grab him before the game tonight."

"I got something else," Alyson said after another few seconds.

"Tell me."

"My sound guy thinks he can figure out what Booker was saying right before he jumped. He accidently on purpose kept a copy of the video, but has to work on it from home. He doesn't want to get in trouble at the office. No one is supposed to still have this. He said he'll know for sure in a couple days at most."

"That would be huge," David said.

"I know, right? Tell me I'm good."

David flashed on the image of her from his computer screen.

"Yes... yes you are."

Manhattan

Gus scribbled his name on the form, folded it, and slid it into a large envelope with other papers. He pulled the protective paper off the envelope's adhesive strip and pressed the flap closed, sealing the contents inside. He initialed across the seam, dropped his pen, and pushed back from the desk.

"Fuck," he said into the quiet of his office.

After a second or two, his eyes drifted across his desk, to a calendar near his nameplate. He started to work out the math. Once the envelope hit the *Out* box, it would take a day for the package to reach Philadelphia. It would take less time than that for the electronic files to get there—as soon as the transfer of custodianship email was sent, Alex could access those files immediately.

Gus could fiddle around with making both of those things happen, but at best, he figured he had no more than three days max until someone started asking about the rest of the original phone call. It wasn't much, but a lot could happen in three days.

Gus was counting on it.

Cincinnati

Mike Coakley awoke with a groan. Average Joe's like him didn't get single rooms, but that wasn't why he was alone. His roommate had a very exacting routine: up at six A.M., two mile run, ten minutes of power lifts with hand weights, thirty minutes of yoga, then off to the ballpark no later than ten A.M. That worked well for Mike because he, on the other hand, usually slept in. This was one of those days.

He groaned again and thought about the debacle of the night before, a thoroughly shitty performance in both ends of the Mets-Reds doubleheader that earned him not one, but two losses. He'd topped it off with several hours in the hotel bar afterward. The soon-to-be raging hangover only added to the weight of Eddie's death, the FBI, and Travis.

"Goddamn it," he said as stared up at the ceiling.

He sat up and looked around and discovered he was wet. Check that, it was more like a small flood. The entire bed—sheets, blankets, pillows, everything—was soaked, as was his hair, t-shirt, and boxers. Always a touch on the big side, meaning overweight, he was used to sweating and had learned to accept it. This, though, was something else.

He tried to remember if he'd been dreaming. Not finding an answer, he scooted across the damp mattress and worked himself off the bed. After striping off the wet clothes, he stumbled to the bathroom. Ten minutes of cold water later, he felt better, but was still bothered by the way his body had reacted to—well, whatever the hell it was reacting to.

He decided it was just a case of nerves, but also decided to dress in layers, to hide things should the sweats come back. It was a good possibility with the pending hangover, recent stress, and bad outing, but at least the extra clothes would mask things until he could get to the ballpark and run it off.

The idea almost died when, halfway through dressing, a massive cramp locked up his left hamstring. As he tried to stretch it out, another spasm rippled along his back, and within seconds, his entire body began to ache. His first thought was the pain was a natural reaction to working both games, the normal tiredness that set in every morning during the season, but as it intensified, he began to realize something else was wrong.

He struggled to finish dressing and made his way to the common area of the suite. His shoulder bag—some might call it a man-purse—was on a table off to one side. He grabbed it and began to hunt for his phone. Before he found the cell, something else caught his eye, Eddie's note. He stared at the folded sheet for a long moment before pulling it from the bag.

With a sigh, he dropped back to the edge of the bed and began to read.

> A lot of people think I'm a coward. I bet a few more will because of what I'm about to do. I can't worry about that. It's too late for me. This is my only way out. I'm already dead. But you guys need to make sure no one else dies. *But no police* - you have to fix this on your own. It's the least you can do after everything I've done for you...

Mike looked away without finishing the rest, refolded the note, and tucked it back inside the bag.

"You're right, Eddie," he said as he stood. "It is too late."

He left the room and went downstairs. His stomach was dancing, but he managed to get through a late breakfast at the hotel's café. He wasn't sure how much was alcohol related, Eddie related, or something else, but the sweats were back. They weren't as severe, and the multi-layered outfit mostly worked to keep any signs of it from being visible to anyone.

After eating, he hailed a cab and made it to the Mets' clubhouse at Great American Ball Park, home of the Cincinnati Reds, without much more than a wet head. Once inside the clubhouse, he quickly changed into his workout gear and hustled out to the field to get in his daily jog around the outfield warning track. The run helped clear his mind and chased away most of the aftereffects of the booze.

He was back at his locker when the next attack came, but it was a different kind of invasion.

"Mike? Hey, Mike, you got a minute?"

He looked up to find David Donovan's smiling face. He shook his head.

"Not if you're gonna bust my balls about yesterday."

"No, no, nothing like that," David said. "I wanted to talk about something else."

Mike used a towel to wipe his face and head as he considered the reporter's words.

"What else is there?" he said.

David leaned in.

"Eddie Booker."

Chapter 20

Citizens Bank Park

Alyson listened intently as David described the conversation. When he finished, she had a million questions in her head, but started with the most obvious.

"Do you think he knows why Booker did it?"

"I do, yes," David said. "Coakley was nervous. I mean, sweating buckets nervous. He's seriously spooked about something and it sure ain't baseball."

Alyson made an odd noise through the phone.

"What was that?" David said.

"Oh, sorry," she said. "That was a bad habit."

"I'll rephrase. What does it mean?"

Alyson laughed.

"It means I'm thinking about what you said. Maybe Coakley's scared about the FBI. Did you mention them?"

"No, but you might be right," David said. "Maybe they're putting pressure on him. It might explain why he sucked so bad last night."

"Or maybe that was because he's old and just plain sucks," Alyson said.

It was David's turn to laugh.

"Yeah, well, there's that, too," he said.

The levity passed quickly. When Alyson spoke again, her tone was more serious.

"OK, so what's next," she said. "Is that guy you called gonna help? What's his name?"

"Thomas Hillsborough," David said. "And he still hasn't returned my calls. I'm beginning to think we're on our own—unless you happen to know someone at the FBI?"

Alyson frowned. Her list of contacts was slim and definitely absent anyone involved with or close to the Bureau. Even if there was someone, no one in her small circle ever shared gossip, at least not *with* her anyway.

"No," she said in a soft voice.

If David caught the disappointment, he let it pass.

"Let me try Hillsborough again. I'll touch base with you in the morning, after I get to D.C."

He was gone before Alyson could reply. She closed her phone and looked out at the playing field below. The press level at Citizens Bank Park was mid-height in the structure, unlike the view David would have once he got to Nationals Park in the Capitol. There, the writers and broadcasters were a lot higher up. Alyson had always thought it was cool because it gave the game a different perspective.

Working with David was doing the same thing. It had only been a few days, but she was seeing things in a new light. Despite the minor setback of not getting help from Thomas, she had to admit it felt good.

And she wanted it to last.

Cincinnati

"What do you mean you don't feel good?" Travis said into Mike's ear.

Mike was at the airport, standing alone near a window in the terminal, away from the rest of the Mets players and traveling party.

It was a continuation of the avoidance mode he'd been in all day. It was tough enough dealing with the odd aches and pains and crazy sweat. He didn't need people asking about it.

"I—I think something's wrong," he said. "We need to tell someone about the notes, about what Eddie was trying to tell us."

"What *was* Eddie trying to tell us, besides the fact he's a stupid motherfucker?"

Travis' tone was more harsh than usual. Mike cringed.

"He was—we have to do *something*," he said through another spasm.

On his end of the line, at his locker room at Citizens Bank Park, Travis dropped to the bench in front of his stall and leaned in as far as he could, to prevent anyone from overhearing his next words.

"We don't have to do a *goddamned* thing, Mike. Eddie ain't my fuckin' problem any longer and neither are you."

"But, but what about the Cure?" Mike said.

"What about it? Christ, man, I told you not to take that shit."

Washington, D.C.

David barely noticed that the Dulles terminal was close to deserted as he made his way toward Ground Transportation. He was distracted by the two messages left on his phone during the flight.

"Mr. Donovan, this is Thomas Hillsborough. I'm afraid I won't be able to assist you."

No reason, no explanation, just no. David knew he and Alyson were making progress, but now, without Thomas' help, he was going to have to regroup. The second message gave him some hope.

"David, I, uh—I need to talk to you about Eddie Booker. I'll call you back."

The message came from Mike Coakley. There was still fear in his voice, but David heard another emotion as well, anger. He wasn't sure if it was directed toward him or something else. The Mets had lost again and dropped a half-game behind the Dodgers in the playoff race. Pretty much all the players were pissed about that, but David doubted it was the reason behind Mike's tone.

He tossed some ideas around his head as he waited for a cab. Outside of him, Alyson, and presumably Mike and Travis, the FBI was the only other place where Eddie's deed was known. But why wasn't it being made public? Sure, they'd given some bullshit reason about why they were dropping the terror level, but nothing concrete. There was no reason to keep the truth a secret, not any longer. It wasn't like Eddie was a terrorist. You'd think that disclosure would help.

"What the fuck is going on?" David said.

Another man standing in the taxi queue turned.

"Yeah, I hear ya," the man said. "These fuckin' guys don't give a shit about us."

David half-nodded, half-shrugged in agreement. Whatever was going on, whatever Eddie had done or gotten into, David began to think he might be the only one who still gave a shit.

Denver, Colorado

Technically, as an umpire, I didn't have a home field. Such would defeat the purpose of the intended neutrality we were supposed to possess. Instead, we were the ultimate road warriors, on the move from late February and spring training until the end of October—and sometimes early November—and the playoffs. It wasn't all bad. I got to visit nice places like Denver, Colorado, and Coors Field, home of the Rockies.

Outside of Citizens Bank Park in Philly, Coors was probably next on my favorites list. It was laid out over seventy-six acres at 20th and Blake streets in Denver's lower downtown. If you were lucky to have a seat along the right field side, a spectacular view of the Rocky Mountains awaited. As an umpire, if you were working first base, you got the same.

That was my assignment for the first game of the series between the Rockies and visiting San Francisco Giants. I'd be lying if I said I wasn't looking forward to sneaking peeks at the peaks between innings. The bombing was still occupying a lot of my thoughts, but the sight of the mountains was going to be a nice change of pace.

In truth, anything would have been better than the crap of the past few weeks.

At least I thought so anyway.

Washington, D.C.

"Hey, has anybody seen Coakley?"

The question came from an assistant to the New York Mets traveling secretary, a young man named Patrick. When no one answered, Patrick began to get worried. His duties were mostly that of a gopher, but on top of the menial tasks was one of slightly higher importance. Patrick had primary responsibility for making sure all players made it to the ballpark on time for road games.

The job usually took care of itself. The majority traveled as a group from the hotel on two team buses. Patrick was in charge of checking off names as they boarded. Some of the veterans—old guys and special guys—were given leeway to arrange for separate travel, a cab, a car, etc.

Mike Coakley was among the former, the old guys, but was anything but special. He used the bus, or was supposed to anyway, but as of departure time, his was the only name not checked on Patrick's list.

"Did you call his room?" someone shouted from the back of the bus.

Patrick nodded.

"Yeah," he said. "That's why I'm asking. There's no answer."

Chapter 21

Denver

With time to kill before my game, I wandered over to a lounge near the Rockies' executive offices. My partners weren't with me yet; I tended to get to the field a tad earlier than they did. The other guys didn't mind. We all had our habits, our own systems, for dealing with the road. You had to. You'd go nuts without it.

Once in the lounge, I grabbed a chewy granola bar from a food station there and settled into a chair in front of a large flat-screen TV mounted to the wall. There were a handful of other people milling around, mostly Rockies staffers, but no one seemed interested in what was on the screen so I commandeered the remote.

The East Coast games were already in process and I picked the Mets-Nationals contest. The screen had a wide shot of the ballpark. The Nats were having another bad year and were long since eliminated from playoff contention, but the noticeable lack of bodies in seats was more pronounced than usual.

"Wow, nobody there," I said out of reflex.

"Not sure I blame them," someone said from behind my shoulder.

I glanced back and shrugged at the guy.

"Eh, maybe," I said. "It still sucks though."

"It does, but we won't have that problem," he said. "I'm hearing it's gonna be close to a full house tonight."

"Nice," I said as he moved away.

It was cool when the parks were crowded, the games were more fun. Still, the emptiness on the screen made sense. There'd been an explosion not quite two weeks ago, and thoughts of terrorism hadn't faded yet, not by a long shot. If it were to happen again, D.C. was probably high on the list of targets. People were still confused and scared. I was too, but at least had some comfort knowing Thomas was trying to figure things out. I mean, I think he was doing that, but I'd kept my promise and hadn't talked to him in the past week. He'd returned the favor. It was refreshing. Refreshing was good.

And again, like entirely too many things in the past two years, it was about to be short-lived.

Washington, D.C.

There was no getting around it, Patrick was in trouble. Not wanting to make everyone late, he'd boarded the bus and traveled to the stadium with hopes that Mike had simply forgotten to inform him of alternate plans. Unfortunately, those hopes had faded quickly, and it was now fifteen minutes past the scheduled arrival and Mike was still missing.

The field manager was not pleased. The general manager was not pleased. The traveling secretary was not pleased. Their collective ire was focused squarely on Patrick, and as he absorbed the wrath, he could see his dream job disappearing right before his eyes. Maybe working at his uncle's accounting firm wouldn't be so bad after all.

"Find him, *now*," the GM said, shaking Patrick back into action.

He ran from the clubhouse as fast as he could, doing the math on the way toward the stadium exit. Nationals Park was located south of the Capitol, adjacent to the Washington Navy Yard, along the Anacostia River. The team's hotel was about two miles north. With traffic, it would take a half-hour to get there, another half-hour to find Mike, and a third to return. Of course, there was still the small problem of that middle leg, actually finding the man.

If Patrick got lucky, a tremendously big IF, things would work out and the game would be somewhere in the middle innings by the time they got back. Barring a major collapse by the starter in the early innings, Patrick figured the plan would work. Mike was a relief pitcher. The team wouldn't need him until later, if at all.

"Later" never came, but not for any reason Patrick could have imagined.

Denver

On another day, I might have missed the content of some chatter between the Nationals broadcast team and their on-field correspondent, a young female. Make that *I would have* missed it because I used to be clueless about such things. But my recent experiences had changed that. And it was a new skill I didn't much like.

"Oh, hey guys, a note about the Mets. Mike Coakley, their long reliever, might not be available tonight. I'm not sure if it's an injury, but we just got word he's not at the park. I'll let you know more as soon as I can..."

If she said more than that, I missed it as I tossed the remote to the nearest person and hustled out of the lounge. I can't say why the comment had bothered me, it just did, and as I walked, I dialed a number on my phone. Thomas answered the call after the first ring.

"I seem to recall a request for lack of contact," he said.

I stopped walking and ducked into a nook in the hallway, just outside the umpires' room.

"Yeah, so sue me," I said. "Listen, it's probably nothing, but I just heard one of the players on the Mets didn't show up for their game in D.C. tonight. I don't even know why it bothers me, it just does."

There was a pause, a *long* one. Thomas was not easily surprised. Correction, I don't think he was ever surprised, but still, the gap was telling. I started to get more nervous.

"Thomas?" I said with a bit more emphasis.

"Does this player have a name?" he said.

The flat tone wasn't completely flat. Or maybe I just thought so. Either way, I lost my place.

"Marshall?" Thomas said, bringing me back.

"Yeah, I'm here."

"The player's name," he said.

OK, no guessing necessary, his voice definitely had an edge.

"Sorry," I said. "Mike Coakley."

"Mr. Booker's client," Thomas said.

It wasn't a question. And it had come out too quickly. He was way ahead of me, as usual.

"Is it bad you sound like you expected that?" I said.

"That would depend on one's definition of bad."

Washington, D.C.

Patrick, the assistant, now close to fully enveloped in panic, scanned the lobby for the hundredth time. No Mike, still, but he did notice a clerk at the front desk doing more or less nothing. Patrick's running toward the man changed that.

"Is everything OK, sir?" the clerk said as Patrick slid to a stop at the counter.

Patrick held up a finger as he tried to check his breathing enough to talk.

"Sir?" the clerk said.

"Can you... can I... can someone help me open a door?" Patrick said through his panting. "One of our players... a player is missing. I mean, I need help to check on one of our players."

"Wait, did you say someone is *missing*?" the clerk said.

"I, uh—no," Patrick said. "I mean, I don't know."

"Sir, let me call security—"

"No," Patrick said, interrupting. "He's not miss—it's just he won't answer his phone and he's not at the field and I can't find him—"

"Sir, please, calm down," the clerk said. "Just stay here and we'll get some help."

"I need to make sure nothing's wrong."

"Sir, we will."

Eight minutes later, the clerk and two rather large gentlemen representing hotel security accompanied Patrick to room thirteen-twenty-nine, Mike's suite. There were sounds on the other side of the door, music or maybe the TV, and what might have been running water. One of the guards turned to Patrick with a shrug, followed by a questioning glance.

"Sure sounds like someone's in there," the man said. "You say he won't answer?"

"No—I mean, *yes*," Patrick said. "I've been trying for an hour, his cell phone and the room phone. I tried knocking, too."

The guard nodded and proceeded to pound a big fist on the steel door. The boom echoed along the hallway before dissipating. After waiting a few seconds, he pounded again and shouted at the door.

"Mr. Coakley? *Mr. Coakley?* Sir, are you in there?"

A tense few seconds passed. The guard tried again.

"Mr. Coakley, are you there? Is everything OK, sir?"

Again, no answer, and the guard turned and looked at his partner. The second guard nodded before the first looked to Patrick.

"OK, do we have your permission to open this door?" the first guard said. "I'm not going in without your say so. You guys are my witnesses."

The second guard nodded again, as did the clerk. Patrick barely noticed.

"Shit, yeah," he said. "*Just open it.*"

Wayne

Thomas revisited his conversation with David Donovan. The reporter had been evasive, adding another tickle to his and Sandy's earlier lack of information, but that wasn't why he had rejected getting involved with the man. That decision was because of someone else.

"I'm not going to like this, but go ahead," Alex said.

"Does the name Michael Coakley mean anything to you?" Thomas said into his phone.

A loud sigh hit his ear.

"Why do you do that?" Alex said.

"I'm sorry?" Thomas said.

"No, that'll be my line as soon as you tell me why you're asking about Coakley."

Chapter 22

Washington, D.C.

"Stop the car," Mike said in a shout.

The cabbie hesitated, but only because of the traffic on both sides of the vehicle. Once it cleared from his right, he veered to the curb. Mike was out before the driver shifted into park.

"Hey—"

The complaint died at the sight of the ballplayer emptying his stomach onto the grass on the side of the road. The driver shouted through the open door.

"Jesus, dude… you OK?"

Mike slowly stood upright and looked around. In front of him was Independence Avenue SW, the eastbound lanes of the split road, just off of Ohio Drive SW. To his north, the Lincoln Memorial, its bright lights reaching into the sky like a beacon.

"Take me there," Mike said as he moved back to the cab.

"You gonna puke in my car?" the cabbie said.

The door slammed shut.

"Just fucking drive," Mike said. "I'll tell you when to stop."

A passing car expressed displeasure at the illegal stop and blasted its horn. The cabbie flipped the other driver the bird before eyeing Mike in the rearview mirror. After a few seconds, he slowly shook his head.

"Man, you better not blow chunks back there."

He shifted the engine into drive and pulled away from the curb. Three minutes later, the cab reached the Memorial grounds. Traffic, both pedestrian and vehicular, was light as the car made a slow pass around Lincoln Memorial Circle.

"We're here," the cabbie said. "You want me to stop anywhere in particular?"

"Not yet," Mike said; then after a pause. "How much you want for your gun?"

The car abruptly stopped. The cabbie spun around.

"Man, get the fuck outta my car," he said. "This ride is over."

Mike held his ground.

"How much for your gun?" he said again. "I know you have one, so how much you want for it?"

The cabbie's head titled to one side as he stared at Mike through the holes in the partition glass. After a few seconds, he scratched at his chin.

"You're fucked in the head, man. Just get out."

"Here's a thousand dollars," Mike said.

The cabbie's eyes bugged out as the player dropped a roll of twenties into the money slot. He quickly grabbed it and started counting.

"The gun," Mike said. "Don't make me come up there and get it."

The cabbie backed off a few inches from whatever he saw in Mike's eyes. After another handful of seconds, he started to laugh.

"OK, man, you win," he said, his hands going up in mock surrender.

His head disappeared for an instant. It came back into sight along with the weapon. For a few seconds, he just sat there, staring at Mike. When there was no reaction, he shrugged and worked a button on his left to lower the front passenger window. Mike began to scoot across the back seat. When he got to the far side, the driver tossed the gun through the open front window. Mike scrambled out after it.

"All yours," the driver said. "Fuckin' thing is stolen, anyway. I don't even know if it works."

"Thanks," Mike said from outside the car.

"Man, you nuts," the cabbie said through the window as it closed.

As Mike picked up the gun, the cab sped away.

"Yeah, that's for sure," he said as it moved off.

When it was out of sight, Mike turned toward the Lincoln Memorial. He was finding it hard to walk, but managed to make it safely across the circle without incident. He dropped his ass onto a short decorative wall adjacent to the sidewalk, along the side of the Memorial. It didn't appear as if anyone had followed, but he wasn't sure. He wasn't sure about a lot of things, but in one of his last moments of clarity, he fished his cell phone from his pocket and dialed a number.

Travis' recorded voice confirmed he'd touched the proper digits.

"I told you we had to do something," Mike said after the beep. "Now it's too late. They're after me. They'll be coming for you next."

The two U.S. Park Police officers working the Lincoln Memorial had no problems with the lack of traffic in and around the park. Thanks to the earlier elevated alert level, most people had taken to staying away from so-called high profile targets. That left the officers to spend most of their recent shifts—this one included—with nothing more to do than sip coffee and enjoy the evening air.

They were at the steps at the back of the structure, the side facing Arlington Bridge and the Potomac River, when the sound of gunshots changed all that. Drawn guns replaced coffee cups as the officers raced around the building. They were joined by four other officers near the southeast corner, at the bottom of the steps facing the Reflecting Pool. All six had similar expressions of confusion.

"Who the hell is shooting?" one said.

The handful of pedestrians that had been in the area were either running away from the Memorial or cowering behind trees, benches, and trash cans—or simply lying on the ground. If invited, at least two of the officers would have joined them.

"*There,*" one said in a shout.

The team turned as one toward the granite stairs. There were two bodies on the steps, halfway up in the center, and another three lying just below the statue of the seated President Lincoln. The officers quickly paired off and began an approach up the stairs, one team in the middle, one on either edge. The two that had come from the back of the Memorial took the central line, the most exposed path.

Both were relieved to find the first civilians alive and unharmed.

"What did you see?" one of the officers said.

"I don't know. Someone just started shooting."

Sirens had begun to fill the air as the officers rushed the bystanders back down and then away from the stairs. From a new position near the Pool, all four turned back as the other two police teams reached the top. The first verbal communication came through the radio from the officers on the left side.

"*We got three down. Looks like two are alive.*"

A voice from the team on the right chimed in.

"*Do you have a visual on the shooter?*"

"*Negative—Wait, wait... I got a gun—*"

There were muffled sounds and static. The voice returned seconds later.

"*Negative on the gun, the shooter is dead.*"

Patrick, the assistant, was sitting on an oversized chair in the hotel lobby. The ninth inning of the game was playing out on a nearby TV. A rout had turned into a nail-biter, but Patrick failed to notice. Like the team, he, too, was hanging on for dear life, trying to comprehend what might have happened to Mike Coakley, overwhelmed by the thoughts. Had he been too late, taken too long to have security open the door? "If only" was going to haunt him for a long time.

Thirteen floors above Patrick, Mike's suite was a wreck. An inebriated rock band couldn't have done a more complete and thorough trashing. Virtually everything in the room was broken or overturned. The dressers, the desks, the side tables, all smashed to pieces. The beds had been pulled apart, the mattresses tossed aside to expose box-springs. The suite's large flat-screen TV was shattered and hanging from the wall by its innards. The bathroom was a splintered mess of broken glass and tiles and leaking water.

The first assumption, from the security guards, was that someone had been looking for something. Blood found in the bathroom changed that thought to something worse. The police had been called and were on their way. Patrick secretly hoped that they'd never arrive.

At least then he might not get fired.

The injured lying on the granite below President Lincoln was a married couple from Columbus, Ohio, in D.C. on vacation. It was the first time they'd ventured more than fifty miles from home. Both vowed it would be the last. They were in serious condition, each having been shot once, the wife in the left thigh, the husband in the abdomen. An excess of fat on both bodies at the entry points helped lessen the damage. From their hospital beds later on, each would make silent promises to never change their diet.

The recent event in New York had provided a nice practice run, and it had taken the police less than three minutes to establish a perimeter around the Memorial. All traffic was redirected away from it and the other monuments. Any vehicles within the barriers were stopped and searched. The plazas were sealed off as well and all pedestrians were hustled into a makeshift command center for questioning.

It was a smooth operation, one the FBI could be proud of, but one more than a few involved would have rather not been repeating. As it had been in New York, this one was going to need a lot of overtime to figure out. The identity of the lone dead body would see to that.

Mike Coakley, major league ballplayer, triple-divorced step-father of three from his second marriage, was dead.

Chapter 23

Philadelphia

Alex was in an elevator, heading down to the FBI parking garage, when his phone beeped. The caller ID indicated a D.C. area code. The call lasted thirty-five seconds and did significant damage to Alex's mood. He was back in his office a minute later. Soon after that, he was standing at the foot of the Lincoln Memorial, Agent Santiago with him.

It had taken just under an hour for them to get to D.C. by helicopter. Alex would have guessed it was less because he spent most of the time on the radio-phone trying to convince various law enforcement types on the scene that the identity of the victim slash possible shooter made this his case, or more precisely, made this a continuation of the Citi Field bombing case. The locals may have wondered about the connection, but they didn't offer much of a protest.

"What the hell is going on, Carlos?" Alex said.

They were standing near Mike's tarp-covered body.

"I wish I knew, sir," Carlos said.

"Isn't baseball supposed to be a fucking game?" Alex said, more to himself than Carlos. "What is all this shit lately?"

Carlos let the question go unanswered as Alex circled the body before kneeling next to it. After a reflexive deep breath, he lifted a corner of the tarp. The granite beneath the body was red, stained by the blood from what was left of Mike's face. Alex looked away, glancing up and to the left, to an ugly splotch on the base of Lincoln's statue, another indication of what the ballplayer had done.

"*Jesus Christ,*" he said under his breath.

He turned back, taking note of the collection of small numbered placards indicating where bullet casings had been found. With a sigh, he lowered the plastic.

"Are all these from the same gun?" he said to Carlos, motioning toward the bullets.

"Too soon to tell," Carlos said.

Alex nodded before eyeing a black object near Mike's feet.

"Do we know anything about the gun yet?" he said.

"The serial numbers are scratched out." Carlos said. "I'd say it's stolen."

"Find out for sure," Alex said in a low voice; then after standing. "And let's find out how it got here and how *he* got here. Check the cab companies. You know the routine."

Carlos had already started the process. He handed Alex a single sheet of paper.

"Here's the preliminary statement from the injured couple."

Alex took the sheet and skimmed through. The elderly couple told of noticing a man near the statue, acting strangely, stomping around, and alternating between mumbles and shouts. He might have been talking on a phone because there was no one else around, and when he pulled out the gun and started waving it, they ran.

Alex folded the sheet and looked up. Carlos met his eyes.

"What's wrong with this picture?" Alex said.

He was using the piece of paper to point at Mike's body. Carlos' expression changed as he failed to find an answer.

"Sir?" he said.

"Where was the couple shot?" Alex said.

Carlos' eyes lit up.

"Oh, right, from the front," he said.

Alex nodded.

"So how'd that happen?"

"Had to be another shooter," Carlos said.

Alex's nod became more pronounced.

"Yep," he said. "Let's figure out what else these people didn't see."

Two hours later, Alex was sitting on a cheap folding chair just outside the command center trailer. If he would have thought about it, he was tired and uncomfortable. He wasn't thinking about it.

"Turn on the news," he said into the phone.

"No need," Thomas said into his ear. "I've been watching. Ms. Hood was kind enough to advise me of the situation."

Alex closed his eyes and tried to pinch back a blossoming headache.

"Tell me again why Marshall was concerned about Coakley. Earlier you said he had a bad feeling. How's that fit in with what happened here?"

"I'd have to see what you're seeing to answer that," Thomas said.

Alex made a sound, something between a sigh and a Bronx cheer. The pinch wasn't working.

"Yeah, that's what I thought."

~*~*~*~*~*~*~

David was only partly surprised by Alyson's sudden appearance in the press box at Nationals Park. Buoyed by—more like *turned on* by—successfully getting a one-on-one interview with Travis, she had blown off the game in Philly and hopped a train to D.C. David didn't mind. Nor did he mind where she took him after the game.

The rumors regarding Ms. Lane were turning out to be very accurate, something he was still thinking about as he stepped out of the bathroom. Alyson was in front of him on the bed, propped up on her knees near the front edge. She was wearing a pajama top and nothing else. David was wearing the matching bottoms, his upper body bare.

"I have to say—"

"Holy shit," Alyson said, cutting him off.

She was staring at a TV on the wall. The color had left her face. David moved to her side.

"What's wrong?" he said.

She pointed toward the screen and turned to face him. There was something in her eyes. David couldn't make it out. It was sort of like the lust she'd displayed earlier, but different enough that he didn't like it.

"What happened?" he said, his voice filled with concern.

"There was a shooting. One dead, two hurt. It was Mike Coakley. He shot himself."

David's eyes widened and he did a quick head shake.

"Baseball-playing-former-Eddie Booker-client Mike Coakley?" he said.

Alyson's expression—whatever it was—deepened. David *definitely* didn't like it.

"Yes," she said. "What the hell is going on, David? Did *we* do this?"

"I have no idea."

Denver

An hour after my game ended I was still in uniform, still in the umpires' locker room, on the phone with Thomas. He'd left a message during the game about Mike Coakley, but I was having a hard time dealing with it.

"This is so beyond fucked up," I said.

I hadn't really meant that for Thomas, but he answered anyway.

"What could you have done differently?" he said.

I looked around the empty room. The rest of my crewmates were long gone. Thomas couldn't see me, but I was shaking my head.

"I don't know... *something*," I said; then after a longer pause. "Fuck me."

"As you are so fond of reminding me, doing 'something' is not your job."

He was right. Fucking guy was *always* right. Still, it didn't help.

"I know it's not my job, but here I am, *again*," I said. "That's what's fucked up about it. I'm kinda getting tired of this shit, ya know?"

"Indeed."

Washington, D.C.

Alyson was straddling David, her knees on either side of his chest. Both were naked, the pajamas on the floor along with the blankets and most of the pillows. What was meant as a reassuring hug and kiss had turned into another round of sex.

"Do you think this is connected to Booker?" Alyson said.

"How could it not be?" David said in a tone closer to annoyed than satisfied.

Coakley's demise wasn't the only reason for his less than happy attitude. Despite the alarming news, Alyson had no problem ignoring it and seducing him. That, maybe more than the shooting, left him out of sorts. He'd finished quickly, but what was left of his erection was still inside her. She either didn't notice or didn't care.

"What do you think we should do about it?" she said.

He moved his hands from her hips and tucked them behind his head on top of the lone surviving pillow. Her skin and curves were pretty much what he imagined based on the photo, but as he eyed her now, he wasn't sure either was worth it. Her aggressiveness was worse than the rumors suggested, but not in a good way. He pushed out a rough sigh.

"I don't know," he said. "Booker was Coakley's agent. They both committed suicide. It has to mean something. Did Mackenzie say anything that might help?"

"About this, no," Alyson said; then after a pause. "But I remember seeing something you wrote, about the steroid connection with Booker. Maybe it's there."

A small beep sounded from a table behind them, from David's laptop, but neither reacted.

"That would make this the worst case of roid-rage ever," David said. "It seems like a stretch if you ask me. I don't know—"

The words faded off as Alyson lowered her body until her chest hit his. The feel of her breasts offset the pinch from her elbows on his shoulders as she propped her chin on her hands.

"I think we need to find out," she said, their faces mere inches apart.

Like her aggressiveness and cavalier attitude toward Mike dying, her use of "we" bothered David. He was beginning to question his decision to work with her, but when she leaned in and licked his chin, he forgot why.

Philadelphia

It took Jason a minute or so to remember where he'd seen it. He rooted through the newspapers on the desk next to the computer and found what he needed near the bottom of the pile, in the Sports pages of the New York *Daily News*. The contact info was at the end of the text of the second David Donovan story.

Working quickly, Jason typed out a new email message:

> To: david.donovan@nydn.com
> Subject: Please contact me immediately - I know why this
> is happening.

He didn't bother adding anything to the body of the email. He pushed *Send*, and within seconds, an electronic receipt came back. Jason sighed in relief and returned his attention to the online streaming video on his computer.

It was the same on every news site, stock stills of the Lincoln Memorial interspersed with shots of police vehicles and flashing lights along the roads surrounding the structure. Jason didn't much care about the pictures as much as the audio. There'd been a shooting. One person was dead, a ballplayer, a name Jason recognized. Bischoff had mentioned it a few times. It was one of several, two of whom were now dead.

Jason's head slowly shook as he watched. If his theory was correct, he knew he had bigger problems than a growing collection of dead hamsters, a lot bigger.

Chapter 24

Philadelphia

Alex read the elderly couples' statements again, his focus mainly on the husband's version. Buried within the man's colorful retelling—besides why the two had never ventured far from home, a trait of mid-westerners Alex didn't understand—was something significant to the case.

"The old man swears he saw a phone," he said. "We didn't find a phone."

"No, sir," Carlos said. "But it fits the theory someone else was there."

Alex began to nod before closing his eyes tightly and scratching at the back of his head. He ended the movements with his chin firmly in the palm of his left hand, his head tilted in that direction. He took a deep breath as he looked around the quiet room. After a second or two, his index finger started tapping against his cheek.

"And the oldsters got shot from the *front*, running *away* from Coakley," he said after exhaling.

"Yes, sir," Carlos said. "Different bullets than those found in Coakley's weapon."

The tapping stopped. Alex closed his eyes again.

"And we're sure Coakley did himself, right?" he said.

"Yes, sir," Carlos said again. "Powder burns, trajectory, fragments, et cetera all say he pulled the trigger. Technically, it's a suicide."

"So was Booker," Alex said under his breath before opening his eyes again.

He looked at his young protégé.

"What's our comfort level on what the old man thinks he heard Coakley say?"

Carlos checked a small notepad he was holding.

"He said Coakley said 'There is no cure.'"

"Yeah," Alex said. "What the hell is that? Was he sick?"

Another agent in the room perked up.

"We haven't found anything that indicates any illness, sir," the agent said. "We should have the complete tox screen shortly, but I'm not sure it will rule out mental issues."

Alex nodded and rubbed at his forehead for a few seconds before continuing.

"OK, listen, I know you've all been going full speed for the past few days, but the holes are still too big. I don't like big holes. Let's get into Coakley's last few hours and see if something shows up, something like Booker's breadcrumbs—"

The rest of the room seemed to hold its collective breath after the sudden stop. Alex looked around at each face.

"There are too many coincidences," he said. "We missed something. Go find it."

Paul Bischoff was sitting in the living room of his condo on 16th Street. The building was among a collection of historic vistas, but Bischoff rarely noticed the architectural beauty in the finely crafted details. He owned the home because a friend had suggested it would make a good investment. Of course, that was before the housing market crash. Now, the only detail Bischoff could see was that he was losing a boatload of money.

The same was true of his business. He had a product no one was buying. "The Cure" didn't work. Eddie Booker was dead. Mike

Coakley was dead. And as it was for Alex Harris, Bischoff knew there were too many coincidences. He also knew enough about math to know it was a trend, a seriously bad one, and it meant things were clearly out of control.

Bischoff was afraid something else was, too.

Jamie and Shady were half of Bischoff's size, but both scared the shit out of him. It was their eyes. He couldn't wrap his brain around the darkness there. The way he figured it, someone could only get that way after seeing some serious crap—or doing some serious crap. Bischoff had doled out his own share over the years, but doubted it compared to that of the Africans. He wasn't particularly interested in testing that theory, but knew the recent visit made it a growing possibility.

Before he succumbed to the thought, a buzzing from his cell phone interrupted. He looked at the caller ID and a shiver ran up and down his spine. Thinking about Jamie and Shady would have barely matched it.

Tentatively, Bischoff raised the phone to his ear.

"Yeah, I know," he said without waiting for the caller to speak.

"Then you know we have a problem."

"Yeah, maybe," Bischoff said.

"*Maybe*, Paul? This thing left *maybe* a long time ago."

Bischoff stood and began to pace. The worry was turning to anger, and the anger was turning his acne scars a sickly-looking maroon.

"I know, all right, you don't gotta fuckin' tell me," he said in an unsteady voice.

"Then what would you have me tell you?"

Bischoff extended the phone and gave it a sideways glance before returning it to his face.

"C'mon, man, cut the shit," he said. "What's that supposed to mean?"

There was a chuckle in his ear.

"How is this shit funny?" Bischoff said.

The chuckle died.

"You're right Paul, it's not. I gave you everything you needed and you fucked it up anyway."

Bischoff shivered again at the darkness in the tone. It reminded him of Jamie's eyes, but as much as the Africans freaked him out, this man on the phone, a man Bischoff knew only as "The Boss," scared him like no other.

"I'll, uh... I'll see what I can do to fix it."

"Yeah, you will."

Wayne

Sandy was sitting at her desk, gently rocking the chair. She was in a thinking mode, her hands repeatedly running through her thick shoulder-length brown hair. It was a mostly subconscious set of movements, something her now-deceased boyfriend always enjoyed—as did Thomas, not that he would ever admit such. After about the twelfth stroke, she grabbed hold and tied the locks into a bun.

"All right," she said. "What am I missing?"

She sat forward and grabbed a folder from her desk. Inside was a company history of Bulge, Inc. She opened the folder and laid it across the keyboard and started to read, not really sure of what it was she sought. Sometimes she was like that, haphazard. It was a method that had worked well in the past.

Maybe it would again.

Washington, D.C.

Distracted first by Alyson and then his real work, covering the Mets games, it wasn't until the morning of his travel day that David found the email from Jason Adley. It meant Atlanta would have to wait. It also meant the girl back at the office would be pissed at him—she hated dealing with cancellation credits—but David didn't really care much about her annoyance. In the scheme of things, it didn't compare to the consequences of what he was about to learn.

"Doctor Adley, David Donovan returning your call—I mean your email," he said after dialing Jason's number.

"No matter what happens, don't ever call me doctor again," Jason said.

David wasn't sure what to make of the words, but pushed past to the point.

"What *is* happening?" he said. "Your email said you know. Can you narrow that down for me? What exactly are you talking about?"

The line went quiet. David was about to ask his question again when Jason's voice sounded. The silence might have been better than what the doctor said.

"I know why Booker and Coakley are dead."

King of Prussia

Being free of David gave Alyson time to think, and it took all of about four minutes into the train ride back from D.C. to decide what she was going to do next. It was no contest. The *right thing* never had a chance. For her, it was all about getting ahead. She'd already stepped on and over a few people to get this far, which was not very far at all, so it was time to go farther.

She didn't care that David had done most of the work. She could see in his eyes he didn't have the guts to go all the way—that she might have misread things never entered her mind. She had no problem going all the way, in bed and elsewhere. David wasn't the first and wouldn't be the last to get used by her. She didn't care if people thought her a whore, she just wanted—no, *needed*—to be noticed for something other than having a perfect ass and tits.

In the scheme of things, "be careful what you wish for" was never so true.

Chapter 25

Wayne

"Aw, damn," Sandy said to the papers in front of her.

Until that moment, digging into the details had felt good. Outside of Alex, it was about the only thing Sandy still missed about the FBI. She'd started as an analyst, her job to dig in the muck, to give the agents what they needed. Now, she did it for herself—and for Thomas. It was the perfect gig, all the fun of the chase without the nuisance of the rules. Fuck the rules. Let Alex worry about them.

Sandy's worry was of being too late with the answers. It had happened before. Sure, she'd eventually found her sister's killer, but Amy was still dead. And sure, she'd helped Thomas end Andrew Singer's life, but Damien was still dead, too. At the end of the day, none of the dead were coming back because she'd been too late. The fear of that ate at her every day. And now, it was happening again.

Eddie Booker was already dead, so were the victims of the blast, and Mike Coakley, but maybe it wasn't too late to save someone else.

She stood and hustled out of her office in search of Thomas.

"The CIA deal got Dukabi to America," she said after finding him in his office, at his desk. "*You* started this."

She hadn't meant to emphasize the "you," it just came out that way, but Thomas didn't respond. That was as telling as one of his eyebrow shrugs, but Sandy pushed on.

"Dukabi let you turn him. It got him out of Kenya no questions asked. You guys set him up, you rewarded him. He had free reign to start the poker games and whatever else he got into. That gave him endless possibilities and access to all kinds of bad things."

If Thomas was thinking about the initial incrimination, he didn't show it.

"Are you suggesting Mr. Dukabi remains connected to the gang?" he said in his best flat tone.

That hadn't been what Sandy was suggesting, not entirely, but she quickly realized it should have been. Some of her anger turned back inward. She'd missed it. He hadn't. She began to nod.

"Well, yeah, I guess I am *now*," she said.

"Continue," Thomas said.

Sandy's nod transformed into a thick frown. How do you mask what you're feeling, Sandy thought as she eyed him, before finding her focus again.

"OK," she said. "Follow the money. Dukabi funnels it back to Africa. That's how the gang got stronger and that's what led them into drug trafficking. You can't play that game without cash."

"You don't believe Mr. Dukabi's stated aversion to drugs?" Thomas said.

"Actually, I do," Sandy said. "That's kinda where all my trails lead. The poker game was a lot easier and safer. Not too many cartels to deal with and every once in a while a client offers up something of interest. The latest example is Booker and Bischoff and the steroids."

Thomas nodded, very slightly, and his hands came up into the steeple.

"Mr. Dukabi somehow lost control," he said.

"Yeah, I think so," Sandy said. "He deals in layers, but is never at the top, the point of greatest risk. That's where we came in. He already knew it would be hard to actually pin any of this stuff on him, just like with Andrew Singer, but he needed to make sure. The more buffers the better, same as always."

"Not *entirely* the same," Thomas said.

Sandy looked at him with questioning eyes. A hint of a smile tickled at his lips, but not one she'd call happy. It was closer to devious, and somewhat surprising. A part of her was annoyed he wouldn't just say it, but the rest of her enjoyed that he was letting her work out the translation. It took her about ten seconds.

"Oooh," she said as the answer came to her. "No deals this time."

Thomas nodded again. It was Sandy's turn to smile.

"Nice."

New York

"What else can I do?" Mark said.

He was at his desk, sitting perfectly still. Gabi watched from the other side, but did nothing to interrupt. He knew it would be a bad idea, and he was trying to stay away from any more bad ideas. He'd had too many lately.

The two had been in the office for over an hour, much of the discussion centered on Mike Coakley's death. That second baseball-related fatality in as many weeks—not counting the bombing victims—had received the obligatory generic statement of sadness, but, as his spoken comment suggested, Mark still wasn't satisfied.

"I took this job because I love the game," he said.

"A good reason," Gabi said.

"Not good enough," Mark said, almost as an aside.

His eyes dropped toward his desk. Several newspapers were spread across the dark wood. Gabi was unable to tell which, if any, Mark was reading. What he could see was a lot of pain in his boss' features, features that usually projected strength. Part of Gabi's job had been to ensure the latter and prevent the former. At the moment, he was doing neither. That more than a few of the omissions were on purpose didn't come up.

"What have I accomplished?" Mark said.

Gabi knew it was rhetorical, a way for Mark to work through the pain. He did not reply. Instead, he let his eyes fall to his Blackberry. His e-mail was open, but there were no answers there, at least in relation to Mark's questions. When he looked up again, Mark was watching him.

"No help, huh?" he said.

The words produced a shot of adrenaline in Gabi that left his body momentarily numb. He hated the sensation. It was why he'd never excelled at sports. He could never handle the rush. He would freeze up from the effect of the chemical instead of using it for energy. He'd gotten better over the years, mostly by avoiding situations where it would occur—or at least better controlling them. He feared this had just become something of the former, something out of his control.

"You still have me," he said, deflecting.

Mark nodded and forced a small smile. Gabi relaxed a few degrees. The panic had been unnecessary. Mark hadn't noticed anything unusual. It wasn't the first time.

"I do," Mark said. "But every time we clean up one mess another surfaces. It's like someone is out to get us, pulling the strings from behind the curtain. The strike, the steroids, the gambling, the umpires, the owners—it's all like a goddamned merry-go-round of shit. No one is ever satisfied. They're never satisfied until we fuck up that is. Then, everyone is happy."

He sat forward and crumbled the newspapers into a huge ball and jammed it into a trash can behind the desk, punctuating the movements by kicking at the bin and sending it bouncing across the office. Gabi watched until it stopped rolling, and then put his eyes back to Mark's. The pain was no longer alone in the man's expression.

"A fucking serial killer almost ruins the World Series," Mark said in an angry tone. "A serial killer, what the fuck is that? I mean, why? And what was that shit at the All-Star Game? I get depressed, too, but I don't go around killing people."

He paused for a few seconds. The anger did not subside.

"And now—and now *this*," he said.

His eyes turned again toward the trash can. It was resting against a large glass display case filled with baseball memorabilia. No one piece was particularly more valuable than the others, not in a marketplace sense, but similar to Thomas' collection, they were very much so to Mark. Gabi never understood the fascination. To him, it was all just a bunch of junk. In his mind, the never-ending love affair with the past was why the game never moved forward. If only Mark would see that, he'd have an answer to some of the questions with which he wrestled.

A sigh from Mark told Gabi today would not be the day for that clarity.

"You need to find out what Booker and Coakley were into," Mark said. "I can't have anyone else die on my watch. Enough is enough."

Gabi nodded and stood.

"I'll figure it out," he said as he turned for the door.

He left out the fact he already knew.

King of Prussia

"Eh, I don't know, Alyson. We could get in a lot of trouble, especially you."

"No guts, no glory," Alyson said with a smile.

She sat back, re-crossed her long legs—Sharon Stone would have been proud—and waited for her boss' reply. He began playing with his bottom lip as he processed the information, his eyes locked on Alyson's legs. She didn't mind. If he needed a touch of extra incentive, so be it, but her story had already done most of the work.

"When did you—how did you get this stuff?" the producer said when he finally looked up again. "There's no way you came up with it on your own."

It was an insult, but like the man's stare, Alyson ignored it.

"I'm not as helpless as you think," she said. "But you're right, I had some help."

The producer nodded and played with his lip some more.

"You gonna acknowledge that help?" he said. "Or do I need to alert Legal?"

Alyson adjusted her legs once again.

"The help has already been properly compensated," she said.

Her wry smile got larger and the producer let out a long, loud sigh.

"Geeze, Aly, that's kinda what I'm afraid of."

New York

Gabi returned to his office and made a phone call. The recipient wasn't surprised. Then again, he never seemed to be.

"I could use your help," Gabi said.

"I understand," Thomas said. "These events are troubling."

"In ways you can't imagine," Gabi said.

If Thomas picked up the slight bobble in Gabi's tone, he didn't let on. Marshall's recent adventures had established the relationship between these two. Thomas found Gabi a capable and trustworthy person. He was also impressed by the man's dedication to Mark. Agreeing to assist was an easy call. There was nothing in his experience to suggest otherwise.

"Ms. Hill and I can be—"

"No," Gabi said, cutting him off. "I'll come there."

Thomas hesitated.

"Very well," he said. "When can we expect you?"

"I'm already on the way."

Chapter 26

Los Angeles

Travis and a teammate were in the trainer's room at Dodgers Stadium. Of the two, Travis was more relieved to be home, and away from the East Coast—not that he planned on explaining that fact, at least not to the man sitting across from him.

"Dude, you OK?" the man said.

Travis looked up.

"Huh?" he said.

The other man motioned with his chin.

"You've been scratching at your face for like ten minutes," he said. "You're bleeding. There, on your cheek."

Travis' brain—the uncorrupted part—caught up, and his hand moved away from his face. He stared at the finger tips. A hint of blood covered each one and had filled in under the tips of the nails. He brought the palm back up and touched it to his jaw. A red spot appeared.

"Whoa," he said; then after wiping the hand on a towel. "Thanks, guess I zoned out."

"Ya sure did," the teammate said. "But your secret's safe with me."

A flash of panic raced across Travis' face.

"*What?*" he said, his voice cracking a bit.

"I'll tell the other guys a woman did it," the teammate said with a chuckle.

"Oh, yeah, sure… thanks," Travis said, the panic subsiding.

The teammate stood and shook his head.

"Dude, if you weren't so goddamned good, I'd seriously wonder about you sometimes."

Travis' phoniest smile covered the fear.

"Guess it's a good thing I'm so goddamned good then, huh?"

He added a chuckle for good measure—also forced—but phony and forced were the best he could do. The situation was a lot of things, but funny wasn't included. He waved at his teammate, and as soon as he was alone, reached down and grabbed his cell phone from a bag on the floor.

Bischoff answered after three rings.

"I'm a little busy right now, Trav," Bischoff said. "I got some problems here."

Travis' eyes had returned to his bloody fingers.

"You're about to have some more."

King of Prussia

"I seriously owe you," Alyson said into the phone. "Can you email the file?"

The phone belonged to a production assistant. He was sitting at his desk, doing his best not to eavesdrop. Alyson's proximity made that extremely difficult. The scent of her perfume was intoxicating enough, but when she'd raised an arm over her head in response to the call, exposing some of her flawless stomach, he nearly lost it.

"Cool, I'll get it at my desk," Alyson said. "Thanks."

She reached in front of the young man to hang up before raising both arms, as if signaling a touchdown. The movements lifted her blouse even more. The PA gave up and stared at the diamond hanging from her belly button. Alyson noticed and winked at him as she lowered the arms. Her hand went to his shoulder and squeezed.

"Nice work, huh?" she said.

More blood rushed to the poor kid's crotch. Alyson caught sight of the growing hard-on under his jeans and smiled.

"And thanks for letting me use the phone," she said in something of a purr.

The PA's mouth fell open a little.

"S-s-sure," he said, his voice cracking like a pubescent teen. "You're, uh—you're gonna rock the world for sure."

Alyson winked again and squeezed harder. Miraculously, the young man's jeans held.

"I already do."

Philadelphia

"I'd say it seems like old times, but I'm not in the mood."

The words came from Alex. He was sitting at the head of the table in the conference room, down the hall from his office. A cast of familiar faces was with him, Thomas, Sandy, Gabi, and Carlos. All five might have wanted to skip the reunion—or at least held it at a bar instead—but the recent events did not afford them either luxury.

The location was no accident. Thomas suggested it after his brief chat with Gabi. Alex wasn't surprised. He was relatively certain whatever was going on was related to baseball. Having Gabi more directly involved made sense. Getting Thomas more involved also made sense now. Alex's earlier annoyance at the man had died under the weight of circumstances.

"So, who wants to start?" he said.

"I'll go," Gabi said; then after adjusting himself in his chair. "As you can imagine, Mark is a wreck. I'm not too far behind. At first I didn't think this was an attack on the game per se. Now, I can't see how it *isn't*. That's why I've asked all the clubs to beef up security at the ballparks."

Alex nodded.

"That's a good idea," he said; then after a pause. "What can you tell us about Booker and Coakley we might not already know? Are you aware of anything we might have missed?"

Dr. Cal Lightman—the lead character from TV's *Lie to Me*—would have easily caught the micro expressions that flashed across Gabi's face as he considered Alex's questions. Lightman was an exaggeration, but Thomas possessed many of the same skills. Unlike the TV doctor, he chose not to express the growing concern at what he was seeing.

"I didn't agree with Mark about reinstating Booker," Gabi said. "His being back in the game was an invitation for trouble. He was never far off my radar, but he was staying clean. Coakley, on the other hand, was never on my radar. He's an average player having an average career. Well, *was*, I should say."

The comments triggered something in Sandy.

"That's not entirely true," she said.

All eyes turned to her with the exception of Thomas'. His remained fixed on Gabi.

"Wouldn't Booker being fired raise a flag?" she said.

Gabi shrugged.

"Not necessarily," he said. "We don't control agency relationships."

"Yeah, but wasn't this more than a simple agency relationship?" Sandy said. "I mean, Coakley was a known steroid user. He wasn't the biggest fish, but he came forward and admitted his use. Booker's other recent client, Mackenzie, now he's a big fish. You've been after him for years. There's no way that didn't register."

Gabi's face experienced a few more micro bursts.

"I'm aware of that aspect," he said in a tight voice.

Alex caught the sudden spike in tempers.

"Sandy, do you have something specific to share?" he said in a commanding tone.

Sandy recognized the tone from her days working for Alex, but ignored it and glanced at Thomas instead. He gave her an almost imperceptible nod. Sandy adjusted in her chair and turned to Gabi.

"Booker was already a known problem. Mackenzie might be, but you haven't been able to prove it. Both players were Booker clients. So were Paul Bischoff and his company. All four, directly or indirectly, were part of the steroid scandals of the past. Marshall told us about rumors of something brewing again on that front. You're pretty damn good at your job. There's no way you weren't aware of all that."

Gabi's reaction was more at the macro level. His eyes narrowed and he began to take long, deep breaths. He was clearly fighting hard to control himself.

"Speaking of jobs, what about yours?" he said. "What's up with you guys and Dukabi? You seem to have missed a few things there, huh?"

That the redirect had gone toward Sandy made sense. Pick on the weakest link, perceived or otherwise. Sandy didn't react to the words, but Thomas made up for it.

"*Many things* have been missed," he said.

The tone was as pointed as Sandy had ever heard. She was sure she knew why. Dukabi's involvement had not been shared with Gabi. It was possible Alex might have done so, but the director's reaction to the tension building in the room told her no.

"OK, guys," he said. "We're all on edge here. It's understandable. But let's not start sniping at each other. We're supposed to be on the same team."

His tone and smile were meant to be reassuring. Whether it worked was debatable.

"Gabi, the good news for you is that these are my cases. You won't have to deal with your friend in New York. You can thank me later."

It took a second, but Gabi got it.

"Ah, yeah," he said. "Director Pappas wasn't my favorite, no."

"The same is true for all of us." Alex said; then after a pause. "Agent Santiago, you're up."

He motioned with his head toward Carlos. The agent nodded.

"Coakley said something odd just before killing himself," Carlos said. "We're not sure if it was intentional or something else, a message maybe. Supposedly, he made mention of *a* cure or *the* cure. We have no idea what that means. Does it mean anything to you?"

The question was directed toward Gabi. His head started shaking, but it conflicted with everything else on his face.

"Uh, no, I can't say that it does," he said. "Sorry."

Sandy's first instinct was to blurt out "That's a lie," but a noticeable shake of the head from Thomas told her not to. It also told her he had reached a similar conclusion: Gabi was hiding something.

Figuring out what that might be would take a little longer.

~*~*~*~*~*~*~

"We need to put out a statement about these rumors. This shit will ruin us."

The words from Bischoff's attorney barely registered. His mind was already fixated on a different kind of statement, one that read: GOING OUT OF BUSINESS.

"Paul, are you listening to me?" the attorney said. "Saying nothing implies guilt. We've been there, done that, in case you forgot."

Bischoff lifted his eyes to meet the lawyer's. At the same time, he began to work his puffy hands as if he were kneading an imaginary ball of dough—or maybe squeezing the other man's skull. The lawyer must have guessed the latter because he started squirming in his chair.

"Why do I pay you?" Bischoff said. "It's not like you ever keep me outta trouble."

The lawyer squirmed a little more.

"I don't think there's anyone alive who could do that."

~*~*~*~*~*~*~

"The situation is no longer acceptable," Dukabi said into the phone.

He was alone at a small table in a coffee shop on Chestnut Street. A cup of something caffeinated was in front of him. The phone was all but lost in the bulk of his massive right hand.

"I agreed to participate with a presumption the outcome was feasible," he said, his voice low, but the tone heavy. "Clearly, I was mistaken."

On the other end of the line, the man known as "The Boss" hesitated before replying.

"It seems we were all mistaken, about a lot of things," he said.

A sound escaped Dukabi's mouth. The people sitting nearby thought it was a cough.

"Do not assume my patience will last," Dukabi said.

"You do the same, Mr. Dukabi."

The cell phone completely disappeared as Dukabi closed it. He dropped it into a pocket on the outside of his jacket before returning his attention to the coffee. A few sips followed. Music of which Dukabi was not familiar wafted through the shop's air, mixing in with the soft voices of the other patrons around him. The white noise was both soothing and annoying.

"This is not acceptable," he said aloud.

A passing server stopped and turned at the words.

"Sir?" the young woman said. "Is something wrong with your drink?"

Dukabi slowly raised his eyes to the woman. Hers widened and she backed off a few steps.

"Yes, my dear, something is most definitely wrong."

Sandy and Carlos headed off with Gabi to start the process of connecting the dots in their respective work. Alex was confident the effort would lead to the truth, happy to have most of his old team back together working on it. That part of the meeting had been positive. The other part, the heightened tensions, had been anything but. Alex was bothered by it, something he aired as soon as he and Thomas reconvened in the director's office.

"What was that stuff between you and Gabi?" he said.

Thomas' reply was a raised eyebrow. Alex sighed.

"Come on, Thomas. We go back too far," he said. "I can see there's something you're not telling me."

"No," Thomas said.

The simple response and flat tone elicited a thick frown from Alex.

"Goddamn it, stop," he said. "I don't need the cryptic shit, not today. There's something rattling around in your head. Tell me."

"Not yet," Thomas said.

"*Not yet?*" Alex said. "As in there's nothing rattling or you're not going to tell me?"

"Yes."

Alex's frustration grew. He stared at Thomas for close to thirty seconds before shaking his head and letting out another loud sigh.

"Goddamn it," he said again. "You're killing me. You know that, right?"

"I would never do such a thing. We've had too many deaths already."

Alex's head stopped shaking. His hand came up and he pinched the bridge of his nose. As much as he was annoyed by Thomas' non-disclosure, the painful accuracy of the man's last words put everything into perspective. He could look past Thomas' personality quirks, but not the truth of the situation.

After a few seconds there was another sigh as Alex looked up.

"Yeah, no shit."

Chapter 27

New York City

David had avoided Atlanta, but couldn't avoid the odd looks he was getting as he made his way to his editor's office. He felt like the sap of the party, the guy with schmutz on his face, but doesn't know it and no one bothers to tell him it is there. In his case, the schmutz wasn't a small spot, but a face full.

"People were right about that fuckin' bitch," the editor said after David took a seat.

"You got the fucking part right," David said.

The editor nodded. He understood. He'd seen it before. It came with the territory. Some people—like Alyson Lane—were just a lot better at it.

"So, what are we gonna do about this?" he said. "What are *you* gonna do?"

David shrugged.

"I'll let you know when I figure that out."

King of Prussia

"The wires are going ape-shit," someone said into the noisy room. "This is awesome."

Alyson smiled at the excitement around her desk. In addition to SNN's repeated airings of her "I stole this but I'm pushing it off as my own" special report, the online version was getting picked up by major news outlets around the country. "Going viral" was taking on a whole new meaning. Requests for interviews were piling up by the minute. Alyson was going to be a busy girl. She didn't mind. Busy was good.

She sat back and closed her eyes, letting the final segment of the report replay in her head. Her smile grew. It had been a rush like none she'd ever experienced, in bed or elsewhere, especially the ending.

"Major League Baseball would have you believe the steroid era was over, a forgotten shadow of the game's dark past. Recent events say otherwise. Eddie Booker was a disgraced ex-player, banned because of gambling problems. But why did MLB fail to mention the man's drug issues, specifically his alleged involvement with painkillers and steroids?

What was the league hiding? Why allow the man back in the game, so close to the players? It was clearly a recipe for disaster, as the latest disclosures have indicated. We now know, thanks to the FBI statement, that Eddie Booker died in a spectacular suicide. The collateral damage, already high, has now extended to Mike Coakley.

The question remains: When and where will it end?"

The full report was cobbled together from David's stories and his as yet unpublished findings, including the email from Jason Adley. Alyson never spoke to Adley—she'd pirated the message from David's computer while he slept. From there, it wasn't hard to scrape together details about Bulge and its shady past. It did take a few edits and an argument with SNN's legal department before she was eventually able to word things in a manner acceptable to all involved while still making the point.

The obligatory "No comment" statements elicited from Bulge and MLB—at the behest of her producer—were positioned within the narrative in such a way that it added meat to the bones of her theory instead of contradictions. Some might say the whole thing was very "Fox News-like," a subtle dance around the connections between the parties involved, a stretching of facts and non-facts alike, enough so to implicate MLB and Bulge and Bischoff as part of a bigger conspiracy.

Alyson didn't care who might get pissed off by the suggestions or how they might react to the disclosures. She *was* rocking the world.

The world would soon rock back.

New York

"I trusted you, Mr. Donovan," a voice said into David's ear. "You said you would help."

David was back at his cubicle desk. The voice in his ear belonged to Jason Adley.

"I know, Jason. I'm sorry," David said. "I was—I *am* trying to help. Lane betrayed a lot of people. I'm as mad as you are."

He closed his eyes. His shitty mood moved a few notches to seriously shitty. Jason's next words didn't help.

"It's too late for mad, Mr. Donovan. Now you need to be scared."

The line went dead. David stared at the phone until a message from Alyson floated into his thoughts. His eyes slid to a stack of paper on the desk. The notes were the basis of the story he could no longer write, thanks to her. If he did, *he* would be accused of stealing. His head began to shake as her words played in his mind again.

I did what I had to.

David's head dropped and he closed his eyes again. Yeah, he thought, you did what you had to, but you got it all wrong, you stupid bitch. He opened his eyes and looked at the notes again. A shiver raced along his spine.

"You're right, Jason," he said to the pile of paper. "I *am* scared."

Philadelphia

It was Alex's turn for the not-so-fortunate honor of being under the harsh glare of the lights shining from D.C. He was not enjoying the exposure. The boss' boss was in full *Wrath of Khan* mode as he berated Alex about Alyson's report, especially the parts suggesting the Bureau was inept at best and in collusion with a cover-up at worst. Alex agreed. Whether accurate or not—he believed not—both points were bad.

"I don't get it," the boss said. "How did this fucking bimbo come up with this stuff? Can someone please explain that to me? Bullshit or not, it seems like she knows a lot more about this case than we do. I'd love to know how that happened. Alex? You got anything?"

As the words settled over everyone like a wet blanket, Alex looked around the conference room. The heaviness pushed heads down and no one held his gaze for more than a second. He shook his, but not because of disappointment with those in the room. His team was working hard. They weren't his problem.

Ninety miles away, listening in as he sat alone in his office in New York, Gus was smiling, happy knowing the latest turn of events gave him a few more days out of the fire. So far, his involvement had been conveniently forgotten. He figured Alyson's report would keep it that way for a while longer. It was why he had called her in the first place and given her some of the inside info about Eddie.

Back in Philadelphia, Alex's features hardened as he refocused on the phone.

"I don't think the reporter should be our focus," he said in a calm tone.

At his end of the line, Gus stopped smiling.

"So what is your focus?" the boss said. "Figure it out, Alex. I don't need this shit."

There was a small double beep and then static from the phone. A few more double beeps followed, signifying a mass exodus from the conference call. Alex reached over and punched a button on the phone to silence the noises. His hand came back and massaged his forehead for a few seconds, trying to erase the pain only he could feel.

After a few quiet seconds, he stood and eyed the rest of the room.

"You heard the man," he said. "Go figure it out."

As soon as he was alone, he pulled out his cell phone. Thomas answered after the first ring.

"I need another favor."

New York City

Mark looked at Suze Keebler with a pained expression. She was standing in his doorway.

"I am officially not available," he said.

"For," Suze said, drawing out the word into a question.

Mark considered her for a few seconds.

"For everything," he said. "Let Media Relations deal with any SNN crap. Don't bother me unless someone is dying. Shit, sorry... I didn't mean that."

Suze shrugged off the remark.

"It's OK. I understand."

She nodded and closed the door. Mark appreciated the nice respite her smiling face had been, but it was another painful reminder. She and Marshall were no longer together, a fact that added to the building melancholy overtaking Mark's soul. The breakup was just one of a now too long line of similar occurrences beating on him.

"I wish I understood," he said to himself after she was gone.

He stood and wandered over to the office's windows. The usually stimulating view failed to stem the tide of despair. He hated feeling like this.

"At least you have more to work with now," he said to the glass. "Gotta be something real in all that bullshit Lane was spewing."

From a chair in front of Mark's desk, Gabi nodded.

"I have some ideas," he said.

Mark turned from the window.

"Then get outta here and quit wasting time talking to me."

He made a motion with his hand. Gabi ignored the rude dismissal. Like Suze, he understood. He left without another word.

After the door clicked closed, Mark moved back to his desk. An index finger pushed a button to reignite his computer monitor. He adjusted the keyboard and stared down at the letters for several seconds.

After a deep breath, his hands went to work, slowly at first, but soon much faster. Words became sentences, sentences became paragraphs.

> From the start, my ambition, my goal as commissioner, was to return this grandest of all American institutions to its former and proper standing. Baseball truly is an undeniable part of the fabric of our society, of its greatness. My actions have been and continue to be directed toward achieving that singular goal.
>
> Some may argue I have failed, but I believe otherwise.
>
> We have made great strides and accomplished much. Regrettably, recent events have taken away from those accomplishments. These events serve as a stark and sobering reminder the naysayers may be correct, that despite our best efforts, the ugliness we have suffered is a permanent scar we cannot remove. These black eyes—

He stopped typing.
"No, that's not right," he said before deleting the last few words. After a few seconds, he started up again.

> There can be no argument that the deaths of Eddie Booker and Mike Coakley represent a catastrophic loss for all of us. Troubled or not, the men were part of our family and they will be missed, but we cannot overlook the fact many others were injured and killed as well. That loss, inflicted on innocent people, is not something I can accept. Nor is it something I can forget.

He stopped again and looked around the office. The modest collection of memorabilia scattered about the room furthered his resolve for what he was about to do. He looked back to the keyboard and resumed typing.

> Effective with delivery of this letter, I am resigning from my position as commissioner of baseball. It is clear to me, now

more than ever, I am no longer suited to handle the duties and responsibilities of this office. The game deserves more. It deserves better.

He stopped again and turned toward the office windows. He wasn't really seeing anything outside. It was all a blur. His mind was elsewhere. The words just typed were the beginning of a path down which he would not be able to return. He had to be sure.

After a minute or so to collect his thoughts, he nodded and continued.

To assist in the transition, I will provide a list of recommendations and remain until a suitable replacement is found. I offer my sincerest thanks to my staff and everyone associated with Major League Baseball. Your time and efforts means a great deal to me. I am forever in your debt for the unselfish and outstanding service. All of you will be missed.

Sincerely and with a heavy heart,
Mark P. Rosenbaum

He stopped and sat back to review the document. On the second read he deleted the final sentence. I'll save that for the day of the announcement, he thought, as he guided the cursor to the *Save* icon and clicked once. As the hard-drive worked, he punched at a button on his desk phone. Suze's voice came through the speaker.

"Yes, sir?" she said.

"I just saved a letter in my Memos folder. Print it on my letterhead and address an envelope to the Executive Committee. Leave both on my desk. I'll sign it later. I'm leaving for the day."

"Are you sure you don't want to get it in today's mail?" she said.

"No. Just set it up. I'll let you know when to send it."

He pushed the button again to silence the phone. A small smile worked onto his face as he pictured Suze. It was too bad about her and Marshall. Maybe they'll reunite, he thought. That would be nice. They're good people.

"Sorry, guys," he said as the image faded.

~*~*~*~*~*~*~

Philadelphia

It wasn't exactly the memo the legal team wanted, but Jason wasn't surprised. He always knew Bischoff was nothing more than a coward hiding behind the false bravado and muscles provided by the steroids. He also knew he, too, was a coward, hiding in the lab and looking the other way, never standing up for what he knew to be right.

But Booker and Coakley and the others in New York changed that. Bischoff could run, but Jason would not.

"This won't work, Paul," he said. "They'll find you."

Bischoff smiled. The redness of the acne scars gave it a Joker-like look—think Heath Ledger's *The Dark Knight* version.

"They ain't gonna find me," he said. "By the time they figure out the release is bullshit I'll be long gone."

Jason shook his head.

"So that's it? You're just going to run away? There are others at risk, risk you created."

"Fuck that," Bischoff said. "I didn't create shit, *you* did."

The insult scored and Jason felt a pang of regret. He watched as Bischoff turned and slid another stack of documents into a shredder. Similar activities were taking place throughout the building. The rats were jumping ship, eager to escape before the vessel went under. Jason thought about the rodents down in the lab. They never had a chance to jump. Bischoff was right about that being Jason's doing.

"I'm not leaving," Jason said.

Bischoff looked up from the whine of the shredder.

"Hey, suit yourself," he said. "Let me know how that works out."

Jason turned and left the office. Alone, Bischoff picked up the pace. Everything had to go, every file, every disk, all of it. Bulge's existence needed to be erased. He could leave nothing, not a shred of evidence that could be hung around his neck later, if—or when—someone did happen to find him.

His verbal instructions to the rest of the employees were very clear on those points. One by one, the staff had come by to confirm their compliance. One by one, Bischoff told them their final pay would be delivered via direct deposit within two days. No one had questioned the promise, most seemingly expecting it. Why it had taken so long to get to this point was the only real mystery.

As nightfall set in, the sounds began to subside. Bischoff's shredder went quiet as well. He wiped the paper dust off his hands and plopped down into the leather chair behind his desk. The chair—like the Bentley, the designer clothes, and the unnaturally-developed muscles—was compensation for his shortcomings.

In the fading light, he thought about that, how his life was nothing more than a charade. Jason was right. Bischoff was a coward, afraid to be himself. As the thought sank in, a tinge of regret nicked at his conscience. It didn't happen often, but he knew others were at risk, people he once considered friends.

"Fucking nerd," he said to a new image of Jason. "Why'd you have to say anything?"

He sat forward in the chair and picked up the receiver from the desk phone. Travis answered after four rings. Bischoff's tone was somber.

"Hey, listen… there's, uh, somethin' I need to tell you."

In contrast to his partner, Jamie had the ability to harness anger, to dole out punishment in strategic bursts, no motion wasted. Each strike had a specific purpose. His formal education and training contributed a lot to that style and its difference to Shady's. It wasn't that the younger man lacked education, but his wild rage could be traced to a more rudimentary source. His family had been butchered, and he was forced to learn to do the same to survive. That left him inclined to submit to lesser emotions. Jamie had no problem with that. It was a nice fallback for when the surgical strikes failed.

Both methods were on Jamie's mind as he spoke into the phone.

"It will be handled," he said in a calm tone.

He closed the phone and motioned with his hand. Shady nodded.

"Of all things, what makes you most angry, my friend?" Jamie said.

Shady worked his mind for an answer.

"Deceit," he said.

"A hideous offense," Jamie said with a nod.

"And betrayal," Shady said.

"Ah, yes," Jamie said. "You are most wise."

Shady smiled. He liked when Jamie commended him.

"And what is an appropriate response to these offenses?" Jamie said.

Shady worked for another answer. Without a word, he picked up a sheath from a table near where the men stood. The blade of the machete sang a song as it slid from the protective sleeve. Shady turned the neatly polished metal in his hand and admired the shine.

"A lesson," he said.

"Again, you are most wise, my friend."

Los Angeles

"Did I wake you?"

The unexpected phone call did in fact wake me, ruining a decent dream in the process, but the worry in Suze's tone was more bothersome. I sat up too fast and my stomach did a few flips.

"Whoa," I said.

"Marshall?"

"I'm OK. I'm up," I said. "What's wrong?"

"Why do all of our conversations start out that way?" she said.

I didn't have the answer. She was right. She was always right. I was the one who'd been wrong, wrong to have ever brought her into my life. She deserved better.

"I wish I knew," I said.

It got quiet for a second or two. It felt more like two hours. Suze broke the silence.

"Me, too," she said.

"So how do I ask why you're calling without making it worse?" I said.

Another quiet came. It was longer than the first one.

"It's Mark," she said. "He's going to quit."

The dizziness of sitting up too fast disappeared, but the knot in my stomach got worse.

"*What?*" I said. "When did this happen?"

"It hasn't yet. He'd be pissed if he knew I was talking to you—to anyone—but he had me prepare a letter. I'm not sure when he's going to send it."

She gave me the details, but I wasn't sure how to respond. I looked around the room for an answer. That didn't help. I really hated the road sometimes. Every hotel room in every city was the same—two beds, a desk, a dresser, a TV, a bathroom. About the only difference were the colors, and even those were duplicated far too often. Having a cool roommate and friend like Bartola Casaba was about the only thing that made it bearable at times. Well, knowing I'd once had Suze waiting somewhere for me had helped, too, but now that was gone.

And another reason was about to disappear as well.

"Shit, Suze, he can't quit," I said. "The game needs him. *I* need him."

Chapter 28

Philadelphia

The steady stream of bodies coming out of the Bulge building reminded Shady of his childhood. The staffers carrying boxes and bags into the darkness had the same hurried and harried look as the villagers of his home, lugging the last of their belongings as they fled the savages bent on destroying everything and everyone. His parents had perished in one such storm of destruction, their fates sealed by the cowardly actions of others.

This night was no different.

"They are afraid," Shady said in his native tongue.

"As they should be," Jamie said.

An unsuspecting man was rapidly approaching from the opposite direction along the walkway. Jamie and Shady changed their pace to intercept the man at one of the dark spots between the lights along the path. The man was carrying two overfilled plastic containers, the kind of phony milk crates you can buy at Staples or Office Depot. Shady adjusted his position, forcing the man directly into Jamie's path. The man stopped just short.

"Oh, hey, sorry, my bad," he said, clearly frazzled by more than the near collision. "I almost didn't see you."

Shady slid in behind the man.

"And now do you see us?" Jamie said.

The man's ragged smile faded into a look of fear.

"Um… can I help you guys with something?" he said.

"Yes."

The word was Jamie's, but the movements came from Shady. His hands were a blur as they grabbed the man's head and twisted in a single rapid motion. The shattering cartilage sounded like a snap of fingers as the shards of cervical vertebrae punctured then severed the spinal cord. In the fraction of a second before the signals to the man's muscles ceased, Jamie's hands took hold of the crates as Shady lowered the body to the grass next to the path.

In the next few seconds, Shady removed the man's ID badge from around the broken neck and posed the corpse, knees up, as Jamie set the crates on either side of the torso. One limp arm was then propped against one of the containers as the other was draped over the man's empty face. Those passing would think he was resting, distraught, trying to find answers for the sudden termination of his job.

Jamie and Shady moved off toward the entrance. In the chaos of activity, no one had seemed to notice the attack or the fact they didn't belong. They arrived unimpeded at their destination, Bischoff's office, a mere three minutes later. Bischoff was alone there, working on the last chores required before departure. His back was to the door and he was oblivious to everything but that task. Some things never changed.

"And I am outta here," he said as he surveyed the space.

The emptiness in front of him was stark and a touch on the eerie side, but not as scary as what he saw when he turned.

"What the fuck are you guys doing here?" he said.

"It seems I should pose a similar query," Jamie said.

Bischoff's eyes went wide and he stumbled back into the office. He banged into the desk, fumbling the shoulder bag he'd been carrying in the process. He left it on the floor as the dark faces of Jamie and Shady slowly moved into the room. When the door shut, Bischoff pissed himself.

"Wait, I can explain," he said as the warmth of the pee began to spread down his leg.

"No explanation is necessary," Jamie said.

Bischoff's hands came up, as if to signal stop. He neither saw nor felt the steel of Shady's blade until after the metal had sliced through his body, leaving him cut almost in half. In the last seconds of his life, he looked down and watched as the contents of his intestines spilled to the floor and joined the urine already there. He'd often wondered what his insides looked like, especially after all the abuse.

Turned out it was as ugly as he'd imagined, like one of Jason's dead hamsters.

~*~*~*~*~*~*~

Thirty minutes later and a few floors below, Jason sat up and tried to get his bearings. He'd fallen asleep at one of the lab workstations. His neck was stiff from the awkward position, but the pain faded quickly, replaced by confusion at the sound of alarms in his ears. It took him a few seconds to realize the noise was not from the lab's fire suppression system, but from the upper floors, the office area.

"Jesus Christ, Paul... what have you done?" he said as he hustled out of the lab.

Growing up with a firefighter father, Jason was accustomed to the scent that hit his nose as he reached the elevators.

"Shit," he said as he began stabbing at the buttons near the lift doors.

The realization that the elevators would be out of service took an extra second.

"Shit," he said again as another realization hit him.

The door to the fire exit stairs was on his right, but instead of going through, he turned and ran back to the lab. Depending on the severity of whatever was taking place above, it was only a matter of time before the secondary Halon gas system there was triggered. He would have little time to escape once that happened, but it was a chance he had to take.

After reaching his computer, he quickly navigated to the necessary files. It would take a minute for the machine to compress and write the files to the 128-gigabyte flash drive plugged into the USB port along the keyboard. As the copy process began, the room began to take on smoke. A tiny beep sounded, signifying the early-warning notice for the Halon. Jason had two minutes before the room filled with oxygen-absorbing gas that would suck the life out of every living thing in the room.

"Shit," he said yet again.

He wiped the smoke from his eyes and checked the conversion status: *88%*. He clicked another icon to open his e-mail. As soon as a new message window appeared he typed out an address and clicked the *Attachment* button. The alarm beep adjusted to a louder pitch. One minute. The smoke was now close to unbearable. Jason coughed several times and pushed on.

A different beep told him the conversion was complete. He pulled the drive from the port as he coughed again. On what he could still see of the screen, the e-mail attachment window was still waiting for a file selection. A piercing siren hit his ears and he looked up to the ceiling.

"Not yet, Goddamn it. *Not yet.*"

Los Angeles

"I thought you should know," I said into my cell phone. "I'm not sure if it makes a difference."

I turned and stared out the window in my room. The L.A. skyline was a fuzzy shadow behind the haze and smog and whatever other nastiness was hanging in the morning air. It was like a veil, but a really ugly one no sane person would ever wear. Underneath the mask wasn't much better, but I had no intentions of taking a closer look. I'd seen enough ugliness lately.

"Mark's departure would be unfortunate, but understandable, given the circumstances," Thomas said into my ear. "He is a proud man."

"He is," I said. "So, did you figure out what's going on yet?"

"No."

"No? That's it?"

The line went quiet. I got the message.

"Sorry, I know you're working on it," I said.

"Your gift for the obvious never ceases to amaze," Thomas said.

"I try," I said.

"Indeed."

Him and that word, funny in an unfunny way, but always appropriate.

"I'm guessing that means we're done here?" I said.

"Yes, for now. Go do your job, Marshall. I'll be in touch."

I knew he would be, but doubted it was going to be for anything good.

Philadelphia

Every news outlet in Philadelphia led its eleven o'clock newscast with a report from the scene of the six alarm fire burning out of control at the headquarters of Bulge, Inc. The vantage points from the various eye-in-the-sky helicopters made for spectacular views of the flames. Bright yellow, orange, and red danced into the black night sky from every window of the building.

Alex stared at the pictures on the small flat-screen TV in his kitchen. On most nights he wouldn't have noticed—or cared. Another fire, ho hum, no big deal.

Except not this time, this was a very big deal.

"What's wrong, Hon?" his wife said when she saw his expression.

He turned to her and the expression changed to something that might have been a smile. It was a look she was used to. No explanation was necessary, but he provided one anyway.

"I need to go," he said.

She smiled and nodded her understanding. In many ways, she was a lot stronger than he. There wasn't much choice in that. The spouses and significant others of him and his team lived in a dangerous world with a lot of risks. Loving someone despite such danger took a strong soul. Mrs. Harris was a very strong soul. She deserved better.

Alex had thought about retirement a few times in the past two years. He had plenty of money to last for a while, that wasn't the issue. It was more a feeling that he couldn't do without the rush of the job, the thrill of the hunt, the quiet satisfaction when all the pieces came together. But now, looking at his wife, a different kind of satisfaction began to set in.

"I love you," he said in a soft voice.

"I love you, too," his wife said as she stood. "Go. And be careful."

She kissed him on the cheek and wiped the moisture away with a thumb. Alex smiled at her and followed with his eyes until she was gone from sight. Maybe I can do without the hunt, he thought, before turning again to the TV.

The smile disappeared.

"But not just yet," he said to the screen.

New York City

"What now, Alyson? Call to see if you can steal a few more ideas?"

"David, I'm sorry," she said.

It sounded sincere, but outside of certain parts of his body—the immature teenager parts somehow turned on at hearing her voice—most of David didn't care. He was bone tired and extremely cranky. Dealing with her was not on his to-do list.

"Whatever. Fuck you," he said.

There was a hesitation before Alyson's voice came back.

"I'm sorry," she said again; then after a pause. "Are you near a television?"

For reasons only Sigmund Freud could explain, an image of her naked body appeared in David's thoughts before he could answer. He quickly chased it away.

"Why, you running another report to fuck me over some more?" he said.

It took about twenty seconds for Alyson to explain. At first, David thought it was bullshit. That faded as soon as he saw the pictures of the fire. His next thought was that Alyson had something to do with the blaze, but he quickly tossed that aside as well. She might have been a razor-clawed succubus, but arsonist was too much of a stretch.

"Goddamn it," he said in a low voice; then after a pause. "Jesus, Alyson, why did you have to steal my story? It wasn't ready. You ruined—"

He stopped himself as Jason's warning came to mind.

"Alyson, *where are you?*" he said in a tight voice.

"I'm still at work," she said tentatively. "Why?"

David's mind raced through a new set of calculations. Of all the possibilities—call the police, call the FBI, call Thomas, call anyone with the capabilities to stop what he feared was happening—the answer he settled on was probably the worst.

"OK, stay there," he said. "I'm coming to get you."

"But—"

"*Just stay there,*" David said, cutting her off. "No matter what, do not leave."

"David—"

He was gone before she could finish. On her end, Alyson hung up and looked around. A few night-staffers were milling about, but the SNN studios were otherwise deserted. A chill raced down her spine. She shivered and wrapped her arms around her body, tightly. All at once she was cold.

"OK, sure, I'll stay."

Chapter 29

Philadelphia

The on-site Philadelphia Police commander was surprised to see the team of FBI agents.

"Crime scene?" he said to Alex. "Are you sure? It's too soon to tell if this was arson."

"Who said anything about *arson*?" Alex said. "And if I wasn't sure, we wouldn't be talking."

He handed the policeman a document. The man read for a few seconds.

"Wow... OK," he said. "What do you need from me?"

"I could use help with the perimeter," Alex said. "Try not to let anyone in or out without my say so. If fire and rescue needs to transport anyone, make sure I know where they're headed. Oh, and if there are any employees still hanging around, round 'em up. We need interviews pronto."

The commander moved off without objection. Alex turned and looked up at the building. He was near the end of the main walkway leading to the parking lot, approximately two hundred yards from the structure. Most of the flames were gone, but a few flickers remained and smoke continued to escape from the gaping holes that used to be windows. Firefighters could be seen and heard inside and around the structure.

"What a mess," he said. "Kinda makes you wonder, huh?"

The question was directed toward Carlos Santiago, standing alongside. The agent didn't respond at first. He was looking at a yellow tarp next to the walkway, about thirty yards closer to the building from where they stood. Alex adjusted his line of sight to match.

"Victim number one?" he said.

A slight shrug rippled across Carlos' shoulders.

"I'll go see," he said.

The round-trip took ninety seconds.

"Deceased male," Carlos said as he rejoined Alex. "It might be an employee, but there's no ID. There are some crates of office stuff next to him. First responders found him there, already dead."

Alex kept his eyes on the tarp.

"They say how?"

"Broken neck," Carlos said.

Alex turned. After a second, his head tilted and a frown worked onto his face.

"Broken neck?" he said. "So how the hell did he get out here?"

King of Prussia

"I'll be there ten minutes, tops," David said into his phone. "I'll call as soon as I hit the parking lot."

"OK," Alyson said. "I'll come—"

"Just wait for me to call first."

David closed the cell and slipped it back into the chest pocket of his jacket. Exactly two hours had passed since he'd left New York by car for King of Prussia. The drive was made shorter by the nagging thoughts he was making a mistake. Being a hero was one thing. Being an idiot was something else entirely. If he wasn't already the latter, rushing to Alyson's rescue instead of calling for help was probably the nail in the coffin.

He still wasn't sure why he was doing it.

Alyson had really screwed things up with her report. Besides messing up too many facts, the timing was all wrong. Things needed to be arranged, precautions needed to be taken. You don't just go off with accusations and incriminations without having all the castle walls properly secured. That kind of thing can get you hurt—or worse.

David had no desire to see anyone else hurt, but the fire seemed like too much of a coincidence. For him, it was a clear signal Alyson's story had touched the wrong nerves. The only question now was whether anyone else saw the signs. If so, well—David tried hard not to think about that, but it did make the last ten minutes of the drive seem more like a hundred.

"I'm here," he said after dialing Alyson again.

In front of him, the outer portion of the lot was empty, those working the night shift having elected to park closer to the building. David followed their lead and headed for a row of spaces to the left of the building's main entrance. Of the six visitor spots, only the one next to the walkway was occupied. He didn't dwell on the black Lincoln Navigator parked there—he pegged it as a car service—and hooked a right into one of the empties, two slots beyond.

That was his second mistake—if you count the mad dash from New York as the first. David wasn't counting, not yet anyway.

He killed the engine, gathered up his stuff, and waited for Alyson to appear in the lobby. From the front seat of the car, he could see two security guards standing behind a reception counter. He knew the burly cop-wannabes were the late-night substitution for the undoubtedly pretty-faced receptionist who manned the station during working hours. His office had a similar system; David relaxed a little.

That was his next mistake.

A minute later, Alyson came through a doorway behind the counter. Both guards followed her with their eyes. David shook his head at the disrespectful ogling as he stepped out of his car. At the same instant, both front doors of the Lincoln opened and two dark-skinned men emerged. As they started for the lobby doors, David hesitated. It took him too long to realize theirs were clearly not the movements of limo drivers.

That was his final mistake.

"Alyson, *NO*," he said in a shout as he started running for the doors. "Stay inside."

Alyson pushed through and stepped out onto the veranda.

"David?" she said.

The dark-skinned men were within fifteen feet of her. One of them, the one on her left, lifted something from beneath his jacket. The image added to Alyson's confusion and she froze.

"Run, goddamn it, *RUN*," David said in another shout.

The man on his right continued toward Alyson, but the other one stopped and turned. David tried to juke past, but his shoes slipped on the cement and he went down awkwardly. The man came forward and stood over him. His dark eyes chased the blood from David's face.

At the door, Alyson's reaction to the second man was similar. She screamed and ran back into the lobby. As both guards rushed forward, the man outside came to a stop at the door. While the guards tended to Alyson, he retreated to his partner. That man was smiling down at David, a gun in his hand pointed at the reporter's head.

"We must go," Shady said in a language David didn't understand.

"Who are you?" David said. "What do you want?"

Jamie's smile grew.

"We are the end, Mr. Donovan," he said in English. "You were warned."

Philadelphia

The police commander rejoined Alex under one of the tents set up in the parking lot. He was carrying a small notepad.

"Here's what I got," he said, reading. "Of twelve employees' statements, no one has any idea where their bosses might be. One did give me this though."

He handed Alex a single sheet of paper.

"Looks a little suspicious," the cop said. "You sure we're not lookin' at arson?"

Alex skimmed through the "abandon ship" email and a new frown formed on his face, the lines cutting deep into his skin. The cop understood. His face had similar lines.

"It might fit, but kind of extreme, no?" Alex said, shaking the sheet.

"Desperate people do stupid things," the policeman said.

"Yes they do," Alex said in a tired voice. "Thanks for your help, Commander. If you and your guys want to take off, go ahead. We can take it from here. Just make sure to leave any paperwork with my team."

"Sure thing," the other man said.

He shook hands with Alex before glancing back at the burned-out shell of a building.

"I'd say have fun, Director, but…"

His words faded into a shrug. Alex nodded.

"I hear ya," he said.

The commander stepped away, and Alex turned and stared up at the charred skeleton. The FBI contingent had grown by two hundred percent in the past six hours, inspired by the discovery of several dead bodies in what was left of the lobby. Unfortunately—or maybe fortunately, it remained to be seen—they were not the bodies Alex needed to find.

"Still no word from Bischoff or Adley?" he said to Carlos.

Carlos was standing just outside the cover of the tent. Several other agents nearby were logging pieces of evidence being brought out of the building. The first hints of sunrise were starting to peek over the horizon. High clouds added an orange-ish glow. It was beautiful, but not enough so to help Alex's mood.

"No answer by phone," Carlos said. "I'm not thinking they're still alive."

Alex couldn't disagree. He simply nodded as he did the math. Not far from where he and Carlos stood, similar men with similar responsibilities were having similar thoughts, and a buzzing sound signaled that those other men were about to add some complexity to Alex's equation.

"Harris," he said after fishing his cell from his jacket pocket.

Twenty seconds later and without another word, he closed the phone and slipped it back into the pocket. Carlos saw the increased annoyance on his boss' face.

"Sir?" he said.

Alex looked up and his head began to shake. After blowing out some air, he started moving away.

"C'mon, son, we just got someone else that's not still alive."

Chapter 30

King of Prussia

"Park there," Alex said as he pointed through the windshield.

Carlos guided the FBI cruiser behind two Upper Merion Township Police squad cars near the SNN entrance and killed the engine. He and Alex got out and looked around. A strand of yellow police tape was attached to a pillar and extended across the entryway to the far end of the Visitors parking area, just past a car there. On the protected side of the tape, halfway from the lobby doors, a yellow tarp rested on the ground. Alex ducked under the tape and headed in that direction. Carlos headed toward the doors.

"Go see what the guards have to say," Alex said. "I'll catch up in a minute."

Carlos nodded and went inside as Alex reached the tarp. The bumps in the plastic told him what lay beneath. An older-looking balding police officer was standing sentry.

"Director Harris," the officer said in a subdued tone. "Good to see you again. Wish it was under better circumstances."

"Same here," Alex said. "Mr. Donovan, I presume?"

He was motioning to the tarp. The officer nodded.

"Yes, sir," the cop said. "Single shot to the forehead."

Alex knelt and lifted an edge of the covering. A grimace quickly filled his face.

"Subtle," he said; then after a pause. "Whataya got in the way of witnesses?"

"Ms. Alyson Lane, reporter, and two night-duty guards, inside. All three gave statements. Mr. Donovan was here to meet Ms. Lane. They were intercepted by two assailants, black. Ms. Lane got back inside, but Mr. Donovan wasn't so lucky. Seems the guards decided against pursuit after seeing the shooting. Perps left in an SUV, but no one got the plates."

Alex lowered the tarp and stood.

"Where is Ms. Lane?" he said.

"Conference room upstairs, one of my guys is with her."

Alex glanced up at the building. He motioned to a half moon of black glass above the entry.

"We'll need the surveillance video," he said. "Can you see that my agent inside gets it?"

"Yeah, sure," the officer said. "So, you think this is related to that fire?"

Alex nodded.

"More than I'd like it to be."

Wayne

Sandy's plan was to start over and rethink everything. Gus Pappas being added to the mix, courtesy of Alex's requested favor from Thomas, was the reason. It was a new wrinkle to the reams of information she'd already accumulated. Somewhere in that data was a trail that led to an answer. It was a maze, but Sandy was very good at seek-and-find. Her father used to marvel at the speed with which she conquered the games. It made him proud.

Sandy loved making the man proud.

"OK, Daddy, I can solve this," she said aloud as she tucked away the memory.

She pulled a clean pad of legal-sized paper from a drawer in her desk. She grabbed a pencil from a collection stored in an old FBI coffee mug and started tapping the eraser on the paper. After a few seconds, she wrote *Dukabi* at the center top. Near the bottom, also centered, she drew a small box and put a question mark inside. The pencil went to her mouth, eraser side in, as she stared at the markings.

"It started with Dukabi," she said to the drawing. "So how do we get to today?"

She wrote *Today* below the little box. To the left of *Dukabi* she drew a short line. At the end of the line she wrote Jamie's and Shady's names. A tail was extended down from *Dukabi* and she labeled it *Booker Suicide*. She drew a short line up from there and wrote *Source*. A short tail was marked *Unexpected*. Left of center on the sheet she wrote *Pappas*.

The pencil then went to her mouth again as she sat back and eyed the schematic.

"Dukabi knew *something*, but the explosion was a surprise," she said. "Why?"

She clicked the pencil against her teeth for a few seconds. Over the next hour, she added more lines, headers, and comments until most of the yellow space was populated. That there were a fair number of question marks annoyed her. The exercise was supposed to answer questions, not add more. The marks meant something was missing, *a lot* of something. She hated when that happened.

"Damn," she said before sitting back and emitting a heavy sigh.

"Looks confusing," Thomas said from behind her shoulder.

Sandy jumped slightly from the sound of his voice.

"Geez, sneak around much?" she said after recovering. "Where did you come from?"

"My office," he said in his best flat tone. "Alex just called."

Sandy did an imitation of the eyebrow shrug, but it wasn't as cool as Thomas'. He ignored it, and reached down and touched a finger to the notepad, once on *Donovan* and then on *Bulge*. The hand retreated and Sandy turned with it to meet his eyes.

"Is an 'uh oh' in order?" she said.

Thomas nodded and pulled a chair up to the desk. She liked his proximity, but put it out of her mind. Duty called, and Thomas spent the next ten minutes reviewing the events taking place nearby. When he finished, Sandy added a few more notes to the schematic.

"Interesting approach," Thomas said. "Does it help?"

Sandy pulled the pad to her lap.

"I don't know," she said. "Ignoring what you just said, I was stuck trying to work out how Pappas fits. Now…"

She trailed off and shrugged.

"Start by telling me about Pappas," Thomas said.

Sandy sat forward and adjusted her bottom in the chair.

"OK," she said. "Santiago took me through all the official stuff. Pappas has some black marks on his record, but no ties to any of the players, at least none that are documented. Did Alex say why he wants us to look deeper at the man?"

"Nothing other than a gut feel," Thomas said.

Sandy's head bobbed for a few seconds.

"Facts would be better, but I trust him," she said.

She pointed to the chart again.

"Anyway, moving on," she said. "Booker committed suicide. Dukabi was surprised by the method more than the fact Booker was dead. That says he thought it was supposed to happen, but in a less destructive manner. Translation: Booker changed the plan. Question: Why?"

"Agreed," Thomas said. "What else?"

"Alex said Pappas was all hot and heavy about the explosion being a terrorist plot, but then, despite the tip, he doesn't bring Dukabi in. We don't need all six degrees of separation to get from Dukabi to any number of terrorist groups. A tip like that, you wring the shit out of it. Doing nothing says Pappas was covering. That's kinda scary in too many ways to count."

Thomas nodded.

"Agreed," he said again.

Sandy took a quick drink from a bottle of water before continuing.

"Next we have Mr. Coakley," she said. "Technically, he committed suicide in that he pulled the trigger on the gun stuck in his mouth, but we know someone else was there and probably helped it along. When the old folks got in the way, Coakley had time to get out that cure comment. That had to be on purpose. Just like Booker, he wanted someone to know what was going on. Turns out someone already did know."

She handed Thomas a piece of paper. It was a written version of Alyson's report.

"There has to be some truth in Lane's work. I think maybe Donovan must have realized that. It would explain why he was so adamant about her not leaving the office. Too bad we can't ask."

"That does add a level of difficulty, yes," Thomas said.

"Just a touch," Sandy said.

The sarcastic comment was more an aside than anything else, one of her traits. Thomas let it pass, like he usually did, and waited. She was looking at him and leaning back in the chair. He could tell she was thinking. After several seconds, she started stroking her hair with both hands—another trait Thomas never minded—but stopped short of tying up the locks this time.

"Donovan's pet peeve is steroids," she said. "We have the rumors about some new product. Booker and Coakley were known users in the past. Bulge and Bischoff are alleged suppliers. Booker owes Dukabi a lot of money. He tries to deliver a message of some sort but it gets messed up."

She stopped and took another shot of water. After the drink she eyed the note pad.

"I think Pappas was buying time until the situation got fixed. Coakley ends up dead in the interim, but then Lane's story comes out. It must have pricked a nerve or two or twenty because then Bischoff tries to run, his company gets burned to the ground and someone tries to end Lane and Donovan."

"Cleaning up loose ends," Thomas said.

Sandy nodded.

"Yeah," she said. "And I'm starting to think maybe our boys from Africa are the cleaners, the proverbial guns for hire."

"Is that another question?" Thomas said.

Sandy frowned as she looked at him.

"Yeah, I think so. As in: Who did the hiring?"

Chapter 31

Philadelphia

After a brief conversation at SNN, Alyson did not protest when Alex asked her to accompany him and Carlos back to the FBI office. They told her it was for her own safety, but she already understood. Someone had just tried to kill her. Explanations weren't necessary.

Once at the FBI building, Carlos showed her to a small interview room. Alex took up station on the other side of the room's two-way mirror. Both could see fear was clearly winning Alyson's battle of emotions. Her eyes were blinking rapidly, the movements interrupted every few seconds by the swipe of a tissue. Outside the loud sniffs and unsteady breaths, she'd been mostly quiet.

"Are you sure there's not something I can get you?" Carlos said.

Alyson looked across the table between them. A fraction of a smile came and went on her lips before she shook her head.

"I'm OK," she said in a low voice.

Carlos glanced at the mirror with a slight shrug, an unspoken question to Alex as to whether he should continue. When there was no response, he refocused on Alyson.

"Ms. Lane, I need to ask a few more questions," he said.

There was another loud sniff before she replied.

"I know," she said.

Her voice was barely more than a whisper. Carlos resisted the urge to stop.

"Why was Mr. Donovan at your office?" he said.

"I told you. He was—he was coming to get me."

"And why was that?"

Alyson's eyes came up. They were red and watery. Carlos did his best to return an understanding expression. There was no way to know if it worked.

"I told him about the fire and he got—he seemed real upset," Alyson said.

"What was your relationship with Mr. Donovan?" Carlos said.

An emotion other than fear flashed across Alyson's features. Carlos—and Alex—caught it before it faded under a deep breath and loud exhale. Training told both men the sounds indicated she was about to make some sort of confession.

"We were working together on Booker and the other stuff. And then we were fucking. And then I stole David's work. And then... and now... *he's dead.*"

Carlos hesitated as he processed the words. They presented a few different directions in which he could take the questioning.

"Can you walk me through everything, starting with your first contact?" he said.

Alyson sniffed again and shifted her position in the chair. Another unsteady breath followed.

"That *was* everything," she said.

"Sorry, ma'am, my fault," Carlos said. "Let me be more specific. Why was Mr. Donovan upset about the fire? Did he give you a reason?"

Alyson wiped at her eyes.

"He said I messed everything up, my story did, I mean. He said he wasn't ready to go public. He didn't have all the pieces yet. I think he meant the fire was my fault."

"And that's when he said he would come and get you?"

Alyson nodded slightly.

"He was in New York. He said I should stay inside until he came. That's what I did."

Carlos gave another understanding nod.

"Go on, ma'am," he said. "Then what happened?"

"When he, uh, called—I mean when he got here, to my office, he called and I came down to let him in. That's when I saw the two men."

She looked away and held back a sob. After recovering, she turned back to Carlos.

"Can you describe the men?" the agent said.

"They were dark," Alyson said.

"Can you be more specific?"

"Their faces, their skin, their hair, their clothes, it was all dark, jet black dark. It—*they* were really scary."

On his side of the glass, Alex turned to another agent there.

"Set up the safe house," he said. "As soon as this is over, I want her tucked away."

The agent nodded and left Alex alone in the dark room. He turned back as Alyson continued.

"David tried to stop them. I think they wanted to kill me, too."

The sobs came again and she could not keep them at bay. Carlos turned to the glass and shook his head. A second later, his phone beeped once, a signal from Alex he should stop.

"Just stay here, ma'am," Carlos said. "I'll get you some water. I'll be right back."

Alex was waiting for him in the hallway outside the door.

"We need to know what Donovan knew," he said. "Get to New York. I'll start the paperwork. Whatever he had is still there. We need to find it before someone else does."

Wayne

Thomas looked up when Sandy stuck her head into his office. He was on the phone with Alex. He set the receiver on the desk and pushed a button to activate the speaker. Sandy took a few steps inside the doorway.

"Ms. Hood appears to have something to share."

"Hey, kiddo," Alex's voice said into the room.

His tone was such that Thomas expected a reaction from Sandy. One came, but it wasn't positive.

"Dukabi is gone," Sandy said in a tight voice.

"*What?*" Alex said through the speaker. "Hang on."

For no other reason than he was who he was, Dukabi had been the first name on the list of potential hiring parties Sandy and Thomas compiled. His running might confirm they'd been correct. It might also mean something else.

"He's gonna be pissed," Sandy said as she moved the rest of the way into the office and sat.

"I believe he is already there," Thomas said.

Alex's voice returned a minute later and confirmed it.

"I'm going to have to call you guys back."

"What happened?" Sandy said.

"I don't know, but you're right, we lost him."

The line went dead. Thomas returned the receiver to the base.

"I called the numbers Dukabi left us, all of them," Sandy said. "They're all disconnected. My gal pal at FBI dispatch hooked me up with the surveillance team. When they went up to the apartment to check, it was empty."

Thomas nodded and the steeple appeared, but Sandy stepped on his thoughts.

"Is he running or being chased?" she said.

Thomas moved the tip of the steeple enough so he could speak over it.

"Based on today's events, I have no idea."

Los Angeles

Distracted by Bischoff's phone call before the game, Travis suffered an oh-for-four clunker—low-lighted by three strikeouts— that helped push the Dodgers another game further back of the Mets in the standings. Things were unraveling faster than a worn out baseball losing its cover, and the news of the fire at Bulge pulled loose a few more threads. Travis wasn't sure there was a needle big enough or strong enough to fix the tattered mess.

Not wanting to talk to the press or anyone else, he retreated to the trainer's room after the game. A few teammates and team personnel came and went, but were sufficiently deterred by the nasty scowl on his face to not bother him. Now, three hours later and still alone, the scowl was gone, replaced by the concerned look of someone afraid of what they saw.

For Travis, it was his right hand. It was shaking, not violently so, but enough to add to his increasingly fragile state-of-mind. The steady flow of sweat coming from every pore wasn't helping. Some might guess the symptoms were those of the early stages of the flu. They'd be wrong. Travis was sick and it was painful, but it was no flu.

Worse yet, just as Mike Coakley had said, there was no cure.

Philadelphia

"Take me through it again," Alex said in a dejected tone.

He was at Dukabi's apartment, standing with the two agents who had been on watch duty there, but that was only part of the reason for the tone. Carlos' trip to New York was almost as bothersome. Ideally, Alex would have asked for and received help from the NYC office in the confiscation of David Donovan's materials. After all the attendant paperwork was secured, the simple request would have been handled without question. People had died, answers were needed. Enough said.

Only Alex didn't ask for help. The suspicion that Pappas was somehow involved in a bad way kept him from making the request. That was why he'd sent Carlos to retrieve the materials instead. He would ask for aid only after getting the word from Alex. No one in New York was to be told of the latest Dukabi development. Alex was handling that directly.

From all appearances, the big man had departed in a hurry, which might explain how he slipped out unseen. Of course, it could have been that the two agents were useless morons because the mass of humanity that was Dikembe Dukabi would be hard pressed to *slip* past anyone.

"You said he got a phone call," Alex said to one of the agents. "What time?"

The agent checked a notepad.

"Eleven-twenty P.M.," he said. "The call lasted eighteen seconds. We didn't get a trace."

Alex's brow knitted as his brain worked on the math. It fit, but didn't equate to good or bad.

"What else?" he said.

The second agent answered.

"The motion detectors stopped an hour later. We figured he went to bed. It made sense."

Alex thought about that and took back his mean thoughts about the men's intelligence. These guys weren't dumb, they'd just been duped—like a lot of people, Alex included.

"I wish the rest of the past four weeks made some sense."

Wayne

"Whataya think?" Sandy said. "Is Dukabi outside looking in or inside looking out?"

"Half-full or half-empty," Thomas said.

"I always look at it directionally," Sandy said.

An eyebrow shrug from Thomas led her to explain.

"If you're pouring something *into* the glass, it gets half-full. If you're drinking *from* the glass, it gets half-empty. It depends on direction, on perspective."

"And if you enter the room and the glass is already there?"

"You find out who left it," Sandy said.

"Precisely," Thomas said.

"OK," Sandy said, drawing out the letters. "I think I get where you're going. We need to start polling the other partygoers on the source of the glass before they all leave, maybe make our presence more noticeable?"

"Everyone likes to be noticed."

Manhattan

"What's this here?"

Gus was at his desk, pointing at something. His assistant was standing next to him. A form was in front of them on the table, the nightly activity roster. Gus was supposed to review and approve the form. It was mostly meaningless government paperwork—mostly.

"Help on a search," the assistant said.

"What search?" Gus said. "Who needed help?"

The assistant leaned in and read the other information on the line in question.

"Agent Santiago from Philadelphia made the request."

Gus did his best not to react.

"What kinda search?" he said.

Outside of New York, someone hearing the tone in the words might have questioned the excessive amount of attitude. As it was, the assistant didn't notice. His tone was about the same. It was a New York thing.

"That reporter, Donovan," the assistant said. "There was a warrant issued for his office and apartment. Four guys went to help."

"*Motherfucker*," Gus said in a mumble before recovering. "Fine… Here… *Go*."

He scratched his name on the form and the assistant scooped it up and headed out. Gus waited until the man was gone before opening a drawer on the right side of his desk and pulling out a cell phone. No one would be tracing anything said on this device.

"You said I should let you know if something comes up. It just did and it ain't good."

Los Angeles

"Hey, Mr. Mackenzie, are you stayin' all night or what? I'm supposed to lock up soon."

Travis slowly opened his eyes. Standing above him was a familiar face, a guard from stadium security. Travis didn't know the man's name. That was the case for most people he encountered. It wasn't a problem he worried about. They all knew *his* name.

"Shit… sorry," he said as he sat up and stretched. "I guess I dozed off."

The guard offered up a disinterested shrug.

"Whatever," he said. "I gotta let the front desk guys know when you're planning on leaving before I go home."

Travis was still in his uniform pants, but his upper body was unclad. He'd given up the fight against the sweat and discarded his shirt, going with a series of towels instead. The guard noticed the pile on the floor as Travis slid off the table.

"Hey, man, you sick or somethin'?" he said.

Travis grabbed a fresh towel from a stand behind the table and wiped his face and chest.

"One of the guys gave me his cold," he said. "No biggie."

The guard nodded.

"Another reason for you to go home," he said.

Travis forced a smile.

"All right, I get it," he said. "I'm leaving. Give me five minutes."

Travis followed the other man from the room, making sure to stay behind to prevent sight of the still-shaking hand. At his locker, he changed into a warm-up suit and jammed the rest of his clothes into a duffle bag. A minute later, he was in his car in the parking lot. After starting the engine, he closed his eyes and let his head fall against the cool glass of the driver-side door.

It wasn't long before an image of Mike Coakley took shape in his mind. Then there was another face, Eddie's. Then Bischoff's came. All were distorted, Travis' subconscious take on the damage done by the suicides and other forces. He opened his eyes and the faces evaporated, the trembling hand taking their place as he stared.

"Sorry Mike," he said in a soft voice. "Guess you were right."

He sat there for a long time, flexing the hand in and out of a fist. He thought about the first time he'd played baseball, with his father, as a toddler. They'd lived in a small two-bedroom apartment, but used the common ground grass area between buildings in the complex as their field. A Frisbee and some other toys served as bases. Travis had an over-sized plastic bat. It made a *whoomp* sound when it connected with whatever ball they might be using that day.

His father was so animated during the games, always adding a colorful play-by-play soundtrack to the action. When the old man died—Travis was eight—he took away more than his son's innocence. Something broke inside. Maybe it was from the realization nothing lasts forever. Maybe it was just what happens to everyone when their parents leave. Whatever the reason, the damage cut deep, and Travis never looked at the game the same after that.

It became less about fun. He took to playing with anger. Some would mistake the anger for passion, for love. Travis no longer felt love, not the way most people did. The anger was nothing more than that, a hatred for what he'd lost, for what had been taken away. His sole focus became to never lose anything again. It was why he worked harder than every other kid and then every other teammate over the years. It was why he had cheated.

The need for more was fed by the hatred, the hatred by the need for more.

As he sat there in the cold car, something inside broke again— or maybe it un-broke. He looked up, a new face in his mind's eye.

"I'm sorry Dad," he said. "But I can still fix this."

Chapter 32

Philadelphia

FBI investigators finished their initial pass through the rubble of the Bulge fire late the following afternoon. The preliminary report showed the blaze had been caused by a series of explosions throughout the building, courtesy of C-4 charges. It would take a few more days to verify that the compound was from the same batch used in Eddie Booker's suicide device.

In the meantime, there was plenty more in the report to keep Alex and his teams occupied. Seven bodies were pulled from the building, to go with the accountant that had been discovered on the walkway. Of those from inside, four were found in or near the main lobby, one was dug out of what was left of Bischoff's office, and the final two were discovered in the sub-levels.

None of the victims had died from the flames.

The four in the lobby were the entirety of the Bulge security team. Two of the bulky men were killed by single gunshots to the head, the other two from blunt trauma and hemorrhaging consistent with damage caused by a machete. The last two had injuries on their forearms, indicating they had tried to protect themselves from the blows.

The body in Bischoff's office was, in fact, Bischoff. Cause of death was a single gaping wound across the stomach, also likely from a machete. In essence, he'd been disemboweled. Alex had witnessed similar attacks during his time in the Marines. He knew, if done correctly, the victim would see the damage before dying, adding to the torturous effect.

He shook off the memory and refocused on the report.

The man found along the walkway had died from a broken neck, as first assumed. From the severity of the injuries and pooling of blood in the body, it was determined he'd been killed at or near the spot at which he was found. The medical examiner concluded someone intercepted him there, killed him, and posed the body to delay detection.

That theory was supported by the fact the man's ID badge was found in the lobby near the dead guards. Evidence there suggested the guards realized the face—or faces—didn't match the ID. Despite a two-to-one advantage, Alex knew they never had a chance anyway.

He stopped reading again and took a drink of coffee from a mug near his phone.

"What a goddamned mess," he said under his breath after swallowing.

The final section of the report centered on the bodies found in the sub-levels. The first one, a production floor supervisor, was found at the foot of the fire stairs in front of the door leading to the lab. Bruising led the ME to a conclusion the man had fallen down the stairs backwards, the fall greatly assisted by a single gunshot to the forehead.

The second body was the more important discovery, that of Jason Adley. He was found in the hallway outside what was left of the lab. The Halon-gas system there had triggered and protected the area from the flames, but the gas was not what killed Jason. At some point after the system fired, the lab had been opened again and thoroughly searched. Based on the damage to both the furnishings and Jason—he'd been decapitated—it appeared the intruders did not find that which they sought.

Alex knew why.

He looked away from the report and eyed a plastic evidence bag resting near the mug on his desk. Inside the zip-bag was a small metallic item, its casing smeared with bile created from whatever Jason had last eaten. The piece of plastic—a computer flash-drive—was found in the doctor's stomach. Alex figured it must have been hard to swallow, especially under the obvious stress of the situation. Something like that probably gave the young doctor gas.

Staring at it now, it was doing the same to Alex.

New York City

Carlos' work procuring Donovan's property in New York was horribly delayed. The first glitch was because the laptop found in the reporter's car at SNN belonged to another reporter who forgot to remove it before David took the car. David's laptop was still in the docking station in his cubicle, but before Carlos could get at it, he had to wait for a resolution of the battle between the newspaper's legal team and the U.S. District Attorney's office as to what did or did not fall under First Amendment, Shield Law, and other legal protections afforded the media.

It was a frustrating wait, but it eventually paid off. The FBI won the arguments, helped along by another use of the Patriot Act, and Carlos found the golden ticket when he accessed David's email. In addition to the earlier correspondence, the Inbox had a new unread message from Jason Adley. The time stamp indicated it was sent after David left New York, but before Jason was killed. The attachment, a zip file, was encrypted, but Carlos deciphered the key courtesy of a simple note in the message body.

The Cure for what ails you is on this file.

An hour later, Carlos was on the phone with Alex, retelling the story.

"Say that again, Agent," Alex said.

"The password was T-H-E-C-U-R-E," Carlos said. "I'm pretty sure now that's what Coakley was talking about. It's some new designer steroid Bulge was working on. It looks like there were some problems and it didn't work. There's *a lot* of stuff in this file."

Alex glanced at the flash-drive on his desk. He could see *128 GB* under the smears. He knew enough about computer technology to know you can store a shitload of data in such space.

"I believe you," he said. "Looks like Adley knew the end was coming and wanted to make sure the info survived if he didn't."

"Donovan has a lot of other files as well," Carlos said. "He and Adley had a running dialogue. It's going to take some time to search through everything and sort this out."

Carlos was in an office a few floors below that of Gus Pappas.

"OK, listen," Alex said. "I'll get Sandy to help you. Just get back here as soon as you can. I don't trust that place."

"What the hell did you guys do?"

Jamie ignored the frantic undertones in The Boss' voice. He was sipping at a small cup of caffè e latte—simply latte in English—at a small coffee shop called Joe's on Waverly near 6th Avenue. Never one for the chain stores, Jamie enjoyed the shop's simplicity. In fact, it had been The Boss who had introduced him to it, and Jamie smiled at the irony.

Shady was with him at a small round table next to the shop's front window. He was reading from a pocket-sized English dictionary. Always practicing, Jamie thought, as he watched his friend. After several seconds, he returned his attention to the phone. He set the cup back on the saucer and adjusted his position, turning further away from those sitting nearby.

"We have done what you asked," he said. "Do not question my actions."

"*Are you insane?*" The Boss said. "I'll question whatever I want. I'm paying you."

Jamie took another sip of coffee.

"You would be wise to refrain from further insults," he said.

A pause followed. Jamie used it to finish off the last of the brew.

"Did you at least get the files?" The Boss said.

Jamie adjusted again and re-crossed his legs.

"We did not," he said. "We have their location. I expect to retrieve them shortly."

There was another pause.

"Do you think maybe you could do it without killing anyone else?"

Jamie let The Boss' words percolate for a few seconds as he watched a parade of pedestrians pass by the glass. A man trying to get to the door of the shop was bumped several times before succeeding. Jamie smiled. With so many people, some were always bound to get in the way.

He refocused on the phone.

"I make no promises."

Carlos signed off for the materials recovered from David's office and apartment and watched the courier disappear with the cart of boxes. He wasn't worried about Alex's warning. The good stuff, David's laptop and notes, was still in his possession—in a backpack Carlos carried—and would remain so until he made it back to Philadelphia.

After leaving the FBI office, he took the Q subway back to Penn Station, a trip that took about twenty minutes. It was after the evening rush, but not so late as to have missed the last Amtrak options back to Philadelphia. After checking the departure schedule, he made his way to the ticket counter. He was jazzed up by the findings. The trip had been a productive effort, not only after the delays, but before as well. Alex was going to be pleased with the harvest. The fruits included answers to some of the questions regarding Gus Pappas.

Carlos was thinking about that as he waited his turn in line. It was probably why he failed to notice the two men eyeing him closely from a nearby bench. When he moved forward to one of the ticket windows, the two men moved into the waiting queue. A minute or so after Carlos finished and stepped away, the two men took their turn at the same teller.

"Good evening, ma'am," Jamie said in a pleasant tone. "Two tickets for the same train as that previous young man please."

The woman backed away from the glass and gave Jamie a skeptical glance. A few seconds passed before she leaned forward again.

"You boys FBI, too?" she said. "I'll give ya the discount, if so."

Jamie smiled and nodded his head ever-so-slightly.

"That would be most generous," he said.

There was no request for ID. The clerk simply prepared the tickets.

"What's with him?" she said as she worked.

She was motioning to Shady. He was ignoring her, his focus fixed on Carlos.

"He is working," Jamie said.

The clerk chuckled and slid two tickets under the glass.

"Whatever that means," she said.

Jamie smiled again and thanked her. A minute later, he and Shady found Carlos near the top of the steps leading to the track for Train 187, the Northeast Regional for Philadelphia, leaving at 9:05 PM. The trip would take approximately an hour and twenty-five minutes.

That was plenty of time.

Chapter 33

Los Angeles

Fifteen minutes before I was supposed to head down to the field for my game, my cell phone beeped. It was my dad.

"What happened?" I said.

My tone came out annoyed, but it was an innocent mistake. I was already in game mode. My dad understood. He was familiar with my mistakes—too familiar actually. He and my mother had become unwilling participants in the mess caused by Andrew Singer when the psycho used their house and my old RV as part of his madness. My mom still wasn't over it. She wasn't ever going to be over it.

"You're gonna be home soon, right?" my dad said.

"Yes," I said very slowly. "Why?"

"We can talk about it when you get here."

"Great, now I'm going to be thinking about that all night. Don't be surprised if you see me on *SportsCenter* later because I screwed up a call or two."

He chuckled in my ear.

"We already see you on TV far too often."

"You're pretty funny, Dad."

"I know. Good-bye, Son."

After he was gone, I stared at the phone for a few seconds before stowing it back in my travel bag. My parents were great people and I loved them deeply, but something told me I wasn't going to like whatever they had to say. I hoped it wasn't bad, but at least I had a few days before they hit me with it.

Turns out I could have used the same luck after the game. That's when Travis Mackenzie hit me with something that left no doubt.

His stuff *was* bad.

North Jersey

"Technology Park is next," a voice said from behind Carlos.

He looked up at the conductor, then out the window. The train was pulling away from the Newark Airport stop. There were only two people out on the platform. Carlos turned back to the interior. It was pretty much the same inside. Amtrak wasn't making any money on this trip.

The media would have everyone believe the lack of travelers was a lingering effect of the bombing. There was some truth to that, but mostly it was nothing more than a case of timing. The earlier trains had been more crowded; that this one was not was merely a happenstance. Some would look back later and shrug it off as wrong place, wrong time.

Others wouldn't get that chance.

Carlos was sitting in a window seat, about mid-car in the second car from the end. He was facing forward, matching the direction of travel toward Philadelphia. In front of him, the backs of four heads could be seen. Carlos failed to recognize any of the heads, the first of several errors caused by the distraction of his work.

Aided by the quiet, he dove back into the notes as soon as the conductor moved away. Alex's urging to return to Philadelphia never really left his mind, but Carlos wasn't dwelling on it. What he was learning about the events of the past few weeks—as well as several occurrences in the months before—was more than enough to keep the director's warning relegated to the fringe.

That, too, was a mistake.

Just after the Trenton stop, a minute or two after ten P.M., Carlos stood. Out of habit and training he lifted the backpack—the contents were vital to the case in more ways than one—and carried it with him as he headed for the Snack Car. He had taken note of the other travelers, but had not necessarily focused on them, which is why he missed it when one of the others stood and followed.

After both disappeared through the cabin door, another passenger stood and moved to a seat behind where Carlos had been. None of the other riders seemed to notice or care about the movements, and it was another ten minutes or so before Carlos returned, carrying a small tray with a beverage and sandwich in both hands. The backpack was hanging from his right shoulder.

As he came through the door, the musical-chairs-playing passenger stood and moved into the aisle, blocking Carlos' approach. The two men smiled at each other with matching "OK, who needs to move?" expressions. Carlos lifted the tray in a shrug, a silent gesture to indicate he felt the load gave him right-of-way. The other passenger smiled and nodded, but did not move.

Carlos took a peek back over his shoulder and saw his reverse path now blocked as well, by a bigger man. A second, longer look revealed it to be a face he recognized. As his head came back around, it dropped and he closed his eyes. Within seconds, as the realization set in, everything good from his earlier efforts disappeared and his expression darkened.

"Idiot."

Said in barely more than a whisper, the single word, an expression of disappointment at the mistakes he now saw but could no longer correct, faded quickly. The errors were confirmed when his ears caught another sound, also from behind. Like the face, he recognized it immediately. He wanted to shout out a warning, but as he turned, he saw that the other two civilians in the car were already as dead as he was about to be.

A heavy sigh escaped his lips as he prepared for the end. His last thought was of Alex, his last words, an apology.

"Sorry boss…"

~*~*~*~*~*~*~

Philadelphia

In the wait for Wilmington-bound travelers on the platform beneath 30th Street Station, the conductor working the rear compartments happened to glance back in at the passengers in the second-to-last car. The different angle revealed something he'd missed moments earlier, a detail on a female rider with her head propped against the window.

On his quick pass down the aisle, the conductor had thought the woman asleep. The new view told him otherwise, and he rushed back inside. There was a trickle of blood coming from the corner of the woman's mouth. After finding no pulse, he shouted for help from the other person in the car, but there was no response. It took but a second to realize that man was dead as well.

Twenty minutes later, the station was closed and all trains in and out, including the commuter lines, were halted. The exits were sealed and Philadelphia and Amtrak police officers rounded up every passenger and worker still in the building—as well as a handful pulled back in from the streets nearby—and ushered all of them into rooms on the upper levels of the building near the administration offices for questioning.

Carlos' body wasn't found until a half-hour after the first FBI team arrived. The agent was in the cabin's restroom, posed on the toilet. The oversight in finding him was only slightly less disturbing than the indignity of the setting. The manner of death was worse. Unlike the two others, killed by single silenced gunshots at close range, Carlos had died from a machete blow to the head. The blade had shattered the skull and impacted the brain, killing him instantly.

The sight of the young agent's lifeless body was made worse by the fact the backpack was missing. All of it added more layers of crap to Alex's growing problems, but at the top of the pile was the fact Carlos had been followed from New York, meaning someone there knew what he had found and what he was carrying back.

"Let's get him out of there," Alex said.

The bark was directed at everyone and no one in particular as Alex stepped back to the platform. The dampness and darkness of the underground cavern was a mirror of his emotions. Only a certain kind of bad guy could so nonchalantly murder a federal agent. It required a complete lack of fear. Not the "he's so brave" kind of fearlessness, but something else, something ruthless and sinister.

Alex knew plenty of the fearless-brave types from his Marine days. He also knew a lot of the other kind, the sick fucks with nothing left in their souls but evil, people able to inflict suffering with no remorse. Damien Hastings and Sandy's sister had fallen victim to one, and now, so had young Agent Santiago and the other passengers on the train. That knowledge didn't sit well with Alex. More than anything, it meant all bets were off.

But Alex was OK with that.

He could be a ruthless son-of-a-bitch, too.

Chapter 34

Wayne

"We'll meet you there," Thomas said.

He closed the phone and walked down the hall to Sandy's office. She was still wrestling with her suspect chart, but the sight of Thomas at the door caused a head tilt and narrowed eyes.

"Oh boy, I think I know that look," she said. "What now?"

"Agent Santiago is dead."

Sandy stared at him for a few seconds before her head dropped into her hands. Thomas moved closer and put one of his on her shoulder.

"We need to go," he said. "Alex needs our help."

Sandy's head stayed down for about fifteen seconds. When it came up again, Thomas saw a look he'd last seen several years ago, in the moments after Damien Hastings had been killed. He'd also been seeing it on himself every morning lately. For him, it was a reflection of the anger growing inside, from knowing he'd had the chance to stop all of this long ago.

Dukabi shouldn't have been turned, he should have been killed. The bullet to the leg should have been delivered to a vital organ instead, inflicting an injury from which the man would suffer and whither and die, just like the villagers had suffered and died, just like Sandy's sister and the other victims of Andrew Singer, just like Damien and now Carlos, just like too many over the years.

"This changes things," Sandy said in a low voice, kicking Thomas loose from the memories.

He looked down at her and nodded. She was in pain and he wanted to do more, but now was not the time. Instead, he made a silent vow to make it stop, if not for him, at least for her.

"Yes, the rules have changed," he said.

Sandy stood and locked eyes with him.

"Goddamn right they have."

Los Angeles

"*Fuck.*"

The shout was followed by the sound of Travis' cell phone slamming to the island counter in the kitchen in his four-thousand-square-foot Santa Monica home. A single person had no real need for so much space. It was excessive and impractical, just like Travis. He and practical had never met. Such traits, both possessed and lacking, were a big part of his present condition.

Had he bothered to check the news—ever—he would already know why no one from Bulge was answering the repeated calls. Sure, Bischoff mentioned the problem with "The Cure," but he didn't say anything about disappearing. And where the hell was Adley? If anyone would know what to do, how to fix things, it was the nerdy doctor. But where was everyone?

Travis turned from the island and stared out the windows toward the ocean. A low-lying fog clung to the beach and water, turning the usual beauty into something that looked like shit. It was fitting because that's how Travis felt as he reached up and wiped another hefty dose of sweat from his brow before turning away from the glass. He needed help, but where to find it remained disturbingly unanswered.

That problem was about to get a lot worse.

Philadelphia

The trip to 30th Street Station didn't take long. Thomas was a skilled driver and fine-car aficionado. Despite the means to do so, however, he never possessed more than one at a time. His latest was a black 2010 Mercedes E550 sedan. Sandy loved both the driving skills and the vehicles in which they were displayed, especially this one, but neither fact mattered at the moment. Her thoughts were elsewhere, on trying to find the answers to the latest seek-and-find.

"It had to be Ibori and his partner," she said.

It came out like a question. Thomas let her answer it without any help.

"They had to be after whatever Carlos found in Donovan's files. But how did they know?"

She was staring out the windshield. The E550 was in the left lane, exceeding the recommended speed limit by nearly double. Like the blur that was the passing landscape, Sandy didn't notice. Her mind was racing almost as fast, the anger keeping most things at bay.

"Alex sent him because he didn't trust Pappas. That makes the fat fuck suspect number one."

She looked up just as Thomas made a subtle move of the steering wheel. The car danced in a smooth arc around a slower left-lane driver. The maneuver barely registered.

"We gotta figure out who was on that phone call with the Dukabi tip," Sandy said.

She shook her head slightly before turning toward Thomas. Her knitted brow told him she was still calculating. He remained silent.

"Don't you think?" she said. "That's gotta be where we find whoever's driving this bus."

"Or at least the location of the next stop," Thomas said without looking at her.

"Good point."

Los Angeles

There was a bathroom down the hall from the kitchen, not more than ten feet away, but Travis barely made it before puking. The majority of the vomit splashed into the toilet bowl, but a few chunks hit the wall as others fell to the floor. Being a regular visitor to the Porcelain God, thanks to his proclivity for partying, the sight of regurgitated food didn't normally bother Travis, but something in this latest batch was both unfamiliar and alarming.

"What the fuck?" he said to the mess.

He slumped back against the wall facing the toilet and tried to remember everything he'd ingested in the past twenty-four hours. Nothing red came to mind, further supporting the notion he was bleeding internally. Those thoughts were helped after a painful burp pushed another small batch of something into his mouth. He leaned forward and spit into the bowl, producing another blotch of blood. He slumped back again.

The coldness of the tiles against his damp skin felt good and he stayed there, unmoving, trying to regroup. After a minute or so, he reached up to a rod above his head and pulled down one of the towels. He wiped at his mouth and chin before using the towel to remove the latest round of sweat. Slowly, his body settled, but it was another few minutes before he fished his phone from his pocket.

"C'mon, Jason, answer the fucking phone already," he said as he waited for the call to connect. "You'll know what to do."

New York

Gabi rolled over and stared at the glowing blue numbers on the nightstand. It took his brain a few seconds to translate, but the answer eventually came to him: Too fucking early. He snatched up the ringing phone lying in front of the clock and pulled it to his face.

"What?" he said in a groggy, but pointed tone.

"Hey, man, I need some help," Travis said.

Gabi almost didn't recognize the voice at first. The usual hubris was missing, replaced by what sounded to Gabi like serious pain. He didn't doubt that. Nor did he care.

"How can *I* help you, Travis?" he said.

There was something of a groan over the line. Gabi pushed himself up to an elbow.

"It sounds like you need a doctor," he said.

"Yeah, no shit," Travis said. "But I can't find the right one."

Gabi got the message and sat up all the way, putting his back against the headboard. His grogginess was gone, replaced by a different kind of emotion.

"And why would I care about that, Travis?" he said.

The ballplayer ignored the bite behind the words.

"Cut the shit, Loeb," he said. "Where the fuck is Jason? He isn't answering my calls."

Gabi looked around the bedroom for a few seconds. Despite the darkness, his mood was brightened by Travis' dilemma.

"You really don't know do you?" he said.

"Know *what*?" Travis said.

Gabi chuckled.

"Adley is dead."

Philadelphia

It didn't take long for the lack of service at 30th Street to wreak havoc on the morning commute. Alex didn't care. No one was getting anywhere near the station until he had some answers as to what had happened on Train 187. The riding public could raise the shit storm of all shit storms. The media could espouse whatever rumors they wanted. None of it was going to change his position until the mess was cleaned up.

He found himself hoping Thomas and Sandy had come with the mops.

"Thanks for coming," he said to Thomas. "I'm hurting here."

The two men were sitting with Sandy on a bench near the Angel of Resurrection statue at the eastern end of the concourse. The angel lifting a fallen soldier was crafted in honor of the Pennsylvania Railroad employees killed in military service during WWII. For Alex, it was a reminder of his fallen soldiers, Carlos being the latest.

"What can we do?" Thomas said.

"Doctor Adley and David Donovan traded a bunch of messages," Alex said. "The last came a few minutes before Adley lost his head in the fire—shit, sorry... that was wrong. I'm tired."

Neither Thomas nor Sandy reacted. Alex recovered quickly.

"We're pretty sure Donovan never saw the last one," he said. "It supposedly had everything we needed to tie all the pieces together."

Thomas' eyebrow moved. Alex intercepted the question without waiting for the words.

"Supposedly because the files were in Carlos' backpack," he said. "Whoever killed him disappeared with it."

"I take it that means Ibori and Okonjo?" Sandy said.

Alex nodded.

"That's our guess," he said.

"Drastic measures to be sure," Thomas said. "We've been wondering how they knew."

"My guess is the answer to that question is in the data," Alex said.

He pulled a plastic bag from the inside pocket of his suit jacket and held it out so Thomas and Sandy could see the contents.

"I thought you said it was gone," Sandy said.

"Doctor Adley was kind enough to give us another copy," Alex said. "I don't trust anyone else at the office to look at it. That's where you come in."

He tossed the bag to Sandy. She caught it and turned it over in her hands. The flash drive had seen better days, but she wasn't deterred by its outward appearance.

"Where can I set up?" she said.

"That's my girl."

Chapter 35

Los Angeles

Travis stared at his laptop screen, finding it difficult to focus on any of the several browser windows open there. One had the story of the Bulge fire and deaths of the company's founders. Another had news about the murder of an FBI agent on a train in Philadelphia. A third had an article on the killing of David Donovan. Most people reading the words wouldn't catch the connections. Travis wished he was one of them.

"Jesus," he said to the pictures. "This shit is outta hand."

He closed the computer and pushed back from the desk. In the process, the promise to his father came back into his thoughts. It was time to act, to fix things. He looked away from the desk, toward a window along the back wall of the living room. Outside, the fog had cleared, the ocean was calm. If only I could be, Travis thought, as he stared out at the water.

The gaze lasted until a tiny beep from his wristwatch pulled his eyes away from the blue canvas. It was nine A.M., time to leave for Dodger Stadium and a pending afternoon game. He closed his eyes and tried to readjust his focus to baseball, but instead, an idea came, a solution for his problems.

"That just might—"

Whatever else he was going to say died when an odd pain rippled through his body. The new sensation was unlike any of the other symptoms he'd been experiencing. It knocked him back in the chair, where he folded over, groaning, as he closed his eyes tightly and did his best to ride out the spasms. In the effort, his mind went back to the episode in the bathroom and the blood.

"What the hell is this?" he said under his breath, through tightly clinched teeth.

It was several minutes before he was able to sit up. Another few passed before he could stand. Once he did, he began to try and work away the aches by stretching and twisting his body, movements similar to his pregame routine. Slowly, the discomfort and other physical manifestations of his illness faded, but they never left his mind. This better work, he thought, as he shook away the last of the pain. I'm seriously fucked if it doesn't.

Stable as he could hope to be, he started for the door, only to be interrupted by the sound of his cell phone. His first inkling was to ignore the call, but that changed when he saw the name on the caller ID.

"Haven't you done enough?" he said after pushing *OK*.

"I'm sorry Travis," Alyson said. "None of this is my fault."

Travis flashed on the locker room incident and subsequent interview—and the Internet pages from moments before. His jaw muscles began to work overtime, as if he had a mouthful of seeds. Too bad he couldn't spit out the bad taste Alyson's words had created.

"Right… you're Miss Fucking Innocent," he said; then after another pause. "Whataya want?"

The snap in the tone was caused as much by Alyson as from the earlier pain.

"I'm sorry," she said again. "I know you're angry with me, but I had to call. I think you're in danger."

Travis winced at a new spasm and looked down at his hand. The shakes were more pronounced than before. A scoffing noise escaped his lips.

"Shit, Lane, tell me something I don't know."

New York

Gabi was at his desk, staring toward the windows of his office. He wasn't seeing anything on the other side. His thoughts, like Marshall's, were locked in the struggle of how best to respond to Travis. The player needed help. Based on the contents of the early morning call, it was the kind of help Jason Adley might have been able to provide were he not dead. The implications of where Travis might turn instead were troubling.

"What's the latest?" a voice said from the doorway, interrupting those thoughts.

It was Mark. Gabi slowly turned from the window.

"Hey, you OK?" Mark said.

His eyes had narrowed into a look of concern. Gabi forced out a smile.

"Yeah, I'm good," he said. "I was, uh, just rebooting."

Mark nodded.

"If only it was that easy, huh?" he said.

"Sometimes it is," Gabi said. "So, what's up?"

Mark's eyes narrowed again as he moved into the office.

"No," he said, drawing out the word. "That's what I just asked you."

Gabi reinforced the phony smile as Mark landed in one of the chairs facing Gabi's desk.

"Yes you did," Gabi said. "Everything is quiet. I have a call into Alex to see if there's anything new. I haven't heard back. No news may be good news."

"I'm not sure it is," Mark said. "I'm thinking he's a little busy at the moment."

He passed several sheets across the desk, copies of the stories about Bulge, Donovan, and the murders on the train. None of it was news to Gabi, but his features slowly darkened anyway as he read. Mark noticed the change, but misinterpreted the meaning.

"I think you were right," he said. "This isn't about baseball."

Gabi looked up. The fake smile was gone.

"Lucky us," he said.

~*~*~*~*~*~*~

Philadelphia

Sandy's efforts on the zip drive hit a snag. Bodily fluids tended to be a harsh environment for sensitive electronics. Recovery wasn't impossible, but would require some tools not currently at her disposal. It would have been easier and more efficient to send the drive back to the office, but Alex did not want it out of his control. He sent an agent to fetch the tools instead. That left Sandy with time to kill, something she hated with a passion.

Her father had drilled the "idle hands" thing into her head as a kid. She still believed it, so she switched gears and launched a new search on her program, using everything Alex could remember about Carlos' work, including the password from Adley's email, hoping it would fill in some of the blanks. Carlos had said everything was linked, but never got the chance to prove it. Sandy was more than willing to give it a try. It was the least she could do for her friend.

As the program churned, she leaned back and let her mind wander. She was sitting in a commandeered cubicle near the Amtrak Customer Service desk. Most the staff was elsewhere, leaving the area quiet. The exception was a collection of managers, standing and chatting nearby. They'd been asked to remain on hand to provide help, a job that had mostly entailed staying out of the way.

They'd been doing a very good job of it.

One, a tall male, pulled away from the group and passed through Sandy's sightline. Without thinking, her eyes latched on and followed the man's movements. She wasn't really focusing on him, at least not until he passed under one of the security cameras attached to the wall. She probably wouldn't have noticed the camera had his head not almost crashed into the lens.

Sandy stood and shouted after the man.

"Hey, wait up."

The man turned. He looked bored. Sandy pointed to the camera.

"Where's the control room?" she said. "I need to check something."

Five minutes and a crash course on the Amtrak security camera system later, Sandy was left alone at the control panel in a small room at the back of the service area. She wasn't entirely sure what she was looking for. She had her notes opened in front of her, to the page with Eddie's activities on the day of the bombing. She wasn't sure why, but the manager's near-miss with the camera had kicked up something she hoped would reveal itself on the videos.

"OK, Eddie, talk to me," she said to the screens. "What were you trying to tell us? Why did you want us to stop you?"

Using the menu of available recordings, she navigated to the time of the package pick-up, minus one hour—the extra time in case the clerk's recordkeeping skills weren't as exacting as hers. She figured that would be long enough to catch the drop-off as well.

A couple of other commands brought the screen directly in front of her to life. She touched *Play*. The image was clear—Carlos would have been impressed with the quality. Before that memory derailed her, she tapped *Fast Forward* once and refocused.

The digital video took on a slide show look, and in just over fifteen real-time minutes, the entire two hours up to Eddie's appearance at the counter played out. As he moved away from the counter, bag in hand, Sandy touched *Pause* and sat back.

"OK, there's the pick-up," she said. "So where the hell was the damn drop off?"

She took a second to compare the screen clock to her notes, but before she could touch *Rewind*, to try again, her phone sounded, a call from the agent who had gone to fetch the tools needed for the zip drive. After telling him where to find her, she looked up at the screen again. Her head bobbed for a few seconds before she turned off the system and stood.

"Hmm, I guess you'll just have to wait," she said to the image.

Leaving the room, she found the bored manager loitering nearby.

"All finished?" he said in a close-to-dead voice.

"No," Sandy said. "Can you set up the entire morning for the same day?"

A nod-shrug managed to make it through the man's apathy.

"Sure," he said. "It'll take a few minutes."

"No rush," she said. "Call me when it's ready. Thanks."

She handed him one of her business cards and hustled off without waiting for a reply. The manager offered up another nod-shrug.

"I guess you're welcome."

~*~*~*~*~*~*~

"This might help," Thomas said.

He handed a large paper cup to Alex and sat down on the bench next to the director. Alex lifted the cup to his nose and took a deep breath. A smile worked onto his face.

"You're right, it does," he said.

Neither said another word for close to two minutes. They simply sat, sipping at the coffee and watching the harried movements around them. The police and FBI personnel had been mostly replaced by an onslaught of commuters, frantic in their attempts to make up for the lost time caused by the murders. It was as if that last point had failed to register on any of the travelers.

Alex shook his head at the collective ignorance.

"The shit people worry about," he said. "Goddamn selfish fucks."

Thomas didn't reply. He was more than willing to afford Alex the opportunity to vent for as long as necessary. His best guess was it wouldn't last. Alex confirmed that seconds later when he finished off the coffee and slammed the empty cup into a trash can.

"All right, enough of that," he said after wiping his hands on his slacks. "How do we stop this—whatever the hell this is?"

"Two reasonable questions," Thomas said.

"You got any reasonable answers?"

"It was a mistake," Thomas said.

Alex's eyes narrowed.

"*What* was a mistake?"

"Dukabi," Thomas said.

"What about him?"

"He's still alive."

"Is he?" Alex said. "It'd be nice to know for sure. Maybe he has the answers."

Thomas hesitated a few seconds before standing. Alex followed suit.

"Lead on my friend," he said. "The floor is yours."

Thomas' hands came together behind his back as the men started walking. He was the picture of calm, but Alex knew the man was deep in thought. He matched the stride, waiting for the expected gem, best guess, theory, or whatever it was his friend was about to put forth.

"I take it the explosives at the fire matched those used by Mr. Booker," Thomas said.

"They did," Alex said.

Thomas nodded, but didn't break stride.

"I take it there is little doubt Dukabi's former associates were responsible for the blaze and murders, including that of Agent Santiago."

"No doubt," Alex said. "We got 'em on video leaving here. They had the backpack."

Thomas nodded again.

"Dukabi's disappearance is troubling," he said. "It suggests he is not the leader of this parade. I believe Director Pappas knew that fact. I suspect the call he received was for something more than a tip, possibly instructions."

Alex's hand came out and touched Thomas' arm. They both stopped walking.

"That has a lot of bad connotations," Alex said.

"Indeed," Thomas said.

Alex's hand moved up to his face. For a minute or so the fingers played with the stubble that had popped out since his last shave— whenever that had been. He ended the movements with a sigh.

"Damn it," he said. "Pappas pushed the terrorism angle so he could keep things under wraps, so he could control it."

They were at the doors at the west end of the concourse. They turned to the right and began to walk again, up the slope leading to the suburban rail ticket windows and tracks. The crowd of pedestrians was thicker there, but neither seemed to notice.

"I agree," Thomas said after a few steps. "I missed it."

"We both did," Alex said.

"Understandable in your case," Thomas said. "You have rules to follow."

The words triggered something. Alex stopped and grabbed Thomas' arm again.

"Speaking of rules," he said. "While Carlos was waiting for the legal guys to finish dicking around, he told me he was going to recheck some of the other case files to pass the time, the original

Booker stuff. Those files would have included the full recording of the call—"

He stopped and his eyes got wide.

"Oh, shit," he said. "That fat son-of-a-bitch."

He turned and motioned for Thomas to follow.

"C'mon," he said. "We're going to New York."

"Yeah, yeah, go," Sandy said. "I should have something by time you get back."

"Call if that occurs sooner," Thomas said.

She pushed *End* and set the cell phone on the desk. After a deep breath, her concentration went back to the zip drive. The repair process she was attempting was very much like surgery. Her patient was in critical condition. One slip could be fatal—in a lot of ways. She blew out the air and tried not to think about it.

"Well, here goes nothing."

Chapter 36

Dodger Stadium, L.A.

After the bottom of the eighth inning ended, I wandered out into shallow left field to wait for the teams to switch sides. The Dodgers had pushed their lead to eight to one, having just scored five times. The win, if it held, would make two in a row. With the Mets having already lost, the playoff race was about to become a virtual dead heat. Things were definitely getting more interesting.

I had no idea just how much so.

"Yo, Connors," a voice said from somewhere behind me.

I turned to find Travis walking toward me. My first thought was that he looked awful. Not an "I'm having a really bad game" awful, but more like a walking-dead-zombie kind of thing. I think I might have backed up a step out of instinct.

"Geez, Trav," I said. "You look like shit."

He coughed. It was an old man sound, like the one my heavy-smoking grandfather used to make before dying of lung cancer. I winced from the memory as much as the goop Travis spit out as the sound faded.

"Are you OK?" I said.

He shook his head. Even that came across as painful to me.

"No," he said, confirming it. "That's why I need your help."

Until that moment, Travis had been near the top of the list of people, athletes or otherwise, that I couldn't see myself helping—ever. He and his kind were the epitome of everything wrong in sports, prima donnas who expected everyone to bow to their every whim. They had it all, but always wanted more. Worse, it was never about the game for guys like Travis. It was about them. And for that reason, part of me hated him.

Still, something in his eyes made me forget about the hatred for a moment.

"Travis?" I said, hesitantly. "Uh, dude, what's wrong? Are you sick? Let's get the trainer—"

"*No,*" he said sharply, cutting me off. "That ain't what I'm talking about."

He looked away to catch a warm-up toss from the center fielder. When he looked back, his expression had somehow intensified. I'd seen similar looks from Thomas, but usually wasn't sure what to make of them. Travis' version was no different. His next words didn't help.

"Just wait for me after the game," he said. "It's important."

He coughed again. If he was doing it on purpose, you know, for effect, it was working.

"Uhhh... OK," I said.

I think I added a shrug, but admittedly, I'm not sure. Confusion reigned supreme and I can only imagine what my face looked like as Travis moved off to finish his warm-up. Thankfully, I didn't have any calls in the top of the ninth. The Dodgers got three quick outs and the game ended without further incident. I left the field with my partners, but didn't mention Travis' request. I didn't understand it, explaining it to someone else would have been impossible.

When the other guys headed out to catch our flight to Philadelphia for the final weekend series, I made up an excuse about needing to run an errand, telling them I'd catch up at the airport. It never happened, again thanks to Travis.

We met in one of the team suites above the field. It took him about five minutes to tell me what he needed. Somehow, it seemed a lot longer.

"That's seriously fucked up," I said after he finished. "I, uh—I have no idea what to say."

I turned and stared out at the grass and dirt below us. I think the grounds crew was working on the diamond, maybe not. It wasn't important. How to respond to Travis was monopolizing my thoughts, and I'm not sure how much time went by before I turned back to him.

"How do I... uh... how am I supposed to react to all this?" I said.

He made the old-man's noise again. I wanted to say "knock it off" but didn't, because it had become clear that he was *not* faking. I think that's why it was so scary. It was too much like my grand-pap, as in "he made that noise and then died." I reached up and rubbed at my face for a second. Travis interrupted the movements.

"You can react by saying 'yes,'" he said, before spitting into a cup he was holding. "You said you'd help. This is the help I need."

What he was asking for was a Thomas-like *save the guy in trouble* scenario. The problem with that, besides the aforementioned fact I sucked as such things, was my being pretty sure Thomas was already doing it, working on the same thing, I mean.

"I don't know, Travis," I said. "Maybe we should call—"

"No, no calls," he said, cutting me off. "If you can't do it, I'll find another way."

I crossed my arms across my stomach. My left hand came up and I leaned into it. After a few seconds, I turned to him again.

"I didn't say I *wouldn't* do it," I said. "It's just—I know some people."

"*No,*" he said with more force. "I can't trust anyone else. Not now."

I thought about Thomas again. All it would take was a call—hell, a ping from the pager—and he'd be there for me, for Travis. I have no idea why I didn't just do that.

"OK, no calls," I said instead. "I'll help."

"Thanks," Travis said.

I kept my eyes on him as he turned toward the field. I realized I didn't know him, not really. Saying I hated him had been over the top. Sure, he often acted like an asshole, but like Thomas always said, it was probably best not to judge a book by its cover.

Sometimes you just had to trust that what was inside was worth it. Thomas knew a lot about trust.

I hoped he was right.

Philadelphia

"Don't you dare... son-of-a-bitch... *NO.*"

The agent helping Sandy wasn't sure how to react.

"What happened?" he said. "Did we lose it?"

Sandy ignored him as she scratched at her nose. OK, it was more like she was trying to rub the thing off her face. At least that's how it looked to the agent. His confusion grew.

"Ms. Hill, are you OK?"

Sandy sat back. Her hands went to her head and she grabbed hold of a lot of hair.

"*No,*" she said sharply. "I'm not OK. *Shit.*"

After a few seconds, she released the grip and sat forward again.

"Sorry, not your fault," she said, motioning toward the screen. "That's all we got."

The agent looked down. A green line had stopped about four-fifths of the way across the length of an indicator bar. The readout above it showed: *91%*.

"Maybe it's enough," the agent said.

Sandy heard it like a question. She looked at him.

"Yeah, maybe," she said. "And what happens if it's not?"

The hours to get to that point would be followed by several more to analyze the data. Luckily, the portion of the drive recovered included Jason Adley's experiment documentation.

The loop for the work was as follows: Step 1: Introduce steroid; Step 2: Observe reactions; Step 3: Document results; Step 4: Repeat Steps 1 thru 3. Step 4 was necessary because a sample of one wasn't acceptable, at least not for any reputable scientist. Results had to be reproduced until there was no doubt.

The doctor had performed forty procedures on his hamsters, counting the original injections and autopsies. Each step was meticulously detailed. Jason was able to successfully reproduce Step 3 every time through the loop. A video told the story. The message had been recorded several hours before his death. Sandy watched it on her laptop.

The doctor was seated at one of the lab's computers, staring into the PC's built-in camera. There were notes and other materials on the table in front of him. The flash drive was resting on top of the pile. Jason's expression and voice were those of a beaten man.

"My name is Doctor Jason Adley. I am—I was—half-owner and lead chemist for Bulge, Inc. My partner, the other half-owner, is Paul Bischoff. Mr. Bischoff is CEO. As both of us are no doubt soon to be arrested, I want this video to stand as my confession. It is being given under no duress and of my own free will. I hope it is taken as such. I will make multiple copies to ensure it survives should I not."

Jason picked up the flash drive and displayed it in front of the camera for several seconds before lowering it and continuing.

"Approximately two years ago I was asked by Mr. Bischoff to create a new product. Mr. Bischoff was of the opinion there was a huge market for this drug, a steroid that could not be detected. It was not the first such claim, but a recently developed process known as Dynamic Combinational Chemistry—or DCC—made the chances of success much greater. I understood such a product would be illegal in every sense of the word, but I deferred to Mr. Bischoff's wishes. I was wrong to do so..."

From there, Jason explained the early work and build-up to creating "The Cure." Sandy couldn't imagine anyone wanting to ingest such a creation, but knew enough about sports to realize why they would. After about twenty minutes, Jason reached the disturbing climax.

"As I have explained, DCC holds great potential for the scientific and medical communities, but I have disgraced that potential with my hideous concoction. The results speak for themselves. Every test subject has died. The Cure is an abomination and I have terminated all work on the project. I have destroyed the remaining project samples in my lab, but several vials remain unaccounted for. I believe Mr. Bischoff removed these samples without my knowledge. I also believe he may have distributed them to unsuspecting victims."

Sandy stopped the video and looked down at her notes, at the chart of names and events.

"Booker and Coakley," she said as she connected a few of the boxes. "Damn it, how did I miss that one? It totally makes sense."

She shook her head before pushing *Play* again. Jason continued.

"Animals do not commit suicide in the sense humans do. In this case, however, there are similarities. Death was a result of mental incapacity as much as physical deterioration caused by the steroid. If a human has ingested the substance, the same result is very likely. Treatment is possible, but some damage is likely permanent. I have included several suggested remedies in my files. Any competent medical doctor will know how to use the information to counteract the effects. They should be effective as long as they are delivered in a timely manner."

Sandy stopped the recording and again looked down at her notes. She used her pencil to circle *Bischoff*, *Booker*, and *Coakley*. After a few seconds, she began to tap the eraser on the paper. Her features slowly knitted into a frown.

"Shit," she said. "Are there more?"

New York

"Three minutes, sir," a voice said into Alex's ear.

He had used director's discretion to commandeer a helicopter to get to New York. Such actions were not his normal style, but the circumstances warranted the exception. Getting there faster was more practical than economical. An agent was dead and another might be behind it. Alex didn't much care if the pencil-pushers in the General Accounting Office understood.

"What do you think?" he said to Thomas through his headset. "Should we go in soft and sweet or use a sledgehammer?"

Thomas turned.

"I don't know the man well enough," he said. "It wouldn't be my place to decide."

"Right," Alex said. "Like that's ever stopped you."

Thomas shrugged his eyebrow before looking away. The New York skyline filled the view through the front window of the chopper. Liberty Island was off to the left side. Thomas had never been inside the statue. He thought about that. There were a lot of similar things he'd never done, kitschy family outing events he'd never experienced. Of course, it wasn't like his life to date had been empty. There'd been more than a fair share of memorable moments, just a few too many where you'd not want family involved.

But what was family anyway? He and his sister were the only two Hillsboroughs left. There were some distant cousins, but Thomas couldn't remember their names. Funny, he thought, *I know the name of every person I've killed, but not my relatives.* From there, his thoughts drifted to Marshall. The umpire was probably close enough to be considered family, but how much of the relationship was real? It was as much a result of a series of tragedies as it was a deep emotional bond.

The latter was there in a sense, driven by those tragedies, but it wasn't developed over time or nurtured by the day-to-day interactions of a "normal" life, the moments when you truly get a glimpse into someone's soul. Sure, the men could read each other better than others could, but what did that really mean? Were they nothing more than extremely observant? Was it merely a game, something played to substitute for a real connection? Was there *any* connection at all?

If not for the fire, their backgrounds, so vastly different, would likely have led each in directions never to have crossed. There's nothing bad in that, like the forgotten names. It's just how life worked sometimes. But their paths did cross, and Thomas would never give up his belief that there were no coincidences in life. Whatever it was, however it had happened, it meant *something.*

He turned back to Alex.

"I suggest the latter option," he said.

Alex smiled.

"Yeah, I thought you would."

Gus was about to leave for the day when he heard a commotion outside his office. He started to lean sideways in his chair to get a better look through the doorway when his assistant appeared there.

"Sir, Director Harris is here—"

The woman didn't finish before Alex exploded into the office behind her, Thomas in tow.

"What the fuck?" Gus said as he stood. "You can't just—"

"Sit down, Pappas," Alex said, cutting him off.

The tone was one Thomas had not heard in a long time, Alex's version of a sledgehammer. He'd almost forgotten how devastating it could be, and Gus' reaction was about as expected. He started shooting daggers with his eyes across the desk at Alex, but when Alex didn't bend, Gus redirected the gaze toward Thomas. It had even less impact there.

"What are *you* looking at?" Gus said to Thomas. "Do I even fuckin' know you?"

Thomas shrugged an eyebrow, but the verbal reply came from Alex.

"*Sit. Down. Now,*" he said.

Gus' eyes got wider as he looked back and forth at his guests. His jaw muscles were working overtime and sweat was streaking down his puffy jowls. After about five seconds, he stopped chewing and plopped back into his chair. The renewed burden of supporting the excess poundage caused the worn seat to creak out a loud complaint. Gus' bitching was almost as loud.

"Fine, I'm sitting," he said. "Now, you gonna explain this or do I have to guess?"

Alex moved to the front edge of the desk, but did not sit.

"Just tell me *why*," he said.

Each word had a bite, but the last took the biggest chunk. Gus seemed to shrink a little.

"I have no idea what you're talking about," he said.

Thomas picked up at least seven micro-expressions in Gus' features. His eyebrow shrugged again. Gus caught it and turned from Alex.

"OK, enough of this shit," he said in Thomas' direction. "Who *are* you?"

"My name is Thomas Hillsborough."

Gus' face went white and he farted. It wasn't funny, but a wry smile filled Alex's face anyway. He was pretty sure some shit had escaped with the gas. If not, it was about to, which had been the outcome he'd been going for. Sledgehammer successfully applied.

"I see you recognize the name," he said. "So, I'll ask one more time. *Why?*"

Several more emotions rippled across Gus' features. None were micro in nature. He tried to adjust his fat and the chair screamed again in protest.

"I, uh—I got nothin' to say," he said. "You guys don't scare me."

Thomas stepped forward.

"Yes, we do."

Chapter 37

Springfield, Pennsylvania

I'd all but forgotten about the mysterious phone call from my father. And then the cab pulled to a stop in front of my parents' house and I saw entirely too much empty space in their driveway.

"Aw, shit," I said mostly to myself as Travis and I got out of the cab.

"Connors?" Travis said, eyeing me closely. "What's goin' on?"

A well-used twenty-eight-foot Rockwood Bayport RV had been my home during my minor league umpiring days. After being promoted to the majors, I couldn't bear to part with it and made a deal with my folks to store it at their place. They would use it every once in a while and so would I, but mostly it just took up space. Well, it used to.

That the Rockwood had been part of Andrew Singer's twisted revenge against Michael O'Hara and his family—and mine—wasn't really on my mind when I'd hatched the idea for helping Travis. Looking at the vacancy in the driveway, I guessed it should have been.

"Uh, we might have a problem," I said to Travis. "C'mon, let's go find out for sure."

We got no more than two steps before the front door to the house opened and my father came out. I don't think an aging, balding, sort of smallish man was what Travis had in mind when he asked for my help. Then again, I'm not sure the ballplayer—once described by my father as "the reason they invented birth control"—was what the old man had in mind when I told him I'd be stopping by.

"Dad," I said, drawing out the word into a question.

"I sold it," he said matter-of-factly before shifting his gaze. "Is this who I think it is?"

Travis turned to me. All I could do was offer up a feeble shrug.

"Dad, Travis Mackenzie," I said. "Travis, this is my father, Sean."

"S'up," Travis said.

My dad just nodded. Neither offered a handshake. This was not going the way I'd planned.

"So, uh, the RV," I said to my dad. "Is that why you called the other day?"

He nodded, but didn't take his eyes off of Travis.

"Shit, Dad, you should have just told me then. Why wouldn't you ask me before selling it?"

He shifted his eyes toward me.

"Your mother almost lost it when we found out you were at the game with the bomb," he said. "It had to go. It's better this way."

"Better for *you* maybe," I said.

I was trying hard not to get annoyed. I'm not sure it was working.

"It's better for you too, Son," my dad said. "I don't know if you're just stuck in some kinda shitty rut or if it's something more, but the fewer reminders the better. We all need to move on."

I understood what he was saying. I also understood moving on wasn't an option, not yet anyway. I was still firmly entrenched in the shitty rut. Worse, without the RV, my parents were going to have to rejoin me there. I closed my eyes for a second and pinched the bridge of my nose as I tried to figure out how to tell him that.

"Yeah, about that," I said after a loud sigh.

My dad's eyes narrowed. He looked at Travis and then back at me. I could see he was doing the math in his head. He used to be a CPA. He was good at numbers.

"I think we'd better go inside."

~*~*~*~*~*~*~

New York

Alex was standing at the window in what used to be Gus' office. This being the government, it would take a few months before that became official, but in the meantime, the office would sit empty as a message to everyone else: Don't be an idiot like the guy who used to work here. The victory was a small consolation for Alex.

"Do you believe him?" he said, turning from the glass.

"Which part?" Thomas said

"That he didn't know this would happen," Alex said.

"Again, which part?"

Alex's brow knitted.

"Oh, I don't know, *all of it*." he said, his tone thick with frustration.

He came around to the front of Gus' desk and leaned on the edge. Thomas was in one of the chairs facing him. His expression was its normal flatness. Gus would have surely taken that over what he'd seen there about an hour earlier. It had even scared Alex a bit, but he got over it fairly quickly. It would take Gus a lot longer.

"I believe he was scared," Thomas said. "I believe he felt he was doing the proper thing, misguided as that was. I believe he feels remorse over Agent Santiago's death. I do not believe he was aware of the true nature of the events."

Alex crossed his arms across his chest and looked around the room. Gus wasn't much for decorations. What he did have was old and cheap. Alex shook his head.

"Yeah, you're probably right." he said; then after a pause. "You don't get into this job to get rich. Seeing people, bad people, become so does get old. I suppose a weak soul might give in to that. Too bad it looks like he lost most of it to our friend from Africa."

He blew out some air and refocused on Thomas.

"Make the call," he said. "It'll be better if he doesn't know that I know."

"Agreed," Thomas said. "It does appear he trusts me."

Alex nodded.

"Yep," he said. "I do, too. That's why we need to get back to Philly. Ms. Hill is gonna want to hear about this. I'm guessing it'll help."

"Indeed."

Cherry Hill, New Jersey

Alyson was staring out a window, but the suburban scenery around the FBI safe house went largely unnoticed. Despite the bright sunshine, her eyes were cloudy with regret—and fear. She would have filed away the betrayal of David as a necessary action in her grand plan. He was nothing more than a token in the game she was playing, but his murder changed that. He was dead because of her.

The game was over.

The Alyson Lane of a week ago would have gladly taken the option of being safely tucked away, a guest of the government for as long as necessary. Hell, she would have found a way to enjoy it. The Alyson of today was no longer so shallow. She knew she didn't deserve such treatment. It wasn't fair.

"I can't just sit here," she said into the still air.

She pushed herself away from the window and walked to the living room. Two agents were there, sitting quietly as they read the newspaper. One of them, a male, looked up as Alyson entered the room. A smile slowly filled his face as he followed her movements. Alyson knew why. It was another thing that wasn't fair.

"Is everything OK?" the agent said.

"No," Alyson said. "I need to speak to your boss."

"I'm not sure Director Harris is available."

Alyson's expression took on even more pain.

"Please," she said. "It's urgent. There's something I haven't told him."

~*~*~*~*~*~*~

Philadelphia

Sandy was equal parts tired, hungry, angry, and annoyed. Learning about Pappas from Thomas added to the bad feelings created by Jason Adley's disturbing confession. The coup de grace was the inability to recover all the data from the flash drive and not being able to do anything about it.

That was why she decided to direct the entirety of her pissy mood toward a renewed effort to find something in the security footage of Eddie's time at the Amtrak baggage counter. She was back in front of the monitors in the security room. The full day's recording was queued up on the main screen. She selected six A.M., the time the counter first opened, and tapped *Play*.

The first traveler appeared at six-oh-two A.M., a woman. She passed a large rolling bag through an opening next to the counter. The Amtrak clerk, another woman, wrote something on a pad and handed the traveler a small ticket. The stub was attached to the bag. Another Amtrak worker came and pushed it over to a metal shelf behind the counter, along one of the walls.

"Simple enough," Sandy said under her breath. "So where the hell is Eddie's drop-off?"

She touched *FFWD* to speed up the recording. During the next hour of real time, four men and six women conducted business at the counter. Dropping off and picking up, nothing unusual in any of the movements. About the only thing Sandy found unusual was that none of the male faces were Eddie and none carried the backpack. Frustrated, she pushed *Pause*.

On the frozen frame, she could see the shelves. She studied the picture. The backpack wasn't there. She fought back the frustration and tapped *Play* again. The clock on the screen rolled past eight A.M., then eight-thirty. More travelers came and went. Again, there was no Eddie and no backpack. Sandy sighed and turned away to stretch her neck. The bones made a few noises, disturbing the quiet of the small room.

"Whoa, where did that come from?" she said after looking back.

She'd looked away for maybe ten seconds, but Eddie's backpack was now resting on the counter. There were no bodies in the shot. Sandy touched *Rewind* and used a slider control to adjust the speed. A dark spot appeared at the lower left of the screen and continued to grow until it became the full form of a person, a man. His head was down and covered by a ball cap, preventing a view of the face.

"Ah, there you are," Sandy said to the screen.

She moved the slider to increase the speed. The man spun in an awkward motion, made more so by the reversed direction of the video. His hand came up to the backpack and lifted it from the counter. He then moved back-first out of the shot along the bottom right. When he was completely gone, Sandy hit *Play* and watched the drop off in normal speed.

The man entered, put the bag on the counter, took his ticket, and walked away. When he was out of the shot, Sandy touched *Stop*. She sat back and took an inventory of what she'd just seen. There was something odd, but what? It took four replays to catch it. Unlike every other video of Eddie, in this one, the person she thought to be him made no attempt to be seen. In fact, he was trying very hard *not* to be seen.

Sandy made note of the exact time before navigating back to the main menu. A few clicks on *OK* took her to a listing of available cameras on the recordings. She selected a different angle, from over the Amtrak clerk's left shoulder. As it played, assumed-Eddie appeared at the door and moved to the counter. His face was obscured by the bill of the cap. The bag came up, the clerk did her thing, and assumed-Eddie left.

As with the first angle, Sandy replayed the sequence four times, all at normal speed. On the fifth pass, she paused the recording at the moment when the best view of the face was available. She could see an ear and part of the chin, but that was it. She closed her eyes for a second and then slowly opened them, seeing but not overly scrutinizing anything on the screen. It was another Thomas trick: Let the picture talk to you.

"Wait a tick," she said after a few seconds.

She reached for a folder on the floor and pulled it to her lap. Quickly flipping pages, she found what she needed and looked back up at the screen. Assumed-Eddie's shirt, barely visible under the overcoat, did not match the descriptions of every other instance of Eddie's sighting. Sandy sat back and played with her hair.

"OK," she said to the image. "You leave the bag, go somewhere and change your shirt, come back and pick up the bag. Not entirely impossible, but still, *why?*"

She reached up and touched *Play* again.

When assumed-Eddie signed for the bag, she had the answer.

"You have greatly miscalculated, my friend," Dukabi said into the phone.

His tone said the person on the other end of the line, The Boss, was anything but a friend. The feeling was mutual.

"No, no way, my calculations were fine," The Boss said. "The mistake was in thinking you could handle things without fucking up. I told you not to involve anyone else. I've been telling you that for years. Apparently, that's a message you never hear."

Dukabi laughed. It was a scary noise. When he spoke again, his deep voice was equally so.

"What you and I have said in the past is no longer relevant."

"What the fuck is that supposed to mean?" The Boss said.

"It means there is nothing left to discuss," Dukabi said. "I have fulfilled my obligations. You will do the same."

A beep interrupted the silence that followed. Dukabi extended the phone a few inches from his face. The name on the ID for the incoming call produced a forceful nod. Dukabi returned the phone to his cheek.

"Your time is short, my friend," he said. "You would be wise to act without further delay."

He didn't wait for The Boss' reply. His large thumb pushed *End* and then *OK.*

"Mr. Hillsborough, I've been expecting your call."

Being summoned to the safe house was only slightly less annoying to Alex than what Alyson said once he got there.

"I didn't know what else to do."

What she had done was pick up David Donovan's bag in the confusing moments after he'd been murdered. The act was captured by the SNN security cameras, but Carlos didn't live long enough to finish reviewing the tapes. Alex felt like crap about the young man's death. Learning the trip to New York might not have been necessary didn't help. He did his best not to take it out on Alyson.

"Why did you wait so long to tell us?" he said.

Alyson started to cry. Alex had not the patience to deal with it.

"Ms. Lane, *please*," he said. "I need your help to make sure no one else dies."

Alyson sniffed loudly and used a finger to smear the tears from her face.

"OK," she said.

"So these files will explain everything?" Alex said.

Alyson nodded.

"Yes, that's what I've been saying. All the stuff we—all the stuff *David* had. He was going to come to you with it. He was trying to do the right thing before I got him killed."

Her head dropped again and the tears returned. Alex hated seeing women cry. It ate as his senses like no other sound. It was probably because his mother used to cry a lot when he was young. In her case, Alex never understood why. It was a mystery he had never solved. Seeing as she was dead now, it would stay that way. Alyson's would not.

"I'll have someone fetch the bag," Alex said as he stood. "We'll bring it here and one of my people will help you go through it."

He didn't wait to see Alyson's reaction. Instead, he turned quickly and hustled to his car. Thomas and Sandy were waiting for him back at his office. He wanted to believe they were about to help make sure his current mystery didn't suffer the same fate as that of his mother's crying. At the very least, he could use the lift.

He would get more than that.

Chapter 38

Springfield

"You didn't think we'd notice someone in the camper?" my dad said.

We were in the basement of my parents' house, my dad's version of a man cave. Two massive leather chairs and a kick-ass entertainment center dominated the setting. It looked like the pictures of the home theaters you might see in the Best Buy circulars in the Sunday paper. My dad called it his oasis, a place to which he could escape.

It was about to become Travis' as well.

"I guess I did," I said. "It seemed like a good idea at the time."

"And *he* was OK with that?" my dad said.

The "he" was accompanied by a motion with his head toward the sofa on the far side of the room. Travis was curled up in a ball there, under a throw cover, sleeping.

"He's here," I said. "I guess that means he was OK."

My dad nodded and rocked his chair a few times.

"Hmmm," he said. "I guess."

Translation of the movements and the noise: You're an idiot, Marshall, but you're my son and I still love you. Oh, and you seriously owe me for this one.

"Did you at least get a good price?" I said after the message sank in.

"It'll pay for our next trip."

That meant he got enough money for their annual European vacation, something they'd been doing ever since my dad sold his firm and retired. It's not like they needed the extra money—the business sale had set them up for the rest of their lives—but at least I was covered for Christmas shopping.

"Nice," I said.

My eyes drifted over to Travis. I sort-of-maybe-but-not-quite felt bad for him. On one hand, he was an idiot for taking an untested steroid—hell, for taking *any* steroid—but on the other hand, I'm not sure he deserved to die, and from what I understood, that's what was going to happen without my help.

The plan—a stretch to call it that at this point—was hashed out during the flight east from L.A. That part was actually pretty cool. Being a celebrity got Travis a lot of free meals. Being a celebrity with a shitload of money got him something else, a lot of favors. An actor friend with a private jet was more than happy to let Travis borrow said jet. The request—"I have to get to New York to see a specialist"—was mostly a lie, but the actor was a huge Dodgers fan and didn't push it. He was just happy to be helping Travis get back on the field.

Of course, that was questionable at the moment. In his present condition, Travis wasn't playing any games any time soon. That would take a few days—if at all.

"You know, that would have been better for your mother."

I turned back to my dad.

"Huh?" I said.

"Your idea, it would have been better to use the RV instead of this."

"Exactly," I said. "That's why you need to keep her out of here."

My dad turned to face me.

"Easier said then done," he said.

We both raised our eyes to the ceiling.

"Yeah, don't I know it," I said.

Travis groaned and rolled over on the sofa. My dad's expression turned over as well. He had a look I hadn't seen in years, one from back in his accounting days. "Professional intensity" is how I'd always described it. It was nice to see it again. I was gonna need the help.

"So, tell me how this works," he said. "What do you need me to do?"

Philadelphia

Despite twenty hours of interviews by various agents, Gus never wavered from the information originally revealed to Alex and Thomas in his office. The interrogations were less stressful than Thomas' had been, but Gus held firm. He gave up the why—several hundred thousand dollars in gambling debts owed to Dukabi—but not the identity of The Boss. Thomas was sure Gus did not know. Alex, not so much, but was giving some latitude to the theory.

He was again in his office, behind his desk, Thomas and Sandy on the other side. He looked disheveled. Sandy was a little better. Thomas was perfectly coifed, as usual. He may have been as tired as the other two, but no one could see it. Alex would have been annoyed by that if he didn't have other itches to scratch.

"All right, Pappas gets a call," he said. "This Boss character that nobody seems to know tells him to pin it on Dukabi or the gambling problem goes public. That means The Boss knew about Dukabi, knew the bombing was coming, and knew about Gus' vices. Who would know all of those things?"

He stopped to take a sip from a large mug. His guests were unsure of the contents. He didn't bother to educate them.

"Anything?" he said after swallowing. "Can you get me there?"

The pleading look and tone was Sandy's cue. She shifted in her chair and took a few seconds to consult the notebook in her lap.

"Not completely, but close," she said. "I couldn't get everything off the drive."

"What did you get?" Alex said.

"OK, as we now know, the new steroid was called 'the Cure,'" Sandy said. "Turns out it was a bust. Every test subject: Dead. In addition to destroying muscle tissue and bone strength, it caused loss of mental capacity in the hamsters. They all went bonkers. But it gets worse. Some of the samples went missing. Adley seemed to think Bischoff took them. I think he, Booker, and Coakley all sampled the stuff. If so, the doctor suggested it might kill them, too."

"Wow," Alex said; then after a pause. "That kinda fits, huh?"

Sandy nodded.

"Yeah, but I don't think any of that was related to Pappas," she said. "He got involved only because this Boss guy forced his hand. It does fill in a blank on Dukabi's reaction though. Booker did not do what The Boss had in mind."

Alex chewed on his bottom lip for a few seconds.

"Meaning," he said, drawing out the word into a question.

"Meaning Booker *was* supposed to do *something*, but the steroids fucked him up and he went overboard. Dukabi was genuinely shocked by the nature of the bombing. It was a screw-up."

"What about Coakley?" Alex said.

"If he was using the steroid, too, the way he went out makes sense," Sandy said. "Hell, he even said so before he shot himself."

Alex flashed on—then pushed aside—the gruesome images from the Lincoln Memorial.

"OK, OK," he said. "So that's what Booker was trying to do, tell someone, right?"

Sandy nodded.

"He made sure everything he did, every movement in the station and the ballpark, got captured by as many eyes as possible," she said. "He practically begged someone to catch him."

"Like maybe he didn't want to do it?" Alex said.

Sandy shook her head.

"No, like maybe so something would stand out."

Alex's eyes narrowed.

"Tell me," he said.

"When the bag was dropped off, it wasn't Booker," she said. "He's right-handed. The person at the drop was left-handed."

Alex's eyes widened and he sat back. He looked at Thomas then back to her.

"Shit, good eye," he said. "You need to come back and work for me."

He was mostly kidding—mostly.

"I kinda already do, seeing as how much you keep hiring us," Sandy said.

Alex shrugged and the levity, what there'd been, quickly dissipated.

"So… we have, what, about three billion suspects?" he said. "How do we shorten the list?"

"We need to find someone close to Booker in physical appearance," Sandy said. "The man at the counter was almost an exact match."

A few seconds passed before Alex turned to Thomas again.

"You're awfully quiet," he said. "What are you thinking?"

An eyebrow moved on Thomas' face.

"Oh what a tangled web we weave, when first we practice to deceive."

Sandy knew the quote, but not why Thomas had used it, at least not at first. She looked at him with a question on her face. Alex's reaction was similar.

"OK, *Marmion* by Sir Walter Scott," he said. "What are you saying?"

Sandy suddenly perked up.

"Oh, shit… I get it," she said. "It's a synopsis of our present situation."

Alex's face brightened and he began to nod.

"Yeah, I guess it is," he said; then after a pause. "So why don't you two quit fucking around and go find me the goddamned spider."

Chapter 39

Cherry Hill

Sandy was more than agreeable to make the short hop over the bridge to the safe house. She agreed with Alex's assessment that Alyson would respond better to a female. Being an attractive woman herself in a mostly man's world, she understood how stupid men could be when distracted. Now was no time for stupid. Of course, there was always the female-female catfight thing, but Alex figured Sandy could handle that if it happened.

It didn't.

The two women seemed to hit it off right away. In truth, Alyson was too frightened to be anything but cooperative. She and Sandy settled in front of a computer on a small desk near the window, in the bedroom of the safe house. Sandy was at the keyboard because Alex couldn't take a chance that Alyson wasn't more than another bug caught in the web. He'd had enough trouble getting the data. He wasn't going to let an errant *Delete* command erase what might be the last chance to get the entirety of it. He tended to trust people, but that only went so far.

Alyson had yet to completely earn it. She'd taken a big step in that direction with her admission that she'd picked up David's bag. The elusive files would go a long way toward filling in the blanks in Sandy's work. At least that was the hope, not just of Alex and Sandy, but also of Alyson. She wanted to make David's death mean something.

"OK," Sandy said. "How do I get in?"

"My user ID is 'A Lane'—one word, no caps," Alyson said.

"Password," Sandy said after entering the ID.

"Rick Springfield, no spaces, but use caps."

Sandy looked up with a questioning expression. Alyson rolled her eyes and shrugged.

"I'm named after one of his songs," she said. "Blame my father."

Sandy understood. Her dad, as great as he was, was also a bit odd.

"Enough said," she said with a grin.

She turned back to the screen and entered the password. The computer booted.

"OK, we're in," she said. "What am I looking for?"

"Open a Firefox session," Alyson said.

Seconds later, a browser window appeared. Alyson's home page was the SNN public site.

"Click on the intranet icon, there, in the corner," she said, pointing.

Sandy did as instructed and a less-splashy page appeared. The cursor was a blinking square in the *User ID* box. She glanced at Alyson.

"Same credentials?" she said.

"Yes," Alyson said. "When the page loads, there'll be an email link on the left… *There.*"

She pointed again. Sandy clicked. Alyson's stomach did a flip. Sandy noticed.

"What?" she said.

"Uh… scroll down."

Sandy did so, and the list of messages cascaded along the window. Alyson watched and the sick feeling grew.

"What?" Sandy said again. "What's wrong? Which message do I need?"

"Keep going, it has to be there," Alyson said.

The list reached the bottom.

"Go back to the top and sort it by date received."

Sandy sorted and re-scrolled. Alyson's expression worsened.

"Try to sort by sender. It'll be the only one from Doctor Adley."

Sandy clicked, the screen reset, the list re-appeared. There were no messages from Jason.

"Oh my God," Alyson said. "*Where is it?*"

New York

"He *still* hasn't sent it?" Gabi said.

He was with Suze Keebler, at a table in a sandwich shop a few blocks from the MLB office.

"No," Suze said. "I'm actually glad. I don't want him to quit."

Gabi's face went through a few expressions before he nodded.

"Yeah, that would suck," he said.

Something in the tone bothered Suze.

"Gabi?" she said. "What's going on? You seem annoyed."

The last part came out more like a question. Gabi was looking off to Suze's left. It was a few seconds before he turned back. Now his expression was all wrong, too. Suze backed away from the table slightly.

"I knew it," she said. "I should never have told you."

Gabi's brow curled into a tighter knot before relaxing into something closer to normal. He couldn't tell if Suze bought it, and overdid the tone of his next words, just in case.

"*Whaaaaat?*" he said, stretching out the word for emphasis. "Of course you should have told me. Why wouldn't you tell me? How am I supposed to help if I don't know what's going on?"

Suze made a face that Marshall used to adore seeing, her "watch out, I'm thinking" look he'd called it. Gabi liked it a lot as well, but unlike the umpire, had never said anything. It was one of a number of regrets he had at the moment, a list that was getting entirely too long.

"I guess," Suze said. "I don't know."

Gabi waved his hands in a "fuggedaboudit" gesture.

"Everything will be fine," he said. "You'll see. It'll all be OK."

Suze smiled.

"If you say so," she said.

It was Gabi's turn to smile.

"I say so."

Suze nodded and seemed to relax again.

"OK, then," she said. "You're the boss."

Philadelphia

"What happened?" Alex said into his phone.

The urgency wasn't necessary. Sandy was way ahead of him.

"It's gone," she said.

She explained how a routine system maintenance process on the SNN mail server had inadvertently deleted all incoming messages for a four-hour block, a window that just happened to coincide with that of Jason Adley's message.

"The collective system Inbox got erased," Sandy said. "If Alyson would have moved the file to a saved folder, we'd have it. She, uh—it doesn't look like she ever moves anything out of her Inbox. It's a really bad habit."

"I get it," Alex said. "She's an airhead."

Sandy shrugged, but he couldn't see it.

"I didn't say that," she said.

"I know, sorry," Alex said. "All right, just come back. Maybe Thomas will have better luck with Dukabi."

"It wouldn't shock me," Sandy said. "He's pretty good at getting answers."

Alex flashed on the visit to Gus' office.

"He certainly is."

"What was Mr. Booker's true task?" Thomas said.

He was with Dukabi in the big man's apartment, the latter having returned after the earlier phone conversation. Agreeing to the meeting wasn't a deal, not like before, but more an understanding.

Dukabi could cooperate and *maybe* end up dead. He could remain hidden and *definitely* end up dead. It wasn't a difficult choice.

"He was to create a diversion," Dukabi said.

The boom in the voice lacked a few of its normal decibels.

"Explain," Thomas said.

His tone was completely normal, meaning it was scarier than the boom, and a shiver raked Dukabi's large frame. The movements were exaggerated by his bulk.

"It was suggested a diversion was necessary to allow time for a situation to correct itself," he said. "It appears Mr. Booker had other ideas."

Thomas took a deep breath. The exhale was ominous. He was losing patience.

"*Explain,*" he said again.

The tone hit home, and Dukabi adjusted his position and brushed at his slacks. After using a handkerchief to wipe his brow, he leaned forward toward Thomas. Like the shiver, the slight movement was exaggerated.

"The original transaction was an exchange," he said. "Certain debts would be forgiven. Certain actions would be overlooked."

Thomas held the big man's eyes as Dukabi continued.

"This affair would likely be over, but the man's illness complicated matters. It was most unfortunate."

"But not entirely unexpected," Thomas said.

Dukabi's eyes narrowed.

"Is that a question or a statement?"

"That depends on how your respond."

Dukabi's eyes relaxed again and he nodded.

"Yes, I suppose so," he said; then after a pause. "For me, it was entirely unexpected. For others, I do not believe that to be the case."

"I need to know about the others."

"Yes, I suppose so," Dukabi said again.

Springfield

A lot of things played into Marshall's agreeing to help Travis. First up was the convenience that the umpire and his crew were already heading east, as were the Dodgers. Marshall's team was working in Philadelphia and then going on to the make-up games in New York. The ballclub had games in D.C. before those final contests. It put them both in the same place, eventually.

Travis worked out an excuse for missing the D.C. series. Being a superstar afforded him leniency not otherwise available to the rest of the team. He shared enough information with club officials to leave them believing he was laid up at home with the flu. The episode in the trainer's room helped the roots of that seed take hold. As soon as he was well enough to travel, he would rejoin the team.

The assistant to the assistant general manager, left behind to make sure that happened, was easily convinced to overlook the fact he was instead spending the weekend alone in Travis' house. The young man didn't make much money. Travis' check doubled it. Sometimes, money *can* buy you everything. The babysitter would get the new car he'd been saving for. Travis would get something else.

Marshall's old RV would have provided a shelter both close enough and far enough from where Travis eventually needed to be, the former allowing him to get to either field as soon as he felt up to it, the latter letting him stay out of view of any prying media eyes. No one—outside of Marshall—would have known where he was.

Of course, the RV's absence complicated things and moved Sean Connors into a more central role. Luckily, he was used to it— and not just because of the Andrew Singer mess. Prior to becoming a CPA, Sean had spent several tours in the Army. One of his assignments had been as a field medic. He knew his way around a medical kit and could handle most of the basics, sort of like a registered nurse, but with slightly different training.

"How long do I have to do this?" Travis said.

The question came as Sean prepared a syringe.

"Until you don't," Sean said.

Travis would have preferred not having the stranger involved, but knew he didn't have that option. Besides the change in venue, the shakes had expanded from his hand to his entire right side. Without help, administering the medicine would have been difficult.

"Now I see where your son gets it," he said as he eyed Sean closely.

Sean ignored the barb and stare as he inserted the needle into Travis' arm.

"*Fuck*... careful, old man," Travis said. "That shit hurts."

He grimaced and squeezed his eyes closed. The expression lasted almost ten seconds.

"I'd say serves you right, but you already know that," Sean said.

Travis nodded as his face slowly relaxed. He stayed quiet as Sean prepared the next injection. All told, he would need to administer six separate shots, three times per day, for the next four days. After that, it would decrease to one per day. The assorted supplements and medicines—another Travis check procured the necessary prescriptions—would counteract most of what "The Cure" had done, but not all. Adley's notes were very clear on that last point.

"Why are you helping me?" Travis said as another needle hit home.

It was as close to an honest tone as had ever come out of the man. If asked, he probably would have said he was merely trying to change the subject so as not to think about the needle, but Sean didn't fall for it.

"I trust my son," he said. "I trust Thomas, too."

"Yeah, who is this Thomas guy?" Travis said. "Connors mentioned him before."

"Most talented man I've ever met," Sean said. "You don't want to fuck with him."

Travis' eyes narrowed.

"I told Connors not to call anyone—"

"Don't get all pissy" Sean said, cutting him off. "You're already dead without his help."

The last needle punctured Travis' arm.

"Fuck me," he said. "Point made—*shit.*"

After a few seconds, Travis stood, shakily at first, but then more steadily. He began to pace the room as Sean cleaned up. The ballplayer was admittedly impressed with the entertainment unit. Sure, it was modest compared to the full theater he had in his California home, but all things considered, it wasn't a bad place to have to shack up for a few days as the treatments took hold.

He was thumbing through a collection of CDs in a tall narrow case when he noticed a photograph on the wall. He leaned in to get a better look. Holy shit, he thought, as he realized what he was seeing. He knew enough to know what someone had to do to get the medal being pinned to Sean's Army Greens. He turned back. Sean was eyeing him. Travis nodded.

"I think maybe *you're* the one I don't want to fuck with."

Sean's features relaxed a touch and his shoulders moved in a tiny shrug. A new voice, a female's, interrupted before either could say another word.

"Sean? Are you going to be down there all day? We need to go shopping."

Both men turned toward the voice. It was Candace, Sean's wife of forty years and Marshall's mother. Sean shrugged and moved for the stairs.

"Talk about someone you don't want to fuck with."

Chapter 40

South Philadelphia

I didn't say a word after Thomas finished explaining where'd he'd been and what he'd learned. We were in the front seat of his car, parked outside Citizens Bank Park. My game was in a few hours, the last in Philly before I had to get to New York. His offer of a ride hadn't triggered anything—well, anything new. He said he wanted to check in on Travis and talk to me about something. It fit.

Now, as I sat there looking at him, *nothing* fit.

"So," I said, before stopping and taking a deep breath. "I guess—"

I cut myself off and let the air escape in a long hiss. Thomas' eyebrow went up. Both of mine went in the opposite direction. I tried again.

"Dukabi doesn't strike me as someone who wouldn't know," I said. "I mean, from what I know, from what you've told me about him, he's very much into the details. Are you sure?"

My frustration was leading to anger. Travis was still hiding in my parents' basement. I needed that to end. That his story about what was going on did not match the one Thomas got from Dukabi only added to my urgency. But the topper, the thing really eating at me, was not being able to tell if Thomas actually gave a shit or not. Most of the time I took that he did as a given, but in the past few days I'd noticed something was off. OK, maybe not *off*—I don't think Thomas was ever off—but let's just say different. Honestly, it was a bit scary. I didn't like it. Not remotely.

I took another deep breath and let it out before turning to face him.

"OK," I said. "So their stories don't match. Who's lying?"

"Both or neither," he said.

I dropped my head and another loud sigh escaped. I loved the man like a brother, but sometimes, his cryptic nature was beyond infuriating. I knew that he knew exactly what was going on and exactly what he was going to do about it. I also knew he had no intentions of just coming out and saying it. Sure, I could read him—more often than not—but that wasn't the point. I liked blunt. Ball, strike, fair, foul, safe, out. I didn't deal in gray. Thomas was gray personified.

I looked hard at him.

"C'mon, enough with the fucking mystery already," I said. "Just tell me."

His eyebrow went up again. I wanted to smack it off his face.

"The most effective lies are those in which the smallest of details are modified," he said. "A complete fabrication requires an escalating volume of additional untruths. It becomes difficult to support the structure."

I knew what he was talking about. Yay, small victory for me, I thought.

"If you wish to strengthen a lie, mix in a little truth," I said.

His expression changed a little. I'd surprised him. Woohoo, two in a row—I was on a roll.

"You're not the only one who took Studies of Religion as an elective," I said. "That Zohar stuff is interesting."

"Indeed," he said with a small nod. "I'm pleased you understand."

"Who said I understand?" I said. "I don't, not remotely. I just get what you mean about the both and neither thing. So, which guy's lies are the ones we need to worry about?"

"That remains to be determined."

I turned back to the window. The ballpark beckoned, the game, my game. It was time to get to work—for both of us. I looked back at Thomas.

"Yeah, well, hurry the hell up," I said. "I'm not sure how much more of this I can take. If Travis is dangerous, I need him out of my parents' house."

"Sean sounded as though he understood the risk."

"I don't care how much he understands," I said, my tone reflecting the return of my anger. "I just want this fucking shit to be over. *All of it.*"

Thomas' expression didn't change, as if it ever did. That just pissed me off more.

"*What?*" I said. "Fucking say something already."

"Everything will be fine," he said.

I shook my head and pushed open the passenger door. I started to get out, but stopped and looked back.

"Go tell that to my mother."

Center City Philadelphia

Jamie and Shady waited until Dukabi passed in front of the parking exit doorway before exiting the car. The Navigator they'd been using was parked illegally on Clover Street, facing 13th Street and the loading area doors for the Wanamaker—now Macy's—Building. It wouldn't take long for the behemoth of a vehicle to draw attention, seeing as how it blocked the narrow alley-like road, but neither man was worried. Drawing attention was the point.

Moving quickly, they hit the sidewalk on 13th and got in step with Dukabi, twenty or so feet behind. Ten seconds later, just as they reached the intersection at Chestnut Street, Jamie pushed a button on his cell phone and the Lincoln exploded. The concussion shattered the windows on the surrounding buildings and sent thick black smoke into the air. It also sent pedestrians scattering in all directions.

Despite the chaos erupting around them, Jamie and Shady held their ground. Diagonally, across Chestnut, Dukabi did as well. It did not take long for his eyes to find those on the dark faces of his former friends. Years ago, before time—and Thomas' bullet—got the better of his legs, Dukabi might have thought of running. On this day, he did not. He simply looked past the frantic crowd passing in front of him and acknowledged Jamie with a single nod of the head. Jamie returned the gesture as he and Shady started forward.

"And so it ends," Dukabi said into the din.

Wayne

Thomas closed his phone, but left it close to his face. The call had been brief. Sandy thought Alex had been on the other end of it, but she began to doubt that assumption. She saw what might have been disappointment as Thomas stared past her, but she wasn't so sure. As it had been to Marshall's eyes, something was off in Thomas' expression. That was new, and as much as Sandy liked to think she was getting better at reading her boss, he was very much still a mystery, a seek-and-find like no other she'd ever attempted.

Unlike Marshall, however, she relished the challenge of solving that mystery.

"What happened?" she said.

Thomas' focus adjusted and he lowered the phone.

"Mr. Dukabi is dead."

The flat tone generated undisguised disappointment in Sandy. She wasn't upset on a personal level—hell, she would have liked to have killed Dukabi years ago—but rather because she knew it changed the dynamics of the hunt. They were rapidly running out of options as to who might know the identity of the elusive spider. Maybe "running out" wasn't right. Maybe they were simply out, as in completely. Sandy tried not to think about that, but it didn't work.

"Fuck," she said.

Sharpness returned to Thomas' eyes. Sandy's outburst was something new. She, too, was still somewhat of a mystery, but unlike for her, discovery was no game for Thomas. It was a necessity, he had to know. It was information needed to stay ahead of the curve, steps beyond everyone else. He'd long ago discovered the power of information, how it can shape and prepare you for even the most unforeseen circumstances.

He had watched and learned from his father, emulating the man's actions and reactions. The family's money didn't just print itself. Thomas' father deftly directed the assets and investments to create more of the same. When the man died, Thomas was ready to step in and continue the process. He was prepared. He was *always* prepared—but not this time.

His eyes narrowed.

"Not a word I expected to hear," he said.

"Sorry," Sandy said with a shrug.

Her tone said she wasn't. Thomas nodded.

"Don't be," he said. "It fits."

A half of a fraction of a chuckle escaped Sandy, but she recovered even faster. The situation wasn't remotely funny, not by a long shot. Her hands came up, palms facing the ceiling, before the fingers interlocked and landed on her head.

"OK, so who's left?" she said.

After a few seconds, she exhaled loudly.

"I got nothin'."

Thomas' hands went to the steeple. Sandy waited. His silence lasted longer than expected and was more disturbing than the earlier look of disappointment, maybe because she was beginning to understand how all of his quirks fit together. It was a lot like the case.

"You don't either," she said.

He nodded slightly.

"That's a big problem, isn't it?" Sandy said.

"Indeed."

South Philadelphia

"Hey," I said to Sandy as I slid into the back seat of Thomas' car.

"Hey, Marshall," she said over her shoulder.

Her smile was clearly forced. I adjusted my eyes toward Thomas. He was eyeing me through the rearview mirror, but I had no idea what he was thinking. I just shook my head. That I was back in the car again so soon was only slightly bothersome. I was either used to it or I'd given up trying to figure it out. I was leaning toward the latter.

Thomas had called and left a message during my game—the Mets beat the Phillies three to two in eleven innings to stay close to the Dodgers. It was a good game, but I'd already pretty much forgotten about it thanks to the call. In it, Thomas said he we had to go get Travis. It sounded simple enough, but a memory of the pregame conversation told me otherwise.

"OK, what now?" I said.

"There's been a development," Thomas said, his flat tone firmly in place.

"I'm sure there has been," I said, as much to myself as to him.

I turned to the window as the car started to move. The sight of the stadium reminded me how much I loved baseball and how much I hated not being able to simply enjoy it anymore. I closed my eyes and pictured buying a new RV and simply driving away. I could go freelance at semi-pro games, like in the old days. No pressure, no spoiled players, no idiot front-office types and inept leadership, just me and the game again. Yeah, that'd be cool.

If only, I thought, as I opened my eyes again and turned back toward Thomas.

"So," I said. "Who died this time?"

Springfield

I knew something was wrong as soon as we turned into my parents' driveway. My dad was waiting for us on the front porch. Our plan—sorry, Thomas' plan—had been to retrieve Travis. With Dukabi's murder, things had gotten worse, as if that was somehow possible. Travis was now the last person alive who may or may not know what the hell was going on. That meant the danger to my folks had increased exponentially. Removing Travis from their lives was the one part of the plan I was OK with.

"I'm sorry," my dad said as he met us in the driveway.

"What happened?" I said. "Are you OK?"

He kicked at a pebble only he saw.

"I gave him the last dose for today and left him alone," he said, not looking at us. "I thought he went to sleep. I went up to the kitchen to sit with your mother. When I went back down to check on him about an hour later, he was gone. He must have gone out the basement door. I never heard him leave."

I looked at Thomas and Sandy, then back at my dad.

"I should have stayed with him," he said.

I shook my head.

"No, Dad," I said. "I shouldn't have involved you in the first place."

His face scrunched up.

"You didn't involve me," he said. "I involved me. I coulda said no."

I reached out and put my hand on his shoulder.

"No, you couldn't," I said. "That's not who you are."

He nodded. We both turned in unison toward Thomas and Sandy. In my case, it was to say: I give up, it's all yours. I think Thomas figured it out because his eyes went to my dad.

"Sean, there's been another death related to the case," he said. "If Mr. Mackenzie somehow learned of it, his response could have been to flee."

My dad glanced at me. I gave him a slight shrug.

"How would he learn of it?" he said as he turned back to Thomas.

He was still trying to help. I wanted him to stop.

"Don't worry about it, Dad, it doesn't matter," I said.

I didn't hold back on the pissy tone. It was meant more as a message for Thomas. Again, he was smart enough to figure it out.

"Yes, Marshall is correct," he said. "This situation is no longer your concern."

A quiet handful of seconds passed. My dad broke it.

"At least you guys know where he's headed," he said.

Between Sandy, Thomas, and me, I'm not sure which of our faces had the bigger look of confusion. I would have voted for mine.

"How the hell would we know *that*?" I said.

My dad looked at me with his "You are the dumbest person alive" face.

"Because he told you," he said in a matching tone. "The other night, remember? After he saw the Mets' score? He said there's no way he's gonna miss those final two games."

I finally caught on.

"Oh, shit. He's headed to New York."

Chapter 41

Two days later
New York City

It was difficult to determine whether the rain that pushed everything back a day was a blessing or a curse. Outside of the weather, nothing else bad had happened, but as the meeting progressed, Mark Rosenbaum realized the latter was still very much a possibility. That everyone else in the small conference room seemed to be expecting it wasn't helping, despite the assurances they were providing.

"I understand your concern, Mark," Alex said. "We're doing everything we can to end this before anyone else gets hurt."

"I... I just don't know," Mark said. "The whole thing bothers me—*a lot*."

The "whole thing" had included a complete airing of the facts around Gus' involvement, the relationship between the deaths, the fire and the steroids, and the situation with Travis Mackenzie. Mark's biggest concern seemed to land on that final aspect.

"You guys still have no idea who's really responsible?" he said. "I mean, how do you stop what you don't know?"

Alex was first to take a shot at it.

"It's what we do, Mark," he said. "Trust me, we'll end it."

Mark blew out some air and sat back in his chair.

"Jesus, I don't know," he said.

"I do," Alex said. "If the killers come, we'll be ready. You have my word."

Sandy recognized Alex's tone from her days with him at the FBI. The fatherly voice used to come out to keep the rest of the staff from falling apart when things were deteriorating. As she remembered it, it also meant he didn't quite believe the words he'd just spoken. She didn't either—and wouldn't until they found the last piece of the puzzle.

"What if that's not enough?"

The question was Gabi's. He'd been unusually quiet—in Sandy's opinion—up until that point. She had attributed it to the stress hovering over everyone in the room. Something she saw changed that. He was doodling on a small pad of paper.

"I didn't realize you were left-handed," Sandy said, motioning with her chin to the pad.

"Yeah," he said, drawing out the word. "And I'm a Leo, too. So?"

A tumbler clicked into place in Sandy's thoughts. She pictured her note pad, the page with the crazy schematic of the case. In her mind, she filled in the blank box in the center of the page, the spot reserved for the source, the spider, The Boss.

Thomas' reaction was more pronounced.

"Avoiding danger is no safer in the long run than outright exposure. The fearful are caught as often as the bold."

"Thomas?" Alex said.

"It's from a poem," Mark said. "Helen Keller, I think."

Thomas nodded. Alex shook his head.

"OK, we're seriously digressing here," he said. "Horoscopes, Helen Keller poems—I think we need to stay focused."

Gabi's eyes were well-focused already. He was staring at Thomas. There was the slightest hint of a curl at the right corner of his upper lip.

"He didn't finish the poem," he said.

"What are you guys talking about?" Mark said.

"He didn't finish," Gabi said, before doing so. "Security is mostly a superstition. It does not exist in nature. Life is either a daring adventure, or nothing."

Sandy caught the almost imperceptible twinkle filling Thomas' eyes. She realized he knew. She looked at Gabi. His eyes said he knew that Thomas knew. All the tumblers were in place. The spider was no longer in hiding.

Gabi Loeb was The Boss.

Yankee Stadium
The Bronx

After the final Sunday of the original schedule, the Dodgers held a one game lead in the National League Wild Card race. One win in the make-up games and they were in the playoffs. With Travis back, most experts felt that was likely. Of course, those experts didn't know what I knew. Travis Mackenzie was a wreck. The extra day brought on by the rain wasn't going to help.

My dad had been right. Travis had headed to New York after slipping out of the house. I think I would have been more impressed by the move if not for one small oversight. He and I were discussing that as we sat alone in the third base dugout of new Yankee Stadium. There were a handful of people out on the field in front of us. None of them gave any indication they thought the sight of me and the player chatting odd. I wouldn't have cared at that point anyway.

"I'm going to go with 'I forgot because I left in a hurry,'" I said.

I set a small bag next to him on the bench. His meds were inside. He looked down at it. A shrug and a scoffing noise followed.

"I didn't forget anything," he said. "I'm done with it."

We looked at each other for ten, maybe fifteen seconds. I broke first.

"I don't get you," I said. "I thought maybe you were going to do the right thing, but now? I don't know. Do you have a martyr complex or something? Dude, you need this stuff or you're gonna die. How is that a good idea?"

He shook his head.

"Connors, you're an idiot," he said. "I'm already dead. You know that. You think the person behind this is gonna let me live? Wake up, man."

"Who *is* behind it?" I said.

He smiled. I'm glad he thought it was funny.

"You'll find out soon enough, *everyone* will," he said.

I was going to ask how, but stopped before the question reached my lips. I didn't want to know. I'd done what I could, more than I should have. I'd endangered myself and my parents—*again*—and risked my career. It was stupid. Travis was stupid. The whole fucking thing was stupid. I'd had enough.

I turned to the field and watched the Dodgers working out around the diamond. The sun was dancing in and out of the clouds. It gave the players' movements a scattered and graceful appearance. It was beautiful. I'd almost ruined that beauty. No more.

I looked back to Travis.

"I know behind that selfish, egotistical, bullshit façade of yours you love this game as much as I do," I said. "I can't believe you'd do something to fuck that up."

He smiled at me again.

"How is this funny?" I said.

The smile disappeared.

"That's just it, Connors, it's not," he said. "I *do* love this game, more than you could ever possibly understand. What I'm doing isn't about fucking that up. It's about *saving* it."

An hour or so later, I was at my locker. I was already dressed for the game, and being on the phone had broken one of my pregame rituals: the phone went off before the uniform went on. Given all the other rules I'd been breaking, I shouldn't have been surprised.

"He knows who's behind it, but he wouldn't tell me," I said into the cell. "I don't know. Maybe he doesn't want to create any more loose ends. I think he's gonna do something stupid. As much as I don't want to care, I couldn't just sit here and not say anything."

Thomas didn't respond. I shouldn't have been surprised.

"*What?*" I said.

The single word question was becoming far too common. My anger was back, but something else came with it and a chill ran along my spine.

"Holy shit, you already know," I said.

I sat back and stared up at the ceiling. It, and everything else around me, was immaculate. It should have been, seeing as how the Yankees spent something like one-point-five billion on the place. That kind of cash buys a lot of perfection. I didn't want to think about what might be coming to mess that up.

"Who is it, Thomas?" I said. "Who's behind this? Who's the boss?"

"Take Mr. Mackenzie's advice," he said. "Do your job and stay out of it."

I think if he was standing next to me I would have punched him—or at least tried to. As it was, the only thing I could do was let out a long sigh.

"Yeah, *now* you tell me."

MLB Headquarters

"What was that shit between you and Thomas?" Mark said.

The tone was a mix of being pissed and confused. When Gabi's jaw muscles flexed, it slid closer to the former.

"What's going on?" Mark said.

The tension lasted another few ticks before Gabi shook it off and found a smile. It was a mask, but he was used to wearing such. He'd been doing it for a long time. He was good at it.

"Nothing you don't know," he said. "I think he was just trying to make a point about how screwed up this thing is."

Mark's brow knitted tighter before relaxing a few degrees.

"It seemed like more," he said. "Are you sure there's nothing I need to know?"

Gabi's smile widened.

"We're good," he said. "Everyone is on the same page."

Mark reached up and scratched at his head. A few odd facial expressions came and went. Gabi tried not to laugh. With Mark, he often found that difficult. It was a big reason for everything that had happened—and for the things about to happen.

"Hey, uh, I've been thinking about what you asked," Mark said. "I'm going to put you at the top of the list. You deserve the shot."

A genuine smile replaced Gabi's artificial one.

"Thanks, Mark," he said. "I appreciate that. I'd rather not see you quit at all, but knowing you want me to have the job means a lot."

They shook hands.

"Don't get too excited," Mark said. "We gotta get through the next couple days still. Please tell me again everything will be OK."

Gabi's smile broadened. How much was still real was debatable.

"You have my word," he said. "Everything will go exactly as planned. *Trust me.*"

Manhattan

Alex's expression was a mix of confusion, determination, and anger. He was rocking in the chair on the business-side of a desk in one of the offices reserved for VIPs in the New York FBI building. Thomas and Sandy were sitting in matching guest chairs on the other side. Both presented their usual picture: Thomas stoically intense, Sandy intensely animated. They'd relayed their theory and were awaiting Alex's reply.

"You guys are sure," he said.

It wasn't a question.

"We are," Thomas said.

Alex crossed his arms. The thumb on his left hand went to his mouth. He tapped it on his lips before pressing it against his upper teeth. Sandy thought for a second he might bite the tip off.

"You OK?" she said.

Alex moved the hand.

"Not really," he said. "This is one helluva deadly web our spider has spun."

"Greed and ambition will do that," Sandy said.

"Talk about misplaced trust," Alex said; then after a pause. "So, everything over the past few years has been connected?"

"Mr. Loeb seeks Mr. Rosenbaum's job," Thomas said. "He orchestrated the incidents to raise doubts into the latter's abilities. His position as head of security gave him the ability to control the situations in sufficient capacity to minimize the damage."

Alex frowned as his brain started to work on the math. When he lost count, he gave up.

"I got a shitload of corpses that suggests otherwise," he said.

"An unfortunate, but necessary component to further the doubts," Thomas said. "The three of us know it as collateral damage."

"Shit," Alex said again in a low voice.

"Indeed."

Chapter 42

Yankee Stadium
The Bronx

A decent but less-than-sold-out crowd showed up for the first game. Interspersed throughout the stadium were several hundred law enforcement types, some obvious, some not so obvious. The exact number of FBI agents in the contingent was something only Alex knew.

Outside, the police presence was more obvious. Bomb-sniffing K-9's, mounted officers, and enough squad cars and vans to fill the playing field made it clear to everyone that things would be different than the last time these two teams squared off.

This game was in the spotlight and under the microscope. It was the only one left on the schedule. The others previously postponed had no bearing on the playoffs. At Alex's behest, Mark canceled those games. He wanted the focus entirely on this single location. If nothing else, it would keep the potential of additional collateral losses to a minimum. There would be no further distractions. This was it.

It was a fragile situation to be sure, but the game, like the show, must go on. In addition to the cancellation request, Alex told Mark that a suspect had been identified and would soon be in custody. The how and when wasn't disclosed. Mark reluctantly accepted that. His job, despite the risk, was to put on his best happy face. He did it well.

"I don't expect anything but great baseball," he said at a pre-game sit down with the writers' corps. "Everything else will take care of itself."

In a lot of ways, that's what he was most afraid of.

Manhattan

"Where are you going to be?" Alex said.

He was with Thomas and Sandy, back at the FBI office. After briefing Mark, they'd spent the rest of the day hashing out the logistics of ending Gabi's scheme. Of course, not everything was in their control. Two dangerous wild-cards were as yet unaccounted for.

"Around," Thomas said.

Alex looked at Sandy. She didn't react to his gaze.

"Do you have to be so goddamned cryptic all the time?" Alex said in a tone that did not hide his frustration. "Screw it, never mind—just be careful."

"Always," Thomas said.

"Hmmm," Alex said. "Get outta here before I change my mind."

He waved them out with a flick of his hand.

"We'll be in touch," Thomas said.

"I have no doubts of that," Alex said.

Sandy sent a tight smile in Alex's direction before leading Thomas out of the office. Alex watched until they were gone from sight. His head began to shake. As much as they were a help, they were a complication, something increasingly difficult to explain to the higher-ups. For some in D.C., it was an insult, a suggestion that the FBI didn't possess sufficient internal resources to handle its responsibilities. Alex knew better, but wasn't sure he wanted to keep fighting the battle.

Some say the definition of insanity is repeating the same actions while expecting different results. Maybe that's what had happened to Booker and Coakley. Maybe it was happening to Alex, the only difference being his wasn't steroid-induced, but rather his natural tendency to reward loyalty, to honor friendship above politics. Mark Rosenbaum had done the same thing. With each crisis he'd turned to Gabi, not knowing the young man was the source.

Alex sighed and turned from the doorway.

It was time to end the insanity.

Three minutes later, Thomas and Sandy were moving through the courtyard at the front of the building. The benches along the paths between the curlicue decorative planters were largely unoccupied. The air was cool, but not cold. In the distance, out past the trees of Foley Square, the sky clung to the last least hint of daylight. At street level, traffic along Lafayette was light. It was eerily quiet, but not the reason for Sandy's concern.

"Why *are* you so cryptic?" she said.

Thomas turned his head slightly.

"He has enough to worry about," he said. "My intentions need not impede that."

"I'm not talking about—"

She stopped herself before taking a deep breath and blowing it out, loudly.

"OK, *fine*," she said. "What are your intentions? What are we doing?"

The tone was pointed. She meant it to be. She was concerned. She thought the FBI should have already arrested Gabi. Thomas, as only he could, artfully presented reasons why that wouldn't be the best approach. That Alex bought into it wasn't entirely surprising. Ibori and Okonjo were still out there. Already more than worthy adversaries, without Gabi as part of the bait, they would disappear. Thomas was not going to let that happen. Still, Sandy wondered whether it was his call to make.

"Alex trusts you," she said. "I do, too. Sometimes you make that harder than it needs to be."

Thomas turned to fully face her. His eyes were intense as he looked into hers.

"I don't wish to make your life difficult," he said.

The intensity matched the look. Sandy held firm.

"Than just tell me what we're going to do."

After a couple of ticks, Thomas' eyebrow went up.

"We're going to end this."

Yankee Stadium

Mets Win! It's One or Done Now!

That would be the headline I'd see in tomorrow's paper. I was mostly happy about that. I had worked first base for the game. It started, the teams went at it, I had a few close calls, there was a lot of excitement and drama and intensity, but that was it. The players played. The umpires officiated. The fans cheered. No one died. Just like it was supposed to be.

That a few observers had expected something else wasn't my problem.

I was one day closer to the off-season and a well-deserved break. The same was true for some of the players. The losers tomorrow would start their vacation as well. As I finished packing up my stuff after the game, I was admittedly thinking about that. I tried not to get too far ahead of myself, though. I would have home plate for the final game. I fully expected it to be as exciting as the first had been.

I hoped that's all it would be.

Travis didn't recognize the number displayed on his phone, but answered the call anyway.

"Nice game, loser," Gabi said into his ear. "Too bad you're a fucking cheater."

"Whataya want, Loeb?" Travis said in a dead-voiced reply.

"You know what I want. You can play along or you can die."

Travis turned his back to the rest of the locker room and sat in front of his stall. He leaned in as far as he could without falling off the chair.

"I'm right here," he said. "Come get me, bitch."

The volume of his voice may have been low, but the undertones were clear. Gabi responded in kind.

"Your loss, tough guy," he said. "Don't say I didn't give you a chance to walk away."

"You were never going to let me walk away," Travis said.

"Maybe, but it's a little late to try and be a hero," Gabi said. "Don't count on a plaque in Cooperstown."

Travis chuckled.

"Like I said, I'm right fuckin' here. Come get me."

The Bronx

"That'll get you in, but after that, you're on your own," Gabi said.

"I understand," Jamie said. "This should be sufficient."

Gabi let out a heavy breath.

"Get it done and disappear," he said. "I'll take care of the authorities."

"And payment?" Jamie said.

"You'll get your money. Just get it done."

Jamie watched in silence as Gabi turned and walked away from the McDonald's where they'd met, back toward Yankee Stadium along 161st Street. After Gabi crossed River Street, Shady stepped forward from the crowd of fans waiting in the lines at the subway entrances and rejoined his partner. Despite the extra police in the area, the two dark faces were no more or less out of place than anyone.

"We shall complete the task tomorrow," Jamie said in his native tongue.

"What of tonight?" Shady said.

Jamie looked around.

"Tonight, we feast," he said.

The fast-food haven on his left—never an option anyway—was crowded. The other restaurants nearby would be as well. That wasn't necessarily bad. It was better to be one face in many.

"Come, let us walk a while," Jamie said.

They began to move east along 161st, away from the ballpark, in flow with most of the post-game pedestrians. They crossed Gerard, then Walton, bypassing the expectedly crowded eateries of those two blocks. When Joyce Kilmer Park appeared on their left, Jamie led Shady up the steps, a few feet past the exposed rock landscape at the corner of the park.

"I know of a place," Jamie said. "Come."

At the top of the steps, they stopped alongside the Lorelei Fountain there. The water was off. A collection of Mums in various colors were planted in the flower beds encircling the statue. A few people sat in front, resting on the short fountain edge, talking or smoking cigarettes. No one paid Jamie or Shady any attention.

No one that is except for the two figures behind their backs, one at the top of the stairs they'd just ascended, the other at the top of the path leading down to Grand Concourse. The first figure, Thomas, went around the left side of the circle after the two Africans moved around the fountain to his right. All three continued north along the path. The second figure, Sandy, turned away and headed back toward 161st.

"Whatever you're gonna do, make it fast," she said in the transmitter near her collar.

"Understood," Thomas said as he got in step behind Jamie and Shady.

A ping followed, telling Sandy he had disconnected their link. He was now on his own. She wouldn't know what he did. She would not be a witness. It was the way he wanted it. And as much as she hated the thought of it, she had not argued the point.

She simply walked away.

Kilmer Park covers the space between 161st and 164th, and Walton and Grand Concourse. The park is dedicated to Joyce Kilmer, journalist and poet, most famous for "Trees," written in 1913. Thomas was very familiar with that work, as were many people. It was an oft-quoted American classic, especially one passage: *"Poems are made by fools like me, but only God can make a tree."*

Thomas didn't believe in God. In his mind, such a concept was nonsensical. He believed in reality, in the truth that came from making a choice and completing a task. Things left to those unseen remained undone. Thomas didn't like to leave anything undone. Sometimes, that meant doing things others might not agree with, things that could be seen as wrong. He couldn't control that part of the equation. Each person had a unique view of the world.

In Thomas' view, the two men on the path in front of him needed to die.

At a fork in the walk, about halfway along the seven acres of green space, Jamie stopped suddenly, reaching out and grabbing Shady by the arm as he did. The younger man's face first showed surprise and then, almost as quickly, shock, as Jamie's eyes went wide and he dropped to the blacktop.

"Hey, what are you doing?" someone said in a yell.

Shady turned his head to find a source. First left, then right, then back around toward Grand Concourse, but he saw nothing. He turned again and looked down at Jamie. There was blood on the path beneath him. Shady kneeled next to it.

"My friend?" he said in his native tongue.

Jamie was silent. A second later, so was Shady.

With the increased presence of law enforcement in the ballpark area, it took less than one minute for a swarm of police officers to arrive where the bodies had fallen along the path. A small crowd of pedestrians had already gathered. Questions were asked, statements were taken, but none of the witnesses could provide anything of use. Whatever had happened to the two unknown men was a mystery police would not soon solve.

Outside of one person who had yet to learn of the situation, no one was going to care.

Alex lowered the second tarp and stood. He was getting tired of identifying dead bodies.

"They're ours," he said to a cop standing nearby. "Thanks."

"Hey, it happens," the officer said. "Two bad guys off each other, maybe they had a lovers' squabble, who knows."

"Yeah, I'm sure that's what it was," Alex said.

A minute or so later, he found Thomas and Sandy sitting on the edge of the Lorelei Fountain. He joined them, but for a minute, no one said anything. The only sound came from the traffic on the street in front of them, surprisingly heavy for the time. Alex thought about that, how this truly was the city that never slept. He'd been holding up that reputation himself in recent weeks.

"Well, I suppose I should be able to sleep easier tonight knowing our friends from the Dark Continent are no longer a problem," he said.

There was no reply.

"Of course, there's the sticking point of how they got that way," Alex said, continuing. "You two have any ideas?"

Sandy made a "beats me" face, but said nothing.

"What about you?" Alex said, redirecting his gaze toward Thomas. "Should I be pissed about this?"

Thomas didn't respond. Sandy knew why. Something was very wrong. In the hour-plus since they'd reconnected, he hadn't said five words. She hadn't pushed it because he was clearly not himself, at least not the "him" she thought she knew. She had never seen him in such a state, not even close. It was scary in a way that left her thinking she didn't want to ever see it again. She was content to just let the puzzle have a missing piece. Some things weren't worth it.

Alex wasn't there yet—or maybe he had seen this piece and knew how to deal with it. Either way, his head began to shake and he let out a long hiss of a breath.

"You're right," he said. "Fuck it. They deserved it."

Sandy almost said something, but decided against it. She simply waited for whatever was coming next, expecting it to be as bizarre as everything else going on.

"OK," Alex said. "I guess I need to hold off on releasing any details of this, right?"

He was looking at Thomas. Thomas' head moved slightly.

"Mr. Loeb needs to remain confident he is in control for as long as possible," he said.

Alex's eyes narrowed.

"Yeah, well, what about me?"

Chapter 43

After leaving the two gate passes that would never be used, Gabi made his way up to Mark's suite. The commissioner was there with a handful of baseball types, guys from the front office and a few representatives from the two teams. Somewhere in the gathering was Mark's likely replacement. Gabi needed that wind to start blowing more strongly in his direction.

He'd done all he could related to that effort, but the weather was hard enough to predict, let alone control. The quantity of dead bodies was testament to that fact. Gabi's plans weren't adrift, but there were a few tears in the sails and the hull was listing badly. He needed the old girl to hold together long enough until he could right her and get her to shore.

"Gabi, come say hello to Senator Miller," Mark said when he saw his protégé.

Gabi moved to where Mark was standing with an older man, near the glass facing the playing field. He shook hands with both.

"Great night for a game, huh?" the senior senator from New York State said.

"It's a great night for a lot of things," Gabi said.

A few minutes of small talk followed before Gabi was able to wrest—or maybe save—Mark from the politician. The commissioner appeared grateful.

"Thanks," he said. "That guy could bore a dead man."

"You looked like you could use an out," Gabi said.

"What I could use is a drink."

Both smiled. Mark's was more genuine. Two minutes later, liquid refreshments were in hand—water for Gabi, scotch on the rocks for Mark—and the men found some empty space away from the other guests.

"How do we look?" Mark said.

"We look good," Gabi said with a nod. "Everything is in place."

Mark's cell buzzed in his pocket, signaling a new text message. As he scanned it, his expression changed to one of concern or confusion or both, Gabi couldn't tell and his went to one of all concern.

"Problems?" he said.

"Um... I, uh... *no*," Mark said. "Hey, um, listen. Hang out here if you want or whatever. I, uh... I gotta go take care of something. I should only be a few minutes."

The smile on his face was as much forced as the words were scattered. Gabi's concerned look changed to something closer to anger, but he quickly pulled on a fresh mask to hide it.

"Anything I can help with?" he said.

"Nah, commissioner stuff," Mark said. "Maybe you'll get the chance soon enough, huh?"

Gabi did his best not to react.

"Hey, that's all I can ask," he said.

When Mark nodded and hustled out of the suite, Gabi felt a sudden change in the wind.

He began to think his boat might not make it ashore.

~*~*~*~*~*~*~

Of the four umpiring positions, I enjoyed working behind the plate the most. You're involved in every pitch. You have to focus and stay focused, but if you think too much, you get in trouble. It was as much a mental strain as a physical one, and when the game ended four hours after the first pitch, I was whipped.

It had started quietly enough, each team trading zeroes for two innings, but then, all hell broke loose. There was rally and response, volley and return, and a lot of runs scored in between. It was ugly and beautiful at the same time, a game to be remembered for everyone involved.

What happened afterward was more so—at least for me.

After taking a long time to get out of my gear, I made my way to the showers and stood in the hot water for close to twenty minutes. The pulsating stream felt good, except on the spots where I'd taken several foul tips. That was a hazard of the job, but not the real reason I was moving so slowly.

My season was over.

It had been a long haul and I was beat up—in a lot of ways—but that wasn't the only reason I was bummed out. I always got that way at the end. Don't get me wrong, it was nice to reach the finish line, but there was always a feeling of emptiness to it. It's hard to explain. You put in so much time and effort, endure the endless travel and almost-daily games, and then, poof, it's over. It was something I'm not sure I would ever get used to.

I didn't mind that the rest of my crew had disappeared by the time I got out of the shower. The quiet gave me time to think. Thoughts of the RV escape plan came and went—I knew I would never do that, at least not this year—chased by thoughts of the bombing and the other deaths.

There were no messages from Thomas. Nothing had happened during the game—on the field anyway. Everything seemed to be quiet. Still, I couldn't help but wonder if the shit, like the season, was really over.

I got my answer as I was drying my hair. A finger tapped me on the shoulder. It was the locker room attendant.

"Sorry to bother you, Mr. Connors," he said. "But Mr. Rosenbaum is outside. He asked if you could come out. I'm not sure why he won't come in."

I looked at the door, then back at the attendant.

"OK, no worries," I said with a shrug. "Just tell him to hang on. I'll be right out."

The attendant disappeared. I threw on a t-shirt and sweat pants and slipped my feet into my running shoes. Mark was pacing back and forth in the hall when I found him. It wasn't frantic, but it wasn't calm.

"Hey, Mark," I said. "Uh, you OK? Did something happen?"

His face took on an expression similar to the pacing.

"A lot of good people wanted the job," he said. "The Executive Committee would have approved whoever I recommended—"

He stopped abruptly and looked around. We were alone.

"Mark?" I said. "I don't understand. What are you trying to tell me?"

He looked up. It wasn't so much pain in his eyes, but fear.

"It was *Gabi*," he said, his head starting to shake. "I—I can't believe it."

"Believe *what*, Mark?" I said, my own fear ramping up. "What was Gabi? What happened?"

When his head stopped moving and his eyes found mine, I got *really* scared.

"He killed all those people."

Chapter 44

Yankee Stadium

"Alex Harris and Thomas called me just before the game started," Mark said. "They told me what was going on and what they were going to do. You can't imagine how hard it's been sitting around with this thing hanging over my head. I wasn't supposed to tell anyone…"

He trailed off. At least I think he did. Honestly, my head was spinning from what he'd just spilled into my lap. Hot coffee would have been more pleasant. That Gabi was the one behind everything didn't make sense. If loyalty had a picture in the dictionary, it was Gabi's face. I mean, we all trusted him, but I supposed now the picture needed to be moved over to betrayal, maybe greed.

"I, I—holy shit, Mark," I said, trying to find something resembling composure. "All of this, it all happened because he wanted your *job*?"

My head wouldn't stop shaking.

"I mean, who… who does something like that?" I said. "I don't get it."

Mark's eyes got big. It surprised me at first. Then it scared the shit out of me.

"What are you doing here?" he said, looking past my shoulder.

The answer was a gunshot. The bullet struck Mark mid-chest. He was thrown back against the wall before falling to the ground. I had no idea where the shot came from. In truth, I had no idea about much of anything. My brain was locking up faster than an engine without oil. The "RUN, you stupid shit" reflex was buried—again—beneath the overwhelming images and sounds: Mark's slumped body, the trail of blood on the wall, the echo of the gunshot.

I'm not sure how long it was before I moved forward and knelt next to Mark's fallen body. He was alive, but struggling to breathe, and when he tried to speak, he coughed up more blood than sound. I took a direct hit from the red spray, but ignored it and leaned closer, not wanting to miss whatever came next. I had the feeling it would be his last words.

"I *trusted* you—"

If there was more, it got cut off by another wet cough, and as the sound died, the sharpness in his eyes went with it and his entire body sagged. Any thoughts of trying to revive him faded, too. There was nothing I could do. He was gone. The answers to my questions were going to have to come from someone else—if they came at all.

"Shit, shit, shit," I said, before reaching down and gently closing his eyes.

After a few seconds I stood, but couldn't stop staring at the growing pool of blood near my feet. It didn't take long before I could see a distorted reflection of myself in the dark plasma.

"What a goddamn mess," I said to my sanguine twin.

"Profound as usual, Connors," a familiar voice said from somewhere behind me.

It was Gabi.

A two-staged click followed. The sound reminded me of the one that came from pulling the chain on the ceiling fan in my parents' kitchen. Yeah, if only, I thought, as I slowly raised my hands.

"I try," I said, before turning.

I knew what I was going to see, but my heart skipped a beat anyway as my eyes were drawn to the darkness at the end of the gun's barrel. The tiny black hole began sucking me in. If nothing else, at least I had an answer for what Mark had been looking at instead of me, and for what his last words had really meant. Those answers were helpful, but not the ones I needed.

After a few seconds, I broke free from the trance and looked up, into Gabi's eyes. The answers there weren't much better.

"And Thomas isn't here to save your ass," he said, as if somehow reading my thoughts. "This time, you're on your own."

And there it was.

"Shit, shit, shit," I said again.

My mind started racing, but all roads led back to an unarguable conclusion, that this was all wrong. "Kill the umpire" had always been just a stupid thing people said out of frustration, a sometimes annoying part of the game. But that was the point: Baseball was a game. It was supposed to be fun. It wasn't this—whatever this was—and it sure as shit wasn't supposed to include any actual murders.

The question of "Why?" was in my head, but I didn't get the chance to voice it.

"Move," Gabi said.

He motioned with the gun and his chin toward the door of the umpires' room, behind me.

"I don't, I'm not—"

He closed in and jammed the gun into my ribs, cutting me off.

"It's a good thing you can umpire," he said. "You're too goddamn stupid for anything else. I said *move*."

He increased the pressure on the gun. I think it cracked one of my ribs. I turned and pulled open the door.

"OK, OK, I'm moving," I said. "Any chance you're gonna tell me what you're doing?"

"Don't worry about it."

I started to turn, probably to ask another stupid question, but never finished. The butt end of the gun crashing into my skull saw to that.

"Thomas?" Sandy said.

He held up a finger as he studied the readout on the pager. Sandy's brow furrowed.

"What is it?" she said, her tone tighter.

Thomas looked up. Sandy's frown was replaced by something closer to wide-eyed surprise. He looked to be genuinely scared. Sandy definitely was.

"Thomas?" she said. "Where is he?"

Thomas' head began to shake.

"I don't know," he said, the tone a few octaves off.

Sandy's fear deepened. Thomas not knowing she could handle. This, though, she could not.

"I don't understand," she said. "He paged—"

The shaking of Thomas' head intensified, cutting her off.

"The page was not from Marshall."

The gentle surf was like the bounce of my mother's knee, the warmth of the water and sun like her hug. I don't think I've ever felt as relaxed. Aw, man, I am soooo glad I decided not to waste the money on a new RV. The tropical vacation was the right call. This was the life—

"Connors? Can you hear me, man? Shit, dude, wake up, you can't be dead."

Hey, who's that calling to me from the beach? Ah, fuck it, who cares? I ain't heading in, not yet. This is too nice—

"Damn it, man, I know you're in there. Come on, Connors, wake up."

Who is that? Seriously, quit bothering me. I just want to stay here—

"Goddamn, wake up."

Wait a minute. I'm not on vacation. I'm—

I lifted my head. A groan escaped as I tried to blink away a massive ball of light in my eyes. Not the sun, I thought, as some of my senses returned. OK, ophthalmic migraine. I'd had plenty of those before, but this one was different—as in painfully so.

I groaned again as I tried to push myself up. A strong hand grabbed my arm.

"Hey, man, take it easy," a voice said. "You got some blood on your head."

I knew the voice. Thankfully, it wasn't Gabi's.

"Travis?" I said. "What the fuck? Where am I?"

From what I could see through the halo of light, he looked as bad as I felt.

"Umpires' room, the floor," he said. "You're OK."

I pushed up to my knees and then sat back on my legs. My hand went to the back of my head and found a sore spot. I guessed that explained the dream: blood equaled warmth and wetness, Travis shaking me equaled bobbing on the waves. I liked the dream options better.

"You look like shit," I said.

I adjusted myself into a regular sitting position and studied Travis. He was sweating heavily and seemed to be shaking a little. That last part may have just been my eyes.

"You're one to talk," he said. "C'mon, we gotta get outta here. Can you get up?"

He helped me to my feet. I took a few seconds to regain my bearings. Everything seemed to be in order in the locker room, but—

"Shit, where's Gabi?" I said. "Did you see him? And what about—"

Travis cut me off with a shake of his head.

"Whoa, dude, settle," he said. "Loeb is MIA. Rosenbaum is dead."

The memory rushed back in. I lost my balance for a second.

"C'mon, man, we gotta go," Travis said. "It's not safe in here."

"But Gabi—"

"Don't worry about him," Travis said. "He's gonna get his soon enough."

The comment chased away the last of my migraine.

"What are you talking about?" I said. "Haven't enough people died already?"

"Not yet."

The plan had been to quietly clear the stadium after the game, to lessen the chance for any further unintended damage from whatever Gabi was planning to do. Prior to that, Alex had stayed in contact with him throughout the game, to keep up the illusion of ignorance, sharing updates on activities that were not actually taking place, in or out of the ballpark. It would continue until the area was clear enough to move in and apprehend Gabi. It had seemed to be working.

Now, Alex wasn't so sure.

"Whataya mean you got a page?" he said into his phone.

"Something's not right," Thomas said. "I'll let you know as soon as I figure it out."

He was gone before Alex could respond.

"Shit," Alex said as he closed his cell. "That ain't gonna do me much good right now."

Sandy's graceful stride kept her at Thomas' side as they ran west along the sidewalk of the inner traffic lanes of 161st Street. Most of the game crowd was gone, but a handful of people were still in Babe Ruth Plaza, some sitting on the low slate wall, others on the benches there. None reacted to the sight of the two runners.

"Which way?" Sandy said as she and Thomas hit the Plaza.

"There," Thomas said.

He pointed to the Press Entrance to the right of Gate 4. Seconds later, two burly guards raised two beefy arms at the same time, their palms out like two big stop signs.

"I don't think so," the guard on Sandy's right said. "No one gets in; police orders."

"Those orders no longer apply."

Thomas followed the words with a blur of thrusts and kicks, leaving the guards unconscious at his feet. Sandy shook her head.

"Subtle," she said.

Thomas ignored the comment as he pulled open the door.

"Go," he said.

Sandy wasn't insulted by the abruptness. It was to be expected.

"You lead, I'll follow," she said.

He did so, making his way into a portico with a twin set of conveyor belts on either side of a metal detector. It looked a lot like the gates at an airport. On the other side, two empty chairs backed a high desk. The former occupants were out of the picture, but Sandy was worried about other obstacles.

"Aren't we about to wake the neighbors?" Sandy said as she eyed the metal detector.

"One can only hope," Thomas said.

Sandy held her breath as he passed under the arch, but the system remained quiet. She followed. Again, there was no sound. She wasn't sure why, but ignored the good fortune and trailed Thomas through a door leading into the Great Hall. The 31,000-square-foot open-air concourse—stretching from Gate 4 to Gate 6—was impressive with its collection of huge banners of Yankee greats lining the glass wall above the walkway.

"Goddamn," Sandy said, looking up, before regrouping. "OK, now what?"

Thomas pointed to another glass wall about ten feet from where they stood. There were several elevator doors on the other side and a lone attendant standing watch inside the vestibule.

"You think maybe he could help?" Sandy said.

"I don't need his help," Thomas said.

"And me?"

He eyed her for a second. Sandy could see the intensity.

"You, I'll take."

"*Shit*," I said. "We gotta go back. I lost my pager."

I stopped and turned toward the locker room. Travis grabbed my arm.

"No," he said. "You need to get outta here."

"But I can get help—"

He squeezed my arm to cut me off. It hurt.

"No, Connors, *enough*," he said in a matching voice. "I got this."

He was facing me. It was not a pretty sight. Between the steady flow of sweat and seriously tired-looking eyes, whatever he had or was about to get, it was going to include a ton of hurt.

"We can get help. It's not too—"

"*No*," he said, again cutting me off. "There is no help, there is no cure, there's only pain."

I stared into his eyes for a few seconds. Past the tired I saw something else, and slowly, I began to understand what he meant.

Chapter 45

Yankee Stadium

The sound of sirens outside the ballpark caused Gabi to turn away from the playing field. He had played along with Alex's obvious game, but knew time was running out, and with it, his remaining options. He could continue to look for Travis and snip the last loose thread, or he could slip away into the dark night before the exits were sealed. He could not do both.

Marshall's pager beeped, interrupting his thoughts. He looked down. The message, the acknowledgment from Thomas, was simple: *Game over.*

Gabi's eyes narrowed as he stared at the words. After a few seconds, he flashed on what he'd said to Marshall before clubbing the umpire over the head: *"Thomas isn't here."* Obviously, that had now changed, and his anger grew.

Not killing Marshall had been a mistake. The minutes wasted on the man should have been nothing more than a split-second to pull the trigger a second time. The idiot deserved to be dead. Gabi wasn't sure why he hadn't made it happen. In the scheme of things, it was stupid.

And so was what came next, but inspired by the blinding hatred erupting from the volcano of a scheme gone terribly wrong, Gabi couldn't see it. He just knew it had to be done.

"Fuck it," he said as he fired the pager into the nearest wall.

It exploded into a thousand pieces. Gabi smiled at the destruction.

"OK, Thomas, let's see how good you *really* are."

The umpires' locker room was on the same level as the Clubhouses, level 000. The press box was a few stories above, level 250. Between the two were the ground level and exits. That's where I should have been headed, but despite his insistence otherwise, I knew Travis needed all the help he could get. I wasn't sure what I could do, but I was going to try anyway, if for no other reason than to honor Mark.

I now knew that everything that had happened in the past few years wasn't my fault. I wasn't destined to find trouble at every turn for the rest of my life, like Suze believed. I'd simply been in the wrong place at the wrong time—a lot of times. I'd missed what was swirling in Gabi's head. Shit, we'd all missed it. But now I had a chance to correct that. The dead deserved the effort.

There was no way I could just walk away. Not now.

"Travis, wait up," I said.

We were near Monument Park, the fabled shrine lifted from old Yankee Stadium and resettled here in the new. The monuments were the holy grail of Yankees baseball. To receive one was a supreme distinction, the highest honor for a Pinstriper—only five had ever been bestowed: Lou Gehrig, Babe Ruth, Mickey Mantle, Joe DiMaggio, and manager Miller Huggins. Those guys were heroes of the game. Sure, it wasn't the game Travis and I were playing at the moment, but the faces gave me a shot of inspiration.

"I'm helping," I said as Travis turned back. "Give me your phone. We can find Thomas."

He stared at me for a few seconds.

"And what if Loeb finds us first?" he said.

I lost a little of my bravado.

"Good point," I said with a tiny shrug.

I looked away from him for a second and caught sight of the wall of retired jersey numbers on either side of the monuments. There was an opening in the center of that wall. The area behind the opening was dark—very dark. I turned back to Travis.

"Hey, uh, you know what my favorite play is?" I said.

Travis' eyes narrowed.

"Are you serious? We don't have time for this—"

I put up my hand to cut him off.

"Suicide squeeze," I said. "Put your head down and run. If your partner succeeds, you score. If he fails, it's a rally killer and you're dead. It's pretty much the ultimate definition of trust."

I motioned with my head back to the opening in the wall. Travis' eyes followed. After a few seconds, he turned back, nodding slightly.

"OK," he said. "So who's running and who's bunting?"

"I'll run, but I was thinking you could take a full cut."

His nod intensified. I pushed out a smile.

"Just, uh, just make sure you hit the right ball, OK?"

"Thomas, I found Mark," Sandy said into her cell phone.

She was just outside the umpires' locker room. She and Thomas had split up at the elevators. Sandy went down, Thomas up. From there, they had planned to search and reconvene back in the middle, on ground level.

The elevator attendant had been told to run. The old man didn't hesitate. After finding Mark's body, Sandy knew that had been a good idea.

"He's dead," she said into the phone.

A noise of some sort came through the line, but she ignored it and pushed on.

"There's another spot of blood on the floor, but I'm not sure whose it is," Sandy said. "There's no sign of Marshall. What should I do?"

"You need to get out of there."

"What's up?" Sandy said. "Did you find—"

On his end, Thomas stopped moving and waited for an explanation for the interruption. He got one seconds later, but it didn't come from Sandy.

"Now I have something you want," Gabi said. "You wanted to play, let's play."

The line went quiet.

"I know you're still there," Gabi said. "You're not as cool as you think. I've seen the way you look at her. Why don't you come show me how much you *really* care?"

The effort to steal a souvenir bat from a concession stand near the Bleacher Café—a restaurant near Monument Park—was entirely too easy. Check that, it was scary easy.

"Uh, Travis, where is everyone?" I said when I got back to him.

"Yeah, I noticed that, too," he said. "We got no time to worry about it now."

He started to move, but stopped when he coughed. It was worse than my grand-pap's noise. This was more like a thousand-year-old-man kind of sound, and when he turned and spit out a wad of blood, I winced.

"Geez, are you gonna be able to do this?" I said.

He recovered and looked at me.

"Don't worry about me," he said. "Just give me the fucking bat and go do your job."

I already thought this plan was nuts, but as he ambled away, using the bat as a crutch, the insanity really set in. Was I really about to trust my life to a guy who was obviously sick—no, correction, obviously *dying*—from whatever shit he'd been ingesting over the years? How could that be a good idea? Then again, the past two years had been nuts, too.

I shrugged it off and started running.

Why fight it now?

"I told you to shut the fuck up."

The words from Gabi were followed by another solid punch to the face. This one shattered Sandy's nose, but it was the impact with the floor that did most of the damage. With her hands bound, there was no way to stop the fall, and her head cracked on the cement. The resulting cut was going to need a few stitches. Gabi didn't care if anyone would ever get the chance to apply the sutures.

"Stay down," he said from above her.

Sandy's eyes were shut, but she wasn't completely out.

"If he doesn't kill you—*I will*," she said in a wobbly voice.

"You can try," Gabi said.

He delivered a kick, mid-body, along her side. The impact broke four ribs, and she let out a yelp. His foot shot out again, breaking two more ribs and collapsing her right lung. It was too much to bear and a second later, she was out. Gabi smiled as he moved away.

"Like I said, you can try."

~*~*~*~*~*~*~

I don't think Gabi expected me to be the one to walk into the Sports Bar. Of course, I wasn't expecting to see Sandy lying on the floor there, so maybe we were even. She was near the bar, her face a mess, blood on the floor around her head. I honestly thought she was dead. If not, she was hurt pretty bad. Either way, it changed things and I wasn't very good at improvisation.

"Crap," I said under my breath as I stepped inside the doors.

OK, Marshall, I thought, as I stared across at her. What are we doing here? Part of me wanted to run over and check on her. Another part just wanted to run, period. *All of me* was scared—sorry, more scared—and I almost forgot what I was supposed to be doing.

Gabi was in the bar, somewhere, and I needed to get him to chase me. How much Sandy's involvement would complicate that was a big unknown. But then, so was something else that suddenly dawned on me. If she was in the ballpark, Thomas must be, too.

I turned back to the doors. The corridor on the other side of the glass was empty. I guess maybe I was hoping Thomas might be there. He usually had pretty good timing, but I quickly realized it was beyond wishful thinking to expect it now. I was on my own for this one, just like Gabi had said earlier.

I turned back toward the bar.

"Hey, Gabi, you forgot about me," I said in a shout.

I waited and listened. There was nothing but silence. I took a few steps toward the bar.

"Guess maybe you're surprised, huh?" I said. "Travis thought you might be."

I was close enough to get a better peek at Sandy. She was breathing. That was a relief, but there still was no response from Gabi and no other movements. I took another couple of steps.

"You know, I never saw you as someone who would hit a girl," I said. "Of course, I never saw you as a murderer, either, so, you know, whataya gonna do?"

"Walk away, Connors."

I stopped and backed up a bit. I couldn't afford to let him get behind me. I knew he already had one gun. There was a good chance he now had Sandy's, too. I couldn't see him passing up another chance to use one of them on me.

"I, uh, I thought about that," I said. "You know, after you tried to bash in my head. I think I'm gonna pass again."

I retreated to within a step of the door and put my hand on it. If things got crazy—and I was pretty sure they were about to—I didn't want to take a chance on fumbling for the handle.

"Bad idea, shithead," Gabi said.

The glass next to my hand shattered. I recoiled out of reflex before recovering and jumping through the jagged opening. Another shot rang out. I felt a burning sensation along my side—similar to the feeling of being hit with a sharp foul tip—but ran through it. The next bullet ripped into a window along the corridor next to me and kicked off another storm of flying glass. A couple pieces bounced off my face, but I kept running.

I wasn't an Olympic athlete, but I knew I could outrun Gabi's short, choppy stride. Of course, he had the great equalizer of the guns, but I made sure not to run in a straight line. It was working until it wasn't, the mistake coming when I jumped down the stairs that led to the monuments and landed awkwardly, twisting my ankle.

As I slid to a painful stop on the granite, Gabi caught up and appeared at the top of stairs behind me. In the slow-motion split-second that followed, I began to scramble and he began to shoot. Another bullet hit me on the same side as the first—my right—this time in the arm. It did more damage than a foul ball, but the adrenaline kept me moving so as to not get hit again.

The opening in the wall was in front of me.

The suicide squeeze was on.

The plan was simple. I was the runner. Travis was the batter. Gabi was the ball. The opening to the alcove was homeplate. My job was to reach the plate before the ball reached the catcher's mitt—in this case, before Gabi shot me again in a place that would keep me down for good.

Travis' job was to make sure that didn't happen, to make contact with the ball so I could safely score. The tweak was he would take a serious full-on homerun swing. Fuck bunting. Of course, I needed to remember to duck.

It was a good plan. At least we thought so.

I dove through the opening and covered my head as I slid all the way to the back wall of the alcove. My heart was pounding and the sound was pulsating in my ears, but that was it, there was nothing else. No crash of bat against skull, no more gun shots, nothing but silence.

In a panic, I twisted my head around, fearing I'd find Gabi standing above me with the guns. Instead, I saw Travis slumped against the inner side of the wall. He was in a sort-of-seated-sort-of-slouched position. The bat was on the ground next to him. At first, I thought he'd connected and then collapsed, but there was no Gabi.

"What the fuck," I said as I scrambled to my knees.

I shimmied across the cold tiles to Travis' side. I found a pulse, but honestly couldn't tell if it was his or mine. I shook him, but he didn't respond.

"Travis? *Travis?*" I said in a suppressed shout. "Shit, please don't be dead."

I shook him again and tried to find some sign of life, but was stopped when I heard a familiar voice on the other side of the wall. It was Thomas'.

"Game over."

Rule 2.00 of the Major League Baseball Official Rules defines four different types of interference: Offensive, defensive, umpire,

and spectator. There are varying consequences and penalties involved to deal with each type, but there is one consistent fact: On any interference the ball is dead.

Gabi had been the ball in my squeeze play. Thomas had interfered. I should have been OK with that, but a lot of me wasn't. I had witnessed a suicide bombing that killed forty-some innocent people. I had watched another explosion erase two people. I'd seen a man get shot right in front of me. I had been kidnapped, beat up, and otherwise run through the shredder in the past couple of years. People I loved and trusted had been hurt—and worse. To say all that stuff left me changed would be an understatement.

What I saw Thomas do to Gabi was worse than all of it.

Every story or partial story or guess on my part about just how lethal of a man Thomas could be paled in comparison to the reality of seeing it in action. The precision of his movements were at once awesome and frightening. The anger in it was far more ruinous. It destroyed the bubble of my childlike fantasy about his life. I would never be able to look at him the same again.

I honestly didn't know if that was good or bad.

An hour or so later, I was propped against the wall near the exit steps for Monument Park. I'd had a visit from a couple of EMTs. Both bullets had gone through and through, they said, and they'd treated my wounds, but suggested a trip to the hospital was in order. I declined. There was still some unfinished business to attend to.

Alex Harris had shown up with a small army of FBI agents. After directing them to do whatever it was they do, he made his way to me.

"You doing OK?" he said.

I looked up and shook my head.

"Uh… no," I said.

He dropped onto the step next to me. He seemed pissed. I think he'd already spoken to Thomas, but I wasn't sure how much was said or if that was behind the bad mood.

"You wanna give me *your* version of what happened?" he said.

The emphasis added to my curiosity, but I held firm. I wasn't sure where Thomas was at the moment, probably checking on

Sandy. That was just as well. I didn't want him to hear what I was about to say. As far as I was concerned, Thomas got there after it was all over. Despite what I'd seen, I wasn't about to admit otherwise. My feelings aside, it was the least I could do for all he'd done for me.

"Travis nailed him with the bat," I said to Alex. "I lost track of how many times. When Gabi kept coming at us I grabbed the gun and squeezed the trigger as many times as I could. It all happened so fast. I guess maybe we got carried away in the moment."

Alex's eyes narrowed. Did he believe me? I didn't know. I guess maybe he wanted to, but that's the beauty of it. Call it umpire's judgment, my version of the truth—and you're not allowed to protest a judgment call, whether you agreed with it or not. Besides, it's not like he could go ask Travis or Gabi. They were dead. I was the only one left—outside of Thomas.

"Yeah, I suppose that could work," Alex said.

A pair of EMTs passed by with Travis' body.

"He would back me up," I said.

"I'm sure he would," Alex said; then after a pause. "Get yourself to the hospital."

He stood and headed up the steps. I nodded and turned back to the field. The auxiliary scoreboard along the leftfield wall caught my eyes. There were a lot of crooked numbers there and a smile worked onto my face. I'd totally forgotten about the game. It had been almost as wild as the one Travis and I had played afterward.

The Dodgers won 11-10, thanks to a ninth-inning, two-RBI double by, of all people, Travis. In the end, I suppose that was a small consolation for the man. Sure, he'd been stupid in too many ways to count, but he was as much an innocent victim to everything else Gabi was doing as I was. OK, maybe not, but he'd suffered enough. He was gone. There was no point piling on.

I turned back to the activity in front of me. Alex was right. I needed to get to the hospital. My entire right side was throbbing from the bullet wounds, but I couldn't find the energy to get up. Instead, I drew up my knees and held on as best as I could as I put my chin on top.

It wasn't from the pain, but after a minute or so, I started to cry.

I'm not sure if the tears were for those who had passed or for me for having somehow survived. I just knew it was sad in more ways than I could comprehend. So many people were gone, some good, some not so good—Buck Walters, Damien Hastings, Andrew Singer and his victims, Eddie Booker and the innocent fans, Mike Coakley, David Donovan, Dukabi and the Africans, Travis, Mark and Gabi— too many to count.

How Thomas had seen to that last one wasn't helping. He might have been used to that stuff, or maybe he was so jaded that it didn't register any longer, but I could never be like that.

I didn't want to be.

I needed to feel, to wear my emotions on my sleeve. To be any other way, to be like Thomas and never show anything to anyone, seemed wrong. I suppose he *did* feel things, but he was so guarded about it. I guess maybe that had something to do with his background, but I don't think I'll ever truly understand it. I'm not sure I wanted to, not now.

I stayed there for I don't know how long and let the tears fall. No one bothered me. That was good. I got it all out.

Eventually, Thomas returned.

"What did you say to Alex?" he said after joining me on the step.

"Does it matter?" I said.

He gave me his best raised eyebrow.

"No, it does not," he said.

"Indeed," I said.

He smiled. I forgot all about the anger. Forgetting was good. I could stand to forget a few more things.

Yeah... if only.

Epilogue

Sandy still had bandages covering part of her face. Her nose had been surgically repaired and was healing nicely. Her ribs were the same, but outside of some sporadic trouble breathing caused by both sets of injuries, she was ready to get back to work. She'd been out long enough.

Like Marshall, she had a few things she'd like to forget, but in the meantime, there was still a puzzle that needed to be solved. Unlike Marshall, she was eager to get back to it.

"So, um, do I still have a job?" she said as she stepped into Thomas' office.

He was standing near the wall of shelves. When he turned, his expression was its normal nothingness. Sandy lost a little of her enthusiasm. She wanted to believe things were going to change, but the empty reaction brought with it some of the old frustration.

"Still holding back, I see," she said, reflecting the emotion.

She watched him closely as he moved in her direction. When he reached her, he delivered a kiss unlike any she had ever experienced.

It lasted for what seemed an eternity. When their lips parted, she was having trouble breathing again, but it had nothing to do with the injuries.

"What do *you* think?" he said as he looked down at her.

For once, there was nothing remotely flat or secretive about his expression. Sandy smiled.

"I think maybe I was wrong," she said in a soft voice.

"Indeed."

###
About the Author:

RALLY KILLER is the third book in Allen Schatz' Marshall Connors Series. Baseball has always been a big part of his life and will continue to serve as the canvas for his future novels.

In addition to the writing, Allen provides finance and accounting consulting services for various clients out of his home office. He has also been an amateur umpire for the better part of the past thirty years. If he's not at his desk, he's probably on a field somewhere.

He currently lives in southwestern Pennsylvania, but hopes to return permanently to the Philadelphia area very soon. He is married and has two adult children, but his two dogs make sure the house remains filled with toys.

Website: www.allenschatz.com
Facebook: facebook.com/AllenSchatzWriting
Twitter: raschatz

~*~*~*~*~*~*~

Coming soon:
LIARS BALL
An all-new mystery—look for it in 2012

Made in the USA
Charleston, SC
10 October 2011